THE FIRE, THE ROSE AND THE CITY

KYMBERLY HASTINGS

ISBN
978-1-960197-01-6 (Paperback)
978-1-960197-02-3 (eBook)

For Gerald Wayne Davenport

LOVER'S STRUGGLE AGAINST THE ODDS

PART I

GATHERINGS

CHAPTER ONE

Late autumn 1944—
Budapest, Hungary

Pacing back and forth inside the gate of the Swedish Ullio Street Embassy House in Budapest, Wolfgang von Friesen could only guess at the uneasy thoughts his two Jewish friends were having. Aral Spigel along with his beautiful golden-haired daughter, Bela, watched him so intently, he sensed they had some misgivings about the sudden move he'd forced them to make to the embassy.

For recently the notorious Adolph Eichmann had been able to gain information through bribery, from people who were willing to identify some of the city's wealthier Jews. And from the expression in Bela and Haral's eyes, Wolf could tell they were still struggling to find their fragile balance in this new environment. "Raoul Wallenberg will protect you as long as you stay here," he assured them.

Wolf was a businessman who frequently used his blond, Aryan good looks to help Ambassador Wallenberg with the Nazis. And he was confident Haral and Bela would be safe here. "Plus *Herr* Wallenberg's secretary inside is holding your passports or Schutz-Passes— Swedish certificates of protection— that will identify you as Swedish citizens, so you won't have to wear those damned yellow stars any more."

"My Bela and I have no words to express our gratitude," said Haral, inclining his head in a gesture of appreciation.

"Not necessary," reminded Jaclyn, Wolf's lovely wife. "Even if my mother's been dead for many years, it doesn't alter the fact that you're still my step-father and Bela my step-sister." She shook her head." It's just that with the city getting more dangerous by the minute, it's safer here at the embassy than at our house."

Haral grinned, his pewter-colored eyes brightening in his tanned face. "Of course we realize it. It's simply I'm afraid that like Bela and myself, you and Wolf aren't very good at cutting deals with the Germans." His eyes flickered to the embassy fence. "Should they break in here and ship us off, like they're threatening."

"No one's good at cutting deals with the Germans," Jaclyn reminded. "So it forces us to do whatever needs to be done."

"Which means," said Wolf, "if the Germans do break in here and try to ship either one of you off, then Jaclyn and I are going to fight them single handed."

Haral looked skeptical as he ran his fingers through his tousled, silver hair.

"But like I told you earlier, staying here at the embassy means the four of us will be separated in the evenings."

"I know," Wolf said, giving his forearm a reassuring squeeze. "But don't forget, Haral, you volunteered to work the long hours helping us make the Swedish passports for the ghetto Jews."

"So what that means," said Jaclyn, glancing at the embassy gate like she was expecting someone. "Is that we'll be stuck together so much, it'll be like you and Bela are still living with us."

* * *

Bela's cheeks warmed with a smile as she reached down and picked up the framed newspaper article about Jaclyn on top of her father's suitcase.

"My well-known step-sister," she bragged, before reading the article silently.

> *Jaclyn Tirand is a French cello player with vibrant, dark hair and a striking pale face. And even though the notoriety she receives from the public pleases her, it's the passionate nature of her music that inspires a compassion in her which makes her a wellspring of joy.'*

"You know that Waffen S.S. Commander Steiner moved on Hungary the day before that article was written," Wolf pointed out. "And I was dumbfounded...I mean it was March of '44, for God's sake. And the Germans were losing the war. So what on earth was he thinking?"

Haral stared at him like he was missing something quite obvious. "I never mentioned it, but in the back of my mind a voice kept nagging me that Hungary was taking too long signing its negotiations with the allies."

"Doesn't matter whether you mentioned it or didn't," said Wolf.

"Our leaders here in Budapest failed to pay attention to the fact that the Germans were running out of supplies and needed Hungary's oil wells near Lake Balaton."

"And as I've said," remarked Haral, "the prevailing opinion was that with the exception of allied air raids— and those Arrow-Cross Nazi thugs, who showed up in October in their green uniforms— Hungary's Jewish population felt relatively safe."

"Which they were—"

"Sorry to intrude," interrupted a familiar voice at the gate, "but *Herr* Wallengberg said I'd find Bela here."

She jerked her head around to see a tall, blond- haired young man, whose warm presence made a thrill go through her each time he said her name. "Yanni! How on earth did you get here?"

"Wolf and Jaclyn."

She turned and gave them each a hug. "I can't believe you arranged for him to stay with us."

A smile tugged at the corners of Jaclyn's red lips. "Why not? Since he needed a safe place too."

Bela hugged her again. "I'll never be able to repay the two of you."

"Think nothing of it," Wolf said. "Because it's pretty obvious from the look in his eyes, how much he cares for you."

Jaclyn's smile increased "And besides, his piano music is like a soul to the universe."

"That it is," Haral nodded briskly. "And he's planning on playing in Palestine the minute the war's over. Which is why he's offered to take Bela and me there."

"And you're going with him?" asked Wolf.

"I'm undecided." He gave Bela's shoulder a light pat. "Because from my experience visiting there, it's still not a safe place for Jews."

"And don't forget, Papa, with its gates closed to immigrants, it's too soon to know what we'll be doing after the war."

"Absolutely. Since our Yanni here is an innocent, gentle soul with lofty ideals that could easily get him in trouble."

"I only want to make Bela happy," he said, stroking her hand.

"Most definitely," Haral agreed.

The young man's gaze dipped. "But what you said the other day, *Herr* Spigel, about my not being much of a survivor is true."

"And you promised me you'd try to do better."

"That I did. But for now it's so cold out here, the four of you are shivering like you need to go inside."

"That's putting it lightly," Haral said, pulling his coat lapels closer together. "Because we could be catching our deaths standing in this chilly air."

Bela reached for her small bag as Yanni picked up her bigger one.

"Neither you nor your father seemed to have brought much stuff," he said, gazing at their luggage.

"That's because Wolf and Jaclyn are still keeping most of it stashed in their house," she told him, shuffling behind her father in her heavy, clunking boots.

"That was kind of them," Yanni replied, giving them a smile of thanks.

"I agree," Bela remarked, unfastening the belt of her brown trench coat as she stepped into the embassy's open hallway.

On the opposite side of it, a man hurried over with two large, cardboard boxes. "I hope you and *Herr* Spigel don't mind sleeping on pallets on the floor."

"Wallenberg." Wolf beamed. "Didn't expect to see you here today."

He set the boxes down and offered his hand. "Change of plans. But I'm glad of it because if you're still of a mind, I discussed it with our Swiss friends, and they said you and Jaclyn can help me speed up things if you'll help them forge twice as many passports by the end of this week."

"We'll help," said Wolf. "And can't wait to get started."

"It can be tricky work when one has to work fast," Wallenberg reminded him.

"Doesn't matter, we're still happy to do it."

"As long as Bela and I can provide music for your embassy guests once a week," said Jaclyn, eyeing Wallenberg coquettishly.

"That's the string your husband pulled to get my approval for your relatives to live here," he teased, ushering them inside to the reception area.

A large number of Jewish families were already crammed in it.

"Since more people are expected to arrive tonight, *Herr* Spigel, you, your daughter, and her friend can sleep on these pallets away from the door." He pointed at them.

"But where will you find the room to put these new arrivals?" asked Wolf, shaking his head.

"Won't be a problem. Since last night the Swiss ambassador and I rented some more properties in Budapest and declared them extraterritorial."

Wolf continued to shake his head. "Anything to keep the Jews from being sent to those terrible camps. But with these new arrivals, can you manage the food? Bela's quite thin, so Jaclyn, Haral, and I have been urging her to eat more."

"Can't say I blame you," said Wallenberg, handing him a large, folded paper.

"The new menu given me this morning is soup twice a day, black bread, cheese, and kosher sausages— when we can get them."

Haral gestured at Wolf. "He's holding my money and will use some of it to cover our expenses while we're here."

Wallenberg brightened at the idea. "And I'm grateful because the more you wealthier Jews can help us, then the more ghetto Jews we'll be able to save." He reached into one of the boxes and pulled out a leather book with a gold flower on its cover. "Here, Bela, this is your new journal."

"*New* journal?" she questioned, surprised at such a lovely gift.

"Your step-sister wanted to buy you one, but I had several unused ones so I told her I'd give you one."

"And I appreciate it." She bowed her head in a gesture of thanks. "Which is why starting tonight, I'll write down all that happens here. And after the war, I'll see if I can get it published."

Wolf put his arm around her. "If you start tonight, Bela, then let your first entry be something uplifting, that you can share with all the newcomers."

"Definitely. Since like us, everything they're familiar with has suddenly been taken from them."

* * *

BELA'S JOURNAL

"I had trouble at first figuring out something to write that would be uplifting. But when I began talking to a lot of the people staying here, I was pleased to learn that most were optimistic the war would be over by the middle of next year— if not sooner. So, I decided to write down their comments.

But before I could do it, Yanni interrupted me.

'I have to slip out tonight to give my cousin's family the blankets and medical supplies I've brought with me. Since they're living in such a hell-hole that if they don't get them, then they'll probably die.'

I was horrified. And immediately told Pa —like I did about most things—and Herr. Wallenberg.

They begged Yanni not to go, with Herr Wallenberg offering to send several of his non-Jewish office workers to go in his place. But Yanni insisted that the part of the ghetto his cousin's family was living in was just as risky for an Aryan as it was a Jew.

Then he did something remarkable. He took my right hand and vowed to me he'd never slip out again. 'Because don't forget, Bela, I love you and want to marry you.' He glanced at the blank page in my journal. 'Even if you are making me wait for your answer until after the war, and we're still alive.'

'I'll marry you,' I promised him, kissing him on the mouth. 'But if Pa doesn't want to go to Palestine—'

'Then we'll do whatever he wants,' he said, returning my kiss.

Yanni was such a gentle soul, that like Pa said, 'He has no business being involved in the dangerous activities connected with the war.' So continuing to worry, I went back to Pa who made Yanni give his word that he'd wake us the minute he got back. Which needless to say, caused us to get little sleep our first night here, as we waited for his return.

But when morning came and Yanni was nowhere to be found, we were frantic. And we feared he'd been put on the run and was possibly doing something suicidal—like striking out for Palestine where his father was a doctor.

Herr Wallenberg contacted his leather-jacketed friend, Karoly Szabo, whose special brigade of Hungarian police immediately began searching for him. But when two days followed and there was no word, they suspected the worst.

Then on the third day the Arrow-Cross militia dumped his body at the embassy gate with a note pinned to it, warning that anyone attempting to sneak out would be shot the same as he'd been.

Naturally everyone in the embassy was deeply grieved—and I let out a loud gasp when I heard. How I'd wanted to marry him. And even now I can hardly stop crying enough to write these words: "Yanni, if my love could have saved you, I'd have seen you had a very long life."

So Jaclyn, concerned, urged me to hug his picture against my heart whenever I could and pray that he was in a much better place than this war-torn world.

'Didn't I warn him his innocence and lofty ideals would get him in trouble?' Pa reminded, tears in his eyes.

But what my father and I failed to consider was the reason we cared about Yanni so much, was that we were birds of a feather. For like him, we let our hearts get the better of us. And like him, it threw us in the enemy's path."

* * *

"I'll have to be more careful when I'm out, Bela," Haral said, fidgeting nervously.

"And when will that be?"

"Soon— according to this note I received."

"Yanni and now you. How can I stand it?"

"Simply by thinking about the lives everyone's trying to save." Her father eyed her steadily. "But regardless of the passports Wolf's helping to make for everyone, he insists on coming with me—"

"Because yours is important work too."

"No more than his." Haral folded the note and tucked it in his pocket. "Which is the reason I don't want him to come."

CHAPTER TWO

"Wake up, Bela," whispered Jaclyn, worried." I've brought your favorite pastry."

She looked at the pastry, then at her step-sister. "Thanks but I'm really not hungry."

But Jaclyn persisted. "It's been three days since you've eaten, and we're all greatly concerned at the way your grief over Yanni is affecting your health. So please, try and get this down."

The gust of frigid air hitting Bela in her face, told her dawn was only a few minutes away. "If I eat it, I'll probably choke."

"Which is why I brought tea—and if that doesn't work then maybe later, some plum brandy."

Seeing the pleading look in her step-sister's dark eyes, she remembered the old days when Jaclyn had loved taking her to the cinema and concerts.

'She's France's gift to Vienna,' the men would say, showering flowers on her after her cello performances. And although their attentions pleased her, she never once let them get in the way of her devotion to her family.

Taking the pastry, Bela bit into it. "Anything for my beautiful step-sister."

"That's the spirit," Jaclyn said, a smile replacing her worried look.

The floor was now covered in a golden light as dawn broke. And **those staying** there quickly rose from their pallets, so they could begin their tedious work assignments.

Usually Bela and her father assisted the group of Hungarians, who helped the Swedes with their forged passports and other protective documents. Work that caused the days to be long and empty, because *one* mistake, and the German consul would throw them all out. *A concern that gave Jaclyn and I little time for our music.*

"We've got to keep all the Jews we can from being sent to Auschwitz," Wolf would continually remind everyone.

* * *

BELA'S JOURNAL

"'But what did the most good,' Wolf informed us, 'was Herr Wallenberg's courageous effort to save a boxcar of Jews bound for Auschwitz, by jumping on top of the car. It was surrounded by armed German soldiers. But even so it didn't stop him from declaring that everyone in it was a Swedish citizen. He then opened a small bag and took out a handful of passports in order to prove it....' Of course, they were made by people like me and Jaclyn here at the embassy. However, not one soldier questioned Herr Wallenberg.

Pa said it was probably because the Germans admired his courage. But I'd like to think the work on these passports— or Schutz Passes— was so meticulous, no one questioned it.

I typed reports and took incoming messages off the clattering machines scattered throughout the building.... Keeping my fingers crossed that it would help the Budapest Jews with these Swedish passports, survive the terrible odds against them.

Which worries me even more since Wolf keeps telling Pa and me, that we should be baptized. Assuring us that if we were, the church promises to give him back-dated baptismal certificates that say we've always been Aryan- Christians.

'A faked conversion, but a necessary one in this suspicious city,' so Jaclyn insists.

And Pa agrees. 'We look Aryan. And Wolf tells me he can get our Aryan- Christian papers without the necessary religious instruction.' Then Pa added, 'I know our religion frowns upon such conversions— the same as it frowned on your mother's request as she lay dying, to take her body to Palestine.... But after all, Bela, we're only human.'

Which is true. So, if Pa thinks we need to be baptized to keep from being dropped in the jaws of the beast, then we should do it. And looking me in the eye, he reminded, 'Throughout history our people have been forced into conversions—fake or otherwise.'

'But after the war, what then?' I asked him.

'There's no reason, we can't go back to being who we were.'

I know he's right about the church papers. Since Herr Wallenberg is receiving rumors everyday that Adolph Eichmann has plans to break into the embassy and round-up all the people who can't prove they're Aryan-Christians. Terrible. Because they'll then be shipped to Auschwitz...where Pa will probably be killed because he's older. And me— since I'm thin.

So Pa told Wolf to use some of the money he was holding for him, to get the papers stating we were Aryan-Christians....Which he did. Although, to our great regret, the Catholic Church refused to hand them over until they conferred with a Cardinal about the baptismal certificates we would get, when we were baptized.

Leaving me to question why they were being so difficult?"

* * *

Bela knew her father felt that way too. 'We've no choice but to wait and continuing doing what we're doing,' he'd insist.

So at times when a different type of help was needed, he'd sneak out of the embassy to both Swedish and Swiss extraterritorial houses to show the Jewish intellectuals—who'd never worked a day with their hands—how to saw and hammer.

It mystified Jaclyn. "Don't you think it's strange, Bela, that your well-to-do banker father can do the work of a common laborer?"

"It is," she said after a silence. "It's just that he doesn't like talking about it."

"Any particular reason?"

"Because he says it's a very sad story."

"Even so, he should tell you while he can."

"Definitely —especially in these fearful times."

So late one evening before bedding down on her pallet, Bela asked him again about his callused hands. And to her surprise, he opened up.

"Growing up, my sweet Bela, my family was very poor. But during the Great War something unexpected happened—"

"Which was?" she broke in, putting her hand on his shoulder.

"I saved the life of a wealthy man's son, whose family took me in."

"Took you in?'

"Yes," he said, a variety of emotions crossing his face.

"Which was extraordinary, don't you think?"

"That it was." She nodded, intrigued by this unexpected turn.

"But what was even *more* extraordinary was that their beautiful, golden-haired daughter fell in love with me."

"Ma," Bela said, trying not to cry.

"Who died after you'd just turned five. And were too young to remember much about her."

"I remember more than you think...but what about her parents?"

"They didn't approve of me at first," he said, shaking his head regretfully. "But eventually came to understand that love often happens when you throw reason to the wind and follow your heart."

"I've never thought of it like that."

"Not many people have." He reached across and took her hand "However, the first time I met your mother, she took my breath away. And I called her my *rose*. Because she was impossible to forget with her long, golden curls and brilliant, blue eyes like yours."

He looked away for a moment like he was attempting to collect himself.

"Eyes her father described as being the striking blue of the heavens of Galilee after a storm. And like hers, your eyes will attract some lucky man, and you'll be his *rose*."

"Me?" she questioned, feeling a faint blush sweep across her cheeks. *'A moon dusted shadow,' Yanni would say, whenever that would happen.*

Haral gazed at her with a curious expression. "Didn't Yanni ever call you his *rose*?"

"He did once, but— "She brushed back a tear. "I told him we shouldn't get carried away because of the war."

"Which will soon be over. And then you'll see that *now*, with Yanni gone, the men will flock to you like the shipwrecked sailors did the sirens."

Bela felt a sudden wave of uneasiness. "Which lets me know I should be careful."

"And you will be."

Then he'd proceeded to tell stories about his long ago world, when he'd danced with her mother in palace ballrooms and gone on romantic river cruises down the Danube.

To Bela it seemed too good to be true. Especially when the other families on their pallets in the embassy, overhearing him, told her it sounded like a fairy tale.

This motivated the sometimes quarrelsome men and women who did the cleaning, to come over and beg him to retell his stories.

And he would. But only on nights when the snow fell the heaviest, and everyone's teeth chattered, would he talk.

"Lost in memories about his courtship," Bela would murmur, as the gloomy shadows, shrouding everyone's face, lifted.

"They love you, Pa," she told him.

"Which takes their minds off things, but—" He looked a little desperate.

"Unfortunately, I won't be here tomorrow."

"Why? Because you're doing some more work for the Swiss or Swedish?"

"At one of the Swedish exterritorial houses where I trained their men."

"And they still don't know what to do?" she asked, her uneasiness increasing.

"They know. But they've managed to acquire two trucks and are in a hurry to put false bottoms in them to sneak some people out."

"What people?"

"Some children. Who're usually killed the moment they arrive at Auschwitz."

A shiver coursed through her. "Then I understand, Pa, but have you told Wolf?"

"I'll tell him tomorrow." There was a lengthy pause before he added, "But he won't be able to go. Because yesterday the Germans found mistakes on a frightening number of the Swedish passports. So new ones will have to be made."

She stood there without moving, thinking about the possible dangers her father might face alone. "Even so, Wolf always helps you."

"I know, but still—"

"Someone should go with you."

"Maybe." He looked down at his callused hands. "But right now there's no one."

"Except me."

"*You?*" he questioned. "Under... no... circumstances."

Fear continued to gouge her. "Why? Because it's dangerous?"

"Very—plus you're needed here."

"Even if I don't do the meticulous work on the passports?" she asked, wishing her fingers weren't so cold and shaky.

"Doesn't matter."

"I beg to differ. Since you'll need someone to help carry your carpentry tools or otherwise the Germans—"

"Will do what?"

"Stop you and take one of the two large toolboxes you'll be carrying."

"There's always the possibility." His lips pressed together as if giving it more thought. "But if Wolf tries to keep you from coming with me, then I'm not going to fight him."

"I doubt he will." She reached for her father's hand. "Especially considering how strict Berlin has suddenly become about these passports or Schutz Passes."

"But haven't they always been?"

"Not like this. Because even with the bribes *Herr* Wallenberg's giving the German and Hungarian authorities, it still isn't stopping them from trying to find mistakes on these papers, we're all so desperately helping his staff make."

* * *

BELA'S JOURNAL

"Birds of a feather — Yanni and I,

My own words came back to haunt me when my first night at the Swedish exterritorial building, the Arrow-Cross militia —siding with armed, black-uniformed Gestapo men — battered down the building's door.

They marched us six abreast to the banks of the Danube and then opened fire.

'Run, Bela!' were Pa's last words, before his body dropped into the Danube. And on the fringe of hysteria, I was ready to leap in after him, when one of the Gestapo men grabbed me and remarked with cold triumph, 'No need to waste

this Aryan-looking rose, with her golden- hair and blue eyes. Because she'll make our Jungs fighting near Lake Balaton quite happy.'

'The men who come from fire—eh.' One of the other Gestapo men laughed.

Trembling, my first instinct was to beg for mercy. But understanding it would do no good, I chose to yell across the Danube at a Gestapo man who sometimes helped Herr Wallenberg with bribes. 'Find a way to get word to Wolf—please!'

Which he did.

However, I later learned he waited a week before he contacted Wolf with the information about me. And when he did, he required a huge pay-off from him... But sadly by that time it was too late. For I was suddenly a prisoner in one of those places for soldiers, or Love Camps as they were called. And bile rose in my stomach each time I thought about the men who came from fire and the depths to which they could sink.

Naturally, when Wolf and Jaclyn learned I was alive, they snapped out of their grief.

'Wallenberg and I bribed everyone we could think of to try and find you,' Wolf told me, when I was finally reunited with him and Jaclyn in Vienna. 'But with the Russians preparing to descend on Budapest, we I had no choice but to pack up and head for Austria.'

'Even so you still managed to rescue me,' I told him.

'Only because we helped one of Adolph Eichmann's clever Gestapo men escape the Russians in Budapest and make it to Vienna,' he explained. 'Which had to be destiny. And when I offered him an exorbitant sum of 'get away' money— plus arranged passage for him and his friend, on a German U-boat headed to South America—he was more than willing to dodge the Russians, buy you out of that Nazi Love Camp, and get you to us in Vienna before Jaclyn and I left for my uncle's chalet in Switzerland.'

'For all the good it did,' I remarked, my illusions shattered.

And Wolf agreed. Because, like me, he understood my life could never be as it had been.

'My survival has made it difficult to accept the death of my people,' I informed him, aware that he and Jaclyn were in training in Switzerland for a possible upcoming Office of Strategic Services or OSS mission in Berlin.

So I volunteered for the training too. Because I saw it as a way I could use my survival to give back.

Especially when several months after our arrival at Wolf's widowed uncle's chalet, I was informed that a former Wehrmacht captain, who'd switched sides, would be meeting us there.

'Unfortunately Albert von Friesen is his uncle as well as mine,' Wolf told me in a slightly bitter tone. 'So I hope it won't bother you.'

'I'll do my best not let it,' I said, despaired, at the unpleasantness of the situation. For this German was joining Jaclyn, Wolf, and me on our special OSS mission to Berlin. A dangerous place to be in the Reich's final days…with Russian machine guns and artillery fire showering the dying city with their suffocating messages of death.

But nevertheless, we had an assignment from London's Grosvenor Square to do whatever was necessary to keep both the Russians and the Germans from locating Albert's brother…. The world- renowned rocket scientist, who'd changed his name to Wilhelm von Lehmann——or von Lehmann— as he preferred to be called for professional reasons.

Both the British and Americans had been searching for him, but to no avail. And since Albert von Friesen had social ties with certain people in the OSS, I thought of him as being a handler, since we were grateful for the training he'd arranged for us. Which, provided von Lehmann could be identified, gave us the opportunity to help the allied intelligence gatherers— working in secret in Berlin— devise a plan to sneak von Lehmann out of the city.

We all feared von Lehmann might not be alive until yesterday, April twenty-eighth. When someone in Berlin sent information to British intelligence implying von Lehmann— and not his doppelganger— was a patient in the Potsdam Hospital…. Because another patient claimed to have overheard this man in the hospital believed to be von Lehmann, say he'd made some preliminary designs under duress, for an improved long-range V-3 Cannon Rocket specifically developed to carry an atomic warhead.

My heart made an unsteady beat each time I thought about the frightening possibilities of such a weapon. But our orders were clear: get to Berlin and either identify von Lehmann, or confirm the patient is his doppelganger. And also, try and locate those papers he's said to have mentioned.

'I hope things will go smoothly between me and this former Wehrmacht captain who's been assigned by the British to help protect me in Berlin,' I told Wolf the day before we left. Biting my lips to keep from saying, 'That after

having been an army whore when we were so close to victory, I never again wanted to be around a German who'd been in the Wehrmacht.'

'All will go well,' Wolf assured me. 'Because you'll only be spending two nights with this man.' He patted my arm. 'So, just call him by his Christian name and treat him like you would a friend.' His voice quieted suddenly, like he had something to say I wouldn't like. 'Because he's expected to arrive from London sometime this evening.'

Words that come back to haunt me every time I recall my meeting with him at Albert von Friesen's chalet. For it was so bizarre it made me gasp. And I questioned whether this was some diabolic joke...? Or just Fate showing a cruel sense of humor?"

CHAPTER THREE

April 29, 1945— Switzerland

Taking a deep, steadying breath, Bela paused before continuing down the sweeping staircase of *Herr* von Friesan's stately chalet. "Please God," she murmured, "may this former German officer the British and Americans have assigned me to work with, be a man who lacks the sense of superiority of the Prussian battle-commanders in Budapest, who gave *Herr* Wallenberg such a hard time."

For if this German is like them, then this meeting here with him could easily wind up in disaster.

Especially, since one of the more experienced girls in the Love Camp was always saying, 'Bela, you're *afraid* because you don't know how to handle the soldiers who come here.'

'Then perhaps it's because I'm of a different spirit,' I'd point out. *A memory that now prayed foremost in my mind as I stepped into the chalet's foyer.*

It was an immense foyer, with its connecting hallway running the length of the house. While high overhead, the light from two chandeliers cast such a dazzling reflection on its mosaic floor, that it looked like a jewel box filled with colorful gems.

"I'm told its exquisite opulence has been known to ease a person's fears and give their mind a rest from the trouble in the world," she recalled writing in her journal. *"And I gaze at this floor in wonder each time I step on it."*

But then— she lifted her head and saw the German. And, immediately, all thoughts about the foyer's beauty left her, as shock more than fear that *gouged her.* "In the name of God!" she gasped, standing frozen to the spot with her brain momentarily stalled.

However, the incredulous look on this former Wehrmacht captain's face, suggested he was having the same problem.

Couldn't be worse if the chandelier with all its crystals had fallen on him, she thought as they stood staring at each other in awkward silence.

Still reeling with disbelief, she wondered if she wasn't hallucinating as she gazed at his peasant-like shirt and pants with suspenders, that covered his tall, well- proportioned frame.

But regardless of his clothes, the longer she stared at him, the more his familiarity became apparent. For this man—even in his loose-fitting clothing—bore a startling resemblance to the Wehrmacht officer in his finely tailored uniform, she was so desperately trying to forget.

Her one-time sex partner serving the German army, whose eyes had looked into hers with a human spark, when she'd led him over to her bed to entertain him at the Love Camp.

Like most such places, the camp was under Gestapo jurisdiction, with soldiers coming in from the military-staging areas nearby. 'We come to this camp for a little pleasure,' they would crow, eager to partake of this *flesh bounty* their government was offering them.

And each time she remembered their drunken breaths and leering faces as they invaded her, she also remembered how close she'd come to throwing herself at the sentries standing guard in their watchtowers, ready to shoot any girl who tried to escape.

Now, after more than two months, the rubicund faces of those soldiers visiting the Love Camp continued to leer at her. With the same expression of the steel-helmeted S.S. man's, when he'd delivered her to the gypsy Madam Kollar, who ran the Love Camp, and ObersturmFuhrer Horst Helmer, who oversaw it.

"And I was such a weakling," Bela later wrote in her journal, *"that I—the same as the other girls— allowed Hitler's gang of inglorious warriors to feast on my body like a flock of savage ravens...since there was nothing else we could do."*

'With often brutal intercourse,' many of the girls in the Love Camp would say, sobbing.

So I'd grown used to looking at the size of a man's penis, because most of our 'honored guests' were beasts.

And if a man had a large penis and slammed into me— as nearly all the soldiers did—then I knew to brace myself and bite back a cry. With the pain shooting through my loins becoming so unbearable, that my tortured body quivered violently whenever the next soldier touched it—"

"Bela," said Jaclyn, intruding on her thoughts. "Our good friend Kurt Ulrich lived in Vienna his first twenty years. So have you two met before?"

Not sure how to answer, her gaze shifted from him to Jaclyn. "Why do you ask?"

"Because he's staring at you like he knows you."

Knows me after our forced intimacy? Of course. And he speaks German with a strong Viennese accent.... But still as stunned as if a bucket of ice water had been poured over her head, she quickly said, "He was a customer who accidentally spilled coffee on my skirt at Demel's."

"Our famous Viennese coffee house?" Jaclyn asked.

"Yes," Bela answered continuing to stare, transfixed, at this alleged German friend— *who came into my life when it was no longer my own.* "And though I realize this coffee spill was a long time ago, the skirt I loved so much was ruined...."

Words that immediately broke Kurt Ulrich's trance, because he stopped looking like he dared not breathe. "And I offered to buy her another, but she refused," he said, smiling ironically as he embellished the tale.

"Refused?" Jaclyn questioned, turning back to her. "Now that surprises me, Bela."

"Well it shouldn't." She shrugged, barely managing to recover her composure as she recalled the OSS warning her, *'Now don't let anything surprise you.'* Then she went onto add, "Because as you know in Vienna, a hand- embroidered wool skirt like I was wearing was a one-of-a-kind piece."

"Which is why I'll always regret my clumsiness," Kurt apologized, taking her hand and bowing in a magnanimous manner. "So I paid for her coffee and pastry, which seemed the very least I could do."

"As I'm sure you've well aware, Bela, Kurt's the man the OSS has assigned to work with you while we're on our special mission in Berlin," said Jaclyn, getting back to their business with them. "And he speaks English like us. Though unlike us, he speaks fluent Russian—the same as von Lehmann." She took Kurt's hand as if mesmerized by his language skills. "But he has no intention of letting the Russians know it, since if they're plotting something concerning us, he'll be apprised of it."

"So that's the reason London's Ros-venor Square sent him?" asked Bela. Resisting the urge to question aloud, ' *How on earth can I manage to be in his presence after what's transpired between us?*'

Ros-venor Square was their shortened name for Grosvenor Square. A name in their present circumstance they found to be too similar to the name *Grossklos*— the surname of their Berlin contact.

"Speaking Russian is not the only reason Ros-venor sent him," said Jaclyn, smiling at him with her usual vibrancy. "Because before he was assigned to the Eastern Front in early '44, his military assignment throughout most of the war was in Berlin. Where he dealt with the Wehrmacht's logistical flow of weapons' manufacture to deliver where needed." She stepped closer to him. "So knowing Berlin like he does means that should we need a guide, we'll have one."

"Then I guess we're fortunate,"said Bela, remembering how Madam Kollar had informed her in the cards she'd taken it upon herself to read for him, '*This Wehrmacht officer and you will meet again, young lady.*'

Jaclyn's smile widened. "So you should be thankful Kurt's your partner....Plus, his mother worked for von Lehmann for many years."

"Qualifications you can't beat," Bela remarked. Although being linked with this man after he'd been one of her '*honored guests*' in the Love Camp, was a complication she didn't need.

The guests acted like pagan forest gods and treated me like they would have done a sacrifice. With the one exception being this wholly familiar man I can't forget...and the last person I ever expected to see in a stately place like this.

"I don't know if Wolf mentioned it," said their host Albert von Friesen, joining them from the library. "But my nephew, Kurt Ulrich, is a former Wehrmacht captain who got captured not too long ago by the British." He paused as if waiting for someone to make a remark about it, but when no one did, he proceeded, "And even if he's still a prisoner- of- war and will remain one after the mission, he's as trustworthy as the other small group of voluntary German prisoners, who're working with the allies to rebuild what they can of their country."

Bela and Jaclyn exchanged looks of surprise.

"Certainly something we weren't expecting to hear," said Jaclyn, shaking her head. "But it goes without saying that being captured by the British is much better than being captured by the Russians. "She squeezed

Kurt's arm. " Since had you fallen into Russian hands, then you'd probably be in prison until you were a very old man."

"No," he corrected. "Until they worked me to death as a young man. Which makes me extremely grateful that the military- transport plane carrying me to Poland had to make a forced landing."

Jaclyn stared at him like she couldn't imagine. "Yet you managed to fall into British hands instead of Russian in that part of the world, so how did it happen?"

"We got hit, had a fuel leak, and had to make a landing in a field at night. Where a special British or *Tommie*—as I call them by their Great War name— reconnaissance patrol was attempting to access the situation between the Germans and *Ivan*. The name we Eastern Front soldiers gave the Russians forces.... And when this Tommie patrol saw us, they took us prisoners and put us on the aircraft sent to pick them up."

"And no doubt the Germans reported you as missing," said Jaclyn, linking her arm through his, *grande dame* like. "Which tells me luck is definitely on your side."

"The British abused him in his first POW camp," Albert spoke up, his paunchy stomach straining against his shiny gray vest. "But the OSS told me they don't want *him* or *us* talking about it because it was a big misunderstanding. So, let's concentrate on how fast they flew Kurt here from London for the mission." He removed a slip of paper from his pocket. "In addition to the latest news, that a second encrypted message has aired on the Morse saying: *"Doktor Grossklos Knows—Action needed."*

"But what about our briefing earlier today?" Jaclyn asked. "When it was brought to our attention that a person in British intelligence has suggested that regardless of these messages, our good doctor could be dead."

Albert gave his head a disapproving shake. "Pure speculation–"

"I agree." Kurt remarked, breaking his flow. "Which is the reason we need to stay focused on the message that implies Dr. Grossklos has information either about von Lehmann and his preliminary designs — or his doppelganger."

As if pleased with his certainty, Albert gave a nod. "Something I'm counting on. Because the good doctor and I became great friends when it was easier to travel between Germany and Switzerland."

"So I heard," said Kurt. "But moving on—" He lifted his eyes to Bela. "How is it I disappear for a few years and come back to discover my cousin Wolf is married to a well-known musician, with a beautiful sister whose honeyed skin is the same color as her hair?"

He indicated the flossy sweep of Bela's curls falling in restless waves above her shoulders.

Since you're the German who visited me at the Love Camp, then you'll remember I have hideous words and numbers the camp tattooed in blue letters between my breasts—Feldhure 101024. 'Because it makes the business here run smoother,' I was told when they put them on me.... Words that now make me want to scream every time I undress!

Most of the time she kept the words and numbers covered with a bandage.

Understanding that, like the yellow star she'd been forced to wear in Budapest, Madam Kollar had said the tattooed numbers were on all the girls because—unknown to the soldiers—most of the girls at the Love Camp were Jewish. A more subtle way than a yellow star, of hiding the fact that sexual relations between Germans and Jews were strictly forbidden.

Even so, it still made no sense to Bela, since tattooed numbers were clearly not a replacement for yellow stars. So she guessed the kindly Madam Kollar was attempting to soften the blow of the tattooed numbers the girls hated so badly, by connecting them with the yellow stars. Because when it came to pleasuring the soldiers awaiting orders to prepare for the next Russian onslaught, it didn't matter.... *Since the Gestapo had made it quite clear to me when they'd grabbed me, that any young, good-looking female — Jewish or otherwise—they could lay their hands on, would do just fine for the staging area soldiers nearby.*

"Bela, please," Jaclyn whispered. "I can tell there's something about Kurt that's disturbing you? Or— "She looked at him. "Is it because you met in happier times before the war?"

"Happier times," she answered, thinking quickly. "Since my life in Vienna always brings back a rich flood of memories."

"As does mine," said Kurt, his tone holding genuine warmth which, considering the circumstances, helped to relax her a little.

He turned to Jaclyn. "But what does Wolf have to say about my being here with the three of you?"

"Just that you're a fellow ally, and he intends to get along with you," she said, glancing in the direction of the library. "Which could explain why he's been busy studying some aerial photographs the British sent him, of the bombed-out ruins of your father-in-law's house in Berlin."

Surprised, Bela turned to Kurt. "So you're married, *Herr* Ulrich?"

"Was." He stared at the mosaic floor for a moment. "My wife and toddler son were killed in a Berlin air raid in November '44."

"Sorry to hear it, but was it while you were on the Eastern Front?"

"Yes—" he began, then stopped mid-sentence when he saw Wolf coming toward him with a photo album tucked under his arm.

"Kurt," Wolf said, placing the album on the foyer's small- entry table before going over to him and shaking his hand. "I must say I'm still surprised the British sent you to us."

"And I must say with the war taking such an unexpected turn, I never expected us to meet again —much less under these circumstances."

Wolf's expression immediately shifted to one of chagrin. "Thought the Germans would win, did you?"

"In the beginning—yes."

"But they forgot that in their conquered countries, there were those like my gorgeous wife here—"He turned to Jaclyn. "Who master-minded not only our escape but our neighbors. When the Russians began their Budapest invasion during the Christmas season of '44."

"Which is the reason I insisted she join the Berlin mission," remarked Albert, ushering the group toward the chalet's dining room.

"His remarks are kind," Jaclyn said,"but there are many women in the resistance who've done far more than I have."

"Maybe, but they're not part of our Berlin mission," said Kurt, taking the hanger Albert handed him from the foyer's coat- rack, with his shirt, slacks, and navy- blue dinner jacket on it.

"These pieces I purchased for you, Kurt, just arrived. But your vest, shoes, tie, and belt came earlier." He indicated a half-closed door." And they're in a package under my desk in the library. So hurry and change."

The chalet's serving woman, Ina, entered carrying a shiny, soup tureen on a large, silver tray. And Albert opened the door for her but kept it closed until Kurt returned.

"As we see, *good people*, dinner is ready." He put his hand on Kurt's shoulder. "Which means you're welcome to sit in the place you find most comfortable."

So as usual, Wolf took his seat next to Jaclyn. But when Bela started to take hers next to Albert at the head of the table, Kurt pulled out a dining chair for her farther down. "I'd be very pleased if you'd sit next to me." He clicked his heels and bowed like a true, *debonair* Viennese. "But would you like to sit here or in the chair next to Jaclyn?"

"Here. "Bela ran her hand across the top of the chair. "And you take the chair next to her."

"Then it'll be my pleasure." He bowed again.

Trying to relax, she took a deep breath. *Is he being a trifle unctuous? Or do I mistrust his friendship? Perhaps a little of both.*

Still, what happens if he tries to pick up where we left off?

After all, he'd turned back to look at her as he'd left the brothel, and his adoring look had managed to deepen her feelings for him. *So what to do?*

Avoid him as much as possible. For even with his hugs and kisses in the Love Camp, she still hadn't forgotten he was serving the German army when she'd been forced to become his sex partner.

That, to my shame, I couldn't protest. And would give people I meet nowadays, a good reason to ask me why? Since if they ever learned I became a field-whore in order to survive, I'd be humiliated and ostracized.

But regardless, in order to carry out their Berlin mission, she owed it to Wolf and Jaclyn to try to get along with Kurt. So even if she did find his intense looks and challenging smile a bit disconcerting in his elegant dinner jacket, she returned his smile as she sat down beside him.

*If everyone supposedly has a double, then I'll pretend he's that Wehrmacht captain's...*aware how the softness in his dark eyes mirrored the same sensitive and responsive nature she'd seen when she'd first met him.

No signs of German ribaldry there. Just his humanity, which given our shared past, makes him dangerous to my heart. On top of which, the shock of deep, brown hair falling across the brow of his handsome face, hints at a fun-loving, Viennese life style. Making me question if in the back of my mind, I want to strike up some kind of relationship with him?

Reaching for his napkin, Kurt smiled again at Bela. "This is marvelous," he said, gesturing at the table, laden with Dresden china dishes filled with pate, Swiss dumplings, *Wiener schnitzel,* and roast goose. "I'd all but forgotten what civilization was like." He was silent for a moment, as if giving it further reflection. "And I'm finding it hard to believe places like this are still standing in Europe."

"So did I when I first came here," said Bela, turning to gaze at the oil painting of a beautiful, Hungarian woman in a gilded frame, hanging above the dining room's sideboard.

"A painting Bela and I consider a sad reminder, "remarked Jaclyn, also gazing at it. "Since like in Budapest, the women in Berlin are bedding the Russian soldiers in order to keep from starving."

Kurt looked disturbed. "So the Tommies told me—"

"Thanks to Ina and Jutta, we now have the chalet's excellent wine for the toast I wish to make," interrupted Albert with a grin. He turned to this other serving girl, who was dressed in old-fashioned black, the same as Ina. And like her, she also carried a tray of wine glasses, overflowing with this excellent wine.

They were the household's two main maids. And since no one was seated on the opposite side of the table, it made it easier for them to move around as they served.

Albert wrapped his beefy fingers around one of the glass's stems. "To the success of my beloved family's mission in Berlin."

His gray eyes glowed with pleasure as everyone at the table clinked their glasses together.

"I've missed good wine," Kurt remarked, sipping his slowly as if trying not to spill any of it on his new jacket.

Which he certainly wears to good effect, with his broad shoulders and slender waist. Bela admired, unable to take her eyes off him.

"How did you and Jaclyn meet?" Kurt asked Wolf, seeming eager to change the subject as he helped himself to a slice of roast goose.

"Through Bela's father, Haral Spigel." He flapped a hand in her direction. "Who was a wealthy banker in Budapest."

"Ah, Spigel," Kurt mused. "A good German name, but also one popular with Jews. When a century ago the emperor, Franz Josef, forced them to take German names."

"Which caused many of my non-Jewish friends to get in trouble," said Wolf. "And though it wasn't easy to get out of Austria, I learned from them which hands to put the money in before I moved to Budapest....And while living there, I applied for Hungarian citizenship and bought an aircraft -parts plant outside the city." He winked at Bela. "And her father became my partner as well as my best friend."

"Quite a story, " said Kurt.

"That it was," Jaclyn agreed. "Since Haral was a Hungarian who'd lived in Vienna and Wolf, an Austrian who'd moved to Budapest. The Pearl of the Danube."

"And when Haral learned a German general requested I return to Vienna, on business for the a week-end," Wolf continued, "he helped me get an invitation to attend a concert featuring his step-daughter, the very talented, Jaclyn Tirand."

"And the party immediately following it," Jaclyn added. "But don't forget he gave you a gift to give me."

"A gift?" Kurt questioned with a curious grin. "Now that was a clever way to bring the two of you together."

"It really was." Jaclyn beamed. "Considering the gift turned out to be a gold-plated lock and key set that had a tiny, sculptured elephant perched on top of it."

"And I was more than happy to deliver it." Wolf grinned in response. "But had trouble giving it to her at the party, because Jaclyn's outstanding performance brought her so much acclaim, that S.S. officers were buzzing around her like flies swarming a honeypot."

"Even so, he caught my attention." Jaclyn laughed, giving him a good-natured nudge. "Especially when he asked me why it was that we'd not met before?"

"And your answer?" Kurt asked.

"Because I was still French and returned home whenever I could."

"It was the same question I asked Bela's father six weeks later," said Wolf. "When Jaclyn and I announced our engagement in Paris, where I was visiting her on a regular basis."

Kurt pointed at the large, white diamond weighing down Jaclyn's well-manicured, left hand. "That's quite a lovely wedding ring."

"It really is." She smiled. "But I treasure this one just as much." She held up a similar diamond in a band weighting down her right hand. "It was the ring Bela's father gave my mother. And it's really Bela's, but she insists I wear it until she makes up her mind to do so."

"Bela's father was Jaclyn's mother's husband," Wolf explained."And they met in Paris where he saw her perform."

"Was he a patron of Vienna's Conservatory?" Kurt asked.

Wolf nodded. "And he was so impressed with her cello playing and Jaclyn's, that he brought the two ladies back to Vienna and made the proper introductions for them at the place."

Kurt glanced from Bela to Wolf. "He must have had a great deal of influence... but where is he now?"

"Dead."

"*Dead?*" Kurt questioned, immediately solemn. "What happened?"

"The war," Wolf said. "But he made me Bela's legal guardian until she comes of age."

"Which— provided the world does not get blown up— I'll do next month," she remarked with a tentative smile.

"A powerful incentive that tells me you'd better get in and out of Berlin before the city dies," warned Albert, with a look of grim amusement.

"True," said Jaclyn, a little breathless as she turned to Kurt. "Which must be sad for you since your wife's family are Berliners."

"It is," he remarked in a strained tone. "Especially the part about the zoo and Zoo Bunker."

Albert turned his attention to Jaclyn. "Kurt met his wife at the zoo."

"T...the zoo? "she said brokenly, clearly surprised. "Where at the zoo?"

"In front of the giraffes," Kurt answered. "Since I've always had a fondness for them and hadn't been in Berlin long,when I decided to pay them a visit."

"And your future wife was there?"

"Yes. And I remarked to her that I'd hate to think what it would be like if a giraffe got a sore throat. And she cringed. As did her cousin and his wife from Cologne who were with her." His dark eyes softened. "And these relatives noticed the immediate attraction between us. So, seeing I was in uniform, they invited me to join the three of them for dinner at a fine restaurant. And afterwards, we four went to my future- wife's hospital, where she worked as a nurse for her father, Doctor Carl Grossklos."

"And then?" Jaclyn asked.

"I bought some flowers for her outside the hospital, and s... she hugged me."

Appearing immersed in the memory, he had difficulty saying the words.

"Which inspired me to kiss her on both cheeks. 'What do you think?' I asked her.

'Was it destiny that brought us together?'

'Absolutely.' She smiled.

And from then on we were rarely apart —even when she had to work nights at the hospital. So, since I was an officer, I asked permission of my commanding colonel to allow me to do volunteer work there in the evenings. And he agreed, as long as I did nothing more than shuffle papers."

Jaclyn's eyes held an uncertain expression. "And Dr. Grossklos. What did he have to say about you and his daughter?"

"The good doctor gave us his blessing and let it be known that in these dangerous times, we needed to marry quickly. In fact— he talked the military into letting me live at his house rather than the barracks." Kurt closed his eyes for a moment as if struck by such an irrevocable sadness, that he hardly dared to breathe. "And we were so anxious for a child, and her father a grandchild, that our wish came true in nine months."

Since it was obvious to everyone at the table the recollection was hard for him, Jaclyn took the liberty of switching the subject to something safer. "But getting back to the animals in the zoo." She pressed her hand against his arm. "Did the British mention anything about their being let out of their cages, shot, and eaten by the Berliners?"

"They did." He frowned. "But that's what people do when they're starving."

Albert leaned forward and poured Wolf some more wine. "Which is another good reason you need to get in and out of Berlin quickly."

"Well isn't that why we're doing what we're doing?" he asked. "Trying our best in the short amount of time we have to confirm von Lehmann's identity. In addition to locate information about his preliminary designs on how to put together an improved long-range V-3 Cannon Rocket with an atomic warhead."

CHAPTER FOUR

Bela arched a brow. "Which as you know, we need to do before this information falls into Russian or German hands."

Albert gave his head a vigorous shake. "If you're lucky. But need I remind you the Morse that came yesterday from a British source in Berlin, continues to suggest that— like the Russians—there's a fear von Lehmann could be dead. And his designs for the improved V-3 rocket destroyed."

Kurt cast an ironic eye at him. "But you know as well as I do, that until we actually get in the city and investigate it, we won't know anything."

"Unstable times," Wolf remarked to Kurt. "Especially with that strange message *"Doktor Grossklos Knows—Action needed."* So tell me, what do you think it is your father-in-law knows?"

"I doubt anything. Since in the last letter I received from him, he wrote that he rarely leaves the hospital."

Jaclyn perked up. "Same as the doctors were doing in Budapest, in their subterranean hospital buried under Castle Hill. And Wolf and I were given the opportunity to help them, but it was urgent we retreat from the city and make it to Vienna."

"It still surprises me the two of you were able to get out of Budapest, with *Ivan* 's troops bearing down so hard, "said Kurt, passing the bread basket to Bela.

"The few that escaped got out on the first wave," said Albert, spearing a small potato with his fork. "But Wolfgang and Jaclyn got out on the third, which was truly amazing."

"How did you manage it, Wolf?" asked Kurt, their eyes meeting.

"For one thing we were able to travel a bumpy, back road into Vienna in our well-kept Mercedes." Then looking preoccupied, he briefly stared past him. "Since the Russians had seized the main road linking Budapest to Vienna."

"But taking that back road route was extremely tricky," Jaclyn pointed out. "In fact, we often saw German and Hungarian troops on the front lines fighting the Russians over the Lake Balaton oil."

"Lake Balaton," Kurt repeated with a slight shudder. "Hard to believe all that was happening not far from the area where von Lehmann often took my mother and me to vacation." A silence passed before he added, "And even harder to believe that in March, a month ago, the fight for Lake Balaton against the Russians is said to be the last German offensive of the war."

Jaclyn's eyes narrowed. "The Russians are certainly a determined group of people. Since they were able to stop most of the German troops in Budapest, from leaving the city."

Wolf took a gulp of wine. "Which considering we were close enough to Budapest, we could see thousands of fires blazing, and hear machine guns and bombs exploding. 'The blood-red sky from the Red Army', we'd say. And in the village where we were staying, we saw bombs ripping the roofs off buildings, causing the main roads to be blocked with enormous pieces of debris."

"And we learned in this unrestful atmosphere, screaming women were being raped with pistols in their faces," said Jaclyn, fidgeting in her chair like she wanted to shut off the thought— "As Russian tanks continued to plow through Budapest, next to our village."

"So we did what we could." Wolf sighed, his face tense. "Which is the reason Jaclyn's long hair caught fire." He half-turned to her. "She was trying to rescue a frightened girl."

"But now." Albert grinned. "After having her hair trimmed in that spiky bob, she looks like an *avante-guarde* French model."

"When they told me in London that Jaclyn and Bela would be posing as secretaries and coming with us, "said Kurt, "I found it hard to believe. But since Jaclyn went through hell on the outskirts of Budapest, then Berlin should offer nothing unexpected." He turned his focus to Bela. "But what about you, weren't you with them?"

Just the mention of the words *Lake Balaton* and its outskirts, unnerved her. But tonight, of course, talking about it couldn't be helped. "We got separated. And Wolf and Jaclyn wouldn't leave, until their friend Raoul Wallenberg, helped uncover the news about my whereabouts." *Which she had no intention of mentioning what some called, the Lake Balaton Love Camp.*

Kurt averted his face from hers, like he knew better than to ask her where she was when she got separated from them. "So that explains why Wolf and Jaclyn left the village on the third wave and not the first."

"My sister and her husband didn't share my experiences," Bela said, feeling strangely obligated to remind him. "But as I later explained to the OSS, I went through a lot where I was." A moment passed as she assembled her thoughts. "And the OSS was so fearful the Russians would capture a rocket scientist like von Lehmann, they honored my request to receive the same training they were giving Wolf and Jaclyn."

Kurt emptied his wine glass. "It's good the Swiss are allowing the OSS to operate here."

"It is," Albert agreed. "Though, it's the Americans who're supposed to be running it. Even if these days, the British seem to have quite a hand in its operation."

Wolf darted a glance at Kurt. "They've only allowed the British to have it, because they know Europe could easily be blown off the map. Which I trust, the London OSS emphasized when they briefed you?"

"They did... but more delicately."

"Delicately?" Jaclyn questioned, her brows rising. "A peculiar word for our upcoming mission."

"I suppose." Kurt shrugged. "But considering von Lehmann's quite possibly being held by the Russians in the Potsdam Hospital, I guess they were afraid that if it sounded too dangerous, I'd refuse to go."

"Relative or not, Kurt," said Wolf," I'm still surprised the OSS allowed you to come on this mission—"

"Why?" Albert cut in sharply. "Because he's a former Wehrmacht captain, who's made his amends? Or because he's a prisoner- of- war?"

"A prisoner- of-war," Wolf snapped. "Since allowing captured German soldiers to volunteer as counter-intelligence agents, sounds to me like those in charge have been drinking." There was a slight hesitation before he spoke again. "Especially when you consider it's well-known that excessive alcohol can bend moonbeams in such a way, that it turns them into a false reality. So whatever makes them think they can trust these Germans?"

Kurt's face darkened. "In my case it happens to be family. And I was being flown from Hungary to Poland since—with *Ivan* advancing there—the Germans were desperate for commanding officers. "He looked around the table at everyone." It was a difficult time. But one I was willing to endure, because my father-in-law was trying to get me transferred to Berlin, on the pretext of attempting to locate von Lehmann."

"However, a month passed before the British discovered his connection with him and with me," said Albert." And when they did, I let it be known in no uncertain terms I wanted him in on this special mission, I was helping the OSS put together to find and rescue my brother."

Wolf gazed at Kurt apprehensively. "Still, Cousin, you and von Lehmann parted on such bad terms that I find it hard to believe you actually volunteered to come along."

"For God's sake, Wolf!" said Albert slamming his fist against the table. "Isn't it clear that von Lehmann's a relative of Kurt's?"

"But not a legal one," he said coldly. "As I'm sure the British kept reminding him."

Jaclyn stared at Ina as she placed a baked *Apfelstrudel* topped with whipped cream, on a china plate in front of her. "Not a legal one, Wolf, like u...uh," she sputtered a bit.

"Bastard," Kurt answered, before Wolf could. "Which is why I carry my mother's name and not the *von Friesen* one."

Jutta put the same dessert in front of Bela. And she started to pick up her fork and take a bite, but slightly flustered, she hesitated. *Wolf was certainly making sure no one in the room missed the fact Kurt was a bastard.* A degrading that bothered her as she recalled Kurt at the Love Camp, taking her in his arms and holding her so tightly against him, it was like the ache in his soul echoed the ache in her own.

Because like her, Kurt had seemed to need the closeness of another human being. Something she would have never thought possible from a German. But once he'd snuggled his head against her chest, she'd been unable to resist his unsettling warmth.

So naturally she'd reached out to him in a way no Jewish girl in her right mind, should ever reach out to an officer in the Wehrmacht. *If only I could hate him…then sitting here beside him wouldn't be so hard.*

"What I'm saying," said Kurt, after a brief silence. "Is that I'm the illegitimate son of Albert's half-brother, Frederick. Who was married and had a four year old boy."

It was obvious Kurt was having difficulty remaining calm because another silence followed. "But sadly my father died of pneumonia while I was still a baby."

Surprised, Jaclyn turned to Wolf. "You mean your father and Albert's had a half- brother?"

"My grandfather was widowed with a son when he married my grandmother— but I thought I'd told you?"

"I don't think so, because I'd remember all those *halves* in your family."

"Probably." Albert laughed. "Since as of now only two *wholes* are left."

"Who are?" Jaclyn asked him, shaking her head like she was struggling to keep it straight.

"Von Lehmann and myself…with Wolf's father, of course, long dead—"

"Only von Lehmann's more like a half than a whole," Wolf interjected. "Because he's an eccentric old man, who uses a made-up professional name rather than his family one."

"Enough, Wolf!" Albert intervened, appearing alarmed at the turn the conversation was taking. "My brother is a genius who likes the name *von Lehmann*. And refuses to be called by his Christian name *Wilhelm*."

"Like you prefer to be called *von Friesen* rather than *Albert*?" asked Wolf, rubbing it in.

"Exactly," said Albert glancing sideways at Kurt. "But do we finish the rest of your story or drop it?"

"You finish it for me."

"Then I'll get back to von Lehmann and the way he took in Kurt, and his mother *Romelia Ulrich*— who'd lost her job in a cheap dance hall. 'I can hardly leave them to beg on the streets of Berlin,' I remembered him telling me. And though my wife was ill, Wolf's father and I would have found a way to help to Kurt and his mother, had von Lehmann insisted it wasn't necessary. And he proceeded to raise my beloved Kurt here, like a son. Enrolling him in the military school he requested, plus paying his tuition so he could earn his engineering degree at Vienna's university."

Jaclyn acknowledged his generosity with a smile. "Sounds like Kurt was lucky to have von Lehmann for a father."

"He was," Wolf agreed. "Though he didn't appreciate it—"

"Didn't appreciate it?" Kurt questioned, raising his voice. "I promised the OSS I'd get along with you, Wolf, but I've heard about enough. And besides you were so opposed to the Nazis, I find it odd you didn't leave what you called the *anti-Semitic* Vienna and join the allies."

"Didn't the OSS explain that to you?"

Kurt shook his head. "Not clearly."

Wolf glowered at him. "In case you don't remember, Budapest was safe from the Nazis until close to the end. So since, later, I was helping *Herr* Wallenberg save as many Jews as he could, I had no intention of leaving."

The sudden animosity between Wolf and Kurt alarmed Bela. Maybe Albert hadn't sensed it until now, but if he had, then what was he doing recommending they be paired together on such a dangerous mission?

"Toward the end, Adolph Eichmann all but shut down the Swedish Embassy in Budapest," Jaclyn explained, giving Wolf a gentle tap on his arm as if to reign in his irritation. "Yet our dear *Herr* Wallenberg, still managed to save many lives."

"Jewish lives," Albert said. "Because by staying in Budapest, Wolf and Jaclyn were able to help Wallenberg negotiate with the German high command." He turned toward Kurt. "To keep the people the Nazis were so hell-bent on slaughtering, from either being sent to those dreadful camps or machine gunned."

Continuing to glower at Kurt, Wolf's eyes widened. "Surely the OSS told you about the concentration camps," he remarked, with a hint of sarcasm.

"We saw a good many pictures, though—" Kurt flinched, his face both tense and defensive. "Goebbels never let the truth get past him."

"Which like many Germans," remarked Wolf in a cutting tone, "leads me to believe you had no knowledge of the atrocities committed in those camps."

Kurt ran his napkin over his mouth. "If a man had a feather of suspicion, he quickly learned to keep his mouth shut."

Wolf uttered a curse. "Like you, Cousin?"

"Yes like me," he stressed. "And besides I wasn't on the front 'till '44, where retreating Wehrmacht soldiers weren't afraid to have open discussions concerning the rumors of the camps."

"Rumors?" Wolf questioned,

"Yes *rumors*," Albert interceded. "So go easy on him, since he lost his family." He gazed at Kurt with a somber look. "And since he was highly decorated for his exemplary expertise in logistics, I'm convinced his estranged, half-brother's family was somehow behind his transfer to that dreadful, Eastern Front."

"Doesn't matter." Wolf flared, his anger intensifying. "Since he heard about those camps but still did nothing."

"What was I supposed to do? "Kurt asked. "I had a family and wanted to keep them safe."

Wolf made a belittling sound in his throat. "You joined the Wehrmacht before you married, so you must have heard something. But then, you always showed an indifference toward Vienna's Jews."

"Indifference?" Kurt asked, looking like he'd been punched in the belly and lost his breath. "I never disliked Jews but kept my distance from them since most were wealthy, and we didn't have much in common."

CHAPTER FIVE

An uncomfortable moment followed as Bela took a long drink. She wished she had the courage to say, *'If you feel like that, you have no business showing yourself in my world here...'* then glancing at Albert, she wanted to ask, *'Could you not have found any other person besides Kurt Ulrich to be my partner?'*

Should the need arise, she had no problem sacrificing her life for Jaclyn and Wolf. But when it came to a former Wehrmacht officer who'd just admitted keeping his distance from Jews, would she be able to do it for him?

Still, he'd done it for her when he'd talked Madam Kollar into tearing up her two reports... but then he hadn't realized she was Jewish.

'You weren't there that November night, Herr Ulrich,' she wanted to say. *'And you didn't see the Arrow-Cross militia and Gestapo order the Jews to take off their shoes before machine gunning them and throwing their bodies into the eternal coldness of the Danube's freezing waters.'*

Suddenly weighed down with this deluge of memories, she shoved her *apfelstrudle* aside. It was hardly kosher food, but after what she'd been forced to eat in order to survive, it hadn't seemed to matter. *There's so much hunger in the world it's not right to waste food. So one of the maids can have it.*

"Please excuse me." She jerked to her feet. "But if I'm accompanying Jaclyn on the piano later, I need to freshen up in the powder room."

"Then do what you must." Kurt smiled, pushing her chair out.

His unwanted solicitude did seem sincere. Prompting her to continue to wonder if down the road, he had hopes of picking-up where they'd left off.

"I need to freshen up too," said Jaclyn, her burgundy, column-style gown clinging to her slender form as she joined Bela.

It was always a source of comfort for Bela to have Jaclyn when she needed someone to talk to.

"My intuition tells me something about Kurt continues to disturb you," said Jaclyn, once they reached the powder room. "Am I right?"

She nodded. "But what really makes me angry is feeling like a child, each time I let it."

"Understandable. Because if I'd been subjected to what you've been, then there's no way I'd be holding up." She stared at Bela in the room's large mirror like she was taking stock of her. "But tell me in detail what is it about Kurt that's affecting you?"

At a sudden loss as where to begin, Bela simply asked, "Aside from being von Lehmann's nephew, why was Kurt Ulrich chosen for this mission? I mean like Wolf implied, shouldn't a prisoner- of- war be kept in a prison camp and not released before the war ends?"

"It does make you wonder," Jaclyn said, reaching into the small, cosmetic bag she kept in the room. "And it surprises me. Which is why I was shocked when I learned he was a prisoner -of -war. Something Albert must have noticed, because at dinner he slipped me a note saying that after the Berlin mission, the OSS had put it in writing that Kurt will remain a prisoner in his custody here in Switzerland—"

"Like a house arrest?"

"Exactly. But written or otherwise, the way the OSS is known to renege on their promises, Albert says he's prepared to fight them if Kurt is forced to remain in Britain."

She dabbed some perfume on her wrists and quickly began rubbing them together. "Because Kurt's convinced he's going back to being housed in a special holding area in Britain with the other captured inmates like himself, who've volunteered to help rebuild their country."

Bela reached for a tissue. "If I were a prisoner- of- war, I wouldn't be willing to go back."

"Of course you wouldn't. But apparently with Kurt, things are different."

"Different?" she questioned, thrown by the words. "In what way?"

"Different because as mentioned earlier, his wife and toddler son got caught in the cross-fires of war and were killed in a Berlin air raid." She allowed a thread of hesitation to pass before adding, "So, he probably feels he has nothing to lose."

An unwanted pang of sympathy gave Bela a mental shake. "Sounds like Kurt might have a death wish."

"Not really." Jaclyn emptied her bag and reached for the red lipstick in it. "Even if I do get the impression Albert feels Kurt's truly willing to take his chances, since he's concerned about the Dr. Grossklos message." Another hesitation followed as she applied her lipstick. "Which he should be. Since the good doctor is a humanitarian, who was daring enough to slip Albert money in order to help the Palestinian Jews smuggle Jewish children into Great Britain."

Bela's brows lifted in surprise. "Quite worthy of him, but does Kurt know?"

"Why do you ask?"

"Because I somehow get the impression Kurt doesn't care much for Jews."

"Well— he did admit he had nothing in common with them." She frowned as if considering it. "But don't forget, my Wolf once claimed he felt the same way. Telling me it was only because he hated bullies so much that he began fighting the Nazis."

"And still is from the way he was talking to Kurt."

"Like so many people." Jaclyn rolled her eyes. "But changing the subject to something more pleasant. Wolf and I gave our word to *Herr* Wallenberg before the Russians took him, that we'd go to Palestine to help the Jewish refugees, he felt certain would be arriving there—"

"In that hostile place?"

"Yes. Because even with all the restrictions, he knew how determined they were to build a new Israel."

"I don't doubt it, since I'd still like to move there."

"So Wolf and I know. Which is why we won't go there without you." She dodged Bela's gaze, like she hated to be the one to say it. "But even so, you'll need those false papers showing you to be an Aryan- Christian—"

"That the church finally gave you?"

"After they thought you were dead. Which fortunately, got you out of Vienna and into Switzerland with us."

"But with Arabs continuing to shoot Jews the way newspapers are reporting, then I'm not sure my papers will work there, without a baptism certificate."

"Why? Because they'll probably be as difficult in Palestine as they were in Budapest?"

Bela stifled a sigh. "That's what I suspect."

"Maybe so," Jaclyn said, applying more lipstick. "But Wolf and I will cross that bridge when we get to it. So in the meantime, don't worry and just think about Palestine."

"Which you both know would be a dream come true for me."

"Same as it is for Wolf and me. Though, he did make me promise not to tell you until after Berlin, but the truth is—" She stopped to dab her cheeks with a bottled, rose-colored stain. "I'm the worst in the world at keeping secrets."

"I know." Bela smiled. "But sometimes it can't be helped."

"Wolf didn't want me to tell you because he feared if you changed your mind about going to Berlin with us, you'd think we wouldn't take you to Palestine."

"I'd never think that after the risks you took to get me out of that Love Camp."

"Still, that's no reason you should feel obligated to make the Berlin trip."

"Think again."

A silence passed as Bela remembered the resourceful Gestapo man who'd explained her presence to Madam Kollar and ObersturmFuhrer Horst Helmer at the Love Camp.

CHAPTER SIX

'There's been a mistake,' the Gestapo man had informed them. 'Because the girl here who's called *Bela Spigel* is *Bela Tirand and* needs to be released at once.' Then reaching into a drawstring bag, he'd handed over several diamond rings and a hefty sum of British pounds to ObersturmFuhrer Helmer.

'A transaction only possible,' Wolf had later explained, 'because I had industrial connections with important, Nazi party officials. And the Russians were bearing down so hard on Budapest, that bribery was easy. Hence, the submarine authority documents to Buenos Aires, which we code-worded as U-boat tickets. So ObersturmFuhrer Helmer and the Gestapo man handling your release, could make their escape from Europe through Denmark.'

"*My release,*" she'd written in her journal. "*Which afterwards I feared would end up being my demise. Since for the several months following it, death appeared to be the only way of ridding myself of all this filth the Germans had put on me.*

And had Wolf not sent that Gestapo man to rescue me, I would have been liberated like the other girls— as the S.S. called it. Which meant either shooting them or working them to death in the freezing cold, before the Russians came.

So I finally came to my senses and thanked God for the luck he'd showered on me—even at the Love Camp. With the stress and tension of having intercourse with so many different men, often causing many of the girls to have severe diarrhea. A problem I was fortunate enough not to have, because the S.S. dealt with those girls by quickly transferring them to a death camp."

"I'll always regret," said Jaclyn, breaking into Bela's wandering thoughts, "that Wolf and I weren't able to find a way to get you and Haral out of Budapest before the Nazis took over."

"You did what you could, but in the end it was Pa and I who made the choice," she said, feeling sorry she never seemed to have the right words to cheer Jaclyn up, when she talked like that. "Which makes me feel bad I mentioned Kurt and worried you." She stared at herself in the mirror as she grappled with her familiar memories of him. "But the truth is, he reminds me of a German officer who visited me at the Love Camp."

"*The Love Camp!*" Jaclyn cried. "And you think there's a possibility Kurt could be that man?"

"They certainly look alike."

Awestruck, Jaclyn gazed at her. "But you did first meet Kurt at Demel's?"

"Yes," she answered, feeling a total fraud. "And never thought I'd see him again."

"I don't doubt it." Jaclyn sighed, shaking her head. "But tell me, this officer who came to the Love Camp, do you remember his rank?"

She thought about the greatcoat Kurt had placed on her bed before he'd left to talk with Madam Kollar. "From what I saw under the poor lighting, there were no glimpses of rank on his greatcoat with its half-belt in back showing. Though, his uniform did look like a captain's." Then remembering the way she'd responded to him, she stopped, embarrassed. "Although he removed his uniform so quickly, I didn't have much time to notice."

"Dear Lord!" exclaimed Jaclyn, crossing herself. "You should ask him—or better yet, let me."

"I'll do it," Bela said, knowing better than to let her.

"Still, sweet baby, if Kurt's abused you, then Wolf and I need to know it."

"But why? Since if he is that man, then he's the only soldier who came to the Love Camp who didn't treat me like a beast."

"Even so." Jaclyn flared. "It doesn't change my opinion about men who visit such places. And besides, Kurt's been toted as being such a devoted family man, that it surprises me to think he would have ever gone to a place like the Love Camp."

Bela's face burned each time she remembered the soul-searching look on his face when he'd stepped over to her bed and started taking off his clothes. The enemy who'd made her feel treasured. And had created such a turmoil of emotions in her, that he'd heightened her shame with the insidious warmth of her desire for him.

Yet here she was... *upset with him*, when she should be *upset with herself*, for not being able to keep her mind off him.

Jaclyn 's brows arched in challenge. "If Kurt and you are going to be working together, you should have some kind of rapport. Which could be difficult if you think he visited you in the Love Camp."

It was, of course. But since she'd promised herself she wouldn't jeopardize their mission together, she suddenly regretted having almost revealed his identity. "Like I said, I'll ask him."

Jaclyn appeared to deliberate for a moment. "As long as it doesn't bother you. Still— considering how he seems to disturb you— this may sound odd, but I couldn't keep from noticing the numerous times he flirted with you at the table. And it was —" She stalled as if not sure how to continue, "Almost like you were enjoying it."

"Then if I was, it clearly means he wasn't the man who visited me at the Love Camp," said Bela, in an attempt to put aside her emotions concerning him and stay focused on their mission.

"Hopefully not." Jaclyn nodded and smiled. "Even if I do get the feeling there's more between you and Kurt than a coffee spill at Demel's. And the real threat for you might not be Berlin, but the way Kurt's stirring your emotions—"

"Surely you don't mean what I think you mean?"

"Only time will tell." She slid her lipstick back in its tube. "So talk with him about what's bothering you. And since you're required to show him those notes you took this morning when that OSS man briefed us, it'll provide you with an excellent excuse to do it."

"That it should," Bela agreed, curious as to how Kurt would act when they were alone together.

"However, understand *this*," said Jaclyn in a firm voice. "The minute we return from our Berlin mission, there's a strong possibility Wolf will confront Kurt about the Love Camp."

"Even if I'm not sure?" asked Bela, trying harder to cover it.

"It won't matter. Since it's not about you, but about what that Gestapo man said to Wolf in Vienna before we left for Switzerland."

Bela lips pursed as a quiver shot through her. "About Kurt?"

"Who else?"

She was appalled. "And this man said *what?*"

"Just a mumble under his breath in a derogatory way, that implied Wolf had a relative who'd visited the Love Camp."

Mystified, Bela shook her head. "But how could he know unless someone told him?"

"Quite possibly someone did. But don't forget, the Gestapo claimed to know everything. And this man was resourceful enough to slip through Russian and German lines to rescue you. So he must have had his sources."

"If Wolf thought Kurt had visited me at the Love Camp, then why did he not object to us being paired together on this mission?"

"Like we've said, Kurt has qualifications like no one else. And besides, since you were in the Love Camp just a little over a month, then I suppose Wolf felt it unlikely you and Kurt would have met there. Or —considering this mission is short but very important — Wolf wouldn't allow himself to think about it."

Bela's curiosity continued to be aroused. "What would happen if Wolf believed Kurt and I did meet at the Love Camp?"

"Then he'll probably try to have Kurt condemned for rape."

"Which makes no sense whatsoever if we're going on a mission together."

"Don't worry," Jaclyn said, dismissing it with a wave. "My husband's just talking nonsense and knows it. Which tells me it's just his way of releasing some of his tension."

"Like he did tonight?" Bela asked, still uncomfortable with the anger between Wolf and Kurt. "He's asked me to treat Kurt like a friend, but clearly he's not doing it."

Jaclyn frowned. "Sounds like my Wolf... but getting back to your notes. Kurt really needs to see them, so be sure and meet with him before he ends up drinking schnapps and smoking with the men in the library." She removed a cigarette from her gold case. "And should you two not get along, then come and get me. Because I'll be in my room for a few minutes."

"Kurt and I *will* get along," Bela assured her, making a concentrated effort to dismiss Jaclyn's uneasiness concerning him. "So go tune your cello like you usually do."

"Then as long as you're as confident as you sound, I guess I'm out of options," she said, giving herself a final look in the mirror before heading toward the door.

* * *

Hardly a night passed Bela's piano music didn't accompany Jaclyn's cello as they entertained the household with some of their most famous pieces. "Your musical accomplishments have grown, Bela," Jaclyn would brag. "And if the world was at peace and we were still living in Vienna, then I'd see you got some great endorsements at the Conservatory."

It pleased Bela to hear her finally say it. But the truth was after Wolf had arranged for her rescue from the Love Camp, playing the piano was the only thing that had kept her from swallowing the white, cyanide capsule the Gestapo man had slipped in her coat pocket in Vienna.

It had been carefully wrapped in a note: "*Liberate yourself—because you'll need this, after being in such a god- awful place.*"

"*No need.*" She'd later scribbled beneath it to remind herself. "*My piano has made me a survivor. Because it's keeping my thoughts focused on the future, and not the past. Making me question my right to live, after the other eighteen girls at the Love Camp died.*"

Bela was still questioning it when she returned to her room and saw Kurt standing in the doorway. "You can come in, *Herr* Ulrich," she invited, calm enough now to greet him with her best smile.

"So we meet again," he said. "As was prophesied."

"Then you deviated from your path—"

"When I became a prisoner- of -war."

Light from the table lamp on her elegant vanity shone through the doorway, casting a circle of bronze over his new shoes and the lovely oriental rug in front of them.

He opened the door wider. "Jaclyn said you had some notes about this morning's briefing you wanted to show me. But before I see them, I'd like to say I thought we'd never meet again—much less end up on a first name basis."

"Certainly an interesting twist when you indicated Hitler possibly had the atomic bomb," Bela didn't hesitate to remind him.

"Information we retreating soldiers were given to give us hope."

Tension crackled inside her. "So it appears Fate brought us together again."

"Meddling with our lives?" The question seemed to hover on his lips.

"I'd rather not think of it like that," she answered, looking away. "Since under the circumstances, whatever past we have is now just our coffee shop adventure at Demel's—"

"That didn't really happen."

"Except with my father, when he accidentally spilled coffee on me."

"And you never told Wolf or Jaclyn?"

Bela turned, avoiding his gaze "I saw no reason to. Though, when I met you at the Love Camp, your speech sounded like you were from Vienna. And since there's always been such a feeling of déjà *vu* between us, it made me wonder if perhaps we did see each other several times at Demel's...or on Vienna's streets."

That gave Kurt pause. "I've thought that myself. But how old might you have been then? Fourteen? Fifteen?"

"Thirteen."

"Interesting? Though for now, I'll remain the man who spilled the coffee, except—" He pointed at the picture on her vanity showing her sitting in a motor bike's sidecar, next to a silver-haired man. "There's a problem with it."

CHAPTER SEVEN

"A problem?" Bela's brows gathered. "What kind of problem?"

"That any man with a brain cell working could never forget a girl as beautiful as you."

She smiled anew. "Still if we did meet, it seems we're having trouble remembering how and where."

"I know. Which I suspect is due to the trauma of the war. However, just before I fall asleep I sometimes see a golden-haired girl drop a napkin at Demel's...which I pick up for her."

"And what does she do?"

"I think probably because of my height, she just stares at me."

"Your height is impressive."

"As is yours."

"That's the first impression of several that I got from you when you entered the brothel. Because I'd seen none like you and had been there for almost a month."

His mouth trembled slightly as he said, "A staggering thought, but you were—and are—such a vision of loveliness that you completely mesmerized me when I saw you." He took her hand. "Even if now, we're going to try and put all this behind us. So I hope you'll find it in your heart to forgive me. Since your short, golden curls and the hint of gray, like quicksilver, flashing in your brilliant blue eyes, simply took my breath away—and still does."

His silken words caught her off guard. "You flatter me, *Herr* Ulrich."

"Call me, Kurt, please," he said, his dark eyes as intense as they'd been in the foyer and at the table.

"Kurt, then it is." She grinned, remembering how she'd been advised to call him by his Christian name. She reached for her notebook with a paper on top of it, beside her vanity. "I'm afraid I wrote so fast this morning that my handwriting's poor. So if you don't mind, I'll have to read my notes to you."

"I don't mind." He glanced at the paper on top of her notebook. "But your handwriting doesn't look that bad." And reaching for it, he began reading. *"So far the battle for Berlin is reported to have lasted fourteen days, with close to a million Soviet casualties."* He held up the paper. "See you've penned your writing with a neat, legible hand."

"I'm glad you think so. But if you read further you'll learn the OSS is quite angry, since by the Yalta Agreement, the Soviet military would be the first ones to enter Berlin."

"And that's a real mistake."

He handed her the paper, and she put it in her notebook. "But what do you think about our cover-story that's getting us into the city?"

"To observe the historical perspective of the war, which Oxford has commissioned Wolf to write a book about." Kurt's voice held a critical tone. "Probably the best they could come up with on short notice.... And you and Jaclyn are supposedly our secretaries doing some co-authoring. Though, I can't imagine who thought that up?"

"The British." She met his eyes disparagingly." Since they claimed bringing women into a war zone made the story more believable."

"A story I feel certain *Ivan's* senior commanders recognized as a scheme."

"They did. And weren't going to allow it until they learned Wolf's wife was Jaclyn Tirand."

"Our famous cello player," Kurt echoed gamely." But I don't see *Ivan* keeping us out of the city if he has plans to use us, like Ros-venor Square has implied."

Bela raised her eyes to him. "Did you ask them for more information?"

"I tried, but they didn't want any dialogue with me." His features hardened. "And all because I kept insisting that bringing two women, without much protection, into a shell-shocked city with bullets whizzing by, was dangerous—"

"—especially when rumor has it over a hundred thousand women from ages eight to eighty in the suburbs, have been raped by the Russians."

"With the Mongols rumored to be doing a good deal of it," Kurt said, lowering his head as if suddenly embarrassed at having done something similar when he'd visited the Love Camp.

"The British insist the four of us *will* have protection," Bela assured him, attempting to ease his disquiet.

"They didn't tell me."

"Why not?"

"Because the OSS kept saying, I'd learn what I needed to know in the final briefing tomorrow." He hesitated."But who's providing us with this protection?"

"Supposedly, some of Dr. Grossklos's White Russian friends in the Red Army who guard the hospital, will be driving us around the city in a truck. And if our man is von Lehmann, they have plans to slip him out of the city the following week."

"And those White Russians are good people," Kurt remarked. "I know, since I was friends with many of them. And I remember feeling sad that such aristocracy had been forced to reside in Berlin for over two decades."

"Definitely not Bolsheviks."

"Still, if they're Russians living in Berlin and plan on surviving the Red Army, then their men are probably being pressured to fight with them." His brows came together with obvious concern. "And it makes me afraid for *us* and *them*, when I think how we'll probably end up looking out for each other."

"Similar to a question that was raised in our last meeting," Bela informed him, reflecting on the dangers they were facing. "Because in my opinion, the four of us working with these White Russians makes us like human shields, standing between Germany's possible atom bomb and the rest of Europe—"

"You've got that right."

"And if that bomb really does exist— and the Soviets get it—then it makes us as fragile as gossamer veils."

"Absolutely," Kurt insisted archly. "When you consider that even at this late date if Admiral Doenitz, the man Tommie intelligence says will replace the *Fuhrer* as Supreme Commander, has the preliminary designs for such a weapon —and if it falls into Stalin's hands— then it would be catastrophic for the world."

Cold fear coursed through Bela. "Making it easy for me to envision the vast number of human beings melting in its deadly flames."

"But until we can actually confirm von Lehmann's status or find his designs, we won't know anything,"

"However, assuming von Lehmann's *not* dead— and not the man in the hospital—then where could he be?" Bela asked, still puzzled by his disappearance.

"Who knows? The allies have captured some of Germany's leading scientists, yet let their most famous one get away—"

"Which certainly raises questions."

"Maybe not." Kurt shrugged. "Because knowing how determined *Ivan's* people can be, they're capable of putting together a long-range rocket carrying a nuclear warhead— with or without, some of Germany's leading scientists."

Bela's breathing quickened. "I sense fear, when I think the only clue the Ros-venor Office can come up with is *"Doktor Grossklos Knows."*

"Something that *does* make me wonder. Considering the Tommies claim to have a report from *Ivan,* saying von Lehmann's body was found in his lab on the city's edge, after some grenades were thrown in it, because someWehrmacht soldiers were believed to be hiding there."

"Probably his doppelganger. Since if they really found von Lehmann, the Americans would be none the wiser."

"Possibly."

Frustration churned in Bela. "And the *Fuhrerbunker*? Did they tell you something about it, they didn't tell us?"

"According to Ros-venor intelligence, *Ivan* has either been killing or brutalizing everyone they can find who's been associated with it—"

"But has still learned nothing?"

Kurt threw up his hands in a gesture of disgust. "That's what the source claimed. Though once the *Fuhrer's* dead, then things will change."

"With the Russians looting the place, the way they're looting Berlin's suburbs"

"Exactly." He pointed at the name *Grossklos* in her notebook." Plus on top of everything else, the way my father-in-law's name keeps coming up in this Ros-venor message, makes me suspect that what he knows is simply another one of *Ivan's* dreamed-up ploys."

"Sounds like it." Bela frowned, worried. "But was your father-in-law friends with von Lehmann?"

"He claims to have never met him. And shortly before my capture, he sent me a letter saying there was speculation von Lehmann was in the country, experimenting with some model rockets."

"Then it definitely seems someone is targeting us—"

"To help them locate *something* or identify *someone*," Kurt replied, shaking his head.

"So perhaps the Russians are *baiting us*, and we're *baiting them*. But getting back to your father-in-law. How long ago was it that his house was bombed?"

"Three months. And he's been living at the hospital ever since."

"Then he must find it comfortable," Bela said, continuing to think about the peculiar message from Ros-venor.

Kurt's mouth curved with a smile. "My father-in-law finds it extremely comfortable. Because he's always had a tiny space in that building, which my lovely wife went to such great care to decorate and make pleasant for him."

"Sounds like you and your wife were quite close."

"Very. She was an only child whose mother had died when she was just five years old."

Like mine, Bela thought.

"And I know we agreed we wouldn't talk about the past, but if we're going to be working together, I think you should at least know that I'd only been widowed a month when I visited the Love Camp." Then like he had an issue with his conscience, he was silent for a moment. "And though I've never forgiven myself for it, I don't want you to think I wouldn't have come back to you if I hadn't been transferred. In fact— " He fell silent again, with the expression on his face one of condolence. "I still don't know how you survived, after having been in such a God- awful place."

Bela drew in her lips thoughtfully. "I don't know either, because I was about to throw myself at the watchtowers, when you showed up."

"And I couldn't return because of my *damned* Wehrmacht transfer."

"No matter. Since most likely your visit was probably the reason I didn't kill myself."

"Like the women in Berlin?"

"Exactly. But since I can't be sure what I might have done, I don't see it's worth discussing."

"Probably isn't. Even if I am disappointed we didn't meet under different circumstances."

"Like Demel's?"

"Yes. And I realize the war and our time together has caused you a lot of pain and sadness, but how are you holding up now?"

"The same as everyone else. "She bent her head, still uneasy with the way he continued to occupy her thoughts. "Some days are good and others bad."

"And Jaclyn and Wolf don't suspect anything about me?"

Bela tensed at the question. "Yes and no...but why do you ask?"

"Because—"Kurt flashed a look of concern at her. "I got the feeling you were upset with me over something I said at the table. Were you?"

Afraid he'd discover she was a Jew, she wasn't about to tell him that his words about not having much in common with Vienna's Jews made her tremble. So she took a second to reply. "I was so upset over the words between you and Wolf that when I went to the powder room, I came close to telling Jaclyn about meeting you in the Love Camp."

Immediately, Kurt's eyes widened in shock. "But you didn't, so what stopped you?"

"Her attitude about men who went to such places."

"Which was terrible, wasn't it?"

"It was. But rather than bungle our mission, I convinced her otherwise."

He exhaled a deep breath. "A powerful relief. And I'm extremely grateful —but what did you do or say that convinced her?"

"I didn't, *you* did."

"*Me*?" He looked confused. "When I wasn't in the powder room with the two of you?"

"Easy. Jaclyn saw the way you were flirting with me at the table, and the way I seemed to enjoy it."

He gazed at her in wonder. "Did you?"

"Yes. Which made Jaclyn decide you couldn't have been the man who visited me at the Love Camp."

"See." He broke into an open, friendly smile. "The more we speak, the better understanding we have between us. So if it's all right with you, I'll keep up my flirting."

"It would be the smart thing to do. Especially after what that Gestapo man told Wolf, when he returned me to him in Vienna."

Kurt tilted his head. "About *me?*"

"Something like that, even though—" She fingered the note in the odds- and- ends box on her vanity, the Gestapo man had dropped in her coat pocket. "When this man delivered me— along with his friend, ObersturmFuhrer Horst Helmer— to Jaclyn and Wolf in Vienna, he mumbled something to Wolf about having a relative in the Wehrmacht, who'd visited the Love Camp."

"What!" Kurt exclaimed. "But how on earth would he know?"

"Can't imagine." Bela shook her head, the uncertainty disturbing her.

"Something that definately raises some questions," Kurt said, lowering his eyes as if overcome with a sudden mixture of guilt and shame. "But surely—" He paused, staring at Bela's hands on her odds-and- ends box. "Wolf must have some idea as to how this particular man knew?"

"Not really. Because like Jaclyn said, this man was resourceful enough to slip through German and Russian lines....Not to mention the Gestapo claimed to know everything."

"Which according to *Herr* Wallenberg, they did. But still—"

"Don't worry," Bela interrupted. "I can probably discredit what the man said by making Wolf angry at him."

"God in his mercy!" Kurt gasped. "You mean he's *here* in Switzerland with us?"

"No. After the U-boat tickets—Wolf's code name for the submarine documents— plus the large sum of money he gave this man and his friend, ObersturmFuhrer Horst Helmer, they're either in South America or headed that way."

"I'll always be in debt to Wolf for getting you out of that Love Camp," Kurt said, briefly shaking himself as he appeared to recall the darkness surrounding her from which it seemed there was no escape. "And I must commend him for his talent at knowing how to bribe the right people."

"Which he learned from *Herr* Wallenberg."

"Who was kind enough to teach him. Though, if this Gestapo man's in South America, then how do you plan on making Wolf angry with him?"

CHAPTER EIGHT

B ela opened her odds-and-ends box. "By showing him what he gave me after we left the Love Camp." She handed Kurt the white, cyanide capsule with the note wrapped around it. *"Liberate yourself—because you'll need this, after being in such a god-awful place."*

"Mother of God!" he practically shouted. "I hope it's never entered your head to take it."

"I...I put it in my mouth once. "She swallowed hard, uncomfortable with the question. "But spit it out immediately."

"Did Wolf and Jaclyn know you had it?"

"No." Bela studied his expression as he held it. "Since I was seriously thinking about taking it."

His eyes locked with hers. "But why would you when you were free?"

"Not from memories. Because before we left for Vienna, ObersturmFuhrer Helmer gave orders to Madam Kollar to see I was wearing no underwear under the loose-fitting dress I had."

"So he could rape you—"

"—beat me."Bela lowered her voice. "Since as a whore, Helmer considered me an inferior being. Which is the reason he gave me whippings with a leather strap whenever we were temporarily out of danger, and the mood struck him."

Kurt's spirits seemed to sink even lower. "That like his cane, must have caused you a great deal of pain."

"It did. But fortunately I was reunited with Wolf and Jaclyn before the Russians arrived, though— " She hesitated, surprised after all she'd been through, to feel her face heat with embarrassment. "I did develop severe diarrhea, once we were on our train headed toward the Swiss border."

"So Jaclyn told me before I came up."

Still jarred by the memory, Bela confided, "I was scared, but refused to let them take me to the hospital, until we reached the border with Wolf's bribe money."

"Good thing Wolf had it." Kurt smiled, clearly pleased with his cousin. "But you're all right now, aren't you?"

"Haven't been sick a day since I've been here. And that's been almost three and a half months."

"Which is good." His smile widened. "With Jaclyn also giving me some pills in a small tin for the Berlin trip, in case I get sick."

"I have some too." Bela reached into her odds- and- ends box again. "But I probably won't need them now that I'm away from ObersturmFuhrer Helmer."

Kurt regarded her with a somber curiosity. "But why did he take such pleasure in punishing you when you were his ticket out of the country?"

"All part of a plot after we got to Vienna, that would make me feel so worthless, I'd kill myself. And I was numb inside and wanted to cry but couldn't. Like I couldn't, when I learned from the OSS that after the brothel closed, the Gestapo made the remaining half-starved girls work for them in freezing weather, before shooting them—"

"Making you the only survivor."

"Thanks to Wolf."

"But what happened to our gypsy or Romani friend, Madam Kollar?" Kurt asked.

"She was always doing whatever she could for us girls —"

"Such as?"

"Like giving us sea sponges to insert when we had our periods, so the soldiers wouldn't be offended."

"Hearing the way the men under my command talked about women and brothels, I'd wondered how you were handling that problem."

"Well now you know—but getting back to Madam Kollar. She was so upset over the way the half-starved girls were suffering in the freezing weather, she helped them anyway she could. Even sharing some of the food the S.S. gave her." Bela's eyes misted as she talked. "And in the madam's weakened condition, without the warmth of her mink coat, she froze to death in a cloth one not fit for Hungary's winters."

"She'll be in heaven for that," Kurt remarked, bowing his head. "But why didn't you tell Wolf what ObersturmFuhrer Helmer had done to you, the minute you arrived in Vienna?"

"Because once he got the money and U-boat tickets, he bragged he'd shoot him."

"Maybe." Kurt appeared to give it some thought. "But since Jaclyn's something of a celebrity, I rather doubt it."

"Even so, it was a risk I wasn't willing to take."

"So you didn't mention it to Wolf then— like you didn't mention the cyanide tablet to him. Since this ObersturmFuhrer Helmer made you feel so humiliated and worthless with his whippings, that you almost took it."

"Exactly. Considering I was coming to despise the numbness inside me that made me feel I had nothing to lose."

"Yet still, you managed to rise above those awful memories," Kurt commended her. "So how were you able to do it?"

"By the grace and beauty of my music." She put the cyanide capsule with its note, back in her odds-and-ends box. "Which allowed me to pretend I was on a tropical island playing my piano under a palm tree."

He placed a reassuring hand on her shoulder. "Then know this, I'll do whatever it takes to keep your spirits up. But first you must give me your word that should I *do* or *say* something that upsets you, you'll let me know."

A sudden pleasantness overcame her. "You have it."

"And I appreciate it." His tense expression relaxed. "But what you should also know, is that I was trying hard not to believe the stories about concentration camps until I wandered into the Love Camp. Then I had to face the ugly truth." He glanced at the oriental rug as if making an effort to control himself. "And I would have found a way to help you, the other girls, and Madam Kollar—had my father-in-law been able to get me transferred to Berlin. But when those *damn* Tommies took me prisoner, then all bets were off —and was I ever furious with them!"

"I can imagine."

"And just thinking about my failure to help you and your friends, gets me so frustrated I start craving a cigarette." His head jutted forward. "So, since you don't smoke, would you mind if I do?"

"Not in the least."

He fumbled for a pack in one of his jacket's pockets. "I've promised myself I'll quit this smoking habit, once the Tommies release me."

"Good idea. " This thoughtfulness she saw in him was identical to that which had been so painfully apparent at the Love Camp. And her anxiety continued to disturb her with the feelings she held for him— her enemy— whenever she recalled how he'd joined his body with hers, unlocking their hearts. *Which was contradictory and against all reasoning. And something I must somehow resolve.*

So in an attempt not to let her confused feelings for him get the better of her, she reached for her notebook and began reading aloud what they'd talked about earlier: *"The U.S. is believed to be working on the atomic bomb— but even so it's still feared the Germans also have plans for it that are near completion. And should the Russians lay hands on von Lehmann's papers—or locate and identify him — then if his papers do offer a fair amount of instruction on how to put together such a bomb and rocket, it could make Stalin as menacing as Hitler."*

Kurt looked at her, determination on his face as he lit his cigarette. "The main reason we have to acquire this information in the very short amount of time we have in the city."

"Which is practically an impossibility."

"Especially since it was less than twenty-four hours ago that the second *"Doktor Grossklos Knows"* message was beamed to a Tommie agent in Rosvenor Square," Kurt reminded. "So by all my calculations, we should have left tonight."

Bela nodded, looking at him without speaking as she pressed her hand against her heart... *struggling to keep it from flying out of my chest.* "But what I want to know is can the OSS name the person who sent this message?"

"They could if they wanted to, but since he's probably in British intelligence, they're hesitant to do it—"

"So in the event the opportunity to locate or rescue von Lehmann *arose*, explains why the OSS had us all on standby."

"Exactly." Kurt drew on his cigarette. "And as soon as word came, the Tommies put me on the phone with Albert to see if I would help Wolf identify von Lehmann. And was I surprised, with the war expected to end the following week. However, the minute Albert recognized my voice, he was overjoyed that I agreed… since von Lehmann and I had parted on such bad terms."

Once again apprehension coursed through Bela at this dissension between the two. "Doesn't sound good for our mission."

"It isn't. Because if von Lehmann and I do meet again, it wouldn't surprise me if he kicked my ass."

Her breath quickened as a sense of dread overtook her. With so much depending on his rescue, then why on earth did this new complication have to raise its ugly head? "It was over your mother, wasn't it?"

"Unfortunately." He shifted his gaze to the rug again. "She was his mistress and loved him, but he refused to make her respectable by marrying her."

"Wouldn't you know?" Bela sighed, shaking her head. It was bad enough to see the hostility between Kurt and Wolf at the table tonight, but this adversity between Kurt and von Lehmann was enough to make her as tense as the strings on Jaclyn's cello.

Clearly aware she was upset, Kurt asked in a gentle tone. "What's the matter? Did what I said about von Lehmann surprise you?"

"Naturally." Her voice dropped in volume as she struggled to hide her misgivings. "But as long as it doesn't upset our mission, then I won't let it get the better of me."

He touched her forearm. "Which I'll make sure doesn't happen. Since if von Lehmann's alive, and the White Russians are able to get him out of Berlin within the next week or two, then I hope we'll end up having more respect for each other than we do now."

"So do I— but one more thing. Why did Albert believe your estranged half-brother's family was behind your transfer to the Eastern Front in '44?"

"Because my mother was staying with some very poor relatives when she gave birth to me." Kurt's face closed like he needed a moment. "And she lived with them for three months afterwards. But apparently I cried all the time, angering the man of the house. Who threatened to slap me if she didn't put me in a Catholic orphanage. A threat that got her so frightened, she sent word to my father. Who, apparently, was as concerned as she was. Since he showed up, *sick*, to tell her he was writing to his three half-brothers…appealing to them to help her out. And he would have done it sooner, had he not been embarrassed he had an illegitimate son."

"So what happened after that?" Bela asked, struggling with the uncertainty of his life.

"When von Lehmann arrived to take me and my mother to Vienna, I later learned from her, that he gathered me in his arms and held me for most of the train trip."

"And did you cry?"

"Not once, so she told me."

"And the reason?"

"Because von Lehmann was very comforting to me."

"But what about your father?"

"He died shortly afterwards. With his wife blaming my mother and I for his death. In fact, she wrote von Lehmann a letter that said one way or another she'd have her revenge: "I'm angry that you allow Kurt and his mother to live like blue-blooded Germans in your house—and sooner or later you'll pay for it"

"And you think it was this woman and your half-brother, who pulled the strings to get you transferred to the Eastern Front?"

"Albert believes it— the same as my father-in-law." Kurt's dark eyes pierced hers as she imagined his past. "But if I hadn't been assigned to the Eastern Front, then I'd have never met you."

Bela could feel her face reddening at this personal message his eyes were sending her. So she quickly handed him the notebook, "I think we should go down now, because my sister's stopped tuning her cello."

"Then I'll follow you."

She turned to leave but paused in front of the round mirror hanging by the door. It was the best place to adjust the chiffon scarf draped around her neck, in order to hide the blue-tattooed words and numbers her bandage covered.

"Your scarf's the same silky lilac as your gown." Kurt noticed, his eyes traveling over her with a glint of wonder, as he inclined his head slightly. "And since your hair is longer now, they both make you look exquisite."

"We were told the Gestapo cut our hair for pillow stuffing."

"Doesn't matter. Your hair was as beautiful then as it is now—which by the way, even if you don't need it, I like your make-up." His gaze seared through her as he admired it. "And I continue to love your perfume."

This magnetism pouring from his dark eyes made her cheeks warm with another blush. Since even if he had been a Wehrmacht officer with whom she had a past, at least he lacked the sense of superiority of the German battle-commanders controlling Budapest.

"What I like best about your gown is the way it compliments your slenderness," he said, with a circular motion of his hand.

She touched one of its pleats. "Jaclyn picked it because she said the way it's draped reminds her of one of those Roman-goddess statues in the Louvre."

"Which it does."

Kurt's keen admiration was as intimate as a kiss. But still uncertain what to do where he was concerned, Bela simply flipped the flower-bud light switch on the wall and headed toward the stairs. "This gown's too elaborate for my tastes. But Jaclyn gave it to me, because she said as her piano accompanist, I needed something elegant to wear."

"It's as perfect for you as your shiny, high heels." He glanced at their brightness as she walked down the steps. "Since a woman with your fine looks should wear only the best."

"Not really," Bela disagreed.... *Plain things suited her better. Because the more fancy and ornate the clothes, the more like a harlot she felt.*

"I beg to differ." He stopped in the middle of the stairs.

"So do others in this household."

"Then believe them." He reached out and took her hand, and its familiarity seemed so natural it was like they were meant to be joined. "When I first arrived here, I caught a glimpse of Jaclyn standing in front of the foyer's mirror, modeling a luxurious, silver- fox coat. And I must say she looked wonderful in it."

"It was a present from Wolf and—"

"One day, " Kurt cut her off," someone's going to give you something like that."

"I have Madam Kollar's mink coat."

"Really." His face was now only a few inches from hers." How on earth did you manage to get it?"

"ObersturmFuhrer Helmer took the coat from her, with one of her winter kerchiefs crammed in its pocket." She turned away, remembering. "Because he said my coat and kerchief weren't warm enough. So, afraid I'd freeze to death before he got the money and U-boat tickets from Wolf, he took her coat."

Kurt drew sharply on his cigarette. "Taking Madam Kollar's fur coat sounds like something that sorry bastard would do."

"It certainly does. With his Gestapo friend dropping the note and cyanide in one of the coat's pockets." A brief moment passed as Bela brushed a tear away. "But in the other pocket I found a note from Madam Kollar, which read: *Each time I look at the cards, they say I must sacrifice myself so one girl can survive... or otherwise no one will ever know what kind of camp we had here.*"

"Which apparently is what she did—but what about your feet?"

"Clogs and wool socks that went up to my knees."

"Certainly not like what you're wearing."

Grinning, Bela glanced at her shiny heels. "With these fitting much better than clogs."

"I don't doubt it. But wouldn't boots have been better than clogs?"

"I was told I'd get a pair when the next batch of clothes arrived from the prisoners the S.S. had killed—"

"Which sadly explains the seductive lingerie I saw hanging over your dresses in your closet... but getting back to Jaclyn. You started to say something else about her when I interrupted you. So please accept my apology and continue."

Impressed he wanted her to do so, Bela's grin increased. "I was just going to say that after several years of marriage, she and Wolf still act like they're madly in love."

"Exactly like my wife and I...." Suddenly Kurt had a faraway look in his eyes as if lost for a moment, in the past. "And she was twenty-one, and I was twenty-three when we married."

"Her death must have been a terrible loss for you."

"It was... but what about your father? How did he die?"

"H...he got shot," Bela had difficulty saying.

"Which must have been a terrible loss for you."

"What war does to us." Their eyes held for several beats as she struggled not to think about the Danube's murky waters closing over his body.

Then she turned and hurried into the drawing room, where Jaclyn was waiting with her cello. "I'm sorry I'm late," Bela apologized, taking a seat beside her at the piano.

"Don't worry, little sister, you're not very. She flashed a cocksure grin at her.

Like she knows the attraction between Kurt and me will soon be spreading all over this chalet. And I'm uneasy... so uneasy. Fearing the secret I share with him will be revealed.

CHAPTER NINE

Kurt took the glass of schnapps Albert handed him. "Every evening Jaclyn pleasures us with her music. And it's my hope you'll enjoy her performance as much as I do."

"I have a great respect for musicians."

"I don't doubt it," remarked Wolf, stepping up and helping himself to another glass of schnapps. "When one considers how well you can play the piano."

"And do you play each time you get the opportunity?" asked Albert, tilting back his head.

Kurt nodded. "But only because my wife enjoyed it."

A grin overtook Albert's features. "She had good taste."

"So everyone said."

Once Jaclyn began playing, Albert, Wolf, and Kurt settled into the deep, reddish- brown pillows on the room's gigantic sofa. An impressive piece that echoed the shade of russet in the weathered- hued colors on the Aubusson rug thrown across the floor.

Kurt liked the elaborate *décor* as much as he did the music, which he found sensuous and deeply moving.

Although, it was Bela's piano accompaniment with its soulful, yet sinuous thread that kept it from unraveling into eroticism.

Eroticism and the painful past. Each time he'd think about it, he'd see a naked girl with shiny curls around her head. Curls so lovely that if they'd been longer, they would have resembled the gold- lame, evening wraps magazine pictures showed cinema stars wearing at Hollywood premieres.

And from the first moment he'd looked into her dazzling blue eyes, he'd worshipped her.

He knew he should have tried harder to protect her. But since his was a collapsing world choking in darkness and ash, there was no place for her... leaving him torn with grief and guilt.

A week before he'd received a letter from his father-in-law: *"It's terrible you were given no time to mourn your wife and son. But remember I'm a doctor who knows some important military people. And since all leaves were cancelled, their refusal to allow you to come home for the funerals has given me more ammunition to convince them to reassign you to Berlin or the Western Front. So please, Kurt, try and hold on a little longer, because I realize the meat-grinding, Eastern Front— as many call it— is a death sentence....Even if there is talk the Fuhrer has an atomic bomb."*

So, he'd been forced to keep his emotions tightly in check, since the Wehrmacht had refused to give him the closure he so badly needed. Plus the wound in his shoulder he'd received in Russia two months ago, still bothered him with its stiffness.

His own mortality seemed imminent. Which is the reason after two glasses of schnapps and the morphine the combat medic had given him for his shoulder, he'd done something unthinkable.... He'd arranged with the corporal driver of his staff car to put chains on it and transport him and an officer friend through the howling, icy wind to the Love Camp.

"Where we can make the most of the night in this Christmas season." His friend, Dieter, had chuckled. "Because I'm still finding it hard to believe it's your first time ever in a brothel."

"Well." Kurt sighed. "When you're in love and happily married, you don't cheat."

"Wouldn't know," Dieter said dismissively. "But this place would really be something if swing music was playing instead of that Schubert music."

"But swing music is forbidden."

"To our great misfortune." Dieter grimaced, proceeding to describe the place as being near the front for the purpose of helping the rank-and-file soldiers— following far behind them in a large truck—forget they'd either be shot to death or end up spending the rest of their lives worked to death in one of *Ivan's* prison camps. "You know." He continued to chuckle. "The reason for this place is that it's a great distraction."

"Like the kind our ancestors used when their women rode naked with their men into battle against the Romans," Kurt remarked, recalling a drawing he'd seen.

Dieter lit a cigarette. "That's what I've been told. Since on a much smaller scale, it's similar to the way our higher-up, field commanders distract us—or rather ease our tensions—by giving us cigarettes and schnapps before we go into battle. The exception being this place. That for some peculiar reason requires we pay three marks a piece... the price of cigarettes. Which is awfully cheap."

"A soldier said we're paying it because it's open at night and not in the afternoon," said Kurt. "Since he maintained the army brothels in other countries close before the sun sets."

Dieter laughed. "Something I've also heard— even though we should be paying to keep the outside of this place from smelling like rats." He laughed again. "But since we're told sex makes us better soldiers, just take what you came for like the rest of us here, shove the girl away, and then walk off."

"But where do the women come from in this place?" Kurt asked him.

"Come from?" Dieter hedged as if trying to find the best words. "They're local whores the government's imprisoned for us. Who've been promised they'll receive protection from us should *Ivan* invade." He quirked his brows. "Their reasoning being that when we have sex, it means we've still got some life left in us. So take note and give that gypsy woman, Madam Kollar, the numbers between the girl's breasts if she doesn't do her job well." He reached in his coat pocket and handed him a blank slip of paper. "But considering we officers get to go first and pick our girls, then you probably won't feel a need to report the one you chose."

Kurt found the remark odd. In fact everything about the place was odd. Since this so-called Love Camp was just a makeshift building with a wall of barbed wire that had razor wire at the top, surrounding it. And sentries on guard in watchtowers. "A prison pleasure house that can be quickly moved," remarked Dieter with a smug expression. "Should the need arise."

But Kurt was skeptical. This place fit the picture of what he'd over heard a sergeant describe as a concentration camp under Gestapo jurisdiction. Something he didn't like thinking about, because if it were true, then he was fighting every day to uphold such inhumanity. Especially when a woman walked past him with the word *Feldhure* and numbers tattooed between her breasts. *The ones he was to write down if she didn't satisfy him?*

With the heavy fog outside, the house's dim, electric lighting made it difficult to read them. And he frowned at the way it drifted through the doors and clouded the room with the icy, night air as the supervising S.S. men— coming back and forth from the waiting area and into the room— obstructed his view even more.

'Why do I get the feeling what Dieter said about this place isn't right?' Kurt considered asking one of the S.S. men. *'Are these women really local whores? Or just some unfortunate girls who've been forced into prostitution?'*

However, noticing how each S.S. man had a crafty look on his face, he doubted they'd tell him the truth.

"I'm leaving, Dieter," Kurt informed him.... But before he could, a golden-haired girl in a blue, pinstriped smock stepped out from behind the gauzy canopy hanging over her bed. And in a simple, innocent voice, she asked him if she could take his greatcoat.

Even without make-up, her face was like something out of a dream, melting his resolve as an immediate sense of *deja vu* swept through him.

"You've got good taste, Captain," Dieter commended him. "Not only is she gorgeous, but she's wearing perfume. So I'll leave you with her." His friend's mouth curved upward as he headed toward a brunette girl, several beds over, who was flashing him a smile.

Kurt marveled at this golden-haired girl. Finding it impossible to take his eyes off her as she hung his fur-lined greatcoat and wool scarf between her sweater and two dresses— with lingerie draped over them— in the open closet next to her bed. *Does beauty like hers still exist in this decaying world?*

Apparently it did.

So in the hopes of riding the swell of life once again, his aching loins couldn't resist being released from his darkness into her glorious fire, as they'd clung to one another in their nakedness.

And before he left, they exchanged kisses one last time.

"I'll never forget you," he'd told her.

But when reality finally returned, he knew for the sake of his lost family he should probably put her out of his mind...which of course, he couldn't.

A young girl in such a dire situation needed prayers — a good many to be exact. And he'd see she got them.

Prayers for his *Goldilock's* safety. Which was all he could do, wasn't it? Something he was reluctant to accept but had no choice. Since he doubted they'd ever meet again, even if Madam Kollar's cards said they would.

Then, remembering his wife and toddler son had only been dead four weeks, he knew it was in his best interest not to dishonor their memory by grieving for this gorgeous, golden-haired girl life had forced him to leave behind.

Yet, here she was at Albert's chalet. *Fate's surprise. The prophecy fulfilled.* The girl from the Love Camp he'd never been able to forget.

An encounter making him question whether meeting her again was an answer to one of his prayers? Or simply God's way of reminding him about his transgression against his dead wife and son? "I should have been in mourning but went to a brothel instead," he said, just as Jaclyn's music stopped. "But I'm not sorry."

His reverie came to an abrupt halt when Albert's barrel chest, shaking with applause, redirected his attention. "Are you talking to yourself, nephew?" he asked, grinning.

"No—just thinking out loud."

"About those two gorgeous, young ladies here?"

"Who else?"

"Then stand up and applaud them with me."

Wolf and the household servants also applauded, as Jaclyn bowed and gestured at Bela to stand beside the piano.

"Play something for us, Kurt," Albert urged.

"On one condition," he bargained with a tight smile. "That Bela will join me in a duet, since I haven't touched a piano in quite awhile."

It was a condition she quickly agreed to. And handing him a music book, she asked him to make a selection.

"A Strauss waltz, of course," he said without thinking. Then remembering how he'd later learned that Strauss and Schubert were played in nearly all the soldiers' brothels, he hesitated before asking, "Will it bother you?"

She gave the book a quick look. "It's a good choice."

So putting his fingers on the keyboard next to hers, he soon found the beauty of her talent offered him a kind of pleasant escape.

And when it ended, he hugged her. Which to his surprise, she returned his hug the way a long lost friend would do.

Albert pointed at the gramophone and told Jutta, to put on the "Blue Danube Waltz."

Then as music once again began rippling through the drawing room, Wolf reached for Jaclyn's slender hand, and they began to waltz.

Loving to dance, Kurt recalled how these past months had made him more aware than ever, how precious time was for him.

Have to make the most of it. Since life is not to be taken for granted.

So, with a hushed intake of breath he went over to Bela, who was tapping her feet to the lilting music. "Would the lovely lady be so kind as to pleasure me with a waltz?"

"Absolutely," she said without hesitation, taking his hand.

He was swept away by her response and quickly ushered her toward the small dancing space.

"Vienna Blood" was now playing, and he spun her several times across the floor.

And her cheeks bloomed with a flush at the way their bodies swayed, until a grinning Albert, surprising them, boldly cut in.

They switched partners several times with Kurt waltzing with Jaclyn, and Wolf with Bela. Then Albert ordered the music be changed and, grinning again, he watched the couples as they began to foxtrot.

The evening ended as it usually did, with everyone joining hands and singing along to a recording of "Blue Moon."

It didn't last long and afterwards, Albert stood in the middle of the group and had Ina take a picture of them with his flash camera.

Then Wolf advised everyone to get to bed early, since he doubted they'd get another good night's sleep until after they'd returned from Berlin.

Still holding Bela's hand, Kurt gave her a swift bow and thanked her for the lovely time. And she returned his thanks by lightly touching his arm, before ascending the stairs.

He recalled the pinstriped smock she'd worn... not exactly imitating bars on a prison, but still it gave him pause. *Why did I ever let myself believe she was a local whore the government had imprisoned? I think I partially knew she wasn't. But after she told me those were innocent girls in the brothel who'd been imprisoned to become field-whores, the fact that I'd forced myself on her, will haunt me for the rest of my days.*

And several months later when the British had shown him and the other prisoners war pictures of the skeletal Auschwitz inmates in their wide-striped, pajama uniforms, all he could see was his *Goldilocks* in her pinstriped smock, when she'd asked to take his greatcoat.

So was Bela Jewish? When sexual relations between Germans and Jews were strictly forbidden? She didn't look Jewish. Which probably meant she was just an unfortunate girl on the threshold of life, the Germans had grabbed when she'd managed to get separated from Wolf and Jaclyn.

And how horrible it must have been after the violation, humiliation, and whippings she'd experienced at the Love Camp.

His abuse from the British had been bad, but hers was unthinkable... making him fear she'd never get over it.

Yet, being with her had made his life suddenly come back to him. And he closed his eyes, asking God to find it in his mercy to forgive him if he'd harmed her in any way.

CHAPTER TEN

L eft to commune with her thoughts in the sanctuary of her bedroom, Bela changed into her long, white nightgown. She wasn't sleepy, so she reached under her pillow for her journal Jaclyn had brought from Budapest and began writing in it. *"Asleep I can sometimes deal with the frightening dreams, but when I awake a different nightmare often begins. Armies have marched over me, making me continue to wonder if death still isn't the only thing that will cleanse me and set me free."*

Reflecting on it, she closed her eyes. But the instant she did, Kurt Ulrich stood next to her bed in his crisp, captain's uniform. Her mind wanted to rebel but couldn't. Forcing her to remember the way he'd stared at her, momentarily speechless, when she'd rushed up to him in her blue smock and clogs.

Since the officers and first nineteen rank-and-file soldiers got to pick their girls, then once they did, Madam Kollar or an S.S. man wrote the girl's number on a chalkboard. And after that Madam Kollar and several S.S. men, began passing out slips of paper to the soldiers, with the girls' numbers on them. 'Yours for the first part of the night. And if you get a number on the chalkboard, you soldiers waiting can either continue to wait or allow me to give you a different number.'

'You'll get fewer complaints, Bela, if you pick your first soldier and don't wait for him to pick you,' one of the more experienced, Love Camp girls had advised her. 'Because for some reason, the night will seem easier if you can halfway tolerate him. So when the second and third soldiers come, you'll be in a slightly better mood.' Then she'd shaken her head as if in warning, ' Just be careful not to give any of the men—officer, S.S. or otherwise—more attention than you have to.'

So, with the pleasant recording of Schubert's "Air Russe" playing in the waiting area, she'd stood behind the gauzy canopy hanging over her bed. It was hardly a cubicle, but it did afford some degree of privacy.

The invincible German world was crumbling. And due to this strategic withdrawal from *Ivan's* forces, many of the soldiers who came to the Love Camp, had open sores and cuts. 'Their anger and discomfort taking its toll on all of us,' Bela lamented, not expecting otherwise as she gazed at the soldiers with medals on their uniforms.

Then she'd spotted a tall German, an officer, who was teary-eyed from the freezing air outside. Yet, his arresting face had a natural gentleness that intrigued her— *unlike many of the officers with whom I've had sex.*

And when she approached him, it immediately seemed they'd known each other in some distant time as he stared at her with a pain in his dark eyes, she sensed was as deep as her own. *A kindred heart.*

A quiver shot through her when he slipped the Iron Cross hanging from his neck, into his tunic's pocket. 'This medal's done nothing but give me a hard time,' he remarked as he stripped down to the double pair of regulation, long-john drawers he was wearing for protection against the cold. 'Can you imagine that?'

'No.' Her fear of him had disappeared, with everything suddenly taking on the glow of a rain-washed sky as she unbuttoned her smock.

Proceeding undeterred after removing his under drawers with their tie-strings, he'd pressed his lips against hers. His strange familiarity sweeping her away with kisses— both light and deep— that seemed to stretch to eternity. *A German speaking to me in the language of heartbeats. With the thrill of anticipation allowing me to rise above the restless rumble of the heavy guns in the distance.*

The passion of his ardor mounted. And in a surge of powerful yearning, they spiraled upward to a world of such great height, it was like a galaxy of light with billions of glowing stars was shining down on them.

It amazed her how easy it was to surrender to his masterful seduction. Offering him the same solace he was giving her as a sweet ache like nothing she'd ever experienced— caused her knees to tremble, at the way she was consumed with his raw possessiveness.

All those men who came to the Love Camp—yet she'd never known anything like this. A balm to her wounded soul.

She lifted her head. *I'm lost! Because his hunger for human love is the same as mine.*

This ecstasy throbbing through her made her feel as valued as a chest overflowing with diamonds as one of his hands held her, while the other gently stroked the wetness of her desire. And she rejoiced at the way her body ached for the fulfillment of their lovemaking when she glimpsed the heart-rending tenderness, in his face.

Then he turned her on her stomach so he could stoke her pleasure point from behind; entering and withdrawing with a precision that left her breathless each time he sheathed himself to the hilt.

Consumed with this overwhelming emotion raging between them tremors, like warm waves, rolled over her. Flooding her with erotic sensations she couldn't imagine existed...and she shuddered. Buffeted by this golden symphony of passion, that pounded her blood so fiercely with its delicious ache, her impatience for release reached a staggering height.

When suddenly he turned her so she was no longer facedown.

'You're doing things to me.' he whispered.

'What I was hoping.'

His mouth seared a path down her chest and onto her abdomen, causing her pulse to take an unexpected leap.

But now she could at least glimpse his expressive eyes as he covered her with the velvety, cocoon-like shelter of his body.

Freed by this delightful joy, her craving for him overrode everything else as their hearts joined in beat, and his tongue explored the rosy peaks of her taut breasts. Forcing her to choke back a cry to keep from begging him—*a German front-line commander*—for the immediate assertion of his manhood. But when he took her hand and guided her to its warmth, her control snapped.

It was unbelievable this man— her enemy— could do something like that to her. But what was even more unbelievable was she had no aversion to him. And she was even regretting not being able to caress the impressive length of his erection, before welcoming him into her body again.

Holding her tightly against him, he brought her to peak after peak of mind-boggling ecstasy, their bodies vibrating in exquisite harmony. Until finally, his eagerness reached explosive proportions, and he lost control. Upsetting her balance, when the shock of his delicious warmth from his fulfillment, flowed into her like a dissolving taper's.

The melting zone. She moaned in complete surrender as he withdrew.

For some time afterwards, their naked bodies—moist from lovemaking— still hovered between worlds. But when the noisy soldiers next to them got up from their mattresses to leave, he began putting on the clothes he'd left in her closet.

She slid her smock over her body. 'Was the officer pleased?' she asked, adhering to the camp regulation that the girls' question their high-and-mighty guests about the treatment they'd received.

He gave her a quick hug. '*Very*,' he said, taking care to adjust his field-gray tunic with its Knight's Cross on the right side. 'But before I leave I have a question.' He reached for his fur-lined gloves. 'Though you don't have to answer if you don' t want to.'

She didn't want to. Because there was always the fear something she'd done or said in their brief time together, might make him suspect she was Jewish.

Still, since he was one of the Love Camp's esteemed guests, she had no choice but to answer him. Fearing that if she didn't, he might change his mind about her treatment of him and give her a bad report. "What is it you want to know?" she asked, after a long and rather tense moment.

'Those marks on your backside. I noticed them when you were lying on your stomach,' he said, reaching under her smock and running his hand over them. 'They looked like punishment, were they?'

Why was he asking? Why did he feel the need to know?

Her voice fled, frightened by this question she was obligated to answer, yet couldn't bring herself to do so.

After a minute passed with no reply, he took her silence as an answer.

'Obviously it happened here, which is why I'd like to know.'

This time when she didn't answer, the hug he gave her was so warm, it felt like she was inside a radiator. 'You can trust me, just tell me why you were punished.'

He was now holding her like he would a dear friend. Like Yanni had held her, making it easier for her to relent and say, 'I disappointed one of ObersturmFuhrer Horst Helmer's friends.'

Immediately his expression turned troubled. 'Somehow I'm getting the feeling the prostitution here is forced.' Then he paused before asking, 'Am I right?'

'Yes,' she answered, not meeting his eyes.

'What I more or less suspected when I came here. But tell me, what instrument did this ObersturmFuhrer Horst Helmer use when he struck you?'

'A..a cane,' she stuttered.

'Across the back of the most beautiful girl in this Love Camp?' Astounded, he shook his head. 'I shudder to think how awful it must have been for you.'

Still uneasy, she nodded. 'If you're learning more about this place than you wish to know, then I'll say no more.'

'No, please do. Because I see young, German men being killed on the front every day and hear the whispers of death camps.' His eyes narrowed as if thinking about them. 'All of which make me question what I'm fighting for?'

'If that's the case, then I know I shouldn't say any more.'

'But you should,' he pressed. 'Since your answer about your punishment marks, confirms I'm fighting in the wrong army— so proceed.'

She looked down at his hand now covering hers. 'When Madam Kollar told me what ObersturmFuhrer Horst Helmer had ordered, I was so afraid I began to cry—like the other girls did. Since we had a unique camaraderie with her.'

'Sounds like this ObersturmFuhrer Helmer made you as afraid as a child waiting for the schoolmaster's whip.'

'He did. With tears pouring down the cheeks of the other girls here. Because when a girl is punished like that, she's stripped naked and made to lie over a stool with her hands and feet tied to its legs.'

'And you were struck how many times?'

'Two.' The word rang with the pain of what she heard within herself. 'I should have been struck by Madam Kollar, but ObersturmFuhrer Helmer wanted to do it... and it was more than I could stand.'

'And you passed out?'

'Came close to it. Because when ObersturmFuhrer Helmer struck me, the pain was so bad it felt like every blood vessel in my body had been hit with a hammer.' Her anxiety intensified as she continued, 'And he prolonged the next blow slow-motion like, because he enjoyed watching me cry and beg him not to hit me again—'

'Better hope I don't meet this Obersturmfuher Horst Helmer, because I'm going to kill him if I do.

'Over me?'

'Over *you*, and all the young women— prostitute or otherwise— he's thrashed like chattel.'

'It won't be easy for you to do.'

'Of course it won't,' he remarked in an exasperated tone.

Considering we're in retreat, and it's rumored I'm being transferred to Poland in a few days due to the shortage of front-line commanders there.' He drew in a sharp breath. 'However, rest assured, I'll find a way... but first let's introduce ourselves. My name is—'

'No!" she objected, with a raised hand. "Madam Kollar has a rule that the soldiers and girls are forbidden to exchange names.'

'So what am I supposed to call you?'

'By my number on my breast or by the name the girls here have given me—'

'Which is?'

'Goldilocks.'

'It suits you. Even if your curls are short.' He smiled, squeezing her hand affectionately. 'And if there's a way I can talk to this Madam Kollar and get you some other kind of work in this place, then I intend to do it.'

'You might, but it won't be as safe as doing this. Because the cooks and secretaries assigned here, last less than a month before the S.S. sends them to a death camp and brings in their replacements.' *'Same as they do the girls here with bad diarrhea,'* she also thought about telling him.

But the fortunes of war were changing and to date, she'd been lucky enough not to have that problem.

'Then how can I help you? ' he asked, clearly at a loss. 'I know the soldiers make complaints or reports, so do you have any?'

'Two.'

'And if you get three?'

'You're either stripped naked and whipped to death, or shot—'

'God!' He gave his head a taut shake. 'What if I speak with this Madam Kollar and give her a good report about you?'

'Since you're a front-line officer, she most likely could find a way to tear up my two reports.'

'Then I'll go see her right now. 'He stood up. 'Because I was planning to inform her before I leave, that your punishment marks aren't healing very well.'

'They're not healing well because at least three or four times since it happened, a soldier or S.S. man has said, *'Punishment— eh,'* and slapped me across the backside.'

'Terrible.'

'It is. And I have to turn on my side or stomach to keep it from hurting.'

'And Madam Kollar hasn't done anything to stop those soldiers from treating you like that?'

'She's tried, but unfortunately those soldiers don't listen to her. So she just gives me salve and that small adhesive patch you saw to cover the worst, in the hopes I'll heal soon.'

'Then I'll have a talk with her about that too. And if she won't listen, I'll remind her I'm a highly experienced officer —and not one of those *damned* rank-and-file servicemen, who seem to be doing a good job of running this place.'

'If you do, be careful.'

'Why?'

'Because this camp is under Gestapo jurisdiction. And they're looking for any reason to flog someone or order them killed in a death camp.' Wishing she could add, *'especially with the war winding down—'* but knew better. 'And I don't want another flogging nor to die in a death camp.'

'I didn't know things were that bad.'

'Then I probably did wrong to tell you.'

'No. Like I said, I've heard some mention of it. So I'll be careful and watch what I say.' He removed his greatcoat and scarf from her closet and laid them next to her. 'How many soldiers come to you a night—two?'

'Most of the time it's more like three. With Sundays saved for the S.S.'

'Then if any soldier comes up, tell him you're with an officer.' And leaning over, he quickly put on his high officer's boots before hurrying to Madam Kollar's cubicle.

His speech sounded like someone who came from Vienna, but since they weren't allowed to exchange names, she thought it best not to ask him.

He wasn't gone long, and when he returned, the former radio singer of folk and gypsy songs, Madam Estrelita Kollar, had her hands tight on his arm.

She was an older, Romanian woman, with wrinkled eyes and a wrinkled neck. But she was wearing a brightly colored dress that looked fit for a theatrical performance, with its colors matching the sequined turban she wore to hide her thinning hair.

'Oh my dear, Goldilocks," she exclaimed, excitement lighting her eyes. 'You should be so grateful to have a front-line commander like this handsome man for a friend. And he gave you such a good report that I found the courage to tear up your two bad reports, I was hiding from ObersturmFuhrer Helmer.'

Bela lowered her head and thanked her.

'And also this handsome, front-line commander is not indifferent to what my cards say about you and him.'

Since ObersturmFuhrer Helmer had forbidden Madam Kollar to read for the girls, Bela had no clue as to what the cards might say about her— much less him.

Perhaps it was something connected with their unexplainable familiarity? And she would have liked to have asked her but didn't dare.

'Madam Kollar gave me a reading,' Kurt informed her. 'Which confirms I'm being transferred to Poland before the end of the week.'

'But you two will meet again, Goldilocks,' she assured her. 'Because your friend here was sent from Russia to us in Hungary, which suggests he's following a winding path of ice crystals. And if deviates, then he won't meet those people. whose eyes are like black mirrors.' Her face twisted as if they were demons. 'Bearers of death and disease, summoned from another dimension—'

'And if he deviates from this path, what then?' interrupted Bela, her curiosity unable to keep her from exercising this bit of courage.

'He'll resume his place, and *you* two *will* meet again.' She took his hand. 'Because my intuition tells me he'll deviate or be deviated from his path.'

'Whatever that means?' Kurt shrugged, shaking his head at the cryptic message.

The sudden complaint from an S.S. man, that a rank-and-file soldier was staying too long with one of the girls, demanded the Madam's immediate attention. So excusing herself, she hurried to address the problem.

'Remember as an officer I can stay as long as I wish, Goldilocks. So I gave Madam Kollar some money, and she's getting a better salve for you.' He waved a hand in her direction. 'Also, she has an S.S. man who's her friend. And it inspired me to give her some extra money, to have him put together and deliver to her a box of tasty food with some chocolate in it.'

Bela smiled. 'She'll like that.'

'Oh but it's not just for her. Since she assures me she'll keep only her portion and see the rest is divided among you girls here.'

It was something she wasn't expecting, so she thanked him, helped him into his greatcoat, and handed him his scarf.

Grinning, he began to talk again. 'It's a gift. And I also requested Madam Kollar not to send you another man tonight. And if one of the girls has to make up the numbers, then my gift should be a *thank you* to her—as well as the others.'

His thoughtfulness made her blood surge from her temples to her toes.

'Besides you'll heal faster if you get more rest," he added. 'Plus there's my ego.'

'Your ego?'

'With the war going like it is, then I'll probably not be back. So I'd like to think I had you all to myself this night.' Then a gap of silence followed, with an emptiness in his eyes, she immediately recognized as coming from his inner heart. ' Since the front can be a very lonely place.'

She wasn't proud of lying next to this German commander but regardless, she was closer to him than she would have liked to think. And she knew that would make it increasingly difficult for her not to worry about him after he left.

CHAPTER ELEVEN

*E*ven though I might never know why it seems we've met before, Bela
thought, *there is one thing I do know. If I later find out he's killed in
battle, I will be sad for him— a German officer of all people.*

'Under different circumstances,' she began, then reconsidering, her
voice trailed off.

'What?'

She shook her head, since what she had to say wasn't worth finishing.

'Then I'll complete your words from my point of view.' He touched her
cheek in a wistful gesture. 'Under different circumstances, I'd buy you a
lovely dress and take you to dinner at a fine restaurant. But since I can't—'
He reached into the pocket of his greatcoat and removed a wrapped,
chocolate bar. 'Madam Kollar knows I'm giving this to you, and she wants
you to eat all of it. So, please accept my humble apology that it couldn't
have been something more.' He bowed his head as he took her hand and
gently kissed her palm.

Once again, she wasn't quite sure what to say. If she said *thank you*, would
it be for the chocolate or the beauty they'd shared on the mattress? Which was
whispered wasn't supposed to happen in army brothels. 'These days I'm not
good at making conversation,' she told him, after a minute had passed.

'You're afraid— I understand. But still, I'd like to ask you one final
question before I leave.'

'What?'

'How do we say *good-bye*? I mean since I now know what this camp
is, I don't want to force you to do something you don't want to do. So *you*
make the decision.'

That certainly caught her attention. 'How would you say good-bye?'

'Well my friend Dieter, who's now in the waiting room ready to leave with me, has a flask, and we could share a drink or.... '

'What?' she asked again.

'We could kiss— if it wouldn't offend you.'

After what they'd shared, of course it wouldn't. 'We'll kiss.'

'What I was hoping," he replied in an appealing voice. 'But would you mind if I kissed you, and then you kissed me?'

'The way we started?'

He nodded.

'Which is the best way to end.'

His engaging smile flashed briefly. 'Then allow me to proceed.'

She closed her eyes as he took her in his arms and pressed his mouth against hers, devouring it. And her knees trembled when his lips—warm and gentle against hers—allowed her once again to drink in the sweet, searing tenderness of his.

Savoring every moment of their departing kiss, it seemed he was reluctant to end it. Although, when he finally did, she realized his yearning for her demanded he kiss her again.

She wasn't surprised at the way his kiss had stirred such warmth in her— both now and in the beginning—when she'd refused to let herself think about who *he* was.

"I got my two kisses, so you don't have to kiss me if you don't want to."

'But I do,' she said, admitting she found it as pleasurable as he did. So savoring the delight the feel of his arms sent through her, she slowly and thoughtfully brushed her lips against his.

And when she raised her head, he whispered in her hair, 'My heart's slamming against my chest, can you hear it?'

'I can.'

'Then keep me in your prayers and thoughts as I'll do you,' he said, putting on his fur-lined gloves. 'Because if it's true the *Fuhrer* has an atomic bomb, then Germany will not be finished as many are saying. And the war will end soon.'

She was curious at the play of emotions she saw on his face but had no intention of saying anything.

'So then, Goldilocks," he said, in a voice spiked with enthusiasm. 'I'll be returning to take you out of here.'

'So you'll keep supporting the *Fuhrer* if he has this atomic bomb?'

'Why not?' he asked, with an expression she had trouble identifying. 'As long as it keeps *Ivan* from breaking in and carrying you off.'

She started to ask him another question, but before she could do it, he spun around and strode toward the door... like he thought it best their conversation end.

'Which it probably should,' she murmured, doubting she'd ever see him again, even if Madam Kollar's cards said she would.

Now Shubert's "Lilac Time Serenade" was playing in the background. And as she'd done earlier at Albert's dinner table, she thought about the way Kurt had turned at the Love Camp door and given her a tender look. *But he couldn't have seen me then, could he? Because I was under my bed's gauzy canopy.* Still, the warmth in his expressive eyes had been impossible to forget.

Having been given little food earlier, she was hungry. So after unwrapping the chocolate bar, she sank down on her bed and began eating it. Of all the men she'd been forced to have intercourse with since she her arrival here, this German officer had treated her as he would have done a sweetheart or a wife. Obliterating her darkness for the moment with this shard of brightness, that had made her pulse quicken and her heart pound. *Except for my dreams, my former life is gone.*

Yet, when she'd looked into his soulful eyes in the aftermath of his fiery possession, a piece of it had returned. And she'd blinked back tears over the extraordinary void she felt after his departure. O-oh how she'd yearned for such affection from someone with a spark of human love. *Will we ever meet again?* she continued to wonder, unable to stop thinking about the dangers tomorrow would bring for him.

Since a commander's life on the Eastern Front was as uncertain as hers. And whose death, like hers, would most likely be buried by the war.

But regardless of the way German duty was aligned with obedience—as her co-workers at the Swedish Embassy were quick to explain about the Master Race—she knew that no matter how hard she tried, she'd never be able to forget this officer who'd shown her such kindness and consideration.

Still how was it possible such decadence could make her feel this way? She questioned, amazed by this unsolved puzzle.

For when he'd taken her in its arms, he'd managed to bewitch her heart, making her feel like a faint spark of purity had returned to her polluted soul. And she'd sprouted wings. *Magic wings.* Which had enabled her to rise above her surroundings and watch as the armed sentries, watchtowers, barking dogs, and barbed wire slowly disappeared into the night.

Kurt's tenderness had been a blessing, even if the guilt following it had been terrible. *Her shame was her punishment.* Because what kind of a Jewish girl found pleasure with an officer fighting with those who'd supported the murder of her father and set her people on fire? *A very wicked one, whom God would never forgive, was the only answer.*

Once again she thought of her father, and how he'd often bragged to his friends about her, *'My virtuous and talented daughter,'* he would say, like it was decided forever.

Yet if he were watching her from above in the act of enjoying sexual intercourse with a Wehrmacht officer, she knew he would judge her severely for the shame of her defection.

Since I lacked the courage to head toward the barbed wire and either get the sentries to fire at me or order the barking dogs to tear me to pieces— the severest Love Camp punishments.

"Kurt Ulrich," she cried, struggling unsuccessfully to sleep. She was quite foggy-headed, but in the hushed stillness, his dream-like reality continued to merge with her memories of him. Making it next to impossible to shake his imaginary image, standing over her bed.

"I recall my experience with you at the Love Camp all too clearly, *Herr* Ulrich," she said. "And considering it, I feel it's better not to remember certain people."

"*Like me?*" he asked, his eyes not moving from her face. "Then you should try to block their memory."

"But you were kind to me," she reminded, taking her handkerchief and wiping a tear from her cheek.

"That I was. But German officers were your enemy, Bela. So if I treated you well, it was only because my heart ached, and I needed someone to hold."

And then he'd disappeared so quickly, it was like a huge stone had been rolled between them. Motivating her to ask God, *"Where were you when the S.S. made a field- whore out of me?"*

* * *

"Bela, wake up," urged Jaclyn, shaking her arm. "What's happened? We heard you cry out, so did you have another bad dream?"

She opened her eyes and gazed at her surroundings. "I thought I saw a German officer in here."

"Here? Impossible," said Wolf, his crimson robe's sash tied around his waist in a hasty manner.

"Are you really sure you want to go to Berlin?" Jaclyn asked, straightening her black peignoir as she sat down on the edge of the bed.

Bela was embarrassed but remained firm in her decision. "Like I said when we were reunited, the intoxication of my deliverance made me forget to mourn the dead. With Berlin the only thing that gives purpose to my survival."

"You have such an inner discipline that if you were Catholic, I swear you'd become a nun," said Jaclyn.

"But since I 'm not, when the war's over, I'll simply have to continue to give my music sixteen hours a day, instead of the usual eight."

Wolf and Jaclyn hugged her and made her promise that if she needed anything, she'd call them.

Bela knew they meant well. But even if she had to stay up the rest of the night, she was determined not have any more dreams or thoughts that made her memories return. *Considering my nightmares are getting worse.* Recalling a recent one where she and the other naked and exposed Love Camp girls had been strapped to their beds facedown, by black-uniformed S.S. men.

"Purgation for their wicked ways," they'd said, before spanking their backsides until they burned with a scorching heat.

And if that wasn't painful enough, the fires of their lust dictated that these men remove their leather belts and replace the brutal spankings with savage whippings across the buttocks, that tattered the girls' flesh.

She was deathly afraid, but no matter the pain, she vowed she'd take the flayings in silence...until the S.S. man, who was receiving such great pleasure in beating her, stopped suddenly— sending the message that something more terrible was in store for her. And listening closely, an awful fear gripped her when she heard the clink of his belt as he unfastened his trousers and stepped closer to her.

The thing she dreaded most was about to happen. And biting her lips, it was all she could do to keep from screaming when he drove into the cheeks of her buttocks in a rush of lust.

Tears of pain immediately followed as *this* slaughter knife of his, scarred her body with its humiliation.

But afraid she'd receive another savage whipping from him—only this time with his baton—she simply lay on her belly, helpless, as he gave her a merciless onslaught of backside grindings, each with a punishing rhythm.

A stark chill swept through her. *"Horrible."* she muttered through clenched teeth.

Even if now, like most mornings, the nightmare of her shame with his vileness would fade when she'd open her eyes and gaze at the snow –capped peaks outside her window. But still, throughout the day, there were often times when thinking about the nightmare would make her buttocks ache, the way they had when ObersturmFuhrer Helmer had struck her with his cane.

Alarm gripped her. *Did I have this nightmare because it was a smothered memory returning from that other, darker side of time? Or... did I have it because it was a premonition of a deadly evil yet to come?*

* * *

Throughout a good portion of the night Wolf and Jaclyn had sat on the sofa by the window in the hallway outside Bela's bedroom Tears sheened in Jaclyn's eyes. Making Wolf swallow hard as he remembered his wife's great pain when she'd learned Bela was in the Love Camp.

"Bela's spirit is still so frail, I pray for her everyday," said Jaclyn, swiping her eyes with a lacy handkerchief.

He gave her hand a loving squeeze. "So do I. But Kurt Ulrich's brought this on her, because several times throughout the evening I caught him flirting with her. And she didn't object."

"She was probably just trying to get along with him, I mean— after what went on in the Love Camp —I don't see how she could ever find pleasure with a man who's a former Wehrmacht captain." She shook her head negatively. "But you were wrong not to allow the OSS to inform Albert that Bela was Jewish."

"Which as you well know she advised me not to do."

"I realize that. Especially after all the money von Friesen gave to help the Palestinian Jews smuggle as many Jewish children as they could to Britain."

"The reason Bela maintained Albert had suffered enough grief and didn't need to learn what had happened to her," Wolf said.

Jaclyn stared at him with a tense, frustrated look. "Still, I believe if he'd known Bela was Jewish, he wouldn't have allowed Kurt to come with us."

"We'll never know. But I'm sure she'll never stop thinking about the Love Camp if she ends up with Kurt."

"None of this would have happened," Jaclyn wept, "if we could have stopped Haral and Bela from working at that Swedish extraterritorial house."

"We tried." Wolf sighed, recalling it. "But since we were saving lives too, Haral and Bela wouldn't allow it."

"That rented Swedish extraterritorial house didn't have it together like it should have had," Jaclyn reminded him. "Because their structure was poorly built, making it easy for the Arrow-Cross militia to burst in."

"How well I know...." Wolf said slumping in despair. *At times, Bela's abuse was beyond what he could handle.* When suddenly, he remembered they were sitting outside her door. And if she heard them, then there was no telling what she might do. "She's got a cyanide capsule— I know it."

"And you've seen it? "Jaclyn asked, rising.

"No. But if I'd been subjected to the wickedness and shame of a soldiers' brothel— plus those terrible beatings by that monster ObersturmFuhrer Helmer—then I'd swallow every one I could lay my hands on."

"Wolf please—"She gave his arm a shake. "We rescued her as soon as we could."

"Which wasn't soon enough. And Haral... poor Haral. "

"Who was born poor but after the Great War died rich," said Jaclyn, her voice dropping. "Which turned out to be his curse."

"And his daughter's," Wolf hastened to add, as a thunderstorm of remorse, intensified the pain of his shattered nerves. "You know when I learned his body was clogging the Danube, with the other bloated bodies, all I could wonder was how many years would the riverbank be red with blood? And how long would it take before Haral's body floated out to the

Black Sea?" A pause. "Since all the rivers reach the sea." Another pause. "Can you believe a thought like that crossed my mind?"

She didn't answer but put her hand impulsively on his shoulder as she gently guided him back to their room. "You advised everyone to get some sleep.... However, we're certainly not."

CHAPTER TWELVE

S everal times in the night, Bela caught herself dozing. But other than that, she wasn't able to sleep because of the lingering, bittersweet feelings she still had for Kurt.

So giving up, she reached for her journal next to her bed and wrote the question she'd been asking herself all night. *"Why did I have this dream about Kurt in my room? Was it because I was feeling guilty at finding enjoyment in his company?"* A question she found difficult to answer. So she turned to the pages she'd written about leaving the Swedish Embassy with her father and began reading them: *'Time is of the essence if we're going to save those children,' Pa keeps reminding me...then, he took my hand. 'Still, Bela, you don't have to go.'*

But I just shook my head. 'Yes I do, because we have our work. Just like the many people here at the embassy....Who've been working twenty-four hour shifts to get the Swedish protective passports ready, for the next boxcar of ghetto Jews slated for Auschwitz.'"

The answer about my enjoying Kurt's company is clearly in these paragraphs...which makes me reluctant to confront the issue because it tells me I was wrong to enjoy his company the way I did.

Regret stabbed her as she pressed her journal against her heart. "But even so, Kurt was there for me when no one else was. And after he'd left me at the Love Camp, I felt empty and drained—"

"Were you saying something to me?" interrupted Ina, entering the room with an armload of fresh bedding.

"No, just myself."

The serving woman grinned, embarrassed, before dropping the bedding in a chair and opening the window. "Enjoy the view, *Fraulein* Bela, while I draw your bath water."

"My intention." She smiled, noticing how beautiful the Alps were on this last day of April.

So sitting up in bed, she stared with a dreamy look at the way each snowy peak was crowned with a sun-gilded turban. "Pure enchantment," she remarked, throwing back her blanket.

And even if she did think it wrong to enjoy Kurt's company, the brightness and beauty of the morning made her reservations about his company temporarily vanish as she looked forward to joining him for breakfast.

She loved to waltz. So waltzing with him last night had been a relaxing escape from her war-torn world. But was it something more...? Like her, he'd seen a lot of death but, regardless, an enthusiasm for life still existed in him that made her hunger to be a part of it.

Which is the reason why no matter what her past connection had been with him, each time he'd squeezed her hand or touched her arm, it had made her feel like he was trying to lessen the echo of her corruption. And help her make the crossing from a world, where she'd lost everything, to one where she was clinging to whatever came her way.

And all this in the hope that at some point, it would give her enough strength to overcome her soul's frayed edges and not fall into an abyss of hopelessness. *Where I'm utterly lost.*

"Bath water's ready," Ina said. "And today it's hot and not lukewarm."

"Probably because some of the snow is melting, and the pipes are thawing."

"Could be, *Fraulein* Bela, but we've just learned it's not the pipes that have given us the most trouble this winter."

Suspecting it had to do with the chalet's heating, she wasn't in the mood to inquire about whatever else it was that had given them the trouble. So she hurried into the bathroom and began her ablutions.

It didn't take long, and after wrapping a towel around her body, she went over to the bedroom's *armoire* across from it, where she removed a pleated, gray skirt and matching twin-set. It would have been another plain outfit had Jaclyn not slipped a pink scarf embellished with scattered pearls around it. Plus there was a note: *"You'll look more stylish if you wear this with your twin- set."*

Shaking her head, Bela not only took her advice but picked up the gold heart bracelet her father had given her when she'd turned sixteen. The Germans had forbidden Jews to own gold jewelry, but Jaclyn had cleverly hidden the jewelry from both families, by sewing the various pieces in the hem of her fox coat.

"Jaclyn and Wolf pamper me, but in reality, I still maintain I need to be pampering them," said Bela, thinking aloud as she slid the bracelet over her wristand headed toward the door.

It was an early six-thirty when she joined Albert and Wolf on the terrace for breakfast. And as usual they were dressed in gray shirts, sweaters, embroidered lederhosen, and white, knee socks.

Jaclyn sometimes slept till late. But after breakfast the two men usually drank a third and fourth cup of coffee, so if she came down sooner, she wouldn't have to eat alone.

"Bela," said Albert, quickly rising and pulling out a chair for her. "You're up early, so what do you want? Your usual light breakfast?"

"What I told Jutta when I was coming down."

Kurt, dressed in embroidered lederhosen, like his cousin and host, soon joined them. "A note on my bed said I should wear this." He handed the note to Albert. "An outfit that greatly pleases me."

"And I stated in this note that the outfit's white, knee socks would show off your well-muscled legs. Which —without a doubt—has impressed Ina and Jutta."

"I'm not sure about that." Kurt grinned. "But I do apologize for being late since I simply forgot to ask what time breakfast was served."

"And I apologize for forgetting to tell you," Albert said, motioning at Jutta to bring him a plate.

"Of little consequence in these perilous times," remarked Wolf. "But what about you, Bela? Did you end up having another sleepless night?"

"Unfortunately." She frowned, not particularly wanting to discuss her sleeping problems with Wolf, in front of Kurt. *Considering all that's gone on— and is going on— between us.*

"If Berlin's keeping you from sleep, then don't let it," said Kurt, patting her hand. "Because I'll be protecting *you* more than the White Russians. And we'll accomplish what we're meant to do there." He paused, his features relaxing slightly. "And then with luck, go back to living our lives similar to the way they were before the war."

Wolf leaned forward in his chair. "We might, but certainly not you, Kurt." He appeared to take delight in reminding him. "Which makes me wonder how many years you think the British will keep you in one of their prisons?"

"Too long." Kurt sighed. "But as was said last night, not as long as *Ivan*."

"Another reason I'll be praying for your safety in Berlin," remarked Albert. "Because even with your good cover-story, I shudder to think what the Russians will do should they learn the truth about what we —their allies— are up to."

Kurt swallowed his coffee. "An unpleasant thought. So please forgive me if I change the subject and ask a question."

"Forgiven." Albert's face brightened. "So ask me, nephew."

"May I go to that lovely stone church in the village down the road, so I can light a candle for my wife and son?"

"Of course. As long as Jaclyn and Wolf go with you and show you the short cut."

"Which we will," Wolf said. "Since there's someone for whom I also wish to light a candle."

"Understandable," said Kurt, reflecting a moment before glancing at Bela. "And you? Will you also be going?"

"No reason not to," she replied, her feelings for him continuing to both surprise and disturb her as his hand squeezed hers.

When she was younger being in a Catholic Church had frightened her. But after her father had married Jaclyn's mother, she hadn't thought twice about covering her head and going with her to St. Stephansdom's Gothic Cathedral in Vienna. In fact, when the Jews in Budapest were being rounded up, Jaclyn would have hidden her with a group of nuns, had Raoul Wallenberg not issued her one of his Swedish passports.

* * *

The morning passed quickly. And an hour or so later Bela, Kurt, and Jaclyn followed Wolf down the winding, cobbled street that ran behind Albert's chalet, to the village's square. The buildings in the village were several centuries old. With many ornately trimmed in baroque-style architecture: while others had stonework carvings decorating them that looked to be from the Middle Ages.

On both sides of the street stood restaurants and shops. One, which specialized in cuckoo clocks and watches, also doubled as a boutique for both ladies and men's clothing. "That's where Albert said he purchased some clothing for me," Kurt remarked.

"And also where we replenished our wardrobes," Jaclyn told him. "Since with the exception of my extraordinary fox coat, I had nothing to wear when I arrived here."

"Nothing?" The revelation appeared to surprise him, and he stopped. "Must have felt like a cave woman wrapped in all that fur."

"That I did. But fortunately, I had a potato- sack looking dress under it, which kept me from standing naked whenever I removed the coat."

He laughed. "Then give my regards to potato sacks."

"Absolutely," she said, stepping close to a flower stand where a woman was selling red roses.

And though Wolf was already in the next block, Kurt went over to the flower seller. "One bunch for Jaclyn and the other for Bela." He bowed, as he removed some coins from the wallet Albert had given him last night and handed them to the woman. "My wife loved flowers, and I hope these two ladies do too."

Jaclyn kissed him on the cheek. "Wasn't expecting this."

"Nor I," said Bela, doing the same.

The church was only a block away, with a frowning Wolf waiting at its door.

But even so, Jaclyn pulled Bela aside. "Were you able to find out anything more about Kurt?"

"Oh. Yes." She smiled.

"Was it bad?"

"Only if you think the compelling power he has over me is dangerous."

"Sounds like a real problem." Jaclyn grinned, sniffing her bouquet.

"Which I feel certain a good many women would love to have."

"You can bet on it," she said, her grip on Bela's arm warm and reassuring.

Once inside the candlelit church, Kurt quickly lit two candles in front of a Madonna and Child, that had a tarnished crucifix behind them. "One for my wife, and one for my toddler son," he informed Bela, staring at their picture in his wallet. "Which after the Tommies took me prisoner was the only thing of mine they allowed me to keep."

She glanced at the photo, noticing his toddler son held a toy giraffe. "What were their names?" she asked with a swell of sympathy.

"Frieda and Erich," he said, genuflecting at the altar in their memory. "But we called *Frieda* by her pet name, *Fresa*."

"And they were killed in an air raid in Berlin?"

"When they were in a building on the Unter den Linden. And it would have been safe had weather conditions not caused bombers to miss their targets and hit the building which—" He looked down. "Exploded."

"It must have been awful."

"It was." He put their picture back. "Since I never saw them again after I left for the Eastern Front. In fact, Carl, my father-in-law, went with me to the train station the morning I left, because Fresa and I had never been apart a day since we'd met. And she was so upset we thought it best she remain at the house with the baby."

Kurt's tenderness continued to move Bela —especially when he offered to light a candle for her father.

Momentarily surprised at what some of her people might have deemed an unwelcome sentiment, she felt at a loss as she stared at the candles. Though, after a moment passed, a sudden calm overcame her, and she thanked him.

Even if later, while writing in her journal, she did ponder what her father might be thinking....*That is provided he's watching me from above the way Yanni—along with other Jews I've known—maintain the dead watch the living.*

She continued to ponder it until the late afternoon, when she informed Kurt that the bald-headed man,who'd briefed them yesterday was here.

"I'm pleased to announce the OSS says the *Fuhrer* died this April thirtieth, at around 3:30 in the afternoon," said this bald-headed man once they were assembled in Albert's library. "And late tomorrow, May first, the Germans are expected to make an announcement about it. Informing the people that General Weilding, Berlin's last commandant, will be signing the official surrender at Tempelhof. Which more than likely will be handled by Soviet General Vasily Chuikov.... And though there's still fighting, the heart of Berlin has fallen or will soon fall."

Everyone stood up and applauded, with Albert shouting, "Champagne!" However, before he could summon Jutta to bring it, this bald-headed, man stopped him.

"Not yet." Then he turned to Kurt and introduced himself, "I'm Mr. Fieszel."

Kurt raised a shoulder and whispered to Bela, "He's pronouncing his name like it's French instead of German."

"Certainly sounds like it."

When she'd met the man yesterday, she'd thought he'd looked as thin as a grapevine trellis, with the suit he was wearing much too large for him. But today, the suit he wore was even larger, with a pocket so big he had trouble removing the small piece of paper inside it. "Here memorize this." He handed Wolf a scribbled copy of an address in Berlin. "It's where von Lehmann could possibly be."

Wolf glanced at it. "It's the hospital where Dr. Grossklos works, which we're expecting to be our first stop."

"And it will be. Even if some of the Russians are continuing to maintain that von Lehmann's dead, and his preliminary designs have been destroyed."

"With no one arresting Dr. Grossklos?" Wolf asked.

"No reason to." Fieszel waited a moment before continuing, "But have you ever considered the Russians might be looking for something besides those preliminary designs for the improved V-3 Cannon Rocket?"

Wolf regarded him with an inquiring gaze. "Anything's possible in that dying city. But what could be more important than locating von Lehmann and his preliminary designs? Or confirming he's dead and his designs destroyed?" He tensed as the muscles of his forearm hardened under his jacket's sleeve. "Or by some ill twist of fate discovering the Germans have him and his papers."

Fieszel smiled wryly. "Perhaps Dr. Grossklos is the only one who knows how the Russians are planning on using you, to lead them to what it is von Lehmann is supposed to know."

"They're baiting us with their cryptic little message," said Wolf, like it was obvious. "Considering they're so busy raping, looting, and killing everyone who gets in their way, they don't seem to have much time to find what they're after."

"Who knows?" Fieszel shrugged. "But then again, if it's something dealing in the realm of the supernatural or science fiction—"

"Like *Buck Rogers*," Wolf cut him short. "Which gives me the feeling that when we get to Berlin, things won't be like you're telling us."

"Just throwing out possibilities," Fieszel remarked with another shrug. "And to remind you to keep an open mind." Then he reached into a fawn -colored bag and handed Wolf the several sheets of thin documents the group would need in order for the Russians to let them in the city. "Your authority papers from Grosvenor Square or Ros-venor— as you're calling it. So put them in your wife's briefcase with her music and never let it out of your sight."

"And the rest of my people don't get them?"

"Only after the Russians have stamped them."

Wolf glared at him. "But why? Can't each member of my party be trusted with *his* or *her* documents?"

"Perhaps." Fieszel hesitated as if disturbed by the question. "But since you're the professed Oxford scholar the British and Americans are paying to write the history of the war, then you'd best hang onto those documents."

"Still, Bela's my co-author, remember? And they claim they're only letting us come, because they're expecting her and my wife to perform for them."

"Of which the OSS views as part of the Russian hard-line. Since as I'm sure you've all said, they would have allowed you in the city without either woman." He then removed some more papers from his fawn-colored bag before asking, "But any more questions?"

"Yes." Kurt glanced at Bela before standing up and addressing him. "The women need protection. So since Wolf and I aren't allowed any weapons, then give us some more details about these White Russians, I'm *told* you mentioned yesterday."

"Simply that being at war is quite different from being at peace," he reminded, his voice cold and exact. "And most of the patients and staff in the hospital—where *Dr. Grossklos* resides—are holed up in its underground basement. Which your White Russian hospital guards in the Red Army, will take you to."

"Will these soldiers be standing over us while we try to locate von Lehmann and his papers?" asked Wolf, like the idea was preposterous. "Seems we're definitely in Soviet hands if it comes to doing that."

"Which you are."

"Wait a minute," said Kurt. "Will they let us talk to von Lehmann in secret? Should the patient there actually be him and not his doppelganger?"

"They're the doctor's friends," Fieszel clarified.

Wolf peered at him. "Since it's peculiar to have White Russians in the Red Army, I'm of the opinion they're trying to keep their people safe from all the raping and looting. Am I right?"

"You are. And naturally they will protect *you*, should you be fortunate enough to come by information about von Lehmann, the Soviets have been unsuccessful at finding."

"Sounds good," said Wolf. "As long as these White Russian guards don't have loose lips with the Soviets."

"They don't. Because they understand a loose mouth kills many a person, but *you*—"

"Me?" Wolf questioned.

"All of you." Fieszel looked at the group. "Until now, you've deliberately heard only part of the story. Though, with your departure imminent, not only has new information surfaced, but the time has come to answer your questions on what to do— should you affirm von Lehmann's identity. And by the way, we're not expecting you to find the papers, because it was concluded last night that the odds are two thousand to one that you won't."

"Unless von Lehmann or his doppelganger knows something we don't," said Wolf with one of his frowns. "But let's get back to this new information. The Russians have von Lehmann or his doppelganger under hospital arrest— do they not?"

"Sort of." Fieszel hedged, then added in a toneless voice, "But they can't be sure who he is, since he has head injuries and is acting like a crazy old man."

Kurt was immediately curious. "So the Russians suspect it's the doppelganger?"

"Who can really say? And if anything, knowing whether this man is von Lehmann's double, or really von Lehmann is what we suspect Dr.Grossklos knows."

"Could be," Wolf replied. "Since it's possible the doctor's found a way to identify him. And realizes it was the doppelganger wearing von Lehmann's name tag, who got killed."

"If that's true, then where was this man in the hospital found?" asked Kurt.

"Unconscious in a ruined, suburb building next to a vacant lot outside von Lehmann's laboratory. With Russian tanks rolling down the street," said Fieszel, like he found it peculiar. "And a briefcase was next to him that had some bound, blank pages inside it."

Wolf shook his head again. "What the hell kind of crazy reason would he be out there with Russian tanks on the street?"

Fieszel cut narrowed eyes at him. "According to Dr.Grossklos, the man claimed he was attempting to do a final test with one of his model rockets."

"*Final*— all right," Wolf chided. "And those Russians took him to Dr. Grossklos's hospital without knowing there was a connection?"

"No. They took him there because it was his request. Plus, the good doctor appears to have been hoarding food and medical supplies— at his own expense—for the past several years to avoid the *chaos* of the other hospitals in the suburbs."

Wolf's face was expressionless. "Smart thinking on the doctor's part, though, I'm still surprised the Russians didn't shoot this man."

"They didn't want to take the chance he wasn't an important scientist," Fieszel replied.

Kurt's brows rose inquiringly. "And those blank papers, what's the latest on them?"

"That they were supposedly secured in a White Russian medic's house—" He stopped as if wondering how best to answer. "And this medic humored von Lehmann by taking them to his house and hiding them."

"And this medic's where?" asked Wolf.

"It's uncertain. Because as things stand now, the Russians have searched this medic's house and surroundings thoroughly and those papers can't be found." Then another moment passed in silence before he proceeded, "Which is creating a problem. Since the fuzzy-headed von Lehmann, or *his* double, somehow managed to convince the Red Army's Supreme

Commander Marshal Zhukov, there was a possibility those blank papers were actually scaled- down, preliminary designs which had been duplicated —with the passion of a monk— in invisible- ink."

"Invisible- ink," Wolf remarked, his eyes darting from Kurt to Jaclyn. "Must have been a challenge for von Lehmann."

"It was," Kurt quickly answered. "Since he saw it as a way to hide some of his achievements from the enemy."

"Which should give the Russians another reason to make sure finding those papers— if they exist— ends up being our job," said Wolf, censure in his tone.

"Exactly." Fieszel nodded. "Even if we did receive confirmation early this morning, that the German atom bomb has now proven to be only a work in progress. And is not part of those invisible-ink papers—"

"Aside from the *Fuhrer's* death, that's the best news I've heard in I don't know when," interrupted Albert. "And certainly now we should have some champagne."

"Mr. Fieszel inclined his bald head. "I agree."

There was a chorus of approval from everyone except Wolf, as Albert rang the bell on his desk to summon Jutta.

"Don't mean to break this mood of jubilation," said Wolf, directing his words to Fieszel. "But if this is true, then what's so important about these papers that the Russians feel they need us to help find them?"

"Rockets... they're all about rockets."

"To get us into space or to deploy nuclear weapons?" Albert asked.

"Both, *Herr* von Friesen," remarked Fieszel. "But before answering any more of your questions, I'm required to inform you about your air departure from Berlin—"

"Which we've been told will be at eight in the evening from Gatow," said Wolf.

And it will be. With the Russians taking you into Berlin and back in one of their trucks." Fieszel turned to Kurt. "Though if you do ascertain it's *von Lehmann,* who's in Grossklos's hospital, then the former communications director, Wehrmacht Colonel Franz Dietrich, will have a plan which will enable von Lehmann to escape from Berlin the following week."

"A Wehrmacht colonel?" asked Jaclyn. "Are you sure we trust him?"

Fieszel's eyes shone straight into hers. "Beyond a shadow of a doubt. Because he's been with us since von Stauffenberg's bomb plot against Hitler, and has been communicating with *Herr* von Friesen's people, trying to save Jewish children by relocating them in Great Britain. But now—" His gaze dropped. "The Russians have him under house arrest, so he can use his equipment to aid them."

"And a man like that is supposed to *help* us?" Wolf asked.

"I know it raises some questions about trusting him," said Fieszel, appearing undisturbed. "But he's fluent in Russian and English. So, before the Russians arrived we worked out a special code with him that's so simple, the Russians don't suspect we're communicating with it."

Looking at him uneasily, Wolf spoke again, "Which has allowed him to tell the Russians all about *us* and our mission, hasn't it, Fieszel?"

"Which, considering the city's fallen—street by street and block by block— was perhaps was the only way the OSS could get you into it," he said, his suggestion side-stepping Wolf's question. "Because regardless, your White Russian escorts from the Red Army will be keeping a close watch over you. Since this Russian Colonel Sokolov is being pressured by Marshal Zhukov, to identify von Lehmann and learn what was on those missing papers."

Once again, Fieszel reached into his fawn-colored bag, only this time he removed a photo of an attractive, dark-haired woman. "This is Vera Tovarishki, Colonel Dietrich's, White Russian mistress. Who works part-time as a nurse for Dr. Grossklos."

"Vera Tovarishki," Kurt said. "She has a house next from my father-in-law's, and my wife and I knew her and her brother quite well."

"Did you ever meet Colonel Franz Dietrich?" Fieszel asked him.

"Once. When he was a patient in the hospital."

"Then you should know he's as exceptional a person as is Vera Tovarishki," he remarked in a confident tone. "And she's taken a flat close to his... but regretfully—" He looked embarrassed. "Colonel Sokolov gave orders that Dietrich's Russian guards were *not* to have sex with her. Although they are fondling her and kissing her."

"*Bad* enough," Jaclyn said angrily.

"But as she tells us on the Morse she and Franz understand the importance of the work they're doing for us, so she's putting up with it."

Kurt gave his head a sharp shake. "Quite a sacrifice."

"But necessary in these desperate times," Fieszel reminded.

"Unfortunately," said Wolf, his brows creasing. "But what exactly are the Russians expecting us to do? Since it doesn't seem they're allowing us to travel around the city like they assured us we could."

Fieszel snorted. "Go to the hospital on the city's outskirts and visit with von Lehmann or his double. Then at some point meet Vera Tovarishki at her house nearby, where the blank papers were supposedly hidden—"

"And start hunting them," Kurt finished.

Bela's eyes focused on Vera's picture. "How are we supposed to find something the Russians couldn't? When it stands to reason they've searched every house and building on the block."

"A new plan. Something we found out about from Colonel Dietrich this morning in a short -wave radio message," Fieszel said, giving her his full attention. "The colonel intercepted a message from Sokolov to Peter and Victor— the two Soviet agents working with him— when they were patrolling in a truck."

"And that message was *what*?" asked Wolf.

"That Colonel Sokolov was ordered by Marshal Zhukov to have Wolf and Kurt confirm the identify of the man in the hospital as either von Lehmann or his doppelganger."

Wolf appeared to study him for a moment. "And just what does he plan on having *us* do if we discover the man in the hospital is von Lehmann? Does this colonel really think we'd tell him?"

"Apparently the colonel has reason to believe this man is von Lehmann— but still this marshal feels he needs your opinion. So the Russians will escort the four of you and von Lehmann, to Vera's house. Where this man will be expected to reproduce some of those missing designs and equations on a drafting board there." He slid Vera's picture back in his bag. "And if he can't, then the colonel is aware that von Lehmann raised your cousin *Herr* Ulrich here, like he was his son, and he'll—"

"Do *what*?" interrupted Wolf.

"See *Herr* Ulrich becomes a Russian prisoner- of-war."

A sudden, chilling silence fell over the room.

Kurt turned to Bela. "I volunteered for this assignment to help identify von Lehmann... and—*now*—I'm on the verge of becoming one of *Ivan's* prisoners?"

CHAPTER THIRTEEN

"I hadn't expected to hear that," said Bela. "And it makes me uneasy." Looking agitated, Wolf stared at Fieszel. "But what happens if it's only von Lehmann's double in the hospital?"

"Then the Russians should have their answer as to who this man really is."

Kurt shook his head again. "Insane. Because if von Lehmann's got multiple head injuries, he can't re-create some of those designs."

"True. But *desperation* often lets you do things you didn't think you could," said Fieszel with a mellow grin. "So if they can make von Lehmann desperate enough by threatening *Herr* Ulrich here, then they're hoping some of his mental faculties might possibly return. And the Russians will have their rocket scientist. But if it's his double, then they'll know it and conclude von Lehmann either died or is hiding somewhere."

"And Kurt will become a Russian prisoner- of- war?" Wolf asked him.

"Colonel Dietrich says it's just a threat to confirm the truth about von Lehmann. So I wouldn't worry about it."

Kurt almost laughed. "What *Ivan* doesn't realize is that von Lehmann and I parted on such bad terms, he'd probably think my ending up a prisoner is what I deserved and—"

"That's where you're wrong," Fieszel broke in. "Vera Tovarishki never met von Lehmann until awhile back at the hospital. But she did recall having seen him many times, wearing a dark suit and standing behind a shrub across the street from her house. Watching your wife, the family maid, and your father-in-law's driver, play with your son. But if the sirens sounded, then a nearby car would pick von Lehmann up—" He reached for Albert's open photo album on the table. "However, von Lehmann wouldn't allow the car to leave, until your wife had grabbed your son and taken him inside to your father-in-law's structurally sound cellar."He pointed at the photos in the album of Dr. Grossklos's bombed-out house and cellar. "A place he made available for his neighbors as well as his family, because he knew if his house went, the cellar would remain."

"And this Vera Tovarishki is certain it was von Lehmann she saw?" Kurt asked.

"Yes," said Fieszel. "Because she took particular notice of him, since he reminded her of one of the legendary *Watchmen* in a cinema she'd recently seen." He took a deep breath, then continued in a tight, reedy voice. "Especially, with von Lehmann coming almost every morning and watching your deceased wife and young son, play together in Dr. Grossklos's front yard."

Kurt was clearly dismayed. "And he never approached them?"

"You'd excluded him from that part of your life, *Herr* Ulrich. So, it seems he wasn't as angry as you thought."

"Something I'll ask him if the man at Grossklos's hospital is really von Lehmann."

"Which leads me to the next question," said Wolf, pulling Fieszel's attention back to him. "How much time do we have before the plane flying us to London tonight —and Berlin tomorrow morning —leaves?"

"A full night," replied Fieszel in his tight voice. "Since you won't be flying out of here to London—"

"Not London!" Wolf sprang to his feet. "If we're not flying out of here to London, then how the *hell* are we leaving?"

"You're flying out of Stuttgart to Berlin in the morning," Fieszel blurted, his face closing as he seemed reluctant to add, "But in order to get there you'll need to take a train that's waiting for you just inside the German border."

"*Train!*" shouted Albert, shaking a fist. "Who thought that up? Since I was personally told by the Ros-venor office that there are still pockets of German soldiers hiding in the woods and —"

Fieszel held up a hand to silence him. "There are. But the Germans in the area your people will be traveling through have surrendered. So there's nothing to fear."

"Not from what my sources are telling me," argued Albert, fast losing patience. "Because it's common knowledge there are still a good many who've refused to surrender. With their battalions making it unsafe for civilians—much less my people— to be traveling by train through the central, German countryside."

"First let me assure you," said Fieszel, "that those isolated pockets of German soldiers are being rounded up by the Americans as we speak."

"Still," insisted Albert. "This train ride makes no sense at all."

"It does when you consider the sensitive nature of your mission."

"Sensitive nature?" Bela questioned.

Fieszel nodded. "An ally kidnapping or planning to kidnap a scientist from another ally."

"Kidnapping!" Albert exclaimed, vaulting from his chair. "Provided von Lehmann's still alive."

"Which apparently the Swiss and British want no part of," remarked Wolf with an unwelcome frankness.

"Correct," said Fieszel. "Because if von Lehmann is alive, the Americans are taking him to the states the following week. And later, should it flashback on your mission, then the British feel it should be up to the Americans to handle the matter with the Soviets."

"Since we're in a such a hurry to get to Berlin, then how far away is this airfield by train?" asked Jaclyn, shifting to a more pressing aspect of their departure.

Fieszel stepped toward her. "If you leave tonight, then you should get there no later than tomorrow morning."

"Which means the airfield *really* is near Stuttgart," replied Wolf, looking uneasy.

Bela's heart jumped. *Were the Americans out if their minds? Even with the allies in control of the area since January, it was still a dangerous place to be.*

"I'd like to get my hands on the American idiot who thought up the idea of a train ride," said Albert with mounting rage. "Because *I* and the OSS have worked very hard planning this mission. But now, so it seems, everything we've planned has been changed by some unknown person who apparently has a great deal of influence."

Fieszel's features tensed. "With all due respect *Herr* von Friesen, you're not going along, so why get so upset?"

"*Upset!*" He sank back down into his chair and tapped his fingers against its leather arm. "My family's at stake! Are you blind not to see it? And this train trip is a delay which means that every minute the Russians continue to plunder Berlin, they have a better chance than we do, of stumbling onto von Lehmann and his papers."

Jaclyn glanced at her watch. "Time is evaporating like expensive drops of French perfume in an open bottle. So surely anyone with a brain can understand that."

"As everyone knows, Switzerland is a neutral country, but the OSS operates here," said Wolf. "With certain people in charge having the good sense to look the other way." He glanced from Fieszel to the group's papers and passports. "So, why don't the British do the same in our case and let us fly out of London to Berlin on an American plane?"

"As I said, it's because London's American OSS office— being operated for a time by the British— refuses to allow it."

"The Germans would be in London if it weren't for the Americans," reminded Albert, his hand cutting a swath through the air. "Can't they see it and give them the go- ahead to do what we want?"

Kurt shifted impatiently. "It's ironic the Americans saved Britain— yet are allowing the Tommies to dictate to them."

"It sounds to me like someone in London's OSS office is making a mountain out of nothing," said Jaclyn. "And the Americans are dumb enough to go along with it."

"That someone is probably a newcomer working there, who's trying to prove himself worthy of the Ros-venor's office big-wigs." Wolf fumed.

Kurt turned to Bela with the flicker of a smile. "Maybe he's blackmailing the Americans to do things his way or he'll tell *Ivan*?"

"With the Americans not having the balls to take him out," Wolf declared bitterly.

Jaclyn tossed her head. "Yet somehow they manage to win wars."

"Remember, you'll have less than twenty-four hours to identify von Lehmann at the hospital," said Fieszel. "So try and learn as much as you can about him and his missing papers. Or otherwise, you'll miss your plane when it returns to land at the Gatow airport, not far from the River Havel."

"What kind of plane is it?" asked Wolf.

"A *Dakoka*." Fieszel handed him a photo. "Which means the pilot will be expecting to pick you up at eight in the evening for your return flight."

"But what if circumstances cause us to miss the plane?" asked Kurt, looking worried.

"Then the pilot will return the following night at the same time to take you to Stuttgart. Where you'll connect with a plane waiting to fly you to London. But try not to miss it because as everyone knows, Berlin's surrounded with war machinery. And there's still heavy fighting—"

"Which lets us know the only way anyone can get in or out of the city is by plane," Kurt finished for him.

Wolf muttered something nobody could understand, then asked in a sarcastic tone, "Is there anything else you feel we should know, *Herr* Fieszel?"

"Isn't identifying von Lehmann and getting information on his missing designs enough?"

"Only Dr. Grossklos knows," Wolf replied. "And *you* do too."

Fieszel looked at him strangely. Then after a few seconds of silence, he remarked, "One last thing, good people. Avoid confrontation with the Russians, even if you see the soldiers treating women and children in a brutal manner."

Bela knew most likely raping women was what he meant. Something that never failed to struck a painful nerve in her. But when she'd agreed to this mission, she'd understood there'd be times she'd have to look the other way. "It's never easy," she said to on one in particular.

"In half an hour, a note Ina just handed me says a car will be waiting," announced Fieszel. "So I guess we'd better have the champagne Jutta's bringing, before you leave."

"I think I hear her at the door now," said Wolf, dropping a cigarette into an ashtray. "So we'll gulp it down, head upstairs, and grab our stuff."

"Train rides always make me want to pee," Jaclyn told Bela. "Which makes me hope this train we're riding on is equipped with a clean restroom."

"If the OSS is providing it, then it should have one."

"One more thing," said Wolf, turning to Fieszel. "How did you learn so quickly about the *Fuhrer's* death?"

"From Marshal Zhukov. Who got word and passed it onto Colonel Sokolov. And since Franz Dietrich has such exceptional equipment, he was able to get a Morse to the OSS with surprising speed—"

"And then what?" Wolf pressed.

"I received a long-distance call from London the minute I arrived here," Fieszel informed him. "But don't any of you say anything to anyone, until the *Fuhrer's* death has been officially announced."

"That's all I wanted to know," said Wolf, shaking his hand.

* * *

In her bedroom Bela told Ina, "Half an hour isn't much time to get dressed."

But the maid smiled, pointing at the clothing neatly laid out on the sofa next to the *armoire* It could be cool at night in the spring. So Bela was grateful for her short-sleeved, brown sweater which, even if it was low-necked, still hid the words *Feldhure*. And like her sweater, her slacks were brown, the same as her tam and laced, sport boots. The boots were similar to the ones the female, Jewish workers had worn in the Swedish embassy. 'Better boots than high heels,' *Herr* Wallenberg was always reminding them. 'In case the Germans storm in and march you off to a train bound for Auschwitz, before I can rescue you.'

'*Makes sense*,' Bela remembered telling him as she tucked her slacks in the boots.

It didn't take long to lace them. And when she finished, she reached for the olive- drab, belted raincoat, similar to the brown trench coat she'd worn in Budapest.

Which due to the spring's chilliness, Wolf had insisted on buying it for her. And she was grateful he had. Especially since it was not only long enough to brush the tops of her boots, but also had a hidden pocket for money.

"A person would have to look carefully to notice you're wearing slacks and not a skirt," said Ina, admiring it like someone would a mink coat or silver evening dress.

Bela was flattered by the maid's interest as she put on her velvet tam. "That's the plan."

The black Mercedes was already waiting on the curved driveway when she came down the stairs into the foyer.

Jaclyn was modeling her new outfit. "Our clothing choices are rather limited, so what do you think?" she asked Bela.

"That it's exactly like mine except for your boots. Which are black and Cossack style."

"I still worry our alleged Russian friends might not understand about my spiky, bobbed hair," she said, putting a black tam over it. "So tell me, Kurt, what should I say if they ask me about it?'

"They won't notice. Because Bela's also wearing a tam. And it makes the two of you look so fashionable, that hopefully it'll *bewitch* this colonel you'll be performing for, as well as his agents."

Grinning, Wolf pointed at Kurt's boots, vest, jacket, and gray overcoat that resembled a Wehrmacht greatcoat with its half-belt in back. "You and Bela look good in your lightweight coats. But tell me, do you think I could pass for an Oxford scholar in this?" He held up part of the belt encircling his khaki- colored coat.

"Most definitely with your suit and tweed vest under it," Jaclyn said. "I know, because I put everything together."

Each person carried a rucksack with a change of underwear and a pair of socks in it.

"And I'm also carrying a medical kit," Kurt said, swinging his sack over his shoulder.

Bela hated to keep admitting it, but the more she was around Kurt, the more he grew on her.

"His soul-searching eyes continue to move me in a way that both surprises and disturbs me. "She'd quickly written in her journal before going down the stairs. *"So naturally, given the right circumstance, I could easily go over the edge with this former Wehrmacht captain... and it makes my heart heavy each time I think about it. Although, considering the way we're being thrown together,* "she'd added, realization falling on her like *a* Gestapo searchlight in a dark alley, *"I fear it's going to be next to impossible not to betray my body with him."*

"Good people," said Albert, stepping from the library to offer his goodbyes to the group. "I will be very lonely tonight. But I'm confident the four of you will bring my brother back to me." He patted the gold vest he was wearing that helped cover his protruding belly. "And when you do, I'm wearing this to the party I'm planning to throw for him."

Hugs followed, with Albert clicking his heels and bowing as he kissed Bela and Jaclyn's hands.

Apparently that was the cue to send Ina and Jutta hurrying over with gifts wrapped in brown paper bags.

"Since you don't have room in your rucksacks for a canteen, each of you gets a package," Ina informed them, holding up one she carried. "Which is better than a bulky canteen because when you open it, you'll find a thermos with hot tea—plus a large assortment of cookies, sandwiches, and chocolate. So put it in your rucksacks."

A sniffing Jutta blotted her eyes. "We didn't want you to be hungry or thirsty on the train."

That earned the maids a warm-hearted hug from each member of the group. "I'll bring you ladies presents from somewhere," promised a watery- eyed Jaclyn.

The servants, along with Albert, waved as the car pulled away.

"Love you," hollered Jaclyn, leaning out the window and blowing kisses at them.

"There's a fair amount of distance between us and the German border," Wolf commented, talking off his hat. "So by the time we get there, it should be quite dark."

"Which means this will be a good time for a nap," said Kurt, also removing his hat.

"Good thing this car's engine has a drowsing purr," Jaclyn remarked.

Kurt nudged Bela. "If it makes you feel like taking a nap, then you're welcome to use my shoulder for a pillow."

But she shook her head, wanting to sleep but like last night, was afraid of the nightmares it would bring.

PART II

JOURNEYS

CHAPTER FOURTEEN

T he road was as lifeless as a bullet-ridden corpse, deepening the gloom in Bela's heart as a heavy darkness hurried to cover not only it, but the dense pines flanking it.

The trees with their silent shadows looked as solemn and alone as a wrecked graveyard in a bombed-out forest. Bringing to mind the bleakness in the Ulloi Street Embassy House at this time of day; when fear had its fingers wrapped around everyone's heart.

Wolf always did his best to boast the morale of the tired workers.

And Bela thought back to how visibly tense she'd been, while she typed reports and took incoming information off the machines on every floor.

"It's starting to rain, Wolf," Jaclyn said, her voice bringing Bela back from the memories flooding her mind.

He opened his eyes. "A soft drizzle is falling everywhere."

Kurt looked at Bela like he wanted to say something. But apparently deciding against it, shifted and stared out the gray window as the driver turned onto a road that led through a primeval-looking forest.

The light was almost gone, making it difficult to see.... *Like Switzerland's cities, that had no light, because it made it easier for the fliers with bombs for Germany to check their positions,* Bela reflected.

Still, she was able to make out a lake with a small bridge spanning it. "With only a few stars above it," she murmured.

The land here looked to be quite fertile, and occasionally tall houses with lights would brighten the hillsides but other than that, there was no sign of life anywhere.

Thick brambles, dark as the oncoming night, sprang up in front of them, making her curious as to how far they'd come. Outside it was probably cooling down from the rain, but inside the car was stifling. So she opened her raincoat and let its sleeves fall down to her elbows.

"Want me to help you take it off?" Kurt asked her.

"This will do," she said as she rolled the coat's sleeves above her elbows.

Then the road dropped into a muddy gulch, with several pieces of broken wood on top of it, which crackled and snapped as the car ran over them.

At the end of the road, a bright beam flashed in the mist several times at the car's headlights as the Mercedes approached it.

"We have to wait," the driver said, stopping.

"Wait?" Wolf questioned. "What's the problem?"

But before he could answer, a man holding a lantern and dressed in black, approached the car. "We take a short walk from here," he informed the group. "So please get out."

"Short walk, eh," remarked Jaclyn with a disenchanted huff. "Our Mr. Fieszel didn't mention that."

Like Kurt, Wolf put on his hat. "Another allied secret, I suppose," he muttered.

Occasional thunderclaps rattled in the distance as they followed a narrow, winding path down a small hill, covered in a tangle of underbrush and fallen leaves. Trees lined the path with their branches above it, interlocked, like arms.

Goosebumps sprouted on Bela's arms. "Almost like a subterranean tunnel," she remarked, turning to Kurt who was beside her.

"Certainly not my kind of place," he said, looking around. "Even if our man says the walk isn't that far."

Which it wasn't.

Breathing the air deeply as she emerged from this silent, cavernous arch of interlocking branches, she caught sight of the train. And she shook her head warily at the rail tracks, reaching out between the beech and pine forests. "This is certainly an isolated spot."

Kurt touched her shoulder. "We're just inside the German border."

Stopping for a moment, a feeling of impending doom threatened to overcome her as she stared at the train's belching locomotive. For with its white blast of exhaust, it reminded her of a beast preparing for a kill.

A German beast. And her soul sagged as she remembered the OSS pictures of the Auschwitz death camp she'd seen. Where against a radiant, blue sky, soot fell day after day, scattering the charred flakes of her people with their shattered dreams. *"Dying stars amid a galaxy of light,"* someone had scribbled on the back of one of the pictures.

For a fleeting instant Kurt's hand pressing against her shoulder, trembled the same as hers. *Did he too feel the menace plucking at their nerves with its ominous chill?* "Like a finger on the high end of a piano," she whispered.

The train was waiting with its conductor staring at them as if he was in a hurry to depart. He was a wiry, leathery-faced man with thick arms and metallic, frosty hair.

"He looks like a sketch of a woodcutter in a museum about the Vikings I visited as a child," Wolf told Kurt as the train whistled.

"We must leave *now*," insisted the conductor. "So get aboard."

"An engine, a coal car, and two railway carriages," Kurt said to him. "But which carriage is for us?"

"The last one." He pointed, before hastening to help Bela and Jaclyn up the carriage's steps. "But the forward one, where I'll be, has a restroom." Then he added, "There's not much light in the rail carriages, so watch yourselves when you step between the swaying, safety plates."

"Just a silver spray of subdued moonlight shining through the windows," Jaclyn remarked. "Because the moon now has a faint cloud cover that gives it a lop-sided appearance."

Wolf put his hat beside Kurt's on a vacant seat. "Don't worry, the cover's already beginning to lift." Then with a grin he added, "Besides if we have to jump off, it's best to be in the last carriage."

"A most comforting thought." Jaclyn frowned. "like going to the restroom on this *damned* train. Which, I imagine, is a bit like going to hell."

"As we agreed earlier, the man who planned this train ride certainly wasn't thinking," said Wolf, in a tone that implied he had something in mind for him after their mission was over. "So hold on tight."

The train lurched forward in a rush of steam and smoke. Then stopped. Then lurched again with beech and pine trees slowly gliding past.

Finally it began moving into the night with an even rhythm, as a somewhat relieved Bela watched Jaclyn, Wolf, and Kurt light cigarettes.

"A smoke before we sleep?" asked Jaclyn, keeping a tight hold on her cigarette. "I doubt it, since the noisy roar of the engine will keep us up all night."

"I'll take the first watch in case we encounter some fighting between the Germans and Americans," said Wolf, his voice rising above the noise.

"And I'll take the second," Kurt volunteered.

"Night is the enemy when a person can't sleep," Bela remarked, stuffing her tam in her raincoat's pocket.

"Well said," Wolf commended her. "As long as you don't forget that when people are very tired, they *do* sleep."

The dense, wooded countryside moved smoothly past the window as the train sped through it. And after a lengthy amount of time had passed, and they were well beyond the border, Jaclyn rose. But having difficulty remaining on her feet, she sank back down like she had a pebble in her boot.

"What's the matter?" Wolf asked her.

"I need to go to the restroom, but the way this train is swaying, I'm afraid I'll lose my balance if I take a step."

"Then hold onto me, and I'll help you get there," he said, clutching his leather briefcase with one arm and sliding the other around her.

"Hopefully, we'll be back shortly," she murmured, the train ride clearly not improving her temper.

Kurt reached out to her so he could get her in motion quicker. "You'd better, so you can get some sleep."

Straining her eyes, Bela stared at Wolf, Jaclyn, and Kurt until they'd moved beyond the train's trembling floor and were safely in the next car.

Several minutes passed before Kurt, leaving Jaclyn and Wolf, returned. And when he did, Bela grinned at him.

"Success," she said, surprised at how easily he'd threaded his way back through the swaying, safety plates between the carriages.

"If I'm seeing things correctly on this bumpy train, the light from our "bomber's moon" is at its highest point. So it looks like we'll soon be scaling a hill."

She turned around in an attempt to see it. But even with the moon at its highest point, the morbid darkness with its empty reflections stared at her through the window with an air of evil, swamping her with feelings of danger.

Suddenly, a blinding flash swept over the window, and she *knew* any minute German boots would step on the train and snatch *her*— like they'd snatched all the Jews who were sound asleep on their pallets, in the Swedish extraterritorial house.

Three thunderous explosions rocked the train carriage, shattering the glass in the window behind her. "The Germans are here!" she yelled.

A frozen nightmare from another time. Only not a nightmare, but a memory returning her once again, to the Swedish extraterritorial house. She bit her lips to keep her teeth from chattering as German stomping feet grew louder and louder.

The Arrow-Cross Militia— accompanied by the jackbooted S.S. men with pistols— burst into the house and ordered all the Jews to get up and dress quickly. Bela's hands shook as she struggled to put on her boots.

'This is part of the Swedish Embassy, and we all have Swedish passports like this,' her father informed them, holding his up for a jackbooted S.S. man to see.

But the S.S. man's response was to snatch it and rip it apart, before knocking him to the floor with the butt of his rifle. 'Shut up, Jewish scum!' he hollered. 'And get moving.'

'Pa!' Bela shouted. She started to rush over to him, but her knees buckled when a different S.S. man with a riding crop, brought it down savagely against her half-naked back.

Another explosion followed— only this time it knocked her against the train's floor. "How'd I get on a train?" she asked. "When I'm at the Swedish extraterritorial building in Budapest?"

She could see the Arrow-Cross, execution brigade now surrounding the building, and she began to shake as they prodded everyone with their rifle butts through the open door.

She and her father scrambled to stay close to each other, but when the shoeless captives ahead of them began falling into the Danube after several rounds of machine gun fire, fear blazed in his eyes. 'In the name of God, Bela, make a run for it!'

Words forever embedded in her brain.

But she was so terrified she couldn't move as she watched him drop into the Danube under a hail of bullets... *his baptism of fire.* 'Pa,' she shouted again.

She was about to leap in the river after him, when a militiaman with Kurt's face suddenly trapped her in his arms. "K...Kurt." She blinked at him in desperation. "What are you doing here? I was standing on the bank of the Danube in Budapest when—"

"We came under a train attack," he said, holding her against his well-muscled body. "And the forward, rail carriages are at the top of the slope, but our carriage is sliding backward into what looks like a marsh. So follow my lead, and we'll jump when it's safe."

Her consciousness was slipping, and his voice was floating in the air as she struggled to get away from him and leap into the Danube. How badly she wanted the water, because it would cleanse her body making it as pure as new fallen snow.

Holding her with one arm and his rucksack with the other, Kurt stood poised at the exit steps in back, ready to leap off the now, slower- moving train. "Every second counts, Bela, so get ready to jump with me." He gulped a quick breath. "And try to land on your feet with your knees bent, so it won't be hard for you to roll if you have to."

And she tried. Jumping off the train headed for Auschwitz to get away from the black-uniformed Germans as they started after her.

Their thundering boots echoed against the ramp as she ran until her strength drained, and she collapsed... but that couldn't be right, could it?

Disoriented, her memories fused together, changing places.

Suddenly, she was in the Danube with its freezing water closing over her. When strangely she heard her name being called by a German— of all people. It was a deep, male voice with a timbre that kept rising as she stared at the moon above.

A moon as full and white as the painting of a vampire's face Yanni once showed me... but why is it now so close? And why am I now lying on the ground and not floating in the water?

CHAPTER FIFTEEN

The German's voice beckoned Bela toward consciousness. "My apologies," said Kurt, gently swabbing her face with a tea-smelling, moist cloth. "But when the explosion caused the coupling to break on our train car, we had to jump. And unfortunately you hit your head quite hard against this birch tree we're under. So I'm afraid you're a bit dazed."

She blinked several times. "*Dazed?*" she repeated, inhaling the scent of damp earth. "Was it the Germans who attacked us?"

"Not sure. But with the country in surrender, it wouldn't surprise me if they still possessed enough demolitions to attack the railway."

"I don't doubt it. But if it wasn't them, then who else could it have been?" she asked, her head spinning as she struggled to collect herself.

"The allies. Thinking they were attacking the Germans who were refusing to surrender. When in reality, they were attacking us."

"Awful." She shuddered as she thought about Germans still roaming the countryside. "But do we know where we are?"

"In the woods and under stars." He reached over and removed the pine needles stuck in her neck.

"That figures." She sighed, hearing an owl hoot in the tree overhead.

"After you hit the tree, you luckily fell against a carpet of birch leaves," he told her, smoothing her hair. "But even so, it didn't keep you from getting stuck by some of those prickly needles from that pine tree next to it."

"And I'm grateful you're able to remove them," she said, gazing at their surroundings. "But where are Wolf and Jaclyn?"

"Last I saw them they were in the other train car with the restroom," he remarked, nodding in its direction. "Since our car was the only one that got separated."

She shoved aside a twig poking her face as she attempted to sit up. "Their carriage was at the top of the hill, wasn't it?"

"Fortunate for them—but you need someone to hold onto you in case you pass out." His arm steadied her. "And I imagine you're thirsty. But don't worry, because I grabbed my rucksack with the thermos of tea in it. Plus I have some pills for a headache in my medical kit."

He held them up, then poured some water in the thermos lid for her.

"But is there enough left for you?" she asked, hesitant to take a sip.

"Of course." He flashed one of his engaging smiles at her. "And if there isn't, then I'm sure if we scout around, there's bound to be a creek where we can refill my thermos. So be my guest."

She drank it quickly, touched by his thoughtfulness as he reached for the thermos again.

"There's more if you want it.", he said.

"Not until we find a creek." "Which we'll probably do in the early morning."

"Hopefully." It had grown foggy, and in an obvious attempt to shield her from it and the cold air, he took her in his arms and cradled her head against his chest in a way that seemed perfectly natural for him to do. "You kept me from being severely injured, Kurt."

"For which I'm grateful." He shivered as a sudden gust of the chilly air made the leaves on the birch tree tremble. "Even if I do regret being forced to let go of you sooner than expected, and you hit that tree."

Instinctively she ran her hand down his arm. "Doesn't matter. I'm just thankful we've made it this far."

Finding comfort in his seductive warmth, her heart struggled again with its conflicting emotions. Making her wish she could get up enough courage to ask him, *'Why was it when you visited the Love Camp, you didn't act like the other German predators, who wolfed me down the way they did? '*

Surely, it wasn't because you saw another way to torture me by bringing me to a momentary ecstasy, which made me lose my emotional control and grovel at your black- booted, German feet. But then that was my fault, wasn't it? Because I was hungry for a spark of human kindness. Still, the compassion in your soul has created a dilemma that makes me feel like I'm a traitor to my people.

"After Berlin, I'll sort this all out," she blurted before she could hold herself back.

"Sort what out?" asked Kurt with a half-hearted grin. "Something about us?"

"After the war."

"Which provided I don't get killed, I'll go back to being a Tommie prisoner."

"I'm certainly praying you won't," she said, keeping her fingers crossed he wouldn't end up a Russian prisoner. "But how do we get to Berlin from here?"

"Offhand, I'd say we need to lay our hands on a short-wave radio, so we can beam a message to Albert." He stared at the moon floating in the sky." And then with luck, he'll be able to triangulate where we are."

"But how long do you think it'll take?"

"Longer than I care to think." He muffled his mouth in her hair. "Which makes it bad, because Wolf and Jaclyn don't know Berlin like I do."

She wiped her eyes with the heel of her hand. "True. But there must be something we can do to keep the Russians from latching onto von Lehmann and finding his missing designs."

Kurt continued to keep her head cradled against his chest. "So one would think," he murmured soothingly. "Although remember, Bela, nobody's a hundred percent certain von Lehmann is alive."

"Maybe not." She took a quick breath, "But I'm willing to bet that if the Russians confirm our man in the hospital is von Lehmann— and is improving— then they might not be so worried about his missing papers."

"The V-3 Cannon Rocket is nothing compared to something out of *Buck Rogers*—like Mr. Fieszel implied."

"There's no doubt. But if the man in the hospital is the doppelganger, then all bets are off."

"Only *Doktor Grossklos Knows,* " he replied, stroking her hair. "Which gives me little faith that after the way the allies have blundered this mission, we won't get to Berlin in time to find out what it is *Doktor Grossklos Knows.*"

Frowning, she tossed back his head. "Certainly appears like it."

She looked up at him, clamping her lips together in an attempt to quell her doubts. "Even though I know Wolf and Jaclyn will be doing all they can to find us and get us there."

"Of that I'm certain. So try not to worry because seeing the stricken look on your face brings back—"

"What?" she asked.

"The longing, guilt, and regret from our Love Camp encounter, when I hurt you without meaning to."

"Kurt—please. Haven't I made it clear you're the one man who didn't hurt me? So don't continue to agonize about it."

He searched her face. "Almost an impossible task with the pain from it pounding me with every breath I take each time I think about it."

"Then think only that your kindness saved me —like I've told you."

"That doesn't make it easier."

"So, I'll keep reminding you." She reached for the solid strength of his arm. "Though it does continue to worry me that you and von Lehmann are at such odds."

"I can understand that. Because it makes it difficult for me to survive with dignity."

"Still if you're admitting it, then there's a decency in you which gives you that dignity."

"What I'd like to believe. And I'm trying to bury my anger, even if von Lehmann raised me with love."

"Yet, you still ended up disliking him?"

"That I did."

She felt a squeezing hurt for him. "So what it comes down to is that if you dislike the person who raised you, then there's a good chance you'll end up disliking yourself."

"I've never thought of it like that."

"You wouldn't, but I do," she said, the memories engulfing her, "because my father and I had a strong bond."

The revelation about ending up disliking himself appeared to bewilder Kurt. "I now it seems like I'm trying to act martyred. And who knows, maybe I am but not admitting it. But like I've said, if I risk myself and help von Lehmann escape from *Ivan*, then maybe he'll see me in a different light."

"Still, he treated you well."

"He did— along with my mother. And we even got to live with him in what was formerly a hunting lodge in the Vienna Woods. **"Although,"** his voice was slightly choked, "his refusal to marry her, made me feel like we were either charity cases, outsiders, extra people or— " he added in a deep tone, "tolerated but not loved."

"Even so, the way he looked after the two of you does indicate he had some feeling for your mother."

"What she wanted to believe. Because as she lay on her deathbed dying of cancer, she kept reminding me how much he loved us." He paused, his heart pounding as if her final words from the past had come back to thump against it.

"I begged him, 'Marry her— please.' But he brushed me off, making me so angry I joined the Wehrmacht."

"So your decision was a kind of vengeance coupled with justice?"

"Exactly. Since von Lehmann hated Hitler and what he was doing to Germany and Austria."

"Yet, he ended up working for him under duress," she said, trying to piece it all together.

"Only because he got careless and didn't make it out of Vienna in time.Which is the reason if I can keep him from falling into *Ivan's* hands, then maybe —"He gazed at her body curled against him. "He might say something that'll make me overcome the great sorrow I feel for the way he treated my mother—"

"Especially after the way he watched your wife and small son from afar."

"Something that, under the circumstances, I'm having difficulty understanding."

His arms around her, she struggled to keep the tears in her eyes from falling, as the warmth from his body in this web of tenderness, threatened her with its passionate message. "It sounds like your life hasn't been easy."

"W...we've all done things we regret. It's just that von Lehmann's refusal to marry my mother when she was dying is something I can't forget."

Bela closed her hand over his, "Which I can understand."

This troubling knowledge continued to disturb her. *Some of which I feel certain is the difficulty I'm having in controlling my feelings for a former Wehrmacht captain.*

"But what you might not understand is this, Bela—" His voice held a surprising tenderness. "That the regret I have over what happened to *you* is far more than I'll ever have over von Lehmann's refusal to wed my mother."

Touched by the way he was unburdening himself to her out here– like he'd done in her room at the chalet— she opened her mouth to make a proper response, but the words wedged in her throat. So all that came out was, "I...I'm having trouble—"

"I know." And leaning over, he kissed her brow in a gentle way that made her feel for moment like there was genuine love between them. "But for now try to get some sleep, while I keep watch."

CHAPTER SIXTEEN

"We've *people* back there!" yelled Jaclyn at the conductor.

"So back up this train at once!" ordered Wolf, grabbing the man's shoulder and shaking it.

"Are you crazy!" he shouted at him. "We just lost a car out there in the middle of that artillery fire!"

"When the light flashed I saw Kurt and Bela jump from their carriage," yelled Jaclyn, her voice wavering between rage and hysteria. "Which means they could be injured and stranded in the middle of nowhere—"

"If they were ordinary people," said the conductor. "But they're supposed to be OSS trained and should know what they're doing."

"Not necessarily," Wolf countered. "And besides we were told the tracks were cleared, and our train wasn't in any danger."

"The allies are in charge. But like I'm sure you were briefed, we do still have some die-hard pockets of German soldiers refusing to give up."

"Small consolation."

"We bought Bela out of hell, only to plunge her in it again," said Jaclyn, tears streaming down her cheeks.

"Jaclyn please—" Wolf implored her. "Remember we found Bela after everyone believed she'd been machine gunned and thrown in the Danube. So believe me, we'll find her again."

"But the odds were better." She sobbed, swabbing at her cheek with the back of her hand. "Because you got a tip from one of Karoly Szabo's police officer friends, and later that Gestapo man—"

"—who claimed to remember seeing a blond girl wearing a brown trench coat, being escorted from the banks of the Danube to Gestapo headquarters."

"I know. But finding her still took well over a month."

"And we wouldn't have succeeded had Raoul Wallenberg not bribed that monstrous Adolph Eichmann, into getting that Gestapo man to help us by bribing him and his friend— that damned OberssturmFuhrer Horst Helmer!"

"Raoul Wallenberg was our angel of mercy then." Jaclyn sniffed, remembering how he'd tragically fallen into Russian hands, never to be heard from again.

Wolf squeezed down on her hand. "Wallenberg may be gone, but if he's in heaven where he should be —and not being worked to death in some Russian prisoner-of–war camp —then we've got a spiritual angel of mercy looking out for us."

"Hopefully. But even so in this wooded countryside with its thick trees, our allied planes are going to have difficulty spotting anyone," Jaclyn continued to argue. "With Bela alone with Kurt, who has no idea she's a Jew."

"And you see that as a problem, after we managed to hide it from Eichmann?" Wolf asked, looking at her in surprise. "Remember Kurt was a Wehrmacht captain and not an S.S. officer. So it could be worse."

"True. And I doubt Kurt would harm her but still—" Her voice trembled. "Don't you remember Albert telling us he'd heard some Wehrmacht soldiers had murdered some returning Jews and were thought to be doing it in this part of Germany?"

"I remember." Wolf's lips twitched. "And I realize there were Wehrmacht soldiers who'd murdered Jews in the past. But if you don't think Kurt will harm Bela, then what's the problem?"

"That she says Kurt looked like a Wehrmacht officer who visited her at that Love Camp."

"*What!*" Wolf yelled, the information appearing to siphon the blood from his face. "So it was true what that Gestapo man said, when he mentioned a relative of mine had visited it?"

Jaclyn nodded. "But could he really know?"

"Only if someone working for the Nazis was from Vienna and knew both Kurt and myself. Plus Bela's stage name is your professional, last name. And since you're known throughout Europe for your music, then I suspect it was someone who was a fan of yours—with my name somehow getting into it."

"Quite possibly," she agreed.

Wolf fished a cigarette from his breast pocket. "It still angers me the OSS forbade us to ask questions about Kurt's Wehrmacht experiences, until after our mission was complete."

"A big mistake, I know—"

"Especially with Kurt allegedly being seen at a place where German soldiers were allowed to rape some of Budapest's more unfortunate, young women... and besides—" He looked out the window at the night-blackened sky as the train raced through the countryside. "Like has been mentioned, Bela wasn't at the Love Camp that long. So what are the odds Kurt could be that Wehrmacht officer who visited her. One million? Two million?"

"Slimmer than you might think," said Jaclyn, inhaling sharply. "When you consider the heavy concentration of German troops trying to stop the Russians from moving in and grabbing the oil wells around Lake Balaton." Then she reminded as an afterthought, "And besides Kurt speaks Russian and grew up in Vienna. So why wouldn't he be assigned to the Eastern Front, where a place like the Love Camp was?"

"Kurt and I were classmates together at the university," said Wolf after a moment's reflection. "But never once did I know him to visit a brothel— like so many of the university men did."

"If he really visited the Love Camp, then maybe he was making up for lost time," Jaclyn replied with a humorless smile." But just so you'll know, I checked with Albert before we left, and he told me in secret that after Kurt was wounded in Russia, he was reassigned to Hungary, not too far from Lake Balaton."

"If he got wounded in Russia, then it serves him right since he was a *damn* Nazi." Wolf flared. "Which from my point of view is just another word for *criminal*."

"But Albert said he wasn't a party member, just a captain in the Wehrmacht with a wife and child he couldn't afford to risk."

"Like I keep saying, he wasn't married when he joined the Wehrmacht. And by being in it, he empowered the S.S." His outburst garnered another disapproving look from the conductor. "But tell me, what's going on between Kurt and Bela, that's got you so worried?"

"Not sure." She frowned, the question disturbing her. "It's just that there seems to be some kind of an attraction between them."

"And that's why you're so upset?"

"No. If she likes him it's fine."

"If he visited her at the Love Camp, then it's nothing short of the *Beauty and the Beast Tale*— which is clearly not fine with me."

"Weren't you planning on asking Kurt after our mission?"

"Of course. Even though I suspected that Gestapo man was probably mocking me with a lie," he said, raising his voice. "Since his friend ObersturmFuhrer Horst Helmer beat Bela with a leather strap, and he did nothing about it."

"Too bad she was so frightened, she didn't tell us until they were gone."

"But she insisted they'd threatened to kill me—"

"When it's daylight, *Herr* von Friesen," interrupted the conductor, "and you get to the Stuttgart airfield, the engineer assures me the Americans will put a plane in the air that will locate the derailed train carriage. And if your friends wave at it, then hopefully the pilot will be able to make a landing nearby—"

"Still it's not the same as stopping this *damned* train," he shot back. "Since with those pockets of die-hard German soldiers in the area, Kurt and Bela have probably moved far away from that rail carriage."

"Our best chance of finding them is *now*," insisted Jaclyn. "Or otherwise, it'll be like looking for a needle in a very large haystack!"

* * *

"Get up, Bela!" Kurt exclaimed. "We have to find a place to hide!"

She rose from her sitting position as his fingers pressed against her wrists, and he pulled her after him.

Once again it seemed the ground was trembling. "What is it?" she asked, jarred by the sudden threat.

"Could be allied artillery. Though I heard German voices nearby *extolling* the *Fuhrer.*"

Rigid with terror, she squeezed his forearm. "If they're deserters, then they'll kill you for your civilian clothes—"

"Provided they know I'm in civilian clothes. Since from a distance, this coat looks like the Wehrmacht greatcoat I used to have." He glanced behind her as the German voices got louder. "Still, I do think it would be wise to find a dead soldier who has a duffle bag, with an extra uniform in it."

"If they can lay their hands on one change of civilian clothes, then the soldier wearing it can steal a vehicle and hide the others in it."

He huddled with her behind several bushes. "I know, and I'll have to take my chances. Because if they find you, they'll think they've found a king's treasure."

Almost the same thing the S.S. man had said to her the night the Arrow-Cross militia, with the Gestapo, had machine gunned her father.

"Come on," Kurt urged, grabbing her hand and dragging her deeper into the darkness of their surroundings. "We've got to get out of here!"

Wild shivers tore through her as a German commander shouted an order at one of his men.

Bela glanced around. *How hard was it going to be to find a good place to hide?* Daylight had yet to break. And a murky overcast still hung in the cold, night sky, making it difficult to see the direction they were headed.

As they hurried through a thicket of brambles, stinging scrubs poked her hands and face. *Like the needles the female German doctor used on me.* She shivered, recalling how the woman had pierced her arm for a blood sample as she lay strapped to a table awaiting the sterilization by cauterization performed on all the Love Camp girls... with very little anesthesia.

The echo of the memory threatened to swallow her. *But since the S.S. men were so quick to slaughter the girls they believed to be disobedient, it often created a shortage for the soldiers, so my virginity was violated before I was sterilized—*

"Get down, Bela!" Kurt said, shaking her arm as if he were trying to shake away her painful memory. "Those Germans are quite near!"

The small cloud passing over the moon suddenly lifted, making it easier to see the soldiers' faces in the misty, white landscape.

And when she saw them, she went cold all over. For less than eighty meters away, four steel-helmeted, brawny Germans—each wearing a white armband with a large, black swastika on it—tramped through forest's roughage and pine cones. "Certainly stupid to be wearing those armbands when they're trying to escape," Kurt remarked, giving them a hostile glare.

One man, a major with slashing, blond brows and a hawk's aquiline nose, carried binoculars, a knotted rope, and a submachine gun.

He seemed full of his self-importance as he ordered the three men with him to hack at the underbrush with their bayonets, making this forested, off-beaten route easier for them to navigate.

A muscle quivered in Kurt's jaw. "Hitler and his twisted ambitions," he said, not taking his eyes off them.

"Are they looking for us?" Bela asked, easing out a shaky breath.

He held her snugly against him as they crouched low. "I don't know, but it's not unreasonable to think they saw us with their binoculars, when we leaped from the train carriage." He frowned at them like he had a deep sense of foreboding. "Especially since the area was lit with its flares, searching for isolated pockets of German soldiers."

Then the major turned suddenly, and Bela jumped like a live wire was attacking her nerve centers. "It's him!" she gasped, taken aback.

"Who?" asked Kurt.

"The S.S. man from my nightmare who did terrible things to me."

* * *

"Terrible things?" Kurt was baffled. "But that major's not in the S.S."

"Doesn't matter." Bela cringed. "I'd recognize his face anywhere."

"From your nightmare?" he asked, after another second of shocked silence had passed.

She nodded. "Which means once again, something terrible is in store for me."

No doubt. Aware she was so upset, it seemed to him she was on the verge of shattering like a terracotta, wine cask. "But this man... did he visit you at the Love Camp?"

"Only in my nightmare."

"There's a certain intimacy in a nightmare. And I don't mean to violate it, but if you're having a nightmare about someone you never met— yet just saw— you need to tell me about it."

"Even if it's embarrassing?"

"Even if it's that." A moonbeam shone on her hand as he slid his beside hers. "Because if it's that difficult to talk about, then you should let me hold you while you do."

Her tears flowed freely as she blotted them with her handkerchief. "It's just that I felt so humiliated in my nightmare—"

"Which considering I visited the Love Camp while you were imprisoned there, will be a humiliation for me as well," he said, keeping his eyes steady on hers. "So don't hesitate to tell me anything you feel I need to know."

She darted another glance in the direction of the major. "In my nightmare we girls in the Love Camp lay on our bellies naked, exposed, and strapped to our beds."

"Total surrender, with plans to abuse you," he said, recalling how his subjugation and helplessness, when the Tommies had beaten him, was similar to hers. And for a moment, he was lost as flashes of the painful memories intensified—

"*Listen* —did you hear that?" She nudged him, returning his attention to the dangers surrounding them.

"Yes. Shuffling feet near our path."

"Is it an ally or a German?"

Kurt turned around to see a steel-helmeted sergeant on the path directly behind them. "A German."

Then in a fairly loud voice, this sergeant said, "Our men need to go a different way, Major, because this path is blocked with broken tree limbs."

"Wouldn't you know," the major grumbled. "Then follow this path ahead of me."

"Good thing they're going another way," Kurt whispered to Bela as the sound of their footsteps lessened.

Her troubled face eased. "A respite for time being."

"But continue telling me about your nightmare, since I need to learn all I can about this man in it, with the major's face."

"Well," she began. "most of the time when I awake from it, I'm so embarrassed thinking about the pain he caused me, I actually hurt."

Kurt drew her closer. "I can imagine," he remarked with a tinge of despair. "But where does this major stalking us come in?"

"An S.S. man stood over each girl's bed with orders to punish her and—"

"This major was the one who stood over yours?"

She took a deep, shaky breath. "Yes."

Gently Kurt rubbed the back of his hand against her cheek. "How did this man punish you?"

"F...first—" She hesitated, obviously having difficulty describing it. "By brutally spanking me... then by whipping me savagely with a leather belt."

"Sounds like this ObersturmFuhrer Horst Helmer is triggering your nightmares," said Kurt, his anger growing. "But I noticed a fading mark on your shoulder at the Love Camp, so someone must have treated you badly before ObersturmFuhrer Helmer gave you those brutal thrashings. So who was it?"

"An S.S. man with a riding crop." She tensed as if to reflect a moment. "And it was a new experience for me since growing up, I never got spanked or whipped with a belt."

Kurt wiped the dampness on her cheeks with his shirt sleeve. "Neither did I," he said, careful not to tell her about the beatings the Tommies had given him. "But what happened after that?"

"The worst."

"I don't doubt it," he said. Brutal spankings and whippings with belts were bad enough in anyone's nightmare. But *this* had to be something of a sexual nature. "So what exactly did this man do in your nightmare?"

She was trembling again. "Invaded me by brutally ramming my pain-racked buttocks with—" She tensed visibly. "His hard as an iron- stake *shaft*." Then she stopped for a moment, before adding, "And he drove faster and faster and deeper and deeper into me."

"Sweet baby!" Kurt gasped, calling her by the name Jaclyn used. "And you'd never been forced to have sex like that in the Love Camp?"

"Several times." Her tears coming faster. "However, when Madam Kollar informed the soldiers that all positions except the missionary one were forbidden, they just laughed and asked her who was she to forbid them? Which angered me. Because the S.S. should have backed her up.

Although at that point in the armies' retreat, they didn't seem to care one way or the other. But, of course, the one day of the week when we entertained the S.S. they did whatever they wanted to do."

A cold sweat broke out on Kurt's chest as her pain made him feel violated too. So he bent his head and kissed her brow before he said, "Unlike some of my rank-and-file men who enjoyed talking about it, I've always shied away from anal sex."

"I could tell, and I was grateful," she said, more tears streaking her face. "Because you don't know how badly I wish I could block out the memory of it, since it nearly killed me." Then looking down, she touched the leaf -carpeted ground. "You see, I'd never been with a man before I got to the Love Camp—"

"What!" Kurt exclaimed, having difficulty believing it. "You mean you were a *virgin?*"

"Yes." She dipped her head slightly. "Who'd never stood naked in front of a man and felt horribly exposed.

" I still marvel you weren't married."

"I might have been had my fiancé, who was my piano partner, not got himself killed"

"He must have been quite talented."

"Very. And his doctor father, working with the British in Palestine, had sent him to Budapest to study music because he had family there."

"Now that's something," Kurt said, retrieving a memory. "Because my father-in-law knew a lot of Tommie doctors. So by chance, do you suppose they knew each other?"

"I suppose if we're lucky enough to get to Berlin, we'll find out."

"Which we most assuredly will."

She rested her cheek against his chest. "Still, even if I do meet Yanni's father later, I don't want him to know what happened to me."

"Can't say I blame you. Because the cruelty of the S.S. often brings terrible grief to friends and family members, who later learn how someone they loved suffered."

"I know it did where Jaclyn and Wolf were concerned."

"Of that I'm certain," he whispered against her hair. "Considering how most, young women with no sexual experience wouldn't stand a chance at knowing how to please the soldiers. And would quickly get the three reports that would get then killed."

"But when did the S.S. ever care? Since it was merely a question of anybody they could lay their hands on."

"Which was certainly unfortunate for you."

"You can't imagine. Because I was terribly ashamed at being made to lose my privacy and stand before the soldiers, naked. And then—"Like she was overcome with shame, she closed her eyes. "With the soldiers having been given the freedom to do anything they wanted to do with me. "Her voice broke several times as a cold sweat, like was on his chest, drenched her forearm. "And the first couple of times I had intercourse was quite painful —with blood oozing from my crotch and caking on my thighs."

His eyes filled with tears. "Almost the same as killing you—considering I was one of those soldiers."

"Stop it!" she said, covering his hand with hers. "Haven't I made it clear you were different from the sixty who'd come before—"

"*Sixty!*" He stared at her blankly, lacking the courage to ask the number that had come after him. "How could I have possibly been different from them?"

"Because you eased into my body like a civilized man." She stifled a sob. "But the majority—particularly the S.S. —spilled themselves in me, like they were trying to infect me with pus from the open wounds dicing their souls."

He shook his head at the way she was describing it. "That sounds about right."

"Especially with my fear of getting an infection."

"Were you afraid of an infection with me?"

"Never gave it a moment's thought."

"Why not?"

She almost smiled. "Because something about the way you kissed me gave me a warm breath of hope."

"Which was definitely my intention," he said, continuing to feel so *very* guilty, of so *very* much. "Though later I heard that in some Love Camps kissing— as well as anal and oral sex— was forbidden, with the S.S. spying on people through tiny holes in the wall."

"Supposedly." Her voice broke again as a deep sob racked her. "B...but I imagine since the Love Camp I was in was so close to the front, it was the reason ObersturmFuhrer Helmer and his S.S. friends, allowed such things. And since our lives depended on how well we could pleasure a man, we were told to smile."

The more Kurt heard, the more her pain threatened his control. "But tell me about that major— your nighttime monster," he said, her nightmare continuing to disturb him as he blotted her damp cheek affectionately. "If we're unfortunate enough to meet up with him, then you should know I'll do my best not to let him hurt you like that."

"I know you'll try." She took his hand. "But without weapons you might not be able to stop him."

"Bela, it's just a nightmare."

"That often keeps me from sleep."

"I can imagine," he said, tears getting in the way as he planted another one of his light kisses on her brow in an attempt to calm her. "And we may have a past but for now, this concern we have for each other's survival is the only thing of beauty we have left in this devastated world. "He stroked her cheek with the back of his hand. "So if I hug you, kiss you gently, and give you reassurances, then please don't take it the wrong way."

She continued to cling to him. "I won't. And I'll do the same for you." She put her arms around his neck. "Because I agree that in these dangerous times, all we have is each other."

"With me vowing to protect you at all costs."

"Words from a very kind and thoughtful man," she whispered, closing her eyes as she rested her head against his chest.

When the night's coldness finally lifted, there was still a predawn blackness. "Best to wait a little longer," Kurt advised.

So he and Bela stayed hidden in the lingering gloom, until a faint, orchid light outlined a group of pewter-colored clouds streaking across the sky.

"A new morning should greet us any time," he remarked, gazing at this world like someone hesitant to claim it as his own. He'd experienced the feeling many times on the front when the purplish, mother-of-pearl light rising in the east had been the signal for a battle to begin.

* * *

"Those Germans will be back, won't they?" Bela asked, frowning like she was trying not to think about what might happen if they found them.

"Not if they find a staircase here in the forest and climb it."

"What?" she asked, tilting her head like she hadn't heard him correctly.

"And old folk tale about children finding a staircase in the woods and climbing it."

"And when they reach the top?"

"A witch greets them— and then eats them."

"Sounds like Hansel and Gretel."

"It does. But what happens to adults?"

"The only adults who climb it are those who believe they have nothing to lose. "His brow furrowed as if reflecting on it. "And then they either disappear forever or someone they know dies."

"Not good." She sighed, shivering in the moist, early morning air. "Especially since those Germans are acting like they have everything to gain."

"I agree." He turned up her raincoat collar. "Which is the reason we need to make it up that slope." He pointed at an embankment with a faint silhouette of snow-capped, forested hills behind it. "Because if we can get to the top, then hopefully we'll be able to have a good view of our surroundings... but first tell me how you feel?"

She touched her head like she still had the pounding headache that his pills had failed to relieve. Although not mentioning it for fear he'd possibly hold back, she simply said with a false bravado, "I'm fine."

"Are you certain?" he asked, stroking her arm. "That was quiet a blow you got last night, so should you feel faint, then you must let me know."

CHAPTER SEVENTEEN

"**I** will. But I'm fine —really I am," Bela said, deeply touched by the way he was looking after her. "So let's start climbing."

He led the way, but as the forest darkened and the underbrush grew thicker, it took them longer than anticipated to reach the top.

"This seems to be a fairly isolated place," he remarked. "So let's stop and catch our breaths."

"You seem to know what you're doing, which is why I didn't mention it, but isn't it possible those Germans will spot us the higher up we go?"

"They won't. Because with the fog moving in, the coverage on the slope is much too thick."

She was as eager as he was to get to the top, so they only stopped for a few minutes before resuming their climb.

But this brutal trek through the dense underbrush made her light-headedness return. And twice she almost fell.

He reached for her hand. "I'll carry you if I have to."

But breathless, she shook her head.

"Then tell me, are you hungry?" he asked, making a slight gesture at his rucksack. "I saw some sandwiches and cookies in it."

It occurred to her they'd been too frightened to eat or drink any of the tea, which could be her problem. "How many sandwiches are left?"

"Four— plus a bagful of cookies."

"Then let's eat two now and two later," she suggested.

"I'm for it. But first we'll need to find a crevice with a barrier of scrubs covering it where we can hide—just in case."

Which to their surprise, turned out to be closer than they thought. "Looks like this should keep us safe," she remarked, entertaining the fantasy of she and her father hiding in a hole similar to this, until the war ended.

Kneeling next to her, Kurt opened the rucksack and handed her a sandwich neatly cut in two halves. "Eat heartily, Bela, since we don't know what lies ahead."

Then he caught her off guard, by offering her part of his. "But I can't," she said, looking at him and shaking her head.

"Please," he began. "A little bit of extra food might keep you from getting light-headed again."

"On the contrary you should take part of mine," she told him. "Because if you end up having to carry me, then you'll need it."

He grinned almost sheepishly. "Jaclyn warned me you could be stubborn."

She laughed. "Did she now?"

"She was just teasing."

In the end they stuck to their original plan, quaffing down their sandwiches and several of the cookies, before drinking some of Ina's now cold tea.

"Not much left." He frowned, stuffing the thermos back in his rucksack, along with his rolled- up jacket, vest, and tie."

She liked the way his suspenders showed, making him look like an average German. "It'll be fine since I won't need anything tonight."

"Are you sure?" he asked, gazing at her the way a man would a beloved wife as he handed her a chocolate bar.

"I'm sure." She smiled, her heart jolting and her pulse accelerating as she remembered how at the Love Camp, his gift had made her feel like her world was not totally lost.

Like *now*. When for a fleeting instant his earlier kiss had turned her back into the innocent girl she'd been when she'd worked at Wallenberg's embassy... with her hope for the future and the happy life she'd believed awaited her. *In my vanishing world of long ago, which after the Love Camp, is a life I doubt I can ever have.*

She gave his arm a meaningful squeeze. "We should divide the chocolate."

"Bela, sweet Bela," he murmured, slipping on his gray overcoat. "I mean it for your enjoyment, not mine. So I refuse to divide."

His gallantry made her heart pound with remembrance.

"So indulge yourself," he insisted.

* * *

Kurt was overwhelmed by her unselfishness in such a dangerous time. And for a moment, he grappled with the urge to scoop her in his arms and kiss her until she was giddy with pleasure; the same as he'd done with her in the Love Camp. But no matter how badly he wanted her, his common sense warned him she wasn't his, so they'd best move on. "Feel like more climbing?" he asked, rising.

She nodded, inhaling the crisp, resinous air several times before standing. Dawn was breaking with the cries of noisy birds overhead greeting its gunmetal light as the sun rose above the distant, forested hills. "How long before we reach the top?"

"If we move quickly, it should take us no more than half an hour."

So plodding along behind him, she had no difficulty matching his long strides.

But after she'd climbed awhile, he had to pause several times to wait for her, since the farther up they went, the steeper the embankment got.

"Be careful," he warned. "Because the dampness on these moss- covered rocks, gnarled roots, and giant ferns might cause you to slip."

She grabbed a tree branch. "That it could."

When they finally reached the top, her brow like Kurt's, was covered in nervous beads of stinging sweat. "Here, take my handkerchief," she offered.

But he declined, pulling out one of his own.

Ocher sunlight now poured through the damp leaves as he gestured at a clearing below. "Look— there's a dirt road running between a line of poplar trees and several unplowed fields."

"And it reminds me of an eel the way it curves around them," she remarked, surveying the scene. "But is that a tiny farmhouse I see in the distance?"

He glanced toward the south, shielding his eyes against the cool, morning brightness. "Appears to be... or a quaint cottage. But its fences and outbuildings look to be in such serious disrepair, that it's probably deserted."

Her gaze swept down to the line of poplar trees. "Then if you don't think those soldiers are hiding there, we should probably check it out."

"What I was thinking."

A C-47 allied plane circled overhead, and they waved at it. "Do you suppose they're looking for us?" she asked.

"Probably. But unless you've got a mirror, they won't be able to see us in all this brush and fog."

"I had one, but regretfully it got left behind in my rucksack."

"Like Wolf and I left our hats on one of the train's vacant seats." He squinted at the sky. "But it doesn't matter, because we should be in open country when the next flier appears."

"With luck we will," she said, with more conviction than she appeared to feel.

The morning fog on the horizon was rapidly getting denser, making the hike down through underbrush, extremely slow. But fortunately the woods running parallel to the dirt road, made it easy for them to keep out of sight.

So Kurt stopped and lit a cigarette.

It was obvious Bela's light-headedness had returned, because grabbing his arm, she slumped against a bush close to the ground. "It's your head again, isn't it?" he asked, putting his hand on her shoulder and squatting down next to her.

"Just a little dizziness."

"And sadly the medicine I gave you isn't working."

"Still, are we safe enough here?"

"For time being." He suspected some of her problem was fear, because she kept looking back like she was expecting any minute to see those Germans. But who could blame her? Since many of the tree limbs in this part of the woods were so twisted and deformed with their mangled roots knocked to one side, that it wasn't hard to imagine they were covering a portal in the ground leading straight to hell.

Clearly a warning that evil was just over the horizon, with this eerie landscape projecting an imminent feeling of danger.

"We could have certainly done without all this dampness," she remarked, frowning. "But my head's stopped spinning, so the sooner we can get to that farmhouse, the better."

"I agree. you need some place dry where you can rest."

Intermittent rains had sprung up for several nights, making the soil so moist, they had to be careful not to leave any evidence of their passing. "Remember, Bela, step only on the protruding roots and branches that I step on."

"What I'm trying to do," she said, putting her foot on them with great care. "But it's not as easy as it looks."

Twigs snapped loudly as prickly shrubs scraped at their clothing. And twice he had to help her duck to keep from getting scratched.

Suddenly, she began sinking in the soil. "It's like quicksand!" he shouted. "So grab my arm and hold on tight!"

He pulled her against him and rested his cheek against hers. "One of the laces on my boot broke and —"She stopped, robbed of speech as large drops of water from one of the leafy branches overhead, began rolling down her cheeks like tears.

"Your boot slid off your foot, and it's sinking." He pointed. "But keep holding onto me while I grab it."

* * *

Bela tensed as she watched him reach through the heavy fog for it. Although, he did it so quickly, it amazed her. And smiling, she informed him, "I was worried you wouldn't get it in time."

"So was I. Since in this soupy terrain you'll need your boots," he said as he removed a small rag from his coat. "But if you're willing to stop for a minute, there's an embankment up ahead where you can sit while I get the mud off it."

"Not necessary," she said, leaning on him while he put the boot back on her foot. "We can clean it once we get to the farmhouse."

He turned toward the southeast. "Up ahead it looks twice as slippery. So stay close enough to grab me and keep stepping where I step."

She made no reply but stared at his disconcerted expression with concerned eyes as he turned and resumed the climb down.

They trekked through the mud like wayfarers in the belly of a tormented beast, until they reached a path lined with rocks that curved to the left.

"Kurt —look!" she called out suddenly. "There're corpses of three German soldiers behind those trees."

He whipped his head around. "And they're bloated with their mouths agape."

"Like in their final, desperate moments they'd begged heaven to open its gates and save them,"she remarked, the look on their faces bringing fearful images to her mind.

"Which they probably did."

She gazed at the bodies, aware they would eventually turn black. "From the way they look, I suspect it was an allied attack that happened less than twenty-four hours ago."

He stepped past her. "Certainly looks like it. So standby while I search them for weapons and anything else we might need."

She leaned toward him as he checked through their pockets.... And he smiled, pleased, when he confiscated a pay book, ID tag, and a Walther PPK pistol, one of the soldiers had strapped to him.

Quickly opening the holster, he removed the pistol, checking for spare magazines, but there weren't any. "A Walther PPK with a silencer on it, but only two shells," he said, handing it to her. "Did the OSS train you to shoot one like that?"

"Of course." she answered, proud to appear self-sufficient. "In fact, the OSS even showed me how to field strip it... but where are their other weapons?"

"Probably scattered in the brush. Which unfortunately, we don't have time to search for."

"Too bad we can't find a submachine gun."

His lips gave a slight twist. "I'm assuming the OSS trained you how to use one?"

"In their advanced training— but look, is that a duffle bag under that bush over there?"

"Appears to be."

"Want me to get it?"

"No, just stay where you are."

"From the twisted shape of the charred trees near that forested hillside, there's no doubt in my mind those soldiers died from a mortar attack," she remarked.

"Definitely." He upended the bag and all its contents tumbled out, scattering on the forest floor.

"Is that a gray, wool scarf?" she asked him, staring at the bag's contents.

"It is." And neatly folded." He held it up. "If the weather gets worse, this should provide a degree of protection."

"It's like the one you wore when you were in the Wehrmacht—"

"And much too warm for here." He put it under her raincoat's collar. "So keep it there for now."

"I will. But what about the soldiers whose things we're going through? Do you think they died from *shrapnel* wounds?"

"More than likely, since those trees are still standing. So I'd venture to say the fire was followed by a heavy rain— but look over there." He gestured with his right hand. "If I'm seeing correctly there's another bag next to that lance corporal's body that appears to be the kind my men carried their extra uniforms in."

"You have good eyes... but if there's a uniform in it, do you think it'll fit you?"

"Hopefully." He went over to the bag, opened it, and held up the uniform. "Like I suspected. And even if this corporal's body is bloated, he does look close to my size."

Bela looked down. "The ground's quite damp, so I'll need to hold your clothes while you change."

"Not necessary since there's a thicket close by."

She grinned slightly. "Kurt, you're not showing me anything I haven't already seen."

"I know, but at a time that wasn't pleasant for you."

"Still, you gave me the hope to hold on until Wolf sent that Gestapo man to get me."

"I'm glad you think that. Though, it's better if you wait under that pine tree across from us and keep a lookout with that PPK."

CHAPTER EIGHTEEN

B ela didn't mind, even if it did make her fidgety to sit and listen to the birds twittering above her. Plus, the abrasive sound the pine tree's branches made as they scratched against the tree next to it, "Is Like someone trying to start a fire," she murmured, the irony hitting her when she gave the charred trees from the mortar attack another look.

Kurt wasn't gone long and when he returned, it was obvious his civilian clothes were now packed in the duffle bag. "I'll need to find a place to hide this bag and its contents once we're close to that farmhouse," he said, staring at several of the larger, broken pine branches on the ground. "Have you any suggestions?"

But she shook her head, not wanting to tell him that seeing him in a sinister, Wehrmacht uniform again, brought back the anguish of what men in such clothing had done to her. And it added an unwelcome tension to her troubled spirits as shivers of apprehension coursed through her. "Kurt—"she uttered.

"Does this uniform bother you?" he asked, standing with stiff, military precision.

"It's a necessary evil," she remarked, looking at the ground for a moment in an effort to avoid this echo from her past... Although, her heart continued to beat rapidly each time she recalled how his dinner jacket at the chalet— like his Wehrmacht captain's uniform he'd worn with such an impressive effect— had offset the uncertainty she felt toward him.

Not to mention the humanity he continued to show her was nothing short of a seductive tenderness, sweeping away the boundaries between them, before circumstances would separate them. *No way I can deny this growing revolution inside me that gnaws at my heart. Nor the long, troubling nights of soul- searching that lay ahead for me... even with this fresh awakening he's given my tormented spirit.*

Clutching his rucksack and the duffle bag, they spent another half -hour hiking down through the thick underbrush on the narrow, dirt path. And they both grinned at how the flocks of birds hastened to take flight from their presence.

Once again her light-headedness returned, and he stopped each time it did, and pulled her against him.

Without a doubt the sway of his attraction for her was getting bolder. Because he was making no effort to hide the longing in his eyes whenever he looked at her. '*My thoughts are spinning and my heart is twisting,*' she was about to say. When, surprising her, he took hold of her hand and remarked with a courtly deference, "Not much farther, my lovely lady."

And thankfully, it wasn't. Because when they finally stood across the road from the cottage, she felt as physically exhausted as he looked mentally. "No hint of warmth in that place," she remarked. "Only the icy uncertainty of not knowing what to expect."

"Which is the reason you need to stay behind those trees," he said, pointing at them. "Because this place may look deserted, but someone could always be hiding in it."

She started to protest, but he handed her his rucksack and gave her the Walther PPK again. "Keep it but stash the duffle bag under the fallen tree behind that Douglas fir." He indicated a tall, evergreen tree. "And wait for me there because if I'm not back in half an hour, then come and look for me."

Given the circumstances she had no choice but to do what he said. So, she sat on the log with the pistol in her lap and again waited under the cover of trees, for time to tick away.

But when the half- hour was almost up, and he hadn't returned, she walked over to a different copse of birch trees. It was a fine morning with the sun dusting the road with its flaxen light, reminding her of the tropical-flower light switch in her bedroom at the chalet. "Makes being in the country feel almost as romantic as cruising on the Danube," she murmured. When glancing toward the southeast, she saw Kurt hurrying across the road.

"We're in luck," he called." That abandoned cottage has a motor bike with a sidecar outside its back door."

"Will it start?" she asked, barely able to contain her excitement.

"No. But I found its tool kit, so I'll make it."

"Then let's go see."

"Not yet." He held up a piece of cloth from an old quilt. "This was inside the tool kit, so I can clean your boot like I promised."

"But I can do it," she insisted, not wanting to appear helpless.

"I know, but it's easier for you to let me."

Like it or not, even if he was a uniformed German, he'd made himself her protector. And when he knelt and began cleaning her boot, her lungs squeezed tight as she struggled with the urge to place her hand on his head and stroke the glossy patina of his dark hair.

After he finished with the boot, he took her hand and smiling, she crossed the road with him to the cottage.

Tall weeds flanked the wooden steps leading to its narrow doorway, making her curious how long it had been since anyone had lived here.

"Be careful. Because you never know what you're going to find hidden in a place like this," he warned as he stepped through the door, looked around, then ushered her inside.

There was no rug on the hard, wooden floor, and its rickety boards made a whining creak under their boots as they stepped on them.

She pressed against him, feeling the emptiness of the cottage's small room as she stared at the long,wooden benches shoved against the walls on each side of it. "It's only furnishings?"

"Afraid so. Which the harvesters probably used as beds," he said, rubbing the back of her hand with his thumb.

"Must have been uncomfortable for them."

"I'm sure."

There was a tiny alcove off to the side that looked like it had once been the kitchen. But there was no sign of a stove or any pots and pans. Just a blackened teapot on the floor with a hole in it, a broomstick, and a long line of dusty canisters and bluish-green jars, many of which had been broken.

"The two windows were closed," he told her. "So I opened them and their shutters slightly, so we could see outside."

A shadow hovered above them and glancing up, she noticed a broken ladder leading to a loft with part of its roof open to the sky. "Do you think there's a main house nearby?"

"If there was it was probably bombed." He shut the door behind them. "Because I found something that makes me suspect someone's lived here recently." He tapped on one of the wooden panels in the wall, and it slid open.

"A secret panel," she said, impressed. "How'd you know?"

"This panel has an oily edge like someone has been handling it a lot. But look, there's a space where one person can hide."

"Only one person?" She moved closer to get a better look. "But is there a lever opening to the outside?"

A sly grin slid across his mouth. "Yes. So a person can make a quick getaway if he or she has to."

Bela contemplated what he'd said. "Don't you find it odd we've stumbled onto something like this?"

"Not in the least. With people here so afraid of what might happen if *Ivan* comes, that many Germans have found ways of adding secret rooms or closets to their houses." He smiled as she leaned closer to get a better look at this secret cupboard. "In Berlin, the *Fuhrer's* ordered, when possible, each block of houses dig escape tunnels from their cellars so they'll all be connected."

"Certainly surprising, but getting back to the motor bike, when do we start repairing it?"

"Now if you like. Though I'd really prefer you to stay inside, since we can't be sure where those Germans are." He glanced out the window, looking vaguely disturbed "Because if they should come around—"

"Which considering the amount of territory we've covered in such a short amount of time, they probably won't. And I was afraid at first, but now that we have a degree of protection, we need to take advantage of it and get that motor bike running."

"I agree. Even though I don't like the idea of your being out there with me."

"Doesn't matter. I helped my father work on his motor bike. And things will go faster if I'm there to hand tools to you."

"Of course they will." He took her hand and held it for a moment. "It's just that I don't like risking you."

"But you won't be. Because the quicker we can get out of here, then the faster we'll be able to get away from those Germans."

"I should hope, but—"He broke off as a new thought appeared to form. "I suppose if the two of us are waving when the next plane returns, then it probably wouldn't be a bad idea for you to remain outside."

"Indeed," she remarked with a sense of certainty. "Because four hands are always better than two. "

"Then I guess I'd better hurry and get to work, so we can get out of here."

"What about the windows? Do we leave them open or closed?"

"Leave them like I have them in case we have to return."

"Which I certainly hope we don't," she said, wondering how long it would take before those Germans showed up.

The task of getting the motor bike to kick-start was surprisingly simple...since its only problem appeared to be the connecting wire on top of a spark plug, which had been cut in half.

"All I have to do is cut the shielding wire in half and attach it to the connection," he told her.

"And it should start right up." She smiled, liking the way things were turning in their favor as she watched him sort through the tool kit while she held it.

The work went so quickly that she could have sworn she heard Jaclyn say, *'A saint is watching over you, with an army of angels.'*

"Wonder who could have left this motor bike here like this?" she asked him, after he finished.

"Doesn't matter, because in war unexplainable things often happen."

He cranked the throttle, and it started with a roar. "So where to, *Fraulein* Bela?" he shouted, grabbing her arm as he helped her climb into its sidecar.

"The nearest village or town," she shouted back, practically in his ear.

"Which should certainly have some way of connecting us to someone in the outside world."

"And if it doesn't, then we'll at least be safe from those Germans."

The bike seemed to be running smoothly as Kurt swerved around the corner of the winding, dirt road and began accelerating down it. He raced the engine full-out, avoiding it's roughness until he came to a belt of pines close to several poplar trees. Then the engine began to misfire and slowing, he shifted down one gear.

"It's the spark plugs again, isn't it?" She frowned as he braked.

"They probably need to be gapped as well as cleaned." He moved slightly on his seat. "This motor bike will get us back to the cottage if we go slowly, and it doesn't die—"

"But the Germans are apt to find us there if they're following us."

"*No* — you'll be safe in that hidden cupboard."

"And *you?*"

"I'm in uniform, so I'll take my chances. But let's hurry and get back. Because I'll need to find something abrasive that'll clean those plugs."

Surprisingly, they got back to the cottage quicker than expected, and Bela found a piece of wadded-up sandpaper inside one of the jars.

" Perfect." Kurt smiled. "Since with this I should be able to get us on our way in less than half an hour."

She started to follow him outside but stopped because he had. "I'm clearly hearing those German soldiers speaking—"

"So am I," he said, cutting his gaze toward the sound of their voices.

"Then what do we do? Stick to our original plan or run?"

"We stick to original plan, because those soldiers are getting closer."

* * *

Kurt knew with those Germans practically in shouting distance, having her hide in the cupboard made her as vulnerable as a butterfly about to emerge from its cocoon. Which meant if they discovered her, it would be the same as returning her to the Love Camp.

"I can handle this, so hurry and get in the cupboard." He slid the Walther PPK in her raincoat's large pocket.

"But not having it makes it dangerous for you."

"I realize that," he said, his heart banging against his ribs. "Just don't argue and get inside that cupboard."

But she hesitated, standing as immobile as if someone had a gun leveled at her. "Please, Kurt, one more thing—"

"What?"

"Be careful." She grabbed his arm like a young recruit in combat, whose emotions were battling the turbulence of the storm, with his fear of death by shell-fire.

"Don't worry, I intend to be."

"I'm counting on it." She tensed, clutching her chest, like her heart was wobbling hard.

But no matter what they did to him as long as he could stop them from treating her like a field-whore, that was what counted.

He went over to the bike, trying not to think about the shaft of uneasiness slicing through him as he removed its plugs. The wadded- up piece of sandpaper was crammed in his pocket, and he took it out to clean them when suddenly, he looked up and saw the four Germans. They were flaunting their swastika armbands as they crossed the road.

And immediately his sense of foreboding increased with a frightening intensity....But like a cornered animal, he remained where he was as they stomped toward him, getting closer and closer.

He had never felt so powerless in his life. Not even when *Ivan's* shells were screaming at him from all directions as their tanks plowed their way through the village, where he and his men were assembled... or several months later, when the Tommies were beating him after his capture.

"Corporal, why are you standing there trying to repair that blasted motor bike?" asked the major, his submachine gun slung over his shoulder as he moved toward him with a swaying gait. The three others with him were passing around a silver flask. And their eyes in their grimy faces were bloodshot from all the drinking they were doing.

"Allied troop movements, Major. And I'm planning on getting away, so I won't end up a prisoner."

"Clever, Corporal," he remarked with an air of confidence. "But have you a weapon or papers you can show me?"

Immediately Kurt felt his jaw go rigid with tension. "I was in a mortar attack, and this is all I have." He reached in his pocket and removed the pay book and ID tag he'd taken off the dead soldier.

"So like us, you're trying to escape from the allies and go where? To South America?"

He nodded.

"The *Fuhrer's* there, you know."

He didn't know but the tales about the *Fuhrer*— dead or otherwise— got wilder every day. "Then who's in Berlin?"

"His *double*," said the major. "And the Americans put him in charge with orders to deal with *Ivan*, before rescuing our beloved *Fuhrer* and putting him and his lovely Eva Braun on a ship headed to Paraguay." He said it in a tone that implied he'd been granted access to information about the former leader, which most people hadn't.

Something Kurt recognized as a ploy this man had dreamed up to make him and his men look important, so he'd hand Bela over to them. "Why would the Americans put his double in charge?" he asked, aware they had yet to learn of the *Fuhrer's* death.

"Because in case you haven't heard, our beloved *Fuhrer* is the new leader of the free world." He paused to shout, "*Heil Hitler,*" and click his officer's boots together. "Which is our reason for not relinquishing our armbands and uniforms, until we can change into civilian clothes."

Kurt shook his head. "And after you do that, then what'll you do? Discard them?"

"Of course not." He looked offended. "We'll put them back on, once we're on a vessel headed to Paraguay."

Did they have the money for such a journey? Kurt wondered, continuing to be surprised by this major's professed revelations.... *If they did, then it was probably stolen.*

"What are you thinking?" the major asked, noticing his look of skepticism. "That we don't have the money to leave?"

"Something like that," Kurt said, half to himself. "But anything's possible."

The major's mouth twisted wryly. "We're due to leave for South America on a German U-boat waiting for us in Denmark." Then grinning smugly, he opened a cognac-colored wallet with several large, rubber bands wrapped around it and waved a wad of American one- hundred- dollar bills in Kurt's face. "And this is going to help us get settled, once we're in Paraguay—" He stopped, cocked his head to one side, and waited as if expecting a reaction from Kurt at being shown such a large amount of money. But when he said nothing, he continued, "We'll make a bargain with you, Corporal, and take you along if you'll help us, but first—" He turned to the stout soldier wearing a Wehrmacht, forage cap and carrying what looked like a bag of ammunition. "Manfred, search our good corporal here and see if he has a weapon."

"What is it you want from me?" Kurt asked the major, pretending like he didn't know.

"Nothing. Other than handing over that golden-haired, young woman I saw jump with you from the train." He patted his binoculars. "So where is she?"

"Not here," Kurt quickly answered.

"Not *here*? "the major questioned, like he didn't believe him. "Then where in *hell* is she, Corporal?"

"I told her to go into the woods and hide until I got this motor bike running," he said. "Which from the looks of it, is going to take several hours or longer."

"While you just stand there cleaning spark plugs?" asked the major, a taunt smile on his lips.

"Have to start somewhere." He shrugged, his uneasiness increasing.

"She's a high-priced, jewel of a woman," remarked a stumpy soldier with blackened teeth, puffing on a cigarette. "And you've simply no right to keep her all to yourself—"

"Who is she anyway, Corporal?" interrupted the major, starting to pace back and forth. "A field-whore?"

"No," said Kurt, easing out his breath. "She's my wife."

"*Your wife*!" His expression bordered on mockery. "Then bring her out here and let us meet her."

"But how can I when I don't *know* where she is?" he asked, trying to sound calm.

"Then how will you find her?"

"She said she'd come back when it's dark."

"Which I seriously doubt," the major remarked. And turning to the soldier closest to him, he ordered, "Heinz, take him inside and see if we can't make him tell us where she is."

"My pleasure." And motioning at the two other soldiers, they jumped on him like a wild boar would have done a crippled deer.

Kurt's fear was now replaced with rage as he struggled with a rough jerk to break away from them. And he might have succeeded, had the major not given him such a fierce kick that it knocked him to the ground.

"Stay down!" ordered the stumpy soldier, grabbing him by the arms.

Heinz's anger flared. "Where's the bitch, Corporal!" he yelled as he helped Manfred drag him into the cottage.

But after a moment passed and no answer came, the stumpy soldier removed his belt, lifted Kurt's tunic, and beat him on the back with bone-wrenching strikes.

Heinz soon joined him. "In war you live from one day to the next, Corporal, "he said, pounding his skull and back with a knotted rope and leather belt, the way he would have punished some poor, despised serf. "So where in fuck is she!"

Please, God, don't let them find Bela, Kurt prayed, trying not to imagine her in their clutches. *The Wehrmacht told us we were knights without fear, God. But if that's true, then why is pain exploding in my head, and I'm clawing at the floor?*

'Life is leaving you,' he could have sworn a voice said. *'Therefore, distract that major before he orders your death.'*

But how could he...? When the way his thoughts were tumbling over each other, all he could do was stare at the man, trancelike, as he watched his evil face fold into a smile.

"Anyone in the room know how much torture a man can stand before he expires?" the major asked, propping a booted foot on one of the dusty benches, before demanding in a pompous voice, "Tell us where she is!"

CHAPTER NINETEEN

urt opened his mouth to say, *'I'd die before I'll tell you,'* but the words stuck in his throat.

He was now surrounded by black, leather boots. And each time he tried to lift his head, all he saw was the swastika on the belt buckles of the soldiers, with the eagle above it, preparing to take flight.

He wanted to take flight too. But his strength was leaving him as the walls of this dilapidated cottage closing in on him, threatened to plug up his breath.

And then he looked up and saw Bela. *Was he dreaming...? She's not supposed to be here, but she is —striping off her clothing and letting it fall piece by piece on the floor beside him. This is madness!*

The first item to go was her raincoat, with the Walther PPK deep inside its pocket. But what chance did a gun with two shells stand against four men with a submachine gun?

So he stared at Bela with a rising sense of panic as she kept removing each garment with no claim to modesty. And then naked, except for her boots, she stood before the major...a plea on her lips.

Savage shocks of fear gouged Kurt. *Don't think about it... even if what she is about to do is as clear to you as the morning's frail, blue light.*

Yet, how could he not think about it? As she stood in front of the major the way she'd stood before him in the Love Camp... like she was nothing more than property owned by the Third Reich.

Reflecting on it, his eyes immediately clouded as he recalled how her dazzling, gold body had made him feel like he'd eluded his foes and taken refuge on top of a crested peak, rising above a burning ocean.

But when she'd locked herself in his embrace, and her pinstriped smock had slid down her arms, he 'd realized his visit to this brothel was not about sating his lusts, but about seeing a glow— like a shaft of sunlight —illuminate her face. So he'd begun caressing each part of her lovely body until his soul melted against hers, and she too was standing on this crested peak.

And then, above this burning ocean, he'd entered her. Giving her several powerful thrusts that had brought her to life with the yearnings they'd sparked, as her cry of fulfillment matched his.

Back then, of course, he'd been equipped to take on the world. But now, rendered helpless by the beatings, he was only half the man he once was— with his skull throbbing like a bullet had splintered inside it. *I'm as useless as one of those pulled up stumps in the woods, with its mangled roots showing. And it's because of me they're making Bela do this terrible thing that I can't stop. Since if I try to brace myself and stand, then everything will go black.*

But battling against the eagle's talons Manfred so proudly sports on his belt buckle, is not the way. For what help can I be to Bela if I get myself killed? So the nightmare swells.

The major handed his submachine gun to the stumpy soldier, who was oblivious to everything, except the naked Bela standing in front of him.

Then nodding at the little man, the major motioned at his other two soldiers to line up behind him for their turn with her.

Of course he gets her first. And he's so anxious, he's already torn off his clothes and scattered them across the floor. "Ah, my kitten." He grinned with a knowing look. "You've a field-whore's mark like I suspected."

And elated, he began shouting out the words from a German drinking song about a girl with golden-hair and tall tits a soldier fucked on the Rhine.

Then flashing a wicked smile in Bela's direction, he pounced on her, spun her around, and sank his teeth into one of her bare breasts.

Kurt's pain-filled body cringed at the horrors his lovely Bela was enduring. *But if I look away from her, it will be the same as abandoning her.*

So he focused on her eyes, letting her know that even with his half -dazed brain, he was still there.

Her blue eyes had now become pools of appeal as they traveled from him, to the stumpy soldier holding the submachine gun and then back to him.

But what did this mean? She was obviously telegraphing him a silent message, but with the shrouded mist fogging his brain, he didn't understand it....

"You're my enemy, Corporal," Manfred broke in, removing his belt with its swastika buckle. "So I'll deal with you as I must." And lifting the belt, he hit him in the forehead with its gleaming buckle.

"M...monster," Kurt stammered.

The pain might have panicked him, had the adrenaline rush from it not stimulated his mental processes. *Bela's terrible nightmare is happening— so I must keep a hold on what has to be done...which means somehow, I have to get the gun out of her raincoat's pocket.*

That's the message she's been sending my fuzzy brain. Has to be. And gasping— with his gaze still connected to hers— it seemed a shadow passed between them as he reached for the Walther PPK.

Time was rapidly dissolving for the old, stumpy soldier and the others from this self-styled Master Race. However, they seemed to be having difficulty getting it through their heads, until he aimed the Walther and fired.

Immediately, Manfred and his stumpy friend gawked in astonishment at their blood -splattered undershirts.

Kurt also gawked, when Bela grabbed the submachine gun from the dying, stumpy soldier and stepping back, fired more bullets at him and Manfred before delivering a spitting death on Heinz.

"W...what in hell—" mumbled the major, a second before she turned the gun on him. And clutching his stomach with a thunderous expression he fell sideways as death overtook him.

"*GOTT MIT UNS!*" Kurt gasped, staring at the major's shattered remains.

* * *

Bela felt herself shaking as she looked down and saw the bandage between her breasts covered in German blood. *The Master Race and their blood of dreams.* How many times in the Love Camp had she wanted to grab a gun and slaughter every German who dared to force himself on her and the other girls? But that was about revenge. Which had become less important with the way her heart twisted each time Kurt's gentle, dark eyes smiled at her.

"You took a great risk to do what you just did, Bela."

"No, *you* did. By keeping my horrible nightmare from coming true."

"If I did, it's only because in war we're either taking risks, getting hurt, making sacrifices— or all three."

"Well said." She smiled, placing a hand on the side of his face." But what about your head?"

"It aches. And I'm feeling a little dizzy. But I don't imagine my injuries are nearly as bad as the bloody bite on your breast that sadistic major gave you."

"Doesn't matter. Since you stopped him from forcing me to have anal sex with him —"

"Bela, stop—*please.*" He held up a hand to silence her. "It gives me chills to think about something that terrible happening to you."

"And it gives me chills to think what could have happened, had you not trusted me enough to pay attention to my nightmare."

"Which hopefully, will put an end to it."

"To that one maybe, but it's not the only one."

"Sad —but getting back to our injuries, where's my rucksack?"

"In the cupboard." She pointed a finger at it.

"Then I'll get it. Because there's a salve inside it that should help." He started toward it, but she grabbed his arm.

"Let me. Since you'll need to take it easy with those bloody marks across your back. And the dried blood on your forehead." She touched it briefly. "Which could possibly mean you have a concussion."

"I'll be all right," he assured her as she stepped over to the cupboard and reached for the rucksack.

"What I'm hoping."

"Still, I keep thinking that if I'd been quicker, that son-of-a-bitch major might not have hurt you."

"I've been bitten before, so it doesn't matter," she said, shaking her head. "But even so I'm amazed you were able to do what you did, in your semi-conscious state." She reached out to brush back a forelock of his dark hair. "But here, take this."

She handed him the rucksack, and he rummaged through it until he found some iodine, salve, a rayon pad, and a roll of cotton gauze.

"We need to see to you first." He held up the tube of salve. "So do I put this salve on your breast or do you want to do it?"

She glanced at the red line. "You'd better, since it's not easy for me to see."

* * *

"Then by all means," Kurt said, his heart threatening to unravel each time he thought about how that horrible major had come so close to raping her.

"Now it's my turn to take care of you." She dampened some gauze from the roll with Ina's left- over tea and sponged the dried blood from his forehead and back, before smearing both with iodine.

"What about this rayon pad?"

"I don't think I'll need it, so you can put it back."

Deeply touched by her efforts, he kissed the fading scar mark on her shoulder before massaging it gently.

Then he put her raincoat around her to cover her nakedness. "The punishment marks on your backside have healed nicely."

"Thanks to that special salve you gave money to Madam Kollar to buy. And Wolf and Jaclyn, who got me to an excellent hospital in Switzerland."

"You're beautiful inside and out, Bela," he whispered. And taking her by the arm, he led her like a wounded comrade, to the two wooden benches against the wall near the door.

Once they were seated, he helped her slide her arms into the raincoat, so it was more snug. "My mind keeps reeling, Bela, and I'm having difficulty remembering exactly what happened." He nodded at the cupboard. "But I'm assuming they found you inside it?"

"They never suspected."She stopped and blotted her suddenly watery eyes with one of the handkerchiefs she kept in her coat pocket. "But when I heard them beating you, I knew I had no choice but to leave the cupboard and circle around through the front door."

"You did *what?*" He was astounded. "You were willing to save my life by allowing the hands of hell to claw at you— the way they did in your nightmare?"

She put her hand on his arm. "Of course, Kurt."

He was at a loss as to how after the Love Camp, she could so willingly sacrifice herself for him.

"I wouldn't have blamed you if you'd shot me, Bela, so why didn't you?"

"Why would I want to do that?" she asked, pressing one of her hands against his cheek. "Because you were once a Wehrmacht captain?"

"Who wasn't any better than the others."

She straightened. "Like I've said, you gave me the warm breath of hope I needed."

"Maybe," he whispered, lightly kissing her on the brow. "But I'm still not exactly sure how, so give me some more detail."

* * *

Bela smiled. "You didn't earn my hatred because, like me, you were suffering too."

"*No*," he said in a dispirited tone. "I keep thinking about how I was forced to leave you in that dreadful place. "His face crumpled. "And later, after I learned that many of the Love Camp women in other parts of Europe were forced to have sex with forty men a day with almost no hygiene, I became so concerned something like that might be happening to you, I nearly lost it when the Tommies took me prisoner." He shifted, staring at the wooden floor. "So I kept up my prayers for you, *liebchen*, asking God to keep you *safe* and somehow find a way to let me know you were."

"And your prayers were answered," she said, gently laying her hand on his forearm. "When you turned up at Albert's."

Kurt kissed her brow again. "And I felt a great relief but under the circumstances didn't quite know what to say to you."

"Like me." She rested her cheek against his shoulder. "But since I gave you the number of men I usually entertained, then you must have figured out that the Love Camp you visited was so close the front, the men didn't come in droves like they did at the Love Camps in Poland... and yes, we did have some hygiene."

"You were quite clean, I remember."

"And unlike many of the soldiers, so were you."

"I tried. Although I do remember after I calmed down, you said you only had two or three men a night. So being familiar with the area where the Love Camp was— and knowing the way the war was going— I realized the military couldn't spare forty men a night for each girl there to entertain." He let out a ragged breath. "But still, it doesn't excuse me for not being able to come up with a way to get you out of that evil place."

"But you couldn't," she said, biting back tears. "Because Wolf understood from the Gestapo man he sent to rescue me, that getting me out was next to impossible unless you were a friend —like this Gestapo man was— with that terrible ObersturmFuhrer Horst Helmer."

"It was awful that Wolf had to bribe those men with money and the means to escape," Kurt replied, shuddering like he had a fever.

Bela tightened her hand on his arm. "What was really amazing was the way you were able to convince Madam Kollar to tear up those two reports I had."

"It did surprise me." He placed his hand over hers." Since it was my first time to be in a brothel."

"I know, but like it or not, we started something that was hard to finish."

His eyes locked with hers. "You wanted what I wanted."

"To create something memorable?"

He nodded. "And I realize I'm making excuses for my behavior, but I had no future when I visited the Love Camp." He hesitated before adding, "Since *Ivan* was slaughtering us so badly, we were literally without hope."

"Still," she said hoarsely," don't you think in such terrifying times that what happened between us could have happened with any of the girls in the Love Camp?"

"Not on your life! " His voice hardened. "And I was about to walk out when you showed up."

"Then you must have felt ashamed."

He nodded again. "For being in a brothel that was like a concentration camp. And later, for disrespecting my wife and son's memory by enjoying myself in it."

"I was ashamed too," she said, her tone mirroring his as she stroked the solid strength of his forearm. "Because the Love Camp was such a terrible place, I had difficulty believing it was possible that the experience we shared could be so beautiful."

"I made love to you, Bela, because I was *in* love with you... if you can believe me?"

"I'm trying, but it's hard when you knew so little about me." There was a lengthy silence as she pondered how he'd feel about her if he knew she was a Jewess.

"That's the beauty of love at first sight," he reminded with the hint of a smile. "Which means I didn't have to know a lot about you."

"Because you're a romantic?" she asked softly." Who was caught in a web of great feeling?"

"Maybe." He grinned. "But at least I'm not a cynic."

She didn't want to talk about it —*couldn't talk about it*—as she closed her eyes, remembering that brief, beautiful moment when this Wehrmacht captain had transported her to another world.

And so she leaned over and kissed him. "After allowing me to climax before you at the Love Camp, I'm not sure what I believe any more."

He took her hand and pressed her fingertips against his lips. "Why? Because you didn't expect a German to act like that?"

"None had before, "she said, still shocked by the driving, urgent need she'd shared with him. "Since you slaked the fires of your own desire, by pleasuring me first rather than yourself."

His mouth curved with tenderness. "O-oh I got pleasure from it throughout—make no mistake. Because when a man cares about a woman, he gets as much pleasure from giving to her as he does receiving from her." He wrapped his arms around her and kissed her on both cheeks. "If I could hold you again like that, do you think it might take away some of those dreadful memories that keep you awake at night?"

"That's a possibility." she said, finding the thought very satisfying. "But no matter how splendid you made me feel, I fear it would be hard for me to forget you were once a captain in the Wehrmacht— "

"That you dislike because I helped empower the people who harmed you."

"No." She placed her head against his chest. "That's the problem. I couldn't dislike you no matter how hard I tried. It's just remembering too much, like thinking too much, can erode the soul and weaken a person."

She braced herself, feeling like something inside her had collapsed. "And after what happened to me and my father, I fear that at some point in the future, I might not be strong enough to put aside those memories and love you like you deserve to be loved."

'*It has to be that way, since I can never give you any children,*' she would have added, had tears not sprung to her eyes each time she thought about how after their mission, they'd be forced to go their separate ways.

* * *

Her disturbingly honest feelings gave Kurt an unexpected jolt. Making him want to say that empowering the enemy in the past was not as important as fighting against the enemy *now*... or rather the past was not as important as the *future*. But considering the horrific tragedy she'd suffered at the Love Camp, he knew better.... With a Gestapo man giving her a cyanide capsule, since he probably thought her too weak to rise above her dreadful memories of the place. *Because her spirit's as frail as cheesecloth. Which like mine, has a yearning for human love.*

So he prayed that given time she'd come to realize it. "Please, *liebchen*, don't be sad."

She shivered in the damp, chilly air. "I...I'm trying not to be."

"Not easy when you're cold," he quickly added. "But with part of the roof open and the stench from those men over there beginning to be noticeable, it isn't nearly as bad as it could be. "He curled his arm around her shoulders. "Of course there're the shutters."

"Just leave them like you had them."

"I think if I can fix one or two minor things, that motor bike will run again. So, we should be able to leave within the next hour."

"Not with your head injury," she said with obvious concern. "I may be cold but even so, you need to rest a bit until you're more stable on your feet. However—" Her gaze fell on his uniform. "If you had the overcoat you left in the woods I'd borrow it... but your corporal's tunic—"

"—is clearly not something you'd wear," he said, finishing for her. "No matter how cold it gets."

"That's the truth." A flash of humor flickered in her eyes. "And I know you're probably thinking I could put on my lightweight sweater and slacks,

158

but with that major's blood streaked all over them, I want to make sure it's dried."

"Can't say I blame you."

She was silent for awhile. *Cold and silent.* So he stared with longing at her.

It seemed she was in a very distant place as his warmth enveloped hers. And it pleased him she was able to lose herself for a brief time, since he suspected she was not fully recovered from that major's brutal assault.

"After we jumped from the train, the Stuttgart doctors will examine us to see if we're still in shape to go to Berlin...." He patted the two wooden benches. "Which tells me we should probably stretch out on these and take a nap."

"I agree. But with your injured head you'll need a pillow, so you'll have to use the rucksack."

"But if I do, then what will you use?"

"Why your shoulder, of course," she said with a partial smile. "Like you offered before we boarded the train."

"What I was hoping you'd say." He chuckled, pushing the benches together.

She peered at his rucksack. "You've got your cigarettes in there, will they get crushed?"

"They're packed tight, so I don't think so." Then before dropping off to sleep, he murmured, *"Liebchen,* at the Love Camp the comfort we gave each other was comfort we hadn't known in a very long time."

"And we lost ourselves *then* like *now.*" The tears in her eyes returning. "In an illusion we both realize will only last for a brief time."

He inhaled deeply. "Still, Bela, it's beautiful to be alive."

"Even in a time like this?"

"And a place like this."

"Yes, a place like this minus those dead Germans," she said, gazing with him at the iridescent rays of sunlight shining through the loft's partially open roof. "Because I somehow get the feeling that long ago in forgotten time, we lived together in a small cottage similar to this."

"Déjà vu... who knows? Maybe we did."

"I'd like to think—"

"Same as me." He placed a hand against her shoulder. "Since it would be encouraging to me to believe we 'd meet again in some future life where there is no war."

"So you believe in reincarnation?"

"Not really. I'm Catholic...but what about you?"

"I believe we're all made from pieces of people—our ancestors—so that could possibly be another reason we get this *déjà vu* feeling."

"Makes sense." He yawned, before closing his eyes and falling into a deep sleep that shielded him for a brief time from the insanity of the world outside.

CHAPTER TWENTY

When Bela and Kurt awoke it was to a low rumbling. "Sounds like a truck's down the road," he said, sitting up. "So hurry and get dressed."

"And allied truck?"

"Possibly." He looked around as if his senses were on hyper-alert. "But we can't be sure."

She sprang to her feet. "We'll need a white flag since you're in a German uniform or—" She paused to catch her breath. "You could always hide in the cupboard?"

"And let them find *you*?" he asked, a puzzled expression on his face. "Not on your life. Because we're not out of danger yet." He glanced through the slightly opened shutters. "That truck coming down the road could have been stolen by some other Germans trying to escape. So if anyone's going to hide, it's going to be *you*."

"Still, we'll make a white flag with this." She reached for her white lace camisole on the floor. "Which can easily be tied around that broomstick over there."

"Later. But first we'd better find out if our guests are Germans." He grabbed the submachine gun. "Because if they are, then I'm going to shoot them."

"I'll find out," said Bela, her stomach flopping like a wet fish on dry land as she peeped through the shutters.

Two English speaking men with American sounding accents stood outside the truck's cab. "The stuttering sound of machine gun fire carries," she heard one of them say. "And it smells bad in there. So you think it came from this place?"

"Certainly sounded like it. But that smell... *damn* Sergeant!"

"Could be worse if it weren't so chilly. But the clean-up crew will take care of it."

Kurt stared at the parts of their makeshift, white flag. "Who do you think they are, Bela, Americans, Canadians, or...?"

"Americans—I think."

"What about their uniforms?"

"A private's and a sergeant's judging from the pictures I've seen. And the sergeant is a blond man like Wolf, who's probably in his early thirties. And the young private has freckles and short hair the color of a carrot."

Kurt shifted, staring at the bodies flung across the room. "But we shouldn't put the gun down until we know for certain. Because there are Germans who speak excellent English and have been issued American uniforms to impede the advance of the American army."

"A frightening thought. But if there were allies nearby, then the submachine gun fire in here could have signaled them, couldn't it?"

"Definitely, but—" He grabbed her hands. "Now that the fog from my brain has lifted, I recall that German major showing me what looked like three thousand American one- hundred- dollar bills—but let me think." He touched the major's tunic on the floor, then blurted, "And they were in a cognac- colored wallet with several rubber bands wrapped around it."

"And I suppose it's in all that discarded, tangled clothing." She frowned, pointing a finger at it.

"Apparently. Since there would be money all over the place if it had taken a hit."

"Then I'd better act fast."

"*No*— wait! It's a dirty job, so let me do it."

"Not with a possible concussion." She gave another quick look out the window.

"Just keep watching these so-called Americans while I hunt for it."

"But Bela—"

"No *buts* about it—just do what I'm asking."

She continued to shiver with chill and fatigue but refused to let it stop her as she hurried toward the scattered pieces of bloody clothing. Any minute and those alleged Americans outside were apt to rush into the cottage with their weapons drawn.

And what a horrible mess they'd find when they did. The major's naked body blackening the floor with a pool of blood. And the nauseating smell rising from it making her wonder if it was her imagination or if the foul odor wasn't getting stronger by the minute?

But determined to find the wallet, it didn't keep her from searching through torn slacks still on human legs and tunics, with an arm missing from one.

Finally, she found *three* of the four missing wallets— two inside a slacks' pocket and the other in an outside tunic's pocket— but with very little money in any of them.

"Find anything?" Kurt asked, turning away from the door.

"Just three tan wallets with coins in them."

"Figures. Since that major was probably holding onto most of the money." He glanced at the other two benches across the room. "But do you remember where his clothing was when you opened fire?"

"On the floor mostly." She looked at it again. "But a piece or two could have been on one of the benches."

"Then there's a possibility the wallet might have taken to the air and landed behind something in this room."

She whirled quickly. "Like that line of canisters and jars near the tiny kitchen."

"The logical place. Considering there's not much else in here where it could have landed."

"I agree." And stepping over to where the broomstick had been, she bent down and looked behind the line of canisters.

At first she only saw only broken glass and a clump of dirt-encrusted, white feathers. *From a dove perhaps? If so it was certainly unexpected.*

She kept up her search for several more minutes until moving two large jars, she saw the cognac-colored wallet covered in pieces of green glass.

And she froze. *It was exactly as Kurt had described, with one of its rubber bands still wrapped around it,*

"See anything?" he asked, redirecting his attention to the door.

"Yes!" Excitement churned inside her. *"It's here* —just like you thought."

"And is it open or closed?"

"Closed. With a rubber band still wrapped around it."

"Now that's surprising."

"It really is considering it's got broken glass covering it."

"If it does, then you'd better let me get it."

"No. If I roll down my raincoat's cuffs, I'll have some protection. So just keep doing what you're doing." She glanced at the slightly open shutters on the windows. "But what about the Americans?"

"They're talking and pointing at this place like they're debating whether or not to come inside."

"Then we've got some time—but even so, I'll hurry."

"Still, Bela, the money's not worth getting cut."

"I beg to differ. Because my intuition tells me we're going to need that money before our Berlin trip's over."

Looking a trifle uneasy, he stared at her. "I certainly hope you're wrong."

"So do I. But with the way this trip's gone so far, I don't think I am." And bending over, she carefully began removing the shards of splintered glass from the stitching around the wallet's edge.

Many of the pieces were stacked three deep, forcing her to go slower than anticipated. And one particularly jagged piece cut through her cuff's binding and grazed her index finger. "Like a snake raising its ugly head," she remarked, straightening her shoulders.

Kurt was pacing back and forth in front of the shutters and the door. "Have you got it yet?"

"Yes," she answered, smiling at its contents before quickly shoving it in her raincoat's hidden pocket. "And the Americans?"

"The sergeant's gone back to the truck and appears to be radioing for back up."

"Still, they could be our chance to get out of here," she reminded, using the major's regulation issued long- john drawers like Kurt had worn, to wipe away the growing pool of blood under her finger.

"Who knows? But is the wallet well hidden?"

"It's in my secret pocket waiting for you."

"*Wrong*—it's yours, and I'm not taking any money from it."

"We'll see about that," she said with a feigned pout.

"*Stubborn, Bela,*" he scolded, looking mildly amused." But switching subjects, just what exactly do we do about those Americans outside? Reveal our presence without any papers to show who we are? Or, provided I've got that motor bike running, we'll leave after they do?"

"That's a hard one to call," she said, thinking about it. "Because we could easily run into more Germans."

"But we have a submachine gun now."

"Still, wouldn't they have one, too?"

"From what we've seen—*yes.*"

In the end the decision as to whether or not to confront the Americans was quite obvious. They'd already lost a day getting to Berlin, and time was of the essence. "I suspect Wolf and Jaclyn paid to have that plane sent over this morning," she told him.

"I'm sure they did." He sighed, like he hated to admit it was a waste of good money. "Which under the circumstances, tells me the smartest thing to do would be to hand ourselves over to the Americans."

Sensing his concern, Bela reassured him with a light kiss on his cheek. "If there was any other way—"

"Doesn't appear to be," he said. And taking her hands in his, he immediately saw the cut on her finger. "*My God!* Why didn't you tell me you were bleeding?"

"Because we have enough worries right now," she said, hearing a rasp of excitement in the American voices as they grew louder and louder.

"That's not the point. We're supposed to be looking out for each other." And turning around, he quickly grabbed the iodine in his rucksack.

She winced at the sting from it as he poured it over her finger and wrapped some tape around it. "I know what we're supposed to be doing, but it still doesn't keep me from wondering if turning ourselves over to the Americans is the right thing to do?"

"We'll know soon enough." He shrugged, giving them another look through the shutters. "Just don't forget to tell the Americans we're journalists on a special assignment for the Tommies."

"Our cover-story. Which has worked for the Russians, so hopefully it will for the Americans."

He grimaced. "Hopefully."

Continuing to be somewhat undecided, they stood arm and arm, staring at the Americans as the seconds ticked by.

Then suddenly Bela stepped in front of Kurt, swung the door back, and began waving their hurriedly made white flag.

"For God's sake!" he shouted. "Get out of the way—"

But she shook her head as she moved toward the Americans. "Don't shoot, we're journalists working for the British on a special assignment. And if you don't believe us, then take a look at these dead German soldiers we killed.'"

The private slapped himself across the brow and spat. "Journalists!" And pointing at Kurt in his German uniform, he burst out laughing. "At least this kraut and his *fraulein* know the war's over."

"Take the kraut prisoner," ordered the sergeant, stepping out of the truck with a submachine gun.

"What about the *fraulein?*"

"Bring her along too." Then he asked, "You call this journalism?" Now it was the sergeants turn to laugh. "From the way those body parts are scattered, I'd say it looks like you got in some kinda brawl."

The private shoved his 45 ACP in Kurt's stomach. "Don't suppose you got papers sayin' you're journalists?"

"They're giving them to us when we get to Berlin," he informed him.

"Berlin?" The sergeant rolled his eyes. "Now I've heard some real stories, so it's no good trying to bluff me."

"But we're not," insisted Bela. "And if you call the Stuttgart airfield and tell them who we are, then you'll know we're telling the truth."

"And just *who* are you?" he asked, scanning her length.

"Bela Spigel. And my partner here is Kurt Ulrich, who's posing as a German lance corporal, to keep from being killed by those soldiers out here who refuse to surrender—"

"Sorry," interrupted the sergeant. "But without papers there's nothing I can do but take you in."

Bela's mind was now in turmoil as the sergeant gestured at Kurt to move toward the door. She had to do something— and *quick.* The proof you need is right here, "she said, opening her raincoat. "See this tattoo *Feldhure*—101024? I'm a Jew and was in an army brothel." She paused, regretting it had come to this. "So if Kurt isn't working for the allies, then why am I standing here with him?"

CHAPTER TWENTY-ONE

The private stared at the word *Feldhure* and the numbers tattooed between Bela's breasts like he couldn't believe it. "Never seen anything like that, have you, Sergeant?"

"I read something about it in an army newspaper from a Jewish man who'd been a German prisoner," he remarked with sudden interest. "But I think he talked about numbers on his arm."

Bela wiped her eyes, afraid to look at Kurt and see his reaction on learning from her own mouth she was a Jew.

Beside her, Kurt was explaining to the sergeant in a loud voice, "Our rail carriage coupling broke —or got blasted— when the firing began. And the train was gaining speed—"

"It was a German train and the allies got it." The man stopped him, in an attempt to clarify.

"No— it was an *allied* one," Kurt emphasized. "Which I suspect got hit by friendly fire."

"Friendly fire?" the sergeant mimicked him.

"Yes. And it was probably the result of an artillery unit being fed coordinates by an aircraft spotter to fire on some German soldiers refusing to surrender."

"This morning a plane was circling looking for us," Bela told him. "So if you were anywhere close, you must have seen it."

The sergeant scratched his head, thinking. "There was a plane circling early, so I suppose it wouldn't hurt to radio that unit near where the train car's coupling broke."

"If anything's to be known, then they should know it," remarked the red-haired private. "But can you handle these two?"

"Of course. And if that *kraut* so much as makes a move, then he's *mine*."

They waited longer than they needed to wait. But when the sergeant returned he was enthusiastic. "Put that gun aside, Private," he ordered. "'Cause a plane should be coming for them in about three hours close to the village where we're holed up."

The private cleared his throat. "Then apparently what they're telling us is true."

Kurt grabbed Bela and gave her a quick kiss, which took her by surprise. "What's the matter? Did you think I wouldn't love you because you're Jewish?" He kissed her again. "On the contrary, if possible, I think I love you a thousand times more. And would even try and do some kosher cooking for you if you wanted me to."

"My very kind and thoughtful Kurt," she whispered, reassured by the warmth of his arms. " Wolf and Jaclyn cooked kosher for Pa and me whenever it was possible."

"But, *liebchen*, it wouldn't have bothered me to learn you were Jewish, so why didn't you tell me?"

"Wolf and I didn't even tell Albert."

" Really?" Kurt looked confused. "And your reason?"

"Because he'd given money to some doctors in Berlin to help the Palestinian Jews save some of the children by relocating them in Britain. But when many still died, he was so deeply grieved, that Wolf and I were afraid if we told him who *I* really was, he'd have a heart attack."

Immediately, Kurt's expression cleared. "Which considering his many health issues, he probably would have."

"The unit up ahead got my coordinates," the private said. "And the plane's going to try to land on something that resembles an airstrip near the village. But they've asked us to stay with you two until it does. And by the way." He smiled. "My name is Richard Corey Kayler, though most folks call me *Torchy*. And the good sergeant here is Hunter Mackery Innis.

So if you're hungry, we've given plenty of food to the villagers... and if you tell us what you want, I'll make certain you get it."

"How about Bratwurst, potato-cakes, Edam cheese—which is my favorite— and Czech beer if they've got it," said Kurt, before turning to Bela. "And you?"

"Are we really hungry after all this?" she asked, her hand on her stomach.

"No." He drew a breath. "But we've got to keep our strength up."

"They've got your Czech beer, Mr. Ulrich," said Torchy.

"Then I'll have a glass or two."

"And I'll have wine," Bela said, losing some of her concern.

Kurt squeezed her hand reassuringly. "Then maybe we'll forget about those rogue Germans for the moment, and our appetites will improve."

"In that case I'll have a tossed green salad and some of that Edam cheese. Or if that's not possible then some buttered noodles and a glazed fruit pastry will be just fine. But first I need to get my camisole and change back into my clothes."

"Then the cupboard's all yours, my lovely lady." Kurt grinned, bowing.

"Is that a secret room?" asked the sergeant, a curious gleam in his eyes.

"Not exactly...but I'll show you after she changes."

Anxious to hurry up and leave, she dressed quickly. And when she finished, she surprised the soldiers by entering through the front door, like she'd done when the Germans were beating Kurt.

"Well I'll be darned." The sergeant shook his head. "That cupboard must have an outside exit."

Kurt smiled at the idea "It does—for a quick getaway."

"Amazing." He pulled out a cigarette and offered one to Kurt. "Is there anything more we can do for you, Mr. Ulrich?"

"Yes." He took a deep drag off the cigarette as he reached for his rucksack. "My clothes are packed in the woods across the road, and I'd like to get rid of this uniform and put them back on."

"Then I'll follow you— but one more thing." Hunter turned back to Richard. "Keep watching for unwanted company, *Torchy*, while I go with Mr. Ulrich and his *fraulein* and help him get his clothes."

"Absolutely, sir, but before you leave I'd like to ask the *fraulein* a question."

"Then ask her, Private."

Richard seemed to fidget with shyness. "My question, *Miss*, is why didn't you Jewish people put up more of a fight?"

"Because they didn't have any weapons," Kurt answered for her, clearly resenting the question. "Now let's hurry, Sergeant, and get my clothes."

They weren't gone long and when he and Bela returned, the sergeant asked him, "What about that motorcycle with the sidecar in back, Mr. Ulrich? Do you want it?"

"Why not?" asked Bela, speaking before he could. "We could keep it as a souvenir of our misadventure."

"And send it where?" the sergeant asked her.

"To Baron Albert von Friesen in Switzerland."

Kurt looked at the sergeant. "But how do we get it *there* from *here?*"

"We got trucks going to Switzerland every day." The sergeant grinned, handing him paper and a pen. "So just write the address where you want it delivered, and I'll see it gets there."

He wrote it quickly and returning the sergeant's grin, gave him back the paper and pen. "We're very much obliged."

"Got to help our journalists." Hunter beamed. "So, you can either get in the truck with us or follow behind on that motorcycle of yours."

"I'd like to follow on the motor bike or motorcycle as you call it," said Kurt." But I need to finish cleaning its spark plugs."

"Then we'll help you get it done," Richard volunteered.

"And I'd be obliged." Kurt grabbed his rucksack before taking a step toward Bela. "Is following behind all right with you?"

"As long as your head's not hurting."

He gave her a one-armed hug. "I'm feeling much better, so ride in the sidecar beside me."

"Be glad to." She lifted her face toward the sun enjoying its warmth.

The motor bike was running sooner than expected. However, before they left the sergeant stepped forward with two aviator helmets and some goggles.

"Better put these on," he advised Kurt. "Cause this one-lane road gets so bumpy up ahead that it really makes the dust fly."

"Then you'll need this to cover part of your face if the dust gets bad," said Bela, removing the gray scarf from under her raincoat's collar.

"Like a western cowboy." Kurt grinned. "But what about you?"

"I can always duck my head, but you can't."

"She's right." The sergeant took the scarf from Bela and threw it over Kurt's shoulder.

"And watch out in Berlin," Richard warned, giving Kurt a hearty handshake, and Bela a warm hug. "Since the way we hear it, those no account Russians can get real mean."

* * *

"That's what the Germans are saying," Kurt replied, leaning slightly against Bela as she tied the scarf around his neck She turned shining eyes toward him, and in the fresh air the events they'd shared earlier appeared to lose some of their unpleasantness.

"It's a lovely day, Bela," he said, swinging his leg over the motor bike's seat.

"A beautiful surprise." A warm glow clearly flowed through her, as his arm brushed against her shoulder when she climbed in the sidecar.

Taken aback by this break from all the tension, he turned toward her, overjoyed, as he cranked the motor bike's engine, opened the throttle, and shot forward.

He smiled as he whizzed down the winding road behind the truck. And taking a deep breath of the cleansing air, he surveyed the road's landscape of tractor trails, abandoned fields, and a small farmhouse with a copse of birch trees in front of it... where flocks of dark-winged birds warbled merrily on their long branches.

He followed the truck through the country's pine-scented hills for miles, slowing down and angling around the rough spots in the dirt road.

"There must be a lake or river around here," said Bela, her voice close to his ear.

"Appears to be, since I saw a narrow path back there leading to a small bridge."

The sky had the same blue brilliance as her eyes, with spangles of silver shining in them from the morning light. And despite her helmet, strands of her golden-hair fluttered in the breeze.

A gleaming mist filled the air with a ray of sunlight piercing it. And her eyes met his with a warmth that made his spirits soar.

He had nothing to look forward to without her. Yet, his future after Berlin would be marked with the desolation of empty days, once they said their goodbyes and parted company.

All too soon— but still a long way off. *'Because unlike peace... which is more sedate, time in war is like a chameleon,'* his father-in-law had pointed out. *'Changing often with its goals and obligations to assure victory.'*

CHAPTER TWENTY -TWO

"The von Friesens have been anxiously awaiting the news of your whereabouts," the pilot told Bela and Kurt as they boarded the plane sent to take them to the Stuttgart Airport. "And *boy* were they ever excited when they learned you'd been found."

"I hope they knew we were too," said Kurt, helping Bela into her seat. He felt around in his rucksack. "We'll finish eating what's left of Ina's sandwiches and cookies once we're in the air."

"I'm for it since we've missed a few meals."

They settled in the plane quickly and began eating. And afterwards, he opened his strong arms to her, and she snuggled against him. "The Germans killed your father, didn't they?"

Her mouth firmed. "The Arrow-Cross militia with the Gestapo tossed his body in the Danube."

"What about your fiancé?"

"Yanni? They killed him too."

"Was he Jewish?" Kurt asked, gazing at her with a haggard expression.

She nodded. His poignant memory never far from her mind. "But I would have married him even if he hadn't been."

"Do you have his picture?"

"In this coin purse in my raincoat pocket," she said, taking it out. "Jaclyn kept my pictures in my journal she brought from Budapest."

"Good for her." He stared at the picture, for a long, solemn moment before saying, "His hair is as light as yours. And like you, he looks Aryan."

"Which helped him with the Germans," Bela remarked, thinking how a lifetime had passed since they'd held each other. "But in the end it was the plain goodness of his innocent heart that got him killed."

"I suppose you miss him like I do my wife."

"I would— had it not been for the shame of the Love Camp.... "Her voice trailed off when she put his picture back. "But now I just try not to think about him because each time I do the pain is so great, it makes me feel like I'm walking barefoot on jagged rocks."

Kurt's chin now rested gently on the top of her head. "I can understand that."

"It would have killed him if he'd lived to learn what happened to me—"

"As it would most men who love a woman," he interjected, before adding in a strained tone, "I've given you my whole heart, Bela, but after what my kind has done to you, I know it's not enough."

Gently, she tugged at his sleeve in supplication. "Still, you mustn't talk about my *Kurt* in such a self-loathing manner, "she scolded, tearing up so badly, she quickly changed the subject. "When my mother died, my father took her body to Jerusalem and buried her there in the city's renowned Jewish cemetery."

"I 'm familiar with it," he remarked, his hand closing over hers. "It's the place where the Jews believe that when the Messiah comes, the bones of those buried there will be resurrected first."

"My father wanted to be buried there and—" She stifled a cry. "And when the war was over, we were talking about moving there."

* * *

The extent of her suffering continued to make Kurt's blood run cold. A wrong he wanted very much to remedy to ease the agony of his mind as well as hers. *'But it's not going to happen, since this past I cannot heal is part of my punishment,'* he came close to saying as he stared out the plane's window with a stoic acceptance of his guilt for so much death.

"I never wanted people—even my innocent, young recruits— to be treated like your father. But honor meant loyalty to the Reich. So I became a highly disciplined soldier whose duty was to follow orders." His pain intensified as this canvas of terrible memories imprinted on his heart returned. "Our *Fuhrer* was a madman to attack Russia, with often chest-high snow in the winter! A coldness that made the simple act of having a bowel movement quite dangerous for three of my men. Who died painfully because they froze to death.

"'Dying like this means we're soiled in the eyes of God,' one of the men uttered as he drew his final breath. While another begged my lieutenant to shoot him."

Bela pressed a finger against his lips. "Kurt—please."

"No, hear me out." He paused, looking imploringly at her. "Even tough I wasn't one of the men pulling the triggers, I was made to witness the slaughter of *Ivan's* partisans— many of whom were women—by my fellow soldiers." He took her hand and held it close to his chest. "Which later became a tacit reminder of my guilt, for being part of an inhumanity that did such terrible things. Because as someone once said, 'we learn the truth about ourselves when we examine our lives closely.'"

"But you killed Russian men, didn't you?"

"Twenty—to be exact. Which I was forced to do to keep them from killing me or my men."

Her voice broke miserably. "I... I realize how you must feel," she stuttered, her fingers trembling in his hand. "But you did what you had to do."

"Like the girls in the Love Camp, who had to be sterilized to keep from having babies."

"You knew that?" she asked, surprised.

"My heart knew it," he said, more pain continuing to pierce him. "There was no birth control at the Love Camp. And now that I know you were Jewish, sterilization was the only way Germans could be allowed to have sex with Jews. It's just that—" His eyes teared up as a moment of breathless silence followed. "After all you'd suffered, my mind had difficulty accepting it."

"I understand." She gulped hard, brushing back tears." And I regret that I could never give you another little boy."

"The OSS discussed medical experiments and sterilizations at the concentration camps, with all of us German prisoners, but never once did I hear them mention the Love Camps. Although it stood to reason that women forced to be barracks-room whores, would be made to undergo something that destroyed their final essence."

"Indeed," she agreed in a dispirited tone. "So I allowed myself to drift into the darkness, since in those days all I could hope for was survival." "In this terrible age of death camps."

"Which meant I was forced to become an army whore with feigned smiles."

"Something that sadly amounted to a slow death," he acknowledged, hugging her hard. "And others may not understand it but nevertheless, like me, you did what you had to do." He gazed into her blue eyes thoughtfully. "Just know this— I don't have to have another little boy. Wolf and Jaclyn don't have children and—"

"They don't have children," she broke in, "because they say the world is too insane to bring them into it."

"Which sounds to me like they have a good point."

"You say that now, Kurt, but you lost a child. And down the road, knowing you'll never have another little boy of your flesh would be quite painful to me, as well as you."

"Then it would be something we'd just have to learn to deal with."

Blinking rapidly, she touched their joined hands. "But if I'm not around, then you wouldn't have to."

God— was there no absolution? It wrenched his heart to hear her say it because after the abuse she'd received, he didn't see her surviving for very long. *And without* her, *my* longing heart has nothing else.

A silence lingered between them until she whispered. "You seem lost in thought, Kurt."

He slanted his head, frowning, at the grim reminder of the circumstances of peacetime and their separation. "I was."

"Was it about Berlin?"

"Always Berlin... but what are we going to tell Jaclyn and Wolf about those Germans we killed?"

"Cut the details and simply say they attacked us, and we shot them."

"Sounds good." He nodded. "And the money?"

"I doubt Wolf would approve of us taking such a large amount to a war-torn city, so we'd better wait until afterwards before we tell him."

"What I was thinking."

She placed her hand on Kurt's arm. But I sense something besides Berlin is bothering you, so it must be about your returning to that prisoner-of -war camp."

"It's not." He shook his head in an attempt to ease her. "It's just something I feel you should know."

"Then tell me," she said in a soothing tone.

"Call me sentimental, melodramatic, or whatever...? " He shrugged, giving her an affectionate look. "But if I'd been a guard at Auschwitz or another camp— " He averted his eyes as the sadness between them allowed another uneasy silence to pass before he proceeded. "And if you'd been a prisoner I couldn't save from the gas chambers, then I'd have pushed my way into the center of the women and died with you."

"What my heart's already told me, Kurt." She clutched his arm tightly. "And I know it's what people would call a sentimental rush, but in the end it's the thought that counts."

"I agree."

Looking like her heart was running over, she grew still. "Even though I suspect if you'd been a guard with a gun, you'd have shot to death as many of the S.S. as you could before it came to our dying together in a gas chamber."

"Possibly... but at the risk of getting myself killed and leaving you to die alone, I don't know."

"It's all hypothetical."

"But the fact that most of the girls in the Love Camp were killed because they were Jewish wasn't hypothetical," he remarked, seeing again the electric, rail-sharp wire wall.

* * *

"Sadly it wasn't." Bela sighed, her tears threatening to return. "And the S.S. chose them because they were Aryan- looking or Kardashian Jews like me."

"Who weren't from the seed of Abraham."

"Correct." She looked away, fighting for self-control as his fingers pressed her hand. "And when the S.S. slaughtered those with three reports—"

"—they called it '*liberated from life,*' like you said. Which is the reason ObersturmFuhrer Helmer tried to get you to kill yourself."

"Which confuses me because the Gestapo man who came to get me—ObersturmFuhrer Helmer's friend— told him I was Aryan."

"But he knew better, don't you think?"

"Probably."

"But what about Madam Kollar?" he asked, turning the conversation. "If I'd *really* believed we'd meet again like she said, I wouldn't have been so upset when the Tommies took me prisoner."

Bela edged forward in her seat. "And if I'd believed her, I wouldn't have been shocked when you showed up at Albert's."

"The Tommies are trying to re-educate *us* German prisoners of war—"

"So the OSS said."

"But did they mention they were showing movies of some of the atrocities at Auschwitz and taking pictures of our faces as we watched them?"

"No. But where did they get these movies? From the Russians?"

"They wouldn't say. But I suspect from the Red Cross, since the Russians had them helping with the sickly Auschwitz prisoners. Though, the way the German prisoners are being treated, this re-education the Tommies are doing is amounting to a huge task."

"Albert mentioned they abused you, but we weren't supposed to be talking about it."

"We're not." He turned to her with an uncertain look. "But since Germany bombed Britain, when the Tommies greeted us prisoners, they called themselves the British S.S. and got aggressive."

"So they tortured you?"

"Let's just say that since they thought I had information they needed—which I didn't—they didn't treat me very well."

"I don't care if we're not supposed to be talking about it, what did they do to you?" she prodded, quite shaken.

"Let's see," Kurt said. "Since I was a commanding officer, the British took away all my clothes but my underpants. Because it lowers a man's self-esteem during an interrogation. And then after calling me a' *fucking German*,' they made me walk in a circle, so they could kick me and give my butt a lick with a schoolmaster's paddle each time I completed it...with bruises easier to explain at the hospital than whip cuts. And it was this abuse that caused my legs and butt to ache with jolts of pain, when they ordered me to clean a staircase with a tiny, damp rag, while they dumped buckets of filthy mop water over my head."

Bela's mouth opened in dismay. "Kurt, your punishment was similar to mine. So why didn't you tell me?"

"Because your inhumane treatment was so incomprehensible, mine wasn't worth mentioning."

Her eyes streamed with empathy. "I disagree... but still they were bound to have known your relationship to Albert and von Lehmann."

"I didn't tell them because I didn't expect them to believe me," he remarked in a crisp tone. "Since I later learned that Albert, like my father-in-law, was having difficulty finding out what had happened to me when it seemed I hadn't made it to Poland."

"Then how'd they find you?"

"Well." He signed, glancing at her self-consciously. "On my second interrogation—where once again I was made to face them in only my underpants, the Tommies told me they owned me body and soul. So, I'd better tell them all I knew.

"They ranted on and on. And when I still had no information for them, they back-handed me in the mouth several times and kicked me. Actions that made me so angry it prompted me to be daring and ask them if slavery wasn't against the Geneva Convention."

Bela shuddered inwardly. "And it angered them, didn't it?"

"Of course... still, I should have known better and kept my mouth shut— even if they were in violation of it. Because then the biggest, meanest guard in the camp threw me facedown, tore off my underpants, and with his boot exerting pressure on my left shoulder, gave me fifteen very hard licks on my bare butt with that schoolmaster's paddle. And afterwards took me to an underground solitary- confinement cell with a wet floor where— wet floor or not— sitting was completely out of the question after the punishment they'd inflicted on me." Then he hesitated... (this way you're still in Bela's point of view, which is good) like he was concerned that even if she'd asked him, it seemed he couldn't help but feel a stab of remorse for exposing her to his abuse. "Undoubtedly a crack in my defenses," he murmured. So as if to fortify himself, he took a deep breath before adding, "Where I was made to spend the night naked."

"Naked on a wet floor!" she exclaimed. "It's a wonder it didn't kill you."

"I was on fire with pain and after they left, I cried. But believe it or not, my pain was still more about what was happening to you than my bruised and battered body—"

"*Me?* At this terrible time in your life?"

"You never left my thoughts. And the next morning when they found me, I was on the verge of pneumonia from being on that wet floor all night. So they rushed me to the hospital."

"Which surprises me."

"Not me. Since I guess they were afraid of the Geneva Convention, Red Cross, or the OSS. Because I remember a nurse asking a doctor why so many German prisoners were in the hospital these days. And what had happened that caused me to fall down the flight of stairs I was cleaning—"

"Which obviously you didn't answer."

"If I did I don't remember because I was semi-conscious and stayed that way most of my time there, giving the Tommies the idea I might talk. So they sent someone to watch over me." He smiled as he informed her what followed. "And did they ever learn a lot."

"About von Lehmann and Albert?"

"And you."

"*Me* again?" she questioned, her hands trembling on his shoulder.

"I was told I kept mumbling about a girl in an S.S. camp called *Goldilocks.* And was so desperate to save her, I was willing to do anything."

Amazed, she shook her head. "Your feelings continue to astound me."

"It's the way I felt. With this time, the Tommies believing me when I said I had no information for them. So I decided to let them know I was related to von Lehmann and Albert....which was a good thing.... Because when I got out of the hospital the Tommies— in conjunction with the Americans — put me with some prisoners who'd volunteered to go back to Germany on dangerous missions that infiltrated the enemy lines."

"A place I'm sure got you better treatment."

He nodded. "We had good food, attended morning classes, played soccer in the afternoon, and saw Hollywood cinemas at night—plus got plenty of rest."

"For which I'm thankful."

He lightly kissed her lips. "As I am for *you*."

CHAPTER TWENTY-THREE

The plane landed. And after it taxied its way to the parking area, Kurt and Bela exited the aircraft. "Welcome back," Wolf said, the minute their feet hit the tarmac.

"We've been so worried about you, "Jaclyn cried, giving Bela a kiss and Kurt a hug, "But how are you two feeling?"

"Like someone who's been attacked by Germans and lived to tell about it," Bela answered.

"When we get back from Berlin, Albert's meeting us in London," Wolf told her. "And we're going to make an official complaint about all this with the Ros-venor office."

"So we're going to Berlin after all?" Kurt asked him.

"You'll have to find out from the medic who's standing over there to check the two of you for possible injuries," he said, pointing at a tent next to a Quonset hut, serving as a terminal. "And the man standing beside him is waiting to brief you."

Kurt looped his arm through Bela's. "Then that's where we're headed."

The examination went smoother than he and Bela had expected. "Your mission's still on," said the medic. "And the *Dakota*, your transport plane, will depart for Berlin at eight tomorrow morning."

Clearly relieved, Jaclyn smiled and pointed at a car on a smooth road beside the runway. "The driver's waiting to take us back to the house where're we're staying. And we'll have dinner late so you can clean up first."

Kurt touched Bela's sleeve. "Then we'd better get going."

It was a short ride and when they got there, a middle-aged woman wearing an apron with a red flower pattern on it, was standing on the porch of a large, two-story house waiting to greet them." *Frau* Bauer," Jaclyn said,"meet *Herr* Ulrich and *Fraulein* Spigel."

"My pleasure." She bowed slightly. "So please come inside."

"*Frau* Bauer manages this place for an elderly man who lives with his daughter,"said Jaclyn, appearing to like the woman and the way she kept the house."

The floor in the entryway had been recently scrubbed with a lemon-smelling wax, that made it shine like a piece of fine porcelain.

"I'm preparing veal, chicken, and a thick lentil soup for your dinner this evening," *Frau* Bauer announced in a friendly voice.

"Then we're living high." Kurt smiled, admiring the white flowers growing in a window box.

"*Frau* Bauer has two children—a boy and a girl," Jaclyn whispered to him. "But sadly her husband was recently killed on the Eastern Front in a bombing."

"In a village?"

"No a field. And his commanding officer thought his men would be safe if they hid under a haystack, but they weren't."

A pang hit him as memories of his own lovely wife and child surfaced. "I can understand how she must feel." He looked over at Wolf. "But which way to the men's bath?"

"This way." He pointed at a long hallway.

Kurt felt a deep sense of relief. "Good we have such a nice place."

It was a late dinner like Jaclyn said. And throughout it, Kurt sat close to Bela, buttering her bread and making sure her wine glass was always full.

Jaclyn and Wolf appeared to take note of his attentiveness. But when Kurt leaned over and planted a kiss on Bela's cheek, Wolf glared at him with a disgruntled look. "At the table?"

"Why not?" He shrugged, inclining his head toward her. "Going to have to shave again, if I keep giving kisses to someone as pretty as you, Bela." He took her hand and caressed it. "Especially since you smell so good."

She smiled. "*Frau* Bauer gave me some make-up and perfume."

"Now that was thoughtful of her," Kurt said, returning her smile. "Very."

* * *

Their rooms were upstairs. And Bela, standing at the foot of the stairs, took one of the keys from *Frau* Bauer, that apparently she'd forgotten to give her earlier.

"The sheets in all the rooms smell like lye soap, because I personally washed them with it," she told her.

Kurt took his key. "Certainly good to hear after what Bela and I've been through."

Jaclyn nudged Bela. "You and Kurt continue to be getting along well, and I'm happy for you."

"He saved me."

"As he says you did him."

Bela's room joined Kurt's, but *Frau* Bauer had given her another key so she could lock the door between them.

"I guess you're already thinking about how hard it is for me to get a good night's sleep with my nightmare problem," Bela remarked as they climbed the stairs. "So if I cry out or something, don't let it bother you."

"Then maybe I should stay with you?"

"Then maybe you should."

"We need to look out for each other as long as we can," Kurt said, standing so close she felt the heat of his body. "And I'd say I'd leave my clothes on, but since I'm leaving them outside the door to be cleaned, then all I've got to sleep in is this heavy, cotton robe *Frau* Bauer gave me."

"Same as this flowery dress under my raincoat."

He slid his rucksack off his shoulder. "Jaclyn said she bought the dress for you from *Frau* Bauer. And I must say it looked wonderful on you at dinner. Though, what's got me worried is how you're planning on getting it to Berlin?"

Bela stifled a yawn. "Don't know, but I 'd hate to lose it since I especially like the way hand- painted, rose buttons go all the way down its front."

"Then let me suggest you roll it up and put it in this." He patted his rucksack lightly.

"And it won't be too crowded?"

"Not at all. Since I'm giving my thermos and medical kit to *Frau* Bauer."

"Then the problem's solved."

"But your dress is made of such thin cotton, I doubt it'll keep you warm.""

"It won't. Which was my great excuse to keep from having my raincoat cleaned when *Frau* Bauer took my slacks and sweater."

"And it was an excellent one—"

"Especially with no place to hide the money but in its secret pocket."

"Lucky for *us*." Kurt glanced at the raincoat, then at her. "But how about in the morning we divide the money in separate packets and oilskin wrap them to keep them dry—"

"But will *Frau* Bauer have oilskin?" Bela interjected.

"If she's like most Germans, who've had to protect their papers and other valuables from leaks caused from by all the bombings."

"Dividing it is a great idea. Since my count shows we have three thousand, five hundred dollars, in one-hundred-dollar bills."

"Wow!" Kurt exclaimed. "That's certainly a little more than I first thought."

"But still you were close."

"Then if we have the money in packets with rubber bands around them, and we're forced to bargain with *Ivan,* we won't have to put all our cards on the table."

"My feeling exactly."

He brushed back a loose strand of hair on her cheek. What would you think if I gave the recently widowed *Frau* Bauer one of those one-hundred- dollar bills."

A smile warmed Bela's mouth. "That it would be the right thing to do."

He opened his arms to her, bringing her closer. "I like being next to you."

"The same as I do you," she said, kissing him and locking her arms around his waist.

"Which later, I hope you don't come to view as a weakness."

"I won't. Considering it was your strength that's sustained me these past two days."

"I was trying to be like a sanctuary for you."

"And you were." She ran a hand down his back. "Even if it does sound a little cold after all you've done for me."

"If it sounds cold, then it's because I'm being realistic." He turned around.

"The Germans murdered your people, so what can you see in me besides protection? That will vanish like a mist once we once we part."

"You know if I could say '*I love you,*' I would."

"But you can't, which I understand— even if we do still have a need for each other." His lips briefly touched hers. "So no one should blame you for the way you feel."

She sat down on the edge of the bed. "Then if you don't mind, hold me so I'll get a good night's sleep."

"Absolutely."

She reached up and lightly stroked his hair. "It smells wonderful."

"I washed it and put the French brilliantine on it *Frau* Bauer gave me."

"She was certainly generous with this French perfume and make-up I received from her."

* * *

Kurt's lips touched Bela's again, only this time it was reminiscent of a goodnight kiss. "If you'll move a little closer to the window, *liebchen*, it'll be easier for me to curl up beside you."

"I will. But it's this quilted bedcover that's taking up the space, so I'll move it." A moment passed as she pushed it to the foot of the bed. "Is this better now?"

"Much. "He smiled, snuggling against her warmth as their bodies joined with a comforting closeness. "I know things are complicated between us but nevertheless, holding you like this is sheer bliss."

"I'm flattered you think that," she whispered, placing a gentle hand on his arm, before pulling the sheet up to her neck.

'*Certainly a night to cherish,*' he was tempted to say, even if the sheet covering her made it difficult for him to feel her bare arms, the way he had on the cottage's hard bench and in the brush.

So much for the intimate sharing of secrets, plans, and dreams., and the pain our separation will bring. For if my dream of having her as my future wife would come true, then she'd have my assurance she'd never be lost in the dark again.

CHAPTER TWENTY-FOUR

T he upstairs bathtub the ladies use is this way, *Frau* von Friesen," *Frau* Bauer told her, turning abruptly and heading down a corridor on the west side of the house.

Jaclyn followed behind her until she saw Bela, waiting in front of it, for the towels and soap *Frau* Bauer was bringing. "It's all right, little sister, if you want to go ahead of me."

But she shook her head. " I'm happy to wait. So help yourself to some of the soap and towels."

Jaclyn smiled. "Wolf's waiting for me downstairs and—"

"Then hurry and get a move on," Bela urged giving her a playful shove. Which she did.

"I can't remember how long it's been since I've seen such a dazzling smile on Bela's lips," she told Wolf as soon as she saw him standing by the desk in the house's entryway.

"Aren't you excited?"

"*Absolutely not.*" He shot an irritated look at her. "Because Kurt's the worst possible man for her."

"Why? Because he was near Lake Balaton on the Eastern Front?"

"That's part of it."

"Well I'm sorry to disappoint you, but from the looks of things he's making Bela happy in a way we never could."

"She probably thinks aligning herself with a German is a way of forgetting the war. Or maybe she feels protected if something like it ever happens again—but *she's* wrong."

"Wrong?" Jaclyn glared at him. "I personally like seeing the familiarity between them."

"Which is obvious," he cut in. "And it continues to disappoint me."

"Something I find difficult to understand."

"O-oh you understand it. It's just that you have difficulty admitting it because you know as well as I do, that familiarity in such a short amount of time can only mean *one* thing—"

"Which is?"

"That Kurt may have known Bela in Vienna, but met up with her again at the Love Camp."

"I doubt that." Jaclyn flared, reacting to the challenge she heard in her husband's voice.

"Since even with that coffee spill, their fateful meeting at Demel's sounded normal to me."

"Not to me, with Bela only thirteen." He shook his head before adding belatedly, "Which is a little young for a man like Kurt, who would have been finishing at the university."

Frustration seized Jaclyn at the disbelief she heard in Wolf's voice. "Kurt's so handsome he was probably her first crush," she said, grasping at possibilities. "Which makes me suspect he humored her with a brief friendship."

"Brief friendship?" Wolf questioned skeptically. "And they didn't become lovers?"

"W...what!" Jaclyn exclaimed, not believing what she was hearing. "You know Bela had restraints and discipline few people have. A puritan's pride... when it came to suitors." Then she continued in a sinking tone, "Since just thinking about what the Nazis did to young girls like her almost killed me."

"Well Hitler took over Vienna not long after she supposedly met Kurt," Wolf pointed out. "And she went to Budapest, and he to Berlin. Where he fell in love with a woman and married her. And later, Bela met up with Yanni in Budapest, who loved her so much he wanted to take her to Palestine after the war—"

"And she loved him too," Jaclyn replied sharply.

"*So... she... said.*" Wolf's tone was chiding as he emphasized each word. "Though, it seemed to me he was more like a brother than a sweetheart."

"Not *to me.*" She regarded him with a speculative gaze. "But what are you suggesting? That there was someone she'd known in Vienna she couldn't forget?"

"Kurt Ulrich. Who married someone else."

"And was about the same age as you, Wolf?"

"Indeed he was." He appeared to reflect more. "It's just that the part about he and Bela, a Jewish girl, meeting in Vienna at a coffee shop eight or nine years ago and never forgetting each other, just doesn't add up."

Jaclyn struggled to keep her voice steady. "How so? Bela looks Aryan, so he probably didn't know she was Jewish."

"Even so something about the time-line isn't right." Wolf's mouth tightened. "Because Bela and Haral left Vienna when she was only thirteen years old, and was too young to go to Demel's without her father or *you.* Which is one of the reasons I intend to question Kurt about his purported friendship with her in Vienna."

"Who *said* Haral wasn't with her?'" Jaclyn frowned, her resentment growing. "He probably was. So I don't know what you think you're going to accomplish by questioning Kurt. Since it's quite obvious he and Bela have feelings for each other."

Wolf shook his head again. "She might, but have you considered he just might be trying to have an affair with her before he goes back to prison?"

His question hit Jaclyn like a blast of cold air. "It's none of our business." she snapped, thinking about the instant attraction she'd seen between Kurt and Bela.

"Maybe, maybe not. Though if Kurt did reunite with Bela at the Love Camp, then what I want to know is why he didn't talk that *damned* ObersturmFuhrer Helmer into giving her some kind of housekeeping job?" He stopped as if reviewing the circumstances. "Or did Kurt have himself a *little time* with her, like the other Wehrmacht soldiers were doing with the girls there?"

Jaclyn tilted her chin in a disbelieving challenge. "Surely you're not going to question him it about that—"

"And *just* why not?"

"Because Kurt and Bela are happy. And that being the case, I'm not worried."

"*You* might not be, but I am," Wolf responded sharply. "Since if he has a past with Bela, then for the sake of our mission I need to know just what exactly it was!"

* * *

Kurt was shaving in the downstairs bath when Wolf barged in on him. "Stay away from Bela!" he warned. "Because things between a German and a Jewish girl can never work out. And if you don't believe me, then wait until the world gets its final death count of all the Jews slaughtered by the Nazis! Why it'll be astronomical. Five million? Six million? Clearly a past we as human beings can't go back and erase."

"I'm going back to prison, and Jaclyn tells me Bela's moving to Palestine with the two of you," said Kurt, staring at Wolf in the mirror. "But in the meantime if I can comfort her in some way that might help her, then I want to do it."

"*Comfort?*" Wolf questioned, followed by an expletive. "Now *what* exactly is that supposed to mean? Exploiting some masochistic affection she feels for you after what you did to her in the Love Camp?"

Resenting the way his cousin lacked the vision to see how much he cared for Bela, Kurt swung around angrily. "What makes you think I was the man who visited her at the Love Camp?"

"Really now—" Wolf sneered. "What's the good of my asking you, after a Gestapo man informed me that a relative of mine in the Wehrmacht had visited the place?" His eyes seemed to blaze with a savage inner fire as he added, "And as I'm sure you've already heard me say, you're the only relative I had who was stupid enough to join the Wehrmacht."

"I love Bela," said Kurt, not hesitating to make his feelings known. "And I know it sounds strange, but it's like I've known her and loved her forever."

More curses fell from Wolf's mouth. "Maybe in some twisted Nazi way, but to my thinking— once a beast always a beast. So be forewarned that if you touch her between now and the end of our Berlin trip, then cousin or not I'll kill you." His tone rang with a chilling-arctic finality— "Because

I've said it before, and I'll say it again, if she ends up with you, she'll never be able to stop thinking about that *God-awful* Love Camp."

Kurt knew Wolf meant it about killing him. But it didn't bother him nearly as much as what he said about the world getting the astronomical death count of the Jews slaughtered by the Nazis. For if that were true, then he greatly feared Bela would not even remain his friend after their Berlin mission was over.

CHAPTER TWENTY-FIVE

Early morning May 2, 1945

"I n case you didn't hear," said Wolf, standing in front of the house where they were staying, "the *Fuhrer's* death was officially announced last night on the radio with the news of the surrender. And because communications in Berlin are poor and many people no longer have radios, a fair percentage of the millions living there may not have heard." He then turned to Jaclyn, Bela, and Kurt. "But the important thing now is *our* mission. So we go to Berlin, identify von Lehmann, and hopefully learn something about his missing preliminary designs for the V-3 Cannon Rocket."

Wolf stared at Kurt. "And if we should happen to identify von Lehmann, then we need to discuss his escape to London with our White Russian friends' plan before the die-hard Nazis or Stalin grab him, but —" He broke off suddenly. "However, should von Lehmann be dead and his designs destroyed, then we'll be expected to confirm it. So the sooner we get on the trail of what *Doktor Grossklos Knows*, the better." He checked his watch. "But for now, our pilot is waiting for us in his *Dakota.*"

BERLIN —9:00 a.m. May 2, 1945 "You can't land," came a voice from a wireless operator to their pilot, seated in front of them in his *Dakota,* as he adjusted the headsets against his ears.

"Can't land?" The pilot looked out the plane's window.

"The Russians like to impress people with their hard-line," Wolf told him. "So just land at Gatow as planned. Since the Russians have the city surrounded."

"I have no intention of doing otherwise." He pointed the plane's nose through the dense plumes of black smoke clouding the city.

Rubber screeched on the shell-marked runway as its wheels bumped against it.

Grimacing, Jaclyn shuddered at the ugly sound. "Rougher than I thought possible."

"Just part of the city's desolation," Wolf reminded. At the end of the runway sat an open truck surrounded by fierce-looking, Russian soldiers with their bayoneted rifles ready for the outsiders. "We give you orders to stay away," yelled a major in halting English. "So why you not listen?"

"Because the four of us have been cleared to visit," said Wolf in a sharp voice. "And I have papers to prove it."

"Who gave you those papers?" asked a captain beside him, in a steely, overbearing tone obviously meant to squelch any opposition.

"His Majesty's Government with the consent of your Lieutenant-Colonel Anton Nikolai Sokolov. "Wolf snapped open his briefcase and handed him the documents verifying what he was saying. "So if you'd take us to him now, we'd be much obliged."

The captain glared at him, then gazed at the documents with reluctance. "But these papers say you should have arrived yesterday."

"I know," replied Wolf, now making a serious effort at diplomacy. "But our train came under fire."

"A train attack?" remarked the stout major in his halting English, shaking his head as though suddenly sympathetic. "I...I surprised you not injured."

"Some of us were," said Wolf.

"Yet you still come?"

"Only because I'm writing a history book about the Berlin invasion. And your Russian colonel agreed when His Majesty's Government informed him that my wife, standing here, is Jaclyn Tirand."

"A name I hear before," said the major.

"As has your colonel," replied Wolf. "Who has allowed our coming as long as my wife and her piano accompanist provide him with a private concert upon arrival."

"Which we really shouldn't have been required to do," said Jaclyn, "even if the colonel does claim to like music."

The major frowned at Wolf. "And your pilot? What about him?"

"Colonel Sololov has made it very plain in this paper he's signed, that the pilot's free to leave," said Wolf. "And he's to return around eight this evening to pick us up... but if he's delayed—"

"Then you stay here under Soviet guard," the major cut him short.

"At Gatow?" Wolf questioned, glowering at him.

"Correct."

A rather tense moment passed before the captain took the liberty of adding, "Since these papers do verify the colonel has agreed you and your team could observe us in the battle for Berlin and take notes for your history book."

"Like I told you," Wolf reminded, irked "Then get in the truck," ordered the captain. "And we'll head to a place not far from Gatow's Central Control."

But Wolf lingered, convinced the German guns on the tower of the anti-aircraft Zoo Bunker were continuing to fire at the Russians.

"You *heard* him—get inside!" shouted one of the officers as his men pointed their bayoneted rifles at the open military truck.

* * *

Same as the Germans did us, Bela recalled. For like Albert had said, '*The city is in torment. With its people taking refuge from the rapes and looting in its gutted -out buildings and ruined houses littered with debris and fallen cables.*'

As she looked beyond the airport, her hand went to her chest. The black smoke from the hundreds of fires still burning were proof to her that nothing in the city had escaped destruction.

But what had Germany done to deserve this? She didn't have to ask as she gazed at the city with dizzied senses. "No light, no darkness, just death and blood," she said, frowning at the smells of smoke and stagnant pools of water from the city's broken mains.

The bodies of three dead German soldiers hung from lamp posts with a large sign reading *Traitors* written in blood. "Berlin's death throes," Kurt remarked, when the truck rolled over a blood-encrusted body in a gray, Luftwaffe uniform. "And sadly the innocent suffer along with the guilty."

When they reached the colonel's newly acquired office, the major pounded on the door with Lieutenant-Colonel Anton Nikolai Sokolov's name on it, until an inside guard swung it back with his rifle butt and bade him come in.

"It does seem they're ready for us," Bela whispered to Jaclyn, looking at a cello, piano, and two benches that had been placed on the far side of the colonel's office. But other than that, there was only a desk, telephone, file cabinet, and four chairs. The back of one had a lopsided portrait of Stalin—Russia's man of steel— propped against it.

"Now that surprises me." Jaclyn told Bela. "But where do you suppose the colonel is?"

"Can't imagine." She looked from the piano to the door. "But wherever he is, we need to hurry and get this concert he's expecting over, because we'll be losing time if he doesn't show up soon."

Jaclyn gazed at the room with a critical squint. "I wish there was some way we could have snuck in."

"Not easy to do when you're surrounded by Russian bullets," Wolf said as he put the briefcase on the colonel's desk. "Which it would have been deemed undiplomatic, since we're supposed to be among allies."

Once again the door swung open only this time, to the obvious relief of everyone, Colonel Sokolov appeared. He wore a peaked, visor hat with a red band around it and a gold badge with the Soviet star in its center.

Bela noted he was a handsome, dark-haired man in his late twenties like Kurt. However, he had a peculiar gentleness in his face that conflicted with the rank he held.

And it surprised her, because the OSS had warned them to beware of such men since they possessed the same arrogance and brutality as a highly-disciplined S.S. officer.

The major gave Sokolov a flawless salute before introducing him to Wolf and the group. "My pleasure," remarked the colonel, in his excellent English. He traded handshakes with them, before removing his hat and placing it on his desk. "And I was especially pleased when I learned that

Fraulein Tirand and *Herr* Ulrich were able to survive the train attack without any serious injuries."

"Jaclyn and I included," said Wolf.

"Naturally, because they're your relatives, and *Herr* Ulrich is a former Berliner—"

"Who's quite anxious to move around the city in the short amount time we have," Kurt spoke up.

The colonel nodded. "Understandable. Since *Herr* von Friesen is writing a book about the Russians securing Berlin with its occupation. And I know all of you wish to observe and take notes as you move through the city—" He glanced at the papers in the open briefcase Wolf had placed on his desk. "Although, that may not be possible today with the information we're receiving about the Freedom Marching Berliners."

"Freedom Marching Berliners?" Wolf questioned.

"Yes. They're making a bit of trouble. So my two agents, Victor and Peter, will be assigned to keep watch over you and your two lovely ladies, who will soon be entertaining me with their music."

"Didn't Fieszel mention those two agents in our final briefing?" Wolf asked Kurt.

"If I remember correctly."

The colonel stepped over to Jaclyn and Bela. "The very talented Jaclyn Tirand." He smiled, giving her hand a warm shake. "The pleasure is all mine."

But before she could respond, he took Bela's hand... allowing it to linger a little too long in his hold. "And you must be the beautiful, young sister I've been looking forward to meeting," he said, making no bones about it. "Which is a pity your brief time here does not give us the opportunity to get better acquainted—"

"Her time is brief here," interrupted Kurt, grasping Bela's hand possessively, "because this young woman and I are being married next week."

A lie...even if it didn't stop Wolf and Jaclyn from exchanging dumbfounded looks with each other.

"Then you're a very lucky man, *Herr* Ulrich," said the colonel, frowning slightly as he turned to straighten the lopsided portrait of Stalin. "But since in these times we snatch what pleasure we can, then we'd best get on with the music these two lovely ladies have so graciously agree to provide me with—" The telephone ringing interrupted him, and he quickly stopped and picked it up.

"Are they working in most parts of the city and suburbs now?" Wolf asked the major.

"Indeed—and all because of *us* Russians."

Immediately the colonel began speaking in Russian like he was under attack, even though the look on his face said otherwise. *A born risk-taker.*

* * *

"What's he saying, Kurt?" Wolf asked in a barely audible voice.

"It sounds like he's arguing that he hasn't made as big a blunder as this Marshal Zhukov— who it seems is calling not far from the Reichstag—is implying" Kurt craned his neck, straining to make an educated guess at what the person on the other end of the phone was saying. "Even if it appears the person he's talking to isn't convinced."

"Too bad." Wolf smiled, the idea clearly pleasing him. "But what else?"

"That valuable scientists have been killed and their information lost, because he's one of the senior commanders who's allowed the Red Army—"Kurt stopped, allowing a heavy silence to fall before adding in a low voice— "particularly the Mongols, who've plundered Berlin's suburbs indiscriminately."

"Couldn't happen to a better person than our Colonel Sokolov," Wolf remarked looking directly at him. With an arrest following his denunciation."

"The way our *ally* Stalin works, "Kurt muttered.

"Exactly." Wolf's mouth curved into a bigger smile. "With the tension in this room about to become thick enough to slice with a razor."

Kurt turned slightly. "So it appears."

Though, to his surprise things didn't.

Wolf blinked several times."This is *really* bizarre," he said, making no attempt to conceal his astonishment. "So what do you make of it?"

"Simply that I suspect Sokolov knows something we don't."

"Like the tale about some important general arriving earlier this morning from Moscow?" Wolf asked, as if there were no other options.

"Exactly—" Kurt stole another glance at Sokolov. "Which makes me angry Stalin didn't send this general here sooner to get the city under control."

"Certainly should have." Wolf agreed. "To help stop this vengeance against the civilians here—"

"My good people," interjected Sokolov, putting the phone on its rest and rising. "The city's surrender was signed at 8:23 this morning—but sadly it seems many of the Berliners are unhappy about it. So, I'm afraid the concert I've been looking forward to will have to be cut to half an hour." He gazed at his four visitors as if making a judicious assessment. "If this is inconvenient, then we'll have to forego the concert altogether."

"Half an hour should be perfect," Jaclyn exclaimed. "She hurried over to the briefcase and handed him several sheets from "Tchaikovsky's "Swan Lake."

"What I was hoping for." The colonel smiled, suddenly bouyant. "Since I read somewhere you studied under a former student of Tchaikovsky's."

"In Paris years ago...but were you able to find a talented German who knew how to tune a cello and piano?"

"The best," he answered, a gleam of pride in his eyes. "Volker Seiffert from Berlin's Philharmonic Orchestra, handled everything earlier."

"Then we'll begin," she said, giving Bela an encouraging pat on her back as they headed over to their instruments. Like at Albert's chalet, the sheer beauty of Bela's musical talent provided Kurt with a kind of pleasant escape. Even if his heart did take a sickening nosedive whenever he thought how this could easily be the last time he'd ever get to see her perform. *Since my wish to be with her won't come true. Like the colonel's, who's deliberately scooting his chair closer to her.*

He stared at this arrogant commanding officer, whose raking gaze drank up Bela's every move.... *The same as Prince Siegfried's had in the ballet when the beautiful swan maiden, Odette, rose with her swan maidens from the mysterious lake.*

The concert came to an abrupt end when the major informed the colonel he had another important call. "My apologies," he said, returning to his desk. "But an urgent matter requires my immediate attention."

The call didn't last long, and when he placed the receiver back on its rest, his look was one of triumph. "You are to go to the Potsdam Hospital first, where supposedly a relative of yours is waiting," he told them, stamping their official documents. "And I know you're in a hurry with your limited time here, but we're expecting some delays—so be prepared."

"And if we are delayed, then where will we wait?" asked Wolf. "In the truck that's taking us to the hospital?"

The colonel nodded. "But then, after you reach the hospital, you are to go with this man there who calls himself von Lehmann, to *Fraulein* Tovarishki's house to search for his missing papers. And like you've been assured, you *will* have protection." He hesitated, regarding him steadily. "However, it'll be from my two N.K.V.D. people, Victor and Peter, who speak English and German. And not the White Russian hospital guards." He gestured at two uniformed men now standing in the doorway.

"Russian Secret Police," murmured Wolf. "I should have known we'd be assigned N.K.V.D. people."

"They've been assisting me, and I'm grateful," the colonel continued, "since I have few soldiers to spare with the Freedom Marcher's situation getting worse." He took a step toward Victor and Peter. "So you'll need to leave with them now, because these Berliners, calling themselves Freedom Marchers, are now close to forty thousand strong."

"What do they want?" Kurt asked him.

"To get to the West away from us Russians— if you can imagine." He shook his head at this apparent discomfiture. "Because it's *we* Russians who have such a strong respect for the rights of all peoples. With our Russian intermediaries courteous enough to order these people to turn back—"

But apparently they're not," Jaclyn remarked.

"No... they keep shouting, '*Better Russian guns than Soviet occupation.*' Which truly shocks me."

Wolf looked at Kurt like he never ceased to be amazed at the Russians and their propaganda. "It seems plans change regularly around this place."

"Only *Doktor Grossklos Knows*," Kurt added, his hand on Bela's arm as the two agents motioned them toward the open door with unseemly haste. "Which is making me continue to suspect there's a *mole* connected with Tommie intelligence, who aired the *Doktor Grossklos* message on the Morse to make sure we'd come."

CHAPTER TWENTY-SIX

Colonel Sokolov was trying not to allow any emotions to play on his face as the four visitors left his office to collect information for the book they claimed to be writing— but really weren't.

Earlier this morning the almighty Stalin had sent Comrade Major-General Joseph Volkov from Moscow... an arrival that immediately spiked dread throughout the senior ranks of the Red Army.

And I'm the exception, Sokolov mused, grinning at the thought. *And the timing couldn't have been more perfect. With destiny bringing those four visitors—or rather British intelligence agents— to the city on the same day the Berliners were Freedom Marching.*

"An excellent excuse to keep them from being driven around and possibly seeing things in the city's shattered ruins, Moscow might not want them to see," he said, rehearsing the speech he was planning on giving the marshal. "As well as giving them time to confirm—as I intend to prove— the man in the hospital is von Lehmann. So we need to keep our visitors out of our way by having them search for the missing papers in Vera Tovarishki's house and cellar, where we've searched so many times."

Obviously, von Lehmann's work had been destroyed in this war-torn city. But Dr. Grossklos was putting him on the mend. And as long as his identity was confirmed by *Herr* von Friesen or *Herr* Ulrich today, then at some point he should be able to re-create the basics of what was on those missing, invisible-ink papers.

"My plans are falling into *place*," Sokolov continued, glancing again at a note from one of his hospital sources that confirmed von Lehmann was making some preliminary designs. "Which certainly makes it easier for me."

The colonel shifted in his chair as he pondered the phone call he'd received in the middle of Jaclyn's *performance*... for it had come from none other than the Supreme Commander himself, Marshal Zhukov. 'The Red Army continues to run wild,' the marshal had snapped in an accusing tone. 'Raping, looting, killing—with much valuable scientific information being lost.' Then he'd stopped, before reminding him in *no* uncertain terms, 'Since the day will come before we know it, Colonel, that the Soviets will come to blows with the West....'

'But didn't we agree these Teutonic people must be held accountable for their crimes against our beloved Mother Russia?' he'd asked, trying not to lose his deceptive calm and lash out at him.

But the marshal didn't answer. 'As I'm sure you're aware, Colonel, the Tartars or Mongols are doing the most damage. Shooting first and asking questions later. With two of Germany's leading scientists recently being killed in one day.' Then he'd paused before adding in a sarcastic tone, 'With General Volkov angry about it — in case *you've* forgotten.'

He hadn't forgotten, since a *von Lehmann* name tag was discovered on a mangled body during some of the heaviest fighting that day. And his death had occurred when three grenades were tossed in his chemical-filled laboratory in the suburbs, because Wehrmacht soldiers were believed to be hiding there.

But if losing von Lehmann wasn't bad enough, then what about his preliminary designs for his V-3 Cannon Rocket, capable of carrying an atomic bomb? Were they presumably destroyed in the ensuing fire? '*I doubt it,*' Sokolov had been prepared to argue. '*Since something of such value would have been kept in a safer place.* '

His thoughts ranged back in time as he remembered how several hours had passed before a survivor was discovered in a ruined building next to a vacant lot outside von Lehmann's laboratory.

He was a befuddled, white-haired man with a brown briefcase, who could possibly be a scientist.

The company commander then ordered his soldiers to search the surroundings, while a major ordered the radio operator in his truck to contact the marshal about this man.

"Take no chances and get him to the hospital at once," the marshal had ordered.

Supposedly, this man had been driven out of his mind by the bombing. Yet he called himself von Lehmann and insisted on being taken to Dr. Grossklos's hospital, because the good doctor and his brother in Switzerland had often visited each other in better times.

'The papers in this briefcase are scaled down preliminary designs that will one day put men in space,' this befuddled man informed the Russian major at the hospital. 'And Dr. Grossklos is such a man of vision, he will not throw them away.'

Later, Sokolov recalled Marshal Zhukov calling him up and informing him he'd received a call from Major Petrov about some important scientific papers believed to have been discovered in a briefcase, belonging to this man in the hospital who called himself von Lehmann.

'So I order you, Colonel, to go immediately to the hospital and retrieve from Major Petrov —who I've assigned to watch over this man— what hopefully are designs for this V-3 Cannon Rocket.'

'*Damn you, Zhukov.*' Sokolov wished he could blurt into the phone. '*Why are you allowing Major Petrov to keep watch over this man? Do you think he can learn something I can't, when he's not the problem solver I am? If you do, then you've got a surprise in store for you... so just hide and watch.*'

But he couldn't have been more wrong. Because upon arrival at the hospital he learned from Major Petrov that the papers von Lehmann— or his double— was so zealously guarding were nothing more than some oilskin-wrapped, blank pages.

'See he's just a crazy, old man!' said Petrov.

'You call me crazy, Major?' The man sat bolt upright. 'You *damn* Russians think you know everything,' he said, shaking a finger at him. 'But just because you can't see something, doesn't mean it's not there.'

'Not there?' the major questioned.

The old man nodded. 'Because these papers are not what they appear to be. And you know why? I had *help* from elsewhere.'

'Help?' That gained Sokolov's attention. 'From who, old man?'

'Beings from an advanced civilization living under the ice in Antarctica.'

'*Antarctica*? Do you take me for a fool—'

'Please, Colonel,' interrupted Dr. Grossklos rushing over. 'The man's experienced some, severe brain damage, so be easy on him since we don't know the truth.'

'Makes it hard, Doctor, when someone's this mentally unbalanced.'

'The *Fuhrer* sent three expeditions down there,' continued von Lehmann or his doppelganger. 'Something I suspect your almighty Stalin— who's ruling like royalty from the Kremlin—failed to tell you.'

But Sokolov's patience was wearing thin; especially when the old man asked Dr. Grossklos to hide the briefcase in the cellar of his shattered house. 'Ive heard enough, Doctor.' He turned to him. 'These papers are worthless to me, so do with them whatever you think best.'

'Then I'll see they're hidden, Colonel,' said the doctor after a moment. 'Because if this man's waking brain does clear, we might be able to obtain some more information about them.'

'I doubt his brain will ever clear,' Sokolov flared, watching the doctor as he stepped over to the square-shouldered, combat medic, Boris Tovarishki.

He was the doctor's next- door neighbor... a White Russian exile, who'd recently received a medical discharge from the Wehrmacht. "Let me go," Tovarishki quickly volunteered. 'Since I know a place where no one will be able to find those papers, without great difficulty.'

The doctor was reluctant at first, but Tovarishki continued to press him, adding with a flash of humor, 'In these grim times we all need a good mystery.'

Even if there was a Russian stranglehold on the city, Boris's house was only three rubble -littered streets away. Which today were strangely deserted. 'No sign of Russian troops on these streets,' a White Russian hospital guard, in a Red Army uniform, had informed the workers there. 'Though the guns in the distance indicate there's still heavy fighting.'

Tovarishki kept insisting he knew the perfect place to hide the papers and promised to get back quickly with news of their whereabouts.

Which apparently he did... but never lived to reveal it. 'Because on his way back he'd encountered three Russian Mongol soldiers with schnapps-drenched brains, dragging a half-naked woman toward a ruined building, 'this White Russian hospital guard searching this ruined building, had reported. 'And they'd shot Boris so quickly that he never knew what hit him. Which was their way of reminding us that they were now the conquerors, and we the conquered Huns— as *Ivan* likes to call us.'

* * *

Sokolov knew that Boris Tovarishki's death might have passed without much talk, had Major Petrov not informed the marshal about von Lehmann's bound, blank pages, and his odd remark about not seeing it didn't mean it wasn't there.

'What's the matter with you, Sokolov!' Zhukov had exploded. 'You mean you let someone take them because you were so stupid, you didn't test them under heat to see if it wasn't some kind of invisible- ink he was referring to?'

'Perhaps—if it had been a letter or message,' he'd argued in his defense. 'But in my opinion, it would have taken a medieval monk in a monastery a very long time to write equations and draw rocket designs in invisible- ink on those pages.'

'Which, in case it hasn't occurred to you,was a surprisingly small amount of pages for something like that,' the marshal had pointed out. 'Particularly since von Lehmann's received much praise for his ability to put a *lot into a* little....So organize a search. '

Adrenline pounded through Sokolov's veins. ' Even with the heavy fighting Marshal?' he questioned. 'Which is only a few blocks away from Tovarishki's house.'

'Doesn't matter, *we've* got to find those papers!'

Which Sokolov, to his shame, agreed; dispatching orders that all houses, cellars, and shops on Boris Tovarishki's block were to be thoroughly searched...not once, but several times.

"With nothing found but the brown briefcase, in which the papers, were carried,"' Sokolov lamented, in the diary-like notepad he kept on his person." The final update I had to give Zhukov, and he thanked me for my forbearance. But nevertheless, continued to remind me that General Volkov was expected to arrive any day. 'And he'll be quite upset for releasing those papers to Tovarishki, ' he reminded me several times."

A sudden knocking on his open, office door returned his attention to the present "Captain Ulyanov," a soldier announced, saluting crisply.

"Then come in, Captain." responded Sokolov. returning his salute "Are you and the major ready to deal with those Freedom Marchers?"

The young, long-limbed officer stepped forward. "The major sent me to inform you we're standing by to do whatever it takes."

"Why? Because General Volkov 's arrival means the Almighty Stalin has sent him here to stop the damage his Soviet commanders are doing, by not imposing more control on the Mongol troops?"

"That's the word being spread."

"And what else? That all the senior Red Army commanders are in for it, because this general's old enough to have been around since the Great Flood?"

The captain fidgeted nervously. "Yes—in a manner of speaking."

"And the reason this general's been around for so long is that he can strike with the fury of an angry cobra each time the need arises for someone to come under his ax? Sokolov allowed a lengthy silence to pass before he reminded, "With no one safe around him, considering wherever he goes, his execution squads leave a bloody trail of death on senior Russian officers and their staffs. Whose careless blunders have made it impossible for them to fulfill their obligation to Mother Russia."

The young man nodded. "Definitely an unpleasant showdown."

"Then have no fear, Captain, because when we stop these Freedom Marchers, it'll give the general a chance to see exactly how good we are at what we do. So go tell Major Petrov that the quicker we can stop this human flood-tide, the better it'll be for us."

"Will do, Colonel." He saluted again, before exiting the room.

The general's arrival was a clear signal to Sokolov that his own arrest was imminent, unless he could positively identify von Lehmann and prove he was getting his senses back by being able to make some preliminary designs. *And ordinarily, I should have been worried, but I'm not. 'Fate has come to save me,'* he wished he could tell Marshal Zhukov. *'Because quite recently I was brought face to face with the Soviet-captured, Colonel Franz Dietrich. A German mole who'd aired messages to London that were decoded by OSS cipher officials. So, naturally, I began questioning him.'*

And in abject fear of torture, the secrets this Wehrmacht communications officer had so carefully guarded, gradually began to surface.

The OSS had trained four people— two of whom were relatives of von Lehmann's. And these people were standing by to get permission from the Soviets to enter the city legally in the hopes they could identify the man in the hospital as von Lehmann, and locate his missing papers.

"Well now." Sokolov reminisced, glancing over the notes he'd taken. *"It would require these four having a very good cover-story to get permission to enter this city. However, I don't doubt they'll have it."*

Giving it some more thought, he had a plan; a risky one but, nevertheless, one that gave him a degree of hope.

The city continued to be a battleground, with bloody fighting between S.S. formations and Russian tanks on practically every street and surrounding areas. So, it would be dangerous for four people to travel from the Elbe to Berlin in a British truck or other vehicle. Which was the reason it made sense to have Colonel Dietrich bait British intelligence with the message, *"Doktor Grossklos Knows."*

For if von Lehmann's identity can be confirmed by his relatives, then it should satisfy Marshal Zhukov and General Volkov.

And being the extraordinary scientist he was, von Lehmann should have no problem re-creating those missing invisible- ink papers as he improved. Of course, he doubted those original papers could be found, with the previous military searches failing to turn up anything. But friends and relatives were known to see things differently... particularly when it came to familiar objects hidden in cellars.

He knew this from experience in his hometown of Smolensk, where he'd located the notebook of poems his mother had written in her youth, in the cellar of her house... a notebook the communal housing people living there, had been unable to find for him.

And this Kurt Ulrich, so Dietrich pointed out, was a British prisoner-of- war who'd once lived in the doctor's, bombed-out house with his deceased wife and son. *A house next door to Boris Tovarishki's house.*

But in the case of the missing papers after all the searching done, Sokolov was coming more and more to believe the inevitable: *Mongol soldiers broke into the house, and finding those bound, blank papers, decided to take them because they'd make good toilet paper. Since after all, they were easy to carry.*

That being his concern, then the report he'd received from Dietrich yesterday, was strengthening his plan concerning *Herr* Ulrich. "Apparently, Bela Tirand *could be* Ulrich's fiancée, "the report read. "With a Mr. Fieszel reporting day before yesterday, that the familiarity between them brings to mind an engaged couple."

'Well done, Dietrich,' Sokolov had praised him over the phone. 'Because when I recently saw the dazzling photo of Bela Tirand in this 1937 Austrian, society magazine Dr. *Grossklos* gave me, I can't tell you how eager I am to meet her. Since even at an early age, she was obviously on her way to becoming one of Vienna's great beauties.'

But other than being Jaclyn Tirand's step-sister, just how did she fit into the family? Was she really a Jew who'd survived a concentration camp, like British intelligence hinted? And if she was, then what in hell was she thinking getting herself engaged to a former Wehrmacht captain…? Something really hard for me to imagine— much less grasp. Considering I acted surprised when Kurt told me he and Bela were getting married—when I met them in my office.

"*No matter,*" he'd noted in his book. "*Because if von Lehmann refuses to draw his rocket designs, then my plan to imprison Kurt Ulrich will surely impress Major- General Volkov, since von Lehmann looks on him as a son. Plus, knowing what I know now will should make Bela desperate enough—with her step-sister's help—to pressure von Lehmann into recreating a few of his missing designs…. So any way I win. With von Lehmann looking on Kurt as a son, and Bela a lover.*"

Far-fetched perhaps, but certainly possible.

Anyway for what it was worth, von Lehmann's relatives didn't appear to be lacking in imagination. "*How I wish I could have questioned them about what they intended on putting in this cover-story book they're writing about the Battle of Berlin. Would it make our Russians look bad?*" Sokolov had quickly written after their departure from his office. "*No doubt. And would they have had a pre-planned answer that would evade this intention? Or would my question have made them grope for one?*"

Their ploy was excellent. So he didn't see anyone objecting if he signed the documents the British had sent him, granting permission for them to enter the city.

And I'll arouse less suspicion with Marshal Zhukov if I keep their visit short. Which means I'll inform the British it should be no longer than a day. "Because confirming von Lehmann's identity and getting some basic preliminary designs from him for further research, shouldn't take any longer," he said aloud. "And I'll pretend to agree to it as long as the lovely Jaclyn and her beautiful step-sister entertain me with their music."

He'd really been looking forward to their visit, so he wasn't trying to be difficult about it. But he'd ordered the men he'd sent to meet the plane, to pretend to be offended by the pilot's audacity to approach the Gatow runway— and threaten him should he land.

He smiled as he mulled it over. Of course it had never occurred to these British agents when they arrived, that he *knew* practically everything there was to know about them... and all thanks to Colonel Dietrich for providing the information.

The phone ringing again, shattered Sokolov's reverie. Only this time he eyed it gamely. *Clearly a reminder to redirect my battle of personal restraint and concentrate on my four visitors, and my plans for using them.*

So he picked it up, listening, as Marshal Zhukov delivered the one sentence message he was expecting. *"Report to Major- General Volkov at once!"*

Certainly a good omen with the general arriving the same day as the four visitors. Because with these pieces falling into place, I'm now in a position to repair the damage I've been accused of doing. Which should greatly surprise Marshal Zhukov as well as Stalin's murdering general.

Another call immediately followed the marshal's, only this time it was from Major Petrov. "Things are continuing to get worse, Colonel," the major informed him. "Wehrmacht soldiers from the Zoo Bunker are leading the Freedom Marchers." His voice was unsteady, like a man panicked. "With the main road to the River Havel and the West jammed with more than forty thousand Berliners. And a few are still able to cross the Charlotte Bridge, even if the fanatical Hitler Youth from the Zoo Bunker have gained control of it."

Sokolov was caught off guard by what he was hearing. "But where are our guns and tanks, Major?" he shouted into the phone. "Haven't we sent the reinforcements they requested?"

"Some arrived, with more are coming. But for now our armies are hiding until the time comes to make themselves known."

"Then our ploy clearly shows the advantage the Red Army holds over the Huns," Sokolov bragged. "And when they do, we'll open fire on these

Berliners— who are so eager to get to the West —and our tanks will crush them."

"I hope you're right," said the major curtly. "With a good many of these crowded marchers trapped on the bridge."

"I am, "Sokolov assured him in an authoritative tone "Because what they need is for Moses to part the River Havel with his staff, so they can cross it..." A brief but tense silence followed as he gave it more thought. "But since Moses was a Jew and considered part of Europe's garbage, then he would have ended up in an oven at Auschwitz."

The major chuckled slightly. "Which is a good thing, Colonel, since Pharoah's *Russian* army can now do whatever it pleases. Without any fear from *Moses* and his God."

CHAPTER TWENTY-SEVEN

J ammed with people, the Potsdam Hospital was bedlam with the buzz of conversation.

Its main ward in the basement was filled with Freedom Marching patients. Though not one would admit it, for fear the Russians would burst into the hospital and either shoot them or take them prisoner. "We were delayed, Doctor, and had to wait in a truck for over an hour," Kurt heard Wolf, from a distance, inform him in a loud voice. "But from what we heard on its radio, we concluded that the march was nothing but a grim butchery...with Berliners being so frightened because of the surrender, they were just trying to get out of the city."

The doctor's eyes shifted over to some of the people. "I'm told a good many did cross the Havel bridges and reach Spandau...." His voice trailed off, as his expression darkened with the agony surrounding him. "But then, the Russians began firing at the people on the bridges, and they fell dead." He gestured at a man waiting to be examined. "And that fellow over there just informed us that the Russian tanks couldn't move, because they had so many body parts stuck in their treads."

Wolf cringed. "What happened after that?"

"The Russians just kept firing."

"And now the River Havel and Charlotte Bridge are red with blood!" shrieked a woman, bumping against the doctor's shoulder as she rushed up. "With the dead splattered everywhere...even in the smooth meadows by the river's banks."

"It was retaliation," said Wolf. "Because after all that the Germans did in London, Warsaw, Budapest, and Minsk what can you expect?"

"Wolf, please." Jaclyn tapped his forearm. "Pull yourself together, since if the Germans hear you, they'll mention Dresden and the awful amount of people who were killed in its bombings."

Jostled by the surging crowd Kurt— in an attempt to bridge the distance—shoved his way through these people, with their desperate faces, as they attempted to get to one of the good doctors. "Father-in-law, is it really you?" he asked, reaching him after a moment.

For a split-second he closed his eyes, trying not to remember that Carl Grossklos's jewel-green ones were the same color as his daughter's. And his burnished hair was as smooth and glossy as hers had been. *All I have left to remind me of Fresa...like Carl says I'm all he has left to remind him of little Erich.*

"Kurt— you made it!" Carl said, giving him a hug. "Colonel Sokolov told me you were delayed because of a train attack, and I was worried. But are you feeling all right?"

"Bela and I are fine." He smiled, putting his arm around her. "With the exception of running head-on into an isolated pocket of German soldiers in the woods."

"Which I hope you took care of."

"I did my best, but wouldn't have succeeded if it hadn't been for my lovely partner here."

Bowing, Carl immediately took her hand. "I saw a picture of you in an old, society magazine, and it honors me to be in debt to such a beautiful and talented young lady like yourself."

"And I'm touched." She gave him a bright smile. "Since I'm Jewish and have no words to express my appreciation for the money Albert said you and your nurse, Vera Tovarishki, slipped to him to save as many Jewish children as you could."

"Still, what we did was not enough—"

"Same thing Raoul Wallenberg said about himself," Wolf piped up.

"I never knew you helped the Jewish children until Bela made a brief mention of it," remarked Kurt, impressed.

"That's because of the censorship on letters," Carl reminded.

"Yet, you dared write me and say a German official was trying to get me transferred from Hungary to Berlin?"

The doctor's features brightened a little. "Not as daring as it sounds. Because that official had a certain kindness and advised me to tell you, since you weren't allowed to attend your wife and son's funerals."

"And I'm in awe of your efforts," said Kurt, placing a gentle hand on his arm. "But before we continue, meet Jaclyn Tirand, one of Europe's foremost musicians. And her husband, Wolf von Friesen."

Carl reached for Wolf's extended hand. "I feel I've known you ever since Albert got a secret message to me about your wonderful work with *Herr* Wallenberg."

"We've been impatient to meet *you*," said Wolf, pumping his hand. "Even if our time here is quite brief."

"Not much opportunity to gather information for your book about Berlin," Carl said.

"Our book." Wolf raised a brow. "Who told you, the colonel?"

"He mentioned it."

"The book was our cover-story," he explained. "But since the colonel has the N. K.V.D. guarding us, rather than the expected White Russians, we won't be going to von Lehmann's, bombed-out laboratory and searching what's left of it...." Wolf sighed, gazing at the floor with what seemed a quiet despondency. "Nor will we be able to check out the two addresses of contacts I received from the OSS in Stuttgart yesterday."

"Who might know something about von Lehmann's missing papers?" Carl asked Wolf nodded. "The OSS doubts we'll find them but, nevertheless, expects us to investigate what we can."

Carl's mouth twisted wryly. "Which will amount to nothing after this Freedom Marching uproar today."

Suddenly, the air was filled with more voices of desperate people surging into the building.

"The melange of motion in this ward befits a carnival, Doctor," said Wolf.

"That it does." He turned to gaze at the hospital's two other doctors as they shuffled past him. "And all because of these unfortunate Freedom Marchers." He pointed at the stretchers carried down the ward's aisle— by what appeared to be friends or family members— with a man or woman stretched full length on each one.

Kurt took a step toward them. "Colonel Sokolov told us the Berliners were making trouble."

Carl's eyes were focused on the passing stretchers. "Which could be the reason Major- General Volkov flew in from Moscow this morning."

"The voice of Almighty Stalin himself." Wolf jeered. "Who continues to maintain Hitler got away."

"Another good reason for the general's visit," said Carl. "But getting back to your cover-story. This hospital is clearly not a reflection of the chaos in the other suburban hospitals, we're trying so desperately to help." He exchanged a nod with one of the nurses nearby. "So, if you should decide to write about Berlin in the future then, with names excluded, I'd certainly be willing to share with you some of the problems that have been dumped in my lap recently from what I call the *field* hospitals. With many of these hospitals in former schools that are overrun with badly wounded German soldiers— most of whom have lice." He exhaled deeply. "And these are *one-doctor* hospitals which are in dire need of medicines, bandages, disinfectants, beds, and ration cards. And when we can get away, we're taking turns going to these hospitals, where the Bolsheviks— not the White Russians in the Red Army— are on guard. And we're bringing to these hospitals some extra supplies I've managed to stash."

Wolf's eyes slid over the faces of Kurt. Bela, and Jaclyn. "Are these understaffed hospitals one of the reasons the women— who've just given birth— are being raped by the Russian Mongols?"

"So you know about that, do you?" asked Carl "After a fashion."

"God!" exclaimed Bela, clearly alarmed. "That's enough to make a person's ears bleed."

"Believe me, young lady, it's happened."

Hearing that, Kurt moved closer to Bela and put his arm around her. "No wonder so many Berliners were trying to escape...but what happened to Horst and Herta Winter? Are they here at the hospital with you—"

"Who are Hans and Herta Winter?" Wolf broke in.

"My wonderful driver and housekeeper," Carl said, his tight expression relaxing. "Who, thankfully, are in Cologne with some of my relatives."

With a doleful expression Jaclyn turned to a nurse holding a man struggling to sit up.

"How many Freedom Marchers were killed today?"

"Not sure. "The man tilted his brow. "But I'm hearing between twenty and forty thousand."

"A terrible massacre." She closed her eyes for a second as if in pain, before turning back to Carl. "But how big is the other ward in this hospital?"

"Not as big as here. "He made a sweeping motion with his arm. "Although it's still so dangerous, we're moving some of our supplies upstairs, since we don't exactly have a subterranean hospital like the one in Budapest."

Wolf shook his head several times. "Even if word has it, Doctor, that the last shot has supposedly been fired from the tower at the Zoo Bunker?"

"I suspect there are many who're *still* refusing to surrender. Since reports coming in are saying there was a final assault on the River Spree, with heavy air support and bloody hand –to-hand combat, forcing Berliners to take cover in basements, cellars, and tube-tunnels under demolished buildings." He gestured at the ceiling. "So it's better to be *down* here, than *up* there."

"We're supposed to be searching Vera Tovarishki's house," Wolf informed him. "Although I suspect we'll end up spending a good deal of time in its cellar."

"Which might not be very comfortable, with a bomb recently striking her chimney stack."

"Still, it's a fairly safe place to stay until our plane returns."

"True...considering the cellar's the only thing left of my house," Carl reminded. "And even if my cellar was at the end of the block with no tunnels, it was comfortable with a large fireplace, though— "He sighed, once again making a sweeping motion with his arm, only this time at the injured Berliners. "My cellar was safe, like a bomb shelter. But it didn't stop the Germans from filling it with debris from the bombings, so the door connecting to Vera's cellar couldn't be opened."

"Did any of my little Erich's things survive?" Kurt asked.

"A few...that Vera put in Boris's leased cellar shop for protection."

"What about little Erich's wooden, rocking horse we had made for him. Did it survive?"

"It's in Boris's cellar...but if it makes you sad, then don't look at it."

"I probably won't."

Bela took Kurt's hand. "Some day you'll have another little boy, and your pain won't be so bad," she practically shouted, as the hospital's noise intensified.

When suddenly echoing through it, a voice hollered, "Kurt!"

It was von Lehmann, and Kurt started toward him, just as an angry looking man, zigzagging his way through the crowd, struck a woman in the mouth. She screamed, kicked him, and was about to kick him again, when Sokolov's two N.K.V.D. agents appeared with their pistols drawn.

Instantly, the cowering people scrambled to take cover as these agents prepared to fire.

"Please—we can't have a massacre in this hospital!" yelled Carl.

"Then these people had better be careful," barked the rugged-looking Victor. "Because Colonel Sokolov's assigned Peter and me to watch after the von Friesens, *Herr* Ulrich, and *Fraulein* Spigel."

"The people here are trying. So don't hurt them," Carl begged.

"If they are, then it's not *hard* enough, Doctor." Victor bristled, shoving one of the stretchers so it shook the man lying on it.

Peter stepped toward him. "We'd better see what's on the floor above us, Victor."

"I agree," he spat, heading toward the staircase instead of the elevator, which didn't appear to be working.

A strained silence followed as the people moved away from the staircase so they could pass.

Carl stood without moving. "A relief for time being." he uttered, before turning back to Kurt. "Which as I'm sure you're aware, with the *Fuhrer* dead, and the British and American allies miles away, Berlin has no government. And the Red Army has gone on holiday."

"Allowing anarchy," Bela said, her vexation evident.

"Especially since the OSS told us not to act independently," Jaclyn reminded. "Since we can't afford a conflict with the Soviets."

"We need to take von Lehmann and head to Vera Tovarishki's, "said Wolf. "So this hospital will be rid of these two agents Colonel Sokolov's assigned to watch us."

"I'll get von Lehmann," Kurt volunteered. "Because he seems to be having trouble navigating his way through the swarm of people."

"But before you do," said Carl. "The four of you need to know I have proof that the man you're taking with you, is *really* von Lehmann and not his double."

Wolf's eyes widened in astonishment. "What kind of proof?"

"Von Lehmann's fingerprints matched earlier ones."

"Earlier ones?" Wolf questioned. "How'd you get earlier ones?"

"From a scrapbook, belonging to my son-in-law here, that survived the bombing of my house."

Instantly a smile played at the corners of Kurt's mouth. "I remember. Since there was a picture of a crocodile I drew as a boy in it, and von Lehmann and I made its back spiky with our handprints."

"Yes," said Carl. "And you wrote a note beneath it, about what the two of you did."

"So this is what *Doktor Grossklos Knows*?" asked Wolf.

"Supposedly." He grinned in earnest. "But please— all of you— call me *Carl*."

Wolf's grin answered his. "Happy to."

The doctor made a slight gesture with his left hand. "One of our nurses is attempting to extricate von Lehmann from that cluster of people across from us. So all of you just stay where you are."

Which they did. Standing very still until the white-haired von Lehmann rushed over and gave Kurt a powerful hug. "Son," he cried, his voice trembling." I can't believe you came!"

Kurt started to say something, but no words came. So he just stood there, helpless, like something was choking him.

Quickly Bela reached in her raincoat and removed a handkerchief. "This should help," she said, wiping it across his face.

He nodded, managing to regain his composure long enough to return von Lehmann's hug. "I've missed you terribly."

"Oh, Kurt, I was so worried when you were in the Wehrmacht that you'd end up a Russian prisoner –of- war. And now here we are—together at last." He reached out to pat Kurt on the forearm. "But that *damned* Colonel Sokolov is threatening me, that if I can't reproduce some of the basics of the designs similar to my invisible-ink ones, he's going to take you prisoner."

"Bela and I were frightened when Victor raised his pistol at everyone," said Jaclyn. "But it's just as frightening to think what this Colonel Sokolov is capable of doing."

"Which I'm not about to let happen," said von Lehmann, momentarily staring at Jaclyn like he knew her. "But to whom do I have the pleasure of speaking?"

"Jaclyn Tirand."

"The well-known cello player?"

She nodded.

An exchange of introductions and greetings followed, with Bela giving von Lehmann a light kiss on the cheek, and Wolf giving him a warm handshake. "Good to see you after all these years, Uncle."

"Same as it is to see you." Von Lehmann sniffed. "And I'm so very sorry that this work I must do for Colonel Sokolov won't allow me to visit with all of you. But if someone has to go to Moscow, then it's better *I* do it than Kurt. Because I'm old, and he's young, with his whole life ahead of him."

"Let's get this straight," said Wolf in a firm voice. "*Nobody's* going to Moscow—or Siberia for that matter."

"But if my head injuries won't allow me to duplicate some of my previous designs, then what?"

Wolf turned to Carl. "How's he coming along?"

"He's doing quite well, because he's on my treatment program. And now even has a job in our inventory control that's helping restore his concentration in a short amount of time."

Von Lehmann's navy-blue eyes flashed impatiently. "But if you could only find my invisible- ink papers." He sighed, shaking his head.

"We're going to try," Wolf assured him.

"And if you do, then you'll give them to the Russians?" He looked worried.

Wolf shook his head. "Of course not—"

"But then you'll have to sneak them out."

"That goes without saying, Uncle," he said, tipping his head in acknowledgment. "Although, I doubt we'll be able to find what the Russians couldn't."

"But what about the designs I make today?" von Lehmann asked "We'll give them to the Russians," Wolf remarked with a glum expression. "And then find a way to get you to London by the end of next week."

Von Lehmann appeared to contemplate it. "But how, if I'm to go with the Russians?"

"Don't worry, Vera Tovarishki has a plan," Carl answered for Wolf.

Von Lehmann's face immediately took on a warm expression. "Of course this beautiful, talented lady does." He swiped at his swollen eyes with a tissue. "And to think her poor brother, Boris, died trying to hide my papers in her house."

"Boris Tovarishki," repeated Kurt, startled. "So he was the medic the Russians killed?"

Carl nodded, his green eyes dark with emotion. "And a witness reported there were two very drunk Mongol soldiers, who shot him, as he was returning to the hospital after he'd hidden those invisible- ink papers—"He faltered as images of Boris's death appeared to flood his mind. "Which sadly is the reason that neither we nor the Russians can find them."

An extended silence followed, with Kurt lowering his head. "Boris was a great skat player. And it was always a challenge for me when I played the card game with him and one of his friends."

Von Lehmann was close to losing control, so Kurt immediately recovered his composure. "Boris volunteered to take them for me, Son," he remarked in a somber tone. "And now look what's happened."

"It's a little awkward to be talking about such things, with our Berlin time ending so soon," Kurt whispered, pressing his arms around von Lehmann's back.

But he continued to sob." I suppose it is. But since we'll have Russians with us, if by chance you do find my papers, you must let me know by asking me if I want a glass of white wine—"

"And then what?"

"We won't be able to talk about it, but at least I'll know." He wept loudly as more tears found their way down his cheeks." I love you, Son, and don't want something bad like what happened to Boris, to happen to you. So please be careful."

"Can I do anything?" asked Bela, stepping over with another one of her handkerchiefs.

"Nothing," said Kurt, taking it and giving it to von Lehmann to replace his tissue." "It's just I'm overwhelmed at how this man who— "His voice faded as von Lehmann buried his face against his shoulder.

"Raised you," Bela completed softly "Yes, raised me, but somehow lost his fatherly feelings for me— "

Feeling awkward, he held his breath for a second. "Yet, still managed to find his way back to me in the middle of this terrible war."

"Doesn't sound like he looks on you as a charity case or outsider," Bela whispered. "Especially, if he's willing to go to Russia in your place."

"Which clearly is something I wasn't expecting to hear," Kurt also whispered, amid more loud weeping from von Lehmann. "Though, whether he admits it or not, he needs me like never before. And I'll be there for him." He gripped von Lehmann's shoulder. "Even if his refusal to marry my mother on her deathbed will always disturb me."

Bela was about to respond, when Victor and Peter walked back into the ward with their long, confident strides and pistols in hand.

"I heard no shots," Carl said to them. "So I trust you found nothing up there?"

"You have fewer patients up there," remarked Victor, "so it makes it much quieter."

"The patients upstairs are the ones who chose to take their chances and remain there," Carl explained. "Because its quietness makes it easier for them to sleep."

But the two N. K.V.D. agents weren't interested in hearing about it.

"Tell us about von Lehmann, Doctor," Victor prodded. "Is he the man we're looking for, like our colonel seems to think? Or is he the doppelganger?"

"Wait and see if he can make a few of his missing designs," Carl answered, with an intense, but enigmatic expression.

"Which he probably can," remarked Peter, his hazel eyes reflecting a cool darkness. "Since from what I'm seeing, von Lehmann appears to be getting along quite well with his relatives...as the colonel was certain he would."

"Of course doubles are trained to do that," Carl reminded. "But as N. K.V. D. agents, I'm probably telling you something you've heard many times before."

"Doesn't matter," said Victor with a smug assurance. "Since if *this* man can recreate some of those basic designs in the next few hours, then we'll know for certain who he really is."

"So let's get a move on," Peter snapped. "Because we don't have that many hours left. And Colonel Sokolov ordered us two days ago to make sure some of his men delivered paper, a drafting board, compass, T-square, ruler, and drawing pencil to Vera Tovarishki's house. Since it would be easier to write equations and make drawings there than at the hospital."

Wolf gave Victor an indignant look. "Why did Colonel Sokolov not try to learn who the two soldiers were that killed Boris Tovarishki—"

"He did. Even offering a reward for anyone with information about them. And also, the missing papers."

The words brought Peter's head around. "But when a soldier is asked to turn against a fellow soldier—"

"So he's learned nothing," said Wolf, glaring at him. He stepped closer to Carl. "But what happens if von Lehmann can't recreate those designs and Kurt ends up a Russian prisoner- of- war?"

"Don't worry, he won't," Carl assured him, glancing at the two N.K.V. D. agents, who stood several feet away. "Because I know for a fact that von Lehmann *will* be able to make a few of his preliminary designs for a rocket."

"Sounds like he's done it for you?"

"He has. And with supplies I got him."

Wolf looked at him in surprise. "You amaze me...but one last thing. How long before the OSS Americans or British working with them, can get him out of here? Next week or longer?"

"Like I said earlier, Vera's got it all planned—"

"Didn't I say we need to get a move on?" interrupted Peter, stepping over.

"All good things must come to and end, Carl," said Kurt, his arms around him.

"We'll meet again soon." He smiled, giving his shoulder a pat. "And in the meantime keep your lovely friend Bela close to your side." He shook her hand again, only this time he kissed it with a good-bye. "But before we go I have a present for all of you."

"Oh my,"exclaimed Von Lehmann, slapping himself across the brow. "And I forgot I'm supposed to deliver it."

"Then hurry and get it," Carl urged, giving him a gentle push toward his private quarters.

He wasn't gone long and when he reappeared, he carried a brown sack and a picnic basket with its cover pulled back, revealing dark breads, Edam cheeses, sausage rolls, pastries, gingerbread cookies, and chocolate bars. "It's from the good doctor and Vera," he announced. "But the cavier, vintage wine, cognac, and *pate* in the brown sack are from Colonel Sokolov, with a written request to be generous and make sure Victor and Peter also get plenty to eat and drink. "

"In that case," said Peter, "I'll appoint Wolf von Friesen to carry it for us while I take his briefcase."

"Which is filled with my wife's music," he reminded, handing it over with a frown.

"And the rucksack," said Victor. "Since this basket's not big enough to carry all the food Colonel Sokolov sent."

"Better get your dress out of it," Jaclyn told Bela. "And wear it under your raincoat like a second wrap."

"Guess I'll have to. "She sighed, like she wasn't particularly fond of the idea.

It didn't take her long to unbutton it and put it on. And then, they started toward the door in single file.

"Wonder what Colonel Sokolov would have done if he hadn't used the massacre of the Freedom Marchers as an excuse to keep us from moving around the city?" Kurt asked her once they reached the lobby.

"He seems quite inventive, so I'm certain he would have come up with another threat that would not allow us to use our cover-story."

Kurt pointed at a bombed building outside. "But do we really need to travel around the city if the papers we're so anxiously seeking are believed to be in Vera Tovarishki's house?"

"Good question."

"Especially now that we've identified von Lehmann and have only one clue as to where the papers could be—" A rifle shot rang out in the distance, and Bela flinched as Kurt held out his arm to calm her. "Though it would have been interesting to have seen more of this war ravaged city."

"My thought exactly." Her lips parted in a smile. "Because who knows? I might really write a book about it someday."

"It wouldn't surprise me. Since it might be interesting to write about Colonel Sokolov threatening to make me a prisoner- of- war, while I'm here."

"I'd say he was desperate."

"Could be. Even if his cool attitude makes me suspect he's got another trick up his sleeve—"

"—that he won't hesitate to use if necessary," Bela finished.

CHAPTER TWENTY-EIGHT

"Vera—please," said Franz Dietrich to his beloved mistress. "After the Freedom Marcher's massacre, any German with a brain will know better than to show himself on the street today."

"I know, "said Vera, glancing at the two Russian guards dozing on his sofa. "Because you've told me *three* times."

"Still, it hasn't seemed to do much good." His place, like hers, was in Berlin's suburbs, and he was sitting in front of his communication equipment monitoring Russian radio messages. "Since reports continue to say that the Red Army sentries will be doubling the guards on all the bridges here."

"Then I'll cross the river close to my house like I did before." She touched the slacks she was wearing that would make it easier to wade through it.

"In one of its underground tunnels that's so very dangerous," he said with a hard expression. "Which makes me angry Colonel Sokolov didn't send that truck for you like he said he would."

"But like he said after the Freedom Marcher's massacre, he didn't have one to spare."

"Still, I find it hard to believe when he's insisting those British agents search your house," Franz remarked, irritated. "While at the same time those two N.K.V.D. agents are standing over von Lehmann as he makes those basic designs Sokolov's so anxious to get his hands on." He stopped and shook his head. "Which tells me, Vera, you don't have to be there?"

"Even so I have the plan for von Lehmann's escape next week—"

"As does the OSS," he reminded her.

"That they do. However, Carl thinks it best if I be there."

Franz looked like his insides were twisting "That's what he told *me*... but what he doesn't realize is that the last time we talked, Colonel Sokolov was sending a truck. So, either let me call him and tell him what's going on, or let me call our enlisted, White Russian friend who transmits for the Bolsheviks. He may be able to get a truck."

"No—time is of the essence." She hated to defy her beloved Franz. But she'd spent a good amount of time planning von Lehmann's escape from Berlin in the next week or two. So it was important she go over the details with the four British agents who would soon be arriving at her house.

Besides Franz might not like to admit it, but she knew the details better than the OSS, so she had no choice but to return to her home. Even though after today's slaughter, he was right when he said no German with a brain would be on the war-ravaged streets of Berlin.

Once again Franz's expression hardened. "And you don't have a stick or pocket-torch, do you?"

"Sokolov's short notice about having no truck hasn't given me time to locate one," she said, trying to hide her concern. "But it doesn't matter because I didn't have either one before."

"What about food? In case you encounter one of those packs of feral dogs whose owners have either died or disappeared."

"I have some oilskin-wrapped food in each of my pockets—"

"Still, call me as soon as you get to your house."

"I will—provided my phone's still working."

"It should be."

One of the two Russian guards who was dozing on the couch began yawning and stretching. "That more aggressive one over there is about to wake up," she said in a whispery voice. "Which means he'll be wanting to lick my face with good-bye kisses and maul my breasts like the Neanderthal beast he is."

Franz crushed her to him. "Then get going!" he urged, his lips brushing against hers as he spoke. "Because if that sorry son-of-a-bitch on the couch makes me any madder, I'll kill him with that butcher knife I keep hidden."

"Please don't," she said, before turning and dashing off.

* * *

Russian soldiers with rifles were patrolling on each bridge. And Vera had to be extremely careful as she listened to them call, "*Slava velikomu Stalinu,*" at one another.

"A sloven, ignorant group of people if there ever was one," she muttered. "Whose revolution forced my family to end up in exile *here*— of all places." She narrowed her eyes at the soldiers. "Which is why I'll forever resist the Soviet regime."

How were such crude people able to do it? And why had the other allies signing the Yalta Agreement, been so stupid as to let them enter Berlin and put this stranglehold on the city?

Nothing seemed to make sense any more. The *Fuhrer's* estimation of Germany's strength concerning super weapons must have been optimistic. Or he wouldn't have made Napoleon's mistake and attacked Russia.

And now these ill-disciplined Bolsheviks were using the excuse of making the Teutonic people suffer, by taking a holiday at the Berliners' expense. And in doing it the chaos in the city had provided the perfect camouflage for Hitler's escape. Such carelessness she felt certain would hamper attempts to destroy his legacy of the Third Reich.

So what did the Americans and British have to say concerning it? She tried not to think about it because each time she did, a secret voice inside her whispered that all the world leaders knew the *Fuhrer* was now on a U-boat headed to South America. *It's truly unfortunate that I can't ask these Russians patrolling the river to let me cross over it to the next suburb, where my house is.*

But after all the brutal rapes in the city, I know better than to show myself.

Women in the suburbs were making themselves scarce, hiding in attics, basements, and root cellars. *With a nurse I know dressing as a man to avoid being raped. And I might have considered it had the Russians not killed Boris, because he was a German man.*

So the safest thing to do is what I'm doing...making my way through the waist-deep, filthy water in one of the underground tube tunnels beneath the river.

The Russians hadn't closed off these subterranean tunnels because they believed nobody could get through them— but little did they know.

Besides, she'd done it before, and she'd do it again, taking her chances in the icy water with its smell like something from a nightmare. But at least it wasn't like being dumped in the middle of a rough ocean; a nightmare she frequently had.

She pinched her nose. *'What those bridge-patrolling Russians need to do is raid a French brothel for perfume and spray this place with it,'* she mentally said, with a fleeting sense of humor.

However, when a corpse from the swollen rottenness of today's massacre floated past, followed by another, and then another, she came close to vomiting as she struggled not to think about this awful slaughter.

The stagnant water was dark as a witch's dream, making it next to impossible to see the submerged rail on the tunnel's floor. And she struggled hard not to trip. But without a stick or pocket-torch, she lost her balance several times and fell.

And each time she did, the water closed over her head with a deadliness that brought to mind a black-uniformed S.S. man she'd seen before the Russians entered the heart of the city. A man whose eyes reflected the all-consuming goal of vengeance as he waded in his jackboots through the blood of the recent AWOL Wehrmacht officers he'd killed.

Then like now, panic threatened to shatter her confidence. So, fearful of joining the sickening parade of corpses floating past, she attempted to scrabble upward...,Though each time she did, the icy water rushing around her waist rose to her throat.

Steadying herself when possible, she continued plowing through the river's darkness, until the water level dropped, and she entered an exit with an uphill slope. And relieved, she worked her way up it.

Quickly stepping out, she saw a street and a ruined building not very far.

'Bravo!' she wanted to shout. *I've now succeeded a second time in making it through a foul-smelling, underground river tunnel. And God willing, I'll never have to do it again.*

Soaked to the skin, she shook her head in frustration as she shivered hard in her wet slacks and boots.

Her house, close to the hospital, was several blocks away from where she now stood. Which wasn't that far, unless she had to make a detour to keep from running into some Russian soldiers.

The familiar street landmarks were all gone. And in most places the roads and pavement lay in piles of concrete blocks torn apart from the bombardment of the city.

"Doesn't look like it did when I was here two weeks ago," she said, stumbling her way through the debris blocking the road.

It made her sad to think of her house with part of its roof now caved in. But fortunately Boris's half of her house's cellar —with the upholstery repair shop in it he'd leased to a friend— was said to be in fair condition. However, on the opposite side of her house was what was left of Carl's house.

She closed her eyes for an instant as she remembered the great dinner parties the doctor had thrown there for his hospital staff.

Kurt's assignment had been in Berlin at that time. With him and his lovely wife always taking care to make sure everyone attending the parties was smiling through the country's extremely uncertain times.

But that was in another life.

So, she'd best turn her attention to the two N.K.V.D. agents shepherding von Lehmann, Kurt, and his friends to her house. *How long will it take them to walk the three blocks from the hospital to my house with all this debris strewn everywhere? Longer than usual. Which gives me time to get out of my wet clothes and clean up.*

She was crossing over to the next block of houses when she heard laughter and two Mongol voices discussing schnapps and women.

"Drunk bastards!" she muttered angrily, hearing their complaints about not being able to find a woman for sexual intercourse.

They were quite near. And if she remained where she was, there was no way she could avoid running into them.

A frightening sense of uneasiness grabbed her as she remembered Carl telling her that so far, it was estimated there'd been a hundred thousand rapes in the city's surroundings.

"Which I'm not about to be their prey and make it a hundred thousand and one," she vowed, darting into a narrow, dirt alley behind one of the larger, ruined houses.

But the soldiers must have seen her because, to her horror, they also darted into the alley.

Still, the ruins provided her with the advantage of seeing them. So she stood there a few seconds, waiting, as she considered her next more.

Finally, her risk-taking nature won out, and she dashed into the street before the soldiers could spot her.

Gasping for breath several times, she prayed she wouldn't lose her footing as she climbed through the wreckage the Russians had yet to clear away.

Her house was now close enough to see its partially caved-in roof. And provided she could reach it, there was a place inside where she could hide.

But how could she, with the Russian voices behind her getting louder and louder? *Holy Father, help me,* she prayed, her heart pounding.

When suddenly out of nowhere, two N.K.V.D. agents appeared.

Surprised, she opened her mouth to let out a cry as Kurt rushed up and threw his arms around her. "Mercy!" she cried. "How on earth did you find me?"

"We had to make detour around all this stone and rubble."

She choked back a tear. "For which words cannot express my gratitude," she remarked, breathing easier as she gave him a vigorous hug.

"And I'm most grateful," he said, planting her a light kiss on her cheek. "But here—meet the rest of my group." He smiled, his hand outstretched in the direction of Bela, Jaclyn, and Wolf.

She blew a kiss at each of them, apologizing for her smelly, wet clothes. Then stepping over to von Lehmann, she gave his arm such a heart-warming squeeze, a tear ran down his cheek.

The Russians soldiers stared at the two N.K.V.D. agents and the women in their entourage, with the envy of the lesser members of a lion pack— not invited to the feast— as they watched their leader devour a recent kill.

"We really should keep going," Wolf advised, glancing from Vera to the Russian soldiers, then back. "Because it looks like they're up to no good. So, the sooner we get to your place, the better."

* * *

To Vera's surprise, the door was half-open when they reached her house, making her immediately suspicious someone was inside. She turned to Victor, behind her, who quickly flipped a switch with wires leading off into the room. "See," he said, "the colonel assured me that von Lehmann— if he is *our* man—wouldn't be making any drawings in the dark."

"How?" she asked, looking at the strange light in her living room.

"Car headlamps and batteries. Which with your window curtains now removed, are creating more light."

"Without much furniture to lay the curtains across," she pointed out, shaking her head. But then she recalled Franz describing the car headlamp lighting the Russians used in the rooms where they tortured their high-ranking, Third Reich prisoners. "It's much stronger than my normal lighting."

"Which is why we Russians like it," said Peter, with a note of pride. "But just as important are these pocket-torches our colonel sent to aid your guests in their searches upstairs and in your cellar."

"As I'm sure they'll need," she replied, watching him remove them from a large box beneath the Black Forest clock on the wall in her foyer.

Fearing for an instant those Mongol soldiers might be hiding in one of the rooms, she thought about asking him, '*What if we have unwelcome visitors?' Of course those soldiers don't know where I live unless— but they've stopped following me, haven't they? So why worry?*

Still, with all the ruined houses and buildings in the neighborhood, is it not possible for a soldier to work his way through them and get ahead of me before I realize it?

Hopefully not, but since she couldn't be certain the uneasiness sweeping through her continued to prick her nerves.

"We're not expecting any more shooting today around here," said Victor. "But since there are Germans out there refusing to surrender, the colonel came two days ago and inspected your understairs storage area." A silence passed as he gave the door a closer look.

"He declared it to be structurally sound and was impressed that two people could be sheltered in it during an emergency."

"Boris made it that way," Vera informed him. "So if we came under attack and couldn't make it to the cellar, we'd have a fairly secure place in the center of this house."

Peter went over and opened the door under the stairs. "Not much room, but still, *three* people could stuff themselves in there if they had to."

"And I'm pleased, but now—" She turned to her four guests. "Franz asked me to telephone him once we arrived. So make yourselves at home while I do it." She fluffed a pillow on the sofa next to her mahogany piano. "And afterwards we'll go upstairs so you can search in the guest bedroom, while I'm in my bedroom getting out of these wet, smelly clothes."

She reached for the phone, counting the seconds until Franz came on the line.

He sounded relieved to hear her voice. Although he gave her some news that intensified the bad feeling sweeping through her.

She had guests in her cellar.

He then went onto inform her that shortly after she'd left, Claus, the father of her distant relative and former neighbor, Gretchen Tovarishki, had called him from a bombed- out building. He, his daughter, granddaughter, and badly wounded son, Guntar Sonntag, had been with the Freedom Marchers. But luckily, when the massacre happened, they'd been able to get away and hide in a root cellar nearby.

"And *now* they're in my cellar!" Vera exclaimed, the phone threatening to fall from her hand at the news.

"Yes... with Guntar seriously wounded from catching *shrapnel* the day before.

So lying on the stretcher his family had made for him, he'd urged them to take him and join the Freedom Marchers heading to the British and Americans on the Elbe."

"And they got to my house this quickly?" But before Franz could answer, the phone went dead.

CHAPTER TWENTY-NINE

A wounded Wehrmacht soldier in my cellar, with two N.K.V.D. agents in my living room, was all Vera could think. *Which is why Kurt and Wolf will need to help me move Guntar and his family into the part of the cellar my brother leased.*

But before she approached them, she had to make sure von Lehmann was comfortable with the drafting board and other supplies Colonel Sokolov had sent. "I hope everything is to your liking."

"Why wouldn't it be, my sweet Vera?" von Lehmann asked, gazing at her, then at the board like he needed to hurry and get started. "But even if it wasn't, I'd figure out a way to do what needs to be done."

"Which means I mustn't keep you." She smiled, moving a folded, lace coverlet as Peter flipped open Wolf's briefcase to show the music inside it. *Why was he doing that?* She watched him as he straightened it on a small, round table across from the stairs.

"That lace coverlet is lovely," said von Lehmann, distracting her.

"It *was*—until one of Sokolov's men pissed on it."

"Why the *damn* nerve of him!"

"It's all right." She quickly took his hand. "Because I know someone whose cleaning skills will restore it."

"Even so, it still doesn't excuse him."

"I know. But once the Americans arrive things will get better."

"And when will that be? Two months or three months?"

"Two months if we're hearing right," Vera replied, continuing to wonder about the open briefcase with Jaclyn's music showing. "But who knows?"

"Then I'd best get busy, since time doesn't appear to be on my side." He reached for some thumb tacks to secure his paper on the drafting board.

"I wish you the best," she said, waiting until he'd begun sketching before she gave her OSS guests their small pocket-torches. "Follow me upstairs so you'll see the disarray my things are in from Sokolov's previous searches."

Wolf gave her kitchen a quick look. "And you're keeping everything overturned like it is in here?"

"Sokolov maintains it'll be easier for you to search the place."

"It probably will be," he remarked, flashing his pocket-torch at the stairs as they started up.

Stepping into Vera's bedroom, it was obvious Sokolov's people had ransacked it like they'd done her cupboards.

All the drawers had been opened with their contents emptied onto the floor.

Bela stared at a broken lamp. "No one's mentioned it, but what exactly do we do if we find those papers the Russians couldn't?"

"What the Russians expect us to do." Wolf grinned. "Hand them over, since we're their allies—"

"No." Vera broke in. "Find a way to smuggle them to London. Which, for the record, no one seems to have figured out yet."

Jaclyn released a long, audible sigh. "No one has because from the looks of everything here, we're not going to find something the Russians couldn't. And like we've said, they didn't know what to do with us after identifying von Lehmann, so Sokolov invented this ruse to keep us busy until our plane returns."

Bela picked up a thin garment from the floor. "Do you have enough clothes here to change out of those wet pieces you're still wearing, Vera?" she asked her.

"Last time I checked I had a shirt, vest, slacks, and a pair of sport boots in the *armoire* in the other bedroom."

Jaclyn turned toward the door. "Would you like me to go and get your things for you?"

Vera glanced at her sideways. "Any other time, but since I have relatives in my cellar who're in trouble—"

"Gretchen Tovarishki?" Kurt asked, interrupting.

She nodded. "You and Fresa's good friend. Who's waiting with her daughter, father, and badly wounded brother—"

"Yes. Guntar Sonntag," he remembered. "Who was in the Wehrmacht."

"The *Wehrmacht!*" Wolf shot back. "So we're helping someone like that?"

"If there'd been no Wehrmacht, then there'd have been only S.S." said Vera, boldly meeting his accusing eyes. "And besides, Guntar was a courier for a general here in Berlin, throughout the entire war. And like the other members of his family, he wanted to do something to help the Jews when they learned about those terrible camps."

"Then how'd he get wounded?" asked Wolf.

"Most likely fighting alongside the general against the advancing Russian forces—"

"Which shouldn't matter," Kurt insisted. "Since my wife and I were fond of the family. So if they need our help, then tell us what Wolf and I need to do."

"Move the family into Boris's part of the cellar that joins mine."

"Then we should hurry before the N. K.V. D. finds a reason to check out *your* cellar," said Wolf, stepping into the hall. "But what about Bela and Jaclyn?"

"I'll tell Victor and Peter they're searching the upstairs," said Vera. "While you men are busy searching my part of the cellar."

"Good thinking," Kurt praised her as he and Wolf followed her downstairs to the living room.

* * *

But when Vera started down the twenty steps leading to her cellar, Wolf stopped midway and asked, "How do we get to Boris's part of the cellar from here?"

"Through that door, with three steps leading up to it and three steps leading down," she answered, flashing her torch at it. "The cellar in this house was quite large, so Boris and I divided it. Which prompted him to put a fireplace in his part and rent it to a friend who did upholstery."

"And this friend is where?" asked Wolf.

"He later got drafted and was killed."

"The door connecting it to Boris's doesn't have a lock," Kurt remarked. "Is it because the *Fuhrer* gave orders that— whenever possible— the cellars of the shops and houses on each block should be connected by doors without locks?"

"Yes," she answered." So people could tunnel through them."

Wolf pursed his lips. "Which hasn't seemed to have done anybody much good with all the rapes."

"In small ways maybe." She looked back at it. "Although with the exception of my cellar connecting to Carl's blocked one, it appears there are no locks on any of the other cellar doors in this block."

"War is chaos." Wolf shrugged, peering at Boris's cellar door.

"And if not the Russians, then it's someone else." Vera frowned. "But let's open the door to Boris's former upholstery shop and quickly move Gretchen and her family into it."

Two candles with flickering yellow lights on a folding card table acted like bookends for the portable radio playing between them.

Their communication equipment appeared to surprise Wolf and Kurt... as did a German Shepherd puppy on a leash.

But they said nothing as Vera introduced Gretchen and her daughter to Wolf.

Obviously remembering her former neighbor, the tall and very blond Gretchen rose from her folding chair and kissed Kurt. "I'm in shock to see you here at this dreadful time."

"What happened when I switched sides and joined the allies."

"Still, you did the right thing."

"I'd like to think so."

Gretchen's twelve year old daughter, Liesel, flashed a wide smile at him. "I kept the birthday present you and Fresa gave me several years ago." She brushed back a strand of her blond hair as she held up a gold, heart-shaped locket she had fastened to a chain around her neck.

"And it pleases me," Kurt said. "But what's your dog's name?"

"*Shay*. And he was a stray who came to us."

"I have a crate in the hall outside my kitchen," Vera told her. "And we can keep him there until I can find a way to get the four of you to the hospital."

"But will the hospital let me keep my dog?" asked Liesel.

"If they won't, Franz and I will keep him for you."

Gretchen's widowed father, Claus, sat in another folding chair at the foot of Guntar's stretcher. He had his rosary and was praying. So, no one said anything to him.

"He's aged since I last saw him," Kurt whispered to Vera. "The merciless lines on his face have deepened, and his hair is now completely gray."

"Life has not been easy for him."

"No it hasn't," Kurt agreed. "Because the pain of his struggle is clearly etched in his face. And it's like a scar from the toil and bitterness of the poverty he endured after the Great War, just so his family could eat."

"Quite sad, but true."

Fortunately, Gretchen had married Vera's cousin, a well-to-do, older White Russian man. And he'd helped his wife look after her family until his death, shortly before Liesel was born.

Then a portion of his money had stopped coming...something no one expected.

But Vera had eased the situation by enlisting Carl's help in investing what was left to get the family through the leaner times.

"Gretchen," said Vera, turning toward the semi-conscious Guntar. "How'd your brother get in this shape?"

"The general he worked for got shot. So two Wehrmacht officers handed him a rifle and ordered him to come with them." She wiped a tear from her cheek. "Although he'd never seen a day in combat."

More questions followed with Gretchen explaining to Vera what Franz had mentioned earlier about Guntar. "He kept insisting we join the Freedom Marchers and get to the British and American allies on the Elbe."

Luckily, they'd been at the tail-end of the human flood of people trying to escape Berlin, or otherwise the Russians would have either shot them or run over them.

Gretchen's voice dropped. "So we went to a bombed-out house nearby, that my husband had once owned, and hid in the root cellar behind it."

"Which was quite a distance from this place," Vera said, assessing the situation. "So how'd you get here this soon with all the danger?"

"Claus found a working phone in a bombed-out building several blocks away and called your Franz—"

"Who did what?"

"Told him to call back in five minutes while he contacted one of your enlisted, White Russian friends to see if he'd been able to get a truck."

Vera was stunned. "Which was extremely dangerous for all of you."

"We know. But we held our breaths and prayed. Because when my father called back, he was told this man had a truck nearby and was coming to get us."

"And just who gave it to him in this city of chaos?" Vera asked with considerable interest.

"Colonel Sokolov. With urgent orders from the marshal to go pick up some dispatches." Gretchen pointed at the radio. "Which I've no doubt are connected with the German surrender today that's being discussed."

Amazed, Vera shook her head. "Why on earth did you bring Guntar to me and not the hospital—"

"Because you have medicines."

"Which aren't nearly as good as the hospital's."

"I know. "But we're hearing the Russians are going into the German makeshift hospitals and either shooting the injured people or taking the ones not in bad shape as prisoners, so they can ship them off to Russia to help with the country's rebuilding."

"Why?" Vera asked "Because they suspect they're Freedom Marchers who managed to escape?"

"They are."

"Which I imagine is happening at these makeshift hospitals where the Bolsheviks are on guard, but I doubt at Carl's."

"Maybe." Gretchen shrugged, looking disconcerted. "But still, you'll help us?"

Frustrated, Vera stared at Guntar. "All depends on how serious his condition is."

Gretchen looked frightened. "And if it's really bad?"

"Then I'll have to find a way to get him moved to the hospital—"

"But first let's move him into Boris's cellar next door," interrupted Kurt. "Where the N.K.V.D. agents aren't apt to search again."

"Still, if you're afraid they'll come in here, then what's to stop them from going in there?" Gretchen asked him.

"Because they've searched Boris's cellar more times than I can count," said Vera before Kurt could answer. "And also Guntar's shivering so hard he needs the warmth of a fireplace with its chimney still standing." She made a circular motion at a pile of fractured bricks. "Something mine no longer has."

* * *

As Kurt and Wolf waited, they listened to the radio as a voice on it said, *"We give thanks to Stalin for this new era of peace in Germany...."*

"New era—eh." Wolf sneered.

"Guntar's Wehrmacht uniform will get him shot for sure," Kurt told Vera. "So we'd better find him some civilian clothes."

"We have some crammed in a large, metal box in Boris's wooden chest, in his cellar, where we're moving him," said Vera. "And lucky for us, the box has a false bottom so you can hide his uniform."

"False bottom?" Wolf asked. "Do the Russians know about it?"

"Hardly. Since you have to upend it and tap on the bottom to get it to open."

"I suppose you've already checked to see von Lehmann's papers weren't there," Kurt remarked.

"The first place I looked after Boris was murdered."

"Then let's move Guntar there before our two N.K.V.D agents upstairs decide to pay us a surprise visit," said Wolf.

When Claus heard him say that he stopped praying."Guntar's suffering so if you can hurry and help me move him, Kurt, I'd be most grateful."

"That's why I'm here."

Everything went quickly as he and Claus moved Guntar, on his stretcher, into the cellar next door.

"Good thing there're only three steps up and three steps down," Wolf said, staring at them from Vera's cellar as he waited to help.

"When I come back I'm getting a very small fire going in the fireplace," she told Gretchen. "So it shouldn't attract much attention."

Then taking Shay by his leash, she started toward her twenty cellar steps. "He'll be safely kenneled," she assured Liesel, "should something unpleasant happen."

After she made her departure, Wolf went to Boris's cellar and helped Guntar out of his Wehrmacht uniform. Then, Claus and Kurt dressed him in some of Boris's clothes in the large, metal box.

"Where do we put his uniform?" asked Claus.

Wolf shook his head as he stared at the cellar's scant furnishings. "If there's room, it'll have to go in this false bottom of the metal box, which we'll put back in that wooden chest in here."

"Should be enough," said Kurt. He turned toward the cellar's unlocked door. "But what's really got me worried is—knowing this place like I do — someone on the street could enter this cellar through this former tailor shop's outside door. Which I presume is unlocked?"

"Anything we can do about this imminent threat?" Wolf asked Claus.

"Not really. Because the outside steps going down to the tailor shop are the only way you can get into Boris's cellar from the street."

Wolf stared at the door. "And this tailor shop's vacant?"

"For a long time." Claus shuddered as he drew in a sharp breath. "Since the Jews, who lived in the house and ran the shop from its cellar, got sent off."

"So the upholstery clients who came to the shop in Boris's cellar, entered from the outside steps leading down into this tailor shop?" Wolf asked, clearly finding it odd. "With an unlocked door leading from this tailor shop into Boris's out-of-business upholstery shop?"

Claus nodded. "And it's awkward, I know. But it was rumored these tailor shop owners had an investment in this upholstery shop."

Wolf's voice grew sharper. "What happened to the lock on the outside door leading into this former tailor shop?"

"It got broken."

"Damn!" Wolf began to pace. "Then we really should *prop* something against Boris's cellar door, since it opens into the tailor shop with its outside, unlocked door—" "But we don't have any big pieces of furniture," Kurt broke in, perplexed.

"Just the four folding chairs and card table we're bringing in from Vera's cellar," said Claus. He turned toward the workbench. "And it's attached to the wall like Boris's wooden chest."

Kurt sighed. "With only two small stools in front of it." He went over and picked one up.

They were across from the workbench where some cardboard boxes, with holes in each one, were stacked. Something he found peculiar. So flashing his pocket-torch at them, he noticed a black, straw hat crammed between two of them. It looked like it might have belonged to Vera. And was so attractive it prompted him to remove it from the boxes and take it over to the workbench.

Wondering what else the cardboard boxes might be hiding, he went back to them and peered through their holes. However, each box was empty. *Another oddity. As was the constricted space between the boxes and the walls.* Since with a small stool in the corner, discarded clothing, and ripped bedding scattered across the plank floor, it looked like someone had been living there. *Probably got in through the tailor shop's outside, unlocked door. Or maybe it was that person, looking for a place to sleep, who broke the lock?*

"But even so, it's a good place to hide Guntar should the need arise," Kurt remarked, thinking aloud, as he turned the boxes so their holes didn't show.

He continued to glance around, averting his eyes from the wooden, rocking horse in the corner he'd glimpsed earlier. *Carl told me it would be here and not to look.*

Although, the memories tearing at his heart made it impossible for his gaze not to drift over to it. And with despair threatening his control, he knew he had to touch it once again. *Little Erich's brown horse with its blond mane, that Fresa and I paid a friend to custom make for him.*

It was Fresa's idea to have the tall, wooden pole put on it. 'It'll make him happy, since you know how he loves it when we hold him and let him ride the merry-go-round at the amusement park,' she'd said.

Kurt's skin heated with shame. *When I marched through the blood of others, why did God not allow me to feel more of their pain?*

"Was it because I was in a world without *Him*, when I joined the Wehrmacht and became part of Hitler's macabre ambitions that caused the deaths of millions of innocent people?" His face twisted with agony as their suffering touched him deep inside. *Obviously it was. Which means losing Fresa, little Erich, and soon Bela, is God's punishment for my wrongdoing.*

But would I have joined the Wehrmacht if von Lehmann hadn't made me feel like a charity case for not marrying my mother, when she was on her deathbed?

The reparations after the Great War had destroyed Germany so badly it was like it was no longer a sovereign nation. 'Germany will rise,' the *Fuhrer* was quick to say. 'Because now the German people will no longer have to look to those who have the money and the power.'

And von Lehmann had opposed everything the *Fuhrer* was offering. *So what better way for me to get back at this man— who'd defiled my mother— than by joining the Wehrmacht?*

However if I'd remained in Vienna I'd have been forced to join anyway. "My only hope would have been to do what Wolf did," he said, continuing to think aloud. "But would I have done it if I'd been given his funds? Or better yet, if I *hadn't* been made to feel like a charity case? Then how would this new hope the *Fuhrer* offered have affected me?"

But not having Wolf's money, he had no way of knowing what he would have done.

Kurt wiped his hand across his eyes when he thought about how his mother never failed to remind him that von Lehmann *did* love them... *even if I might never understand why such a kind and thoughtful man had refused to marry her...probably not.*

Yet, it did wrench his heart each time he thought about von Lehmann hiding behind a bush so he could watch Fresa play with little Erich.

Now Kurt wanted to go upstairs and hug his frail shoulders, but knew better. "With two N.K.V.D. watching him while he makes those *damned* drawings, I'm not about to distract him."

"What?" Vera asked him, returning to the cellar. She'd freshened up. Her dark hair was combed, and she was wearing a clean shirt, vest, slacks, and laced up boots similar to Bela's. *Though* both her hands were full, with a medical bag in one, while in the other was a box lid with two candles, coffee cups, a coffee pot, and a thermos with a label on it reading *tea*.

"I was just thinking about von Lehmann and those two agents."

"Well everything seems all right so far." She shifted nervously. "But hold your breath."

CHAPTER THIRTY

K urt took the box lid from her.

"If you don't mind brewing a pot of coffee in the fireplace, I'd certainly be grateful," she said. "Because that way I can take Guntar's temperature and pulse, so I can get a better idea about his condition."

"Anything to help Guntar and his father,"

Kurt motioned at Wolf, who was listening to the Russian propaganda on the radio.

"I forgot to ask, Vera, but is it all right for me to play this radio?" He jammed his hands in his coat pocket as he turned to her for an answer.

"We need to hear the news the Russians are putting out. So as long as it doesn't get noisy in here, it shouldn't matter," she said, putting her medical bag on the table and unzipping it. "I've got morphine and sleeping pills in here. Plus some prontosil for infections Carl gave me." She handed the thermos to Claus. "This wasn't in the basket I helped prepare at the hospital for our guests yesterday, but it looks like today somebody put a thermos of tea in the bottom of it. So for the time being, give Guntar two pills from each of my three medicines here and have him swallow them with this tea." Her fingers lightly brushed his temples. "Because like it or not, his fevered face is telling me we've got to find a way to get him to the hospital."

Gretchen began laying out Guntar's pills. "The hospital's only three blocks away, so why can't we just take Guntar and walk there?"

"Because we have marauding Russian Mongols in the neighborhood, looking for women to rape," Vera replied in a crisp tone.

"Did you tell Franz?"

Vera released a tremulous breath. "I had no way, Gretchen, with my telephone dead. And given our present situation, I didn't think it wise to ask Victor or Peter to have someone radio him until I can feel them out about your presence here."

"So what do we do just wait?"

She nodded. "While I try and get Victor or Peter to come with Kurt, Wolf, and myself while we walk you to the hospital." Vera's gaze drifted in its direction. "Where the four of you need to remain until it's safe."

Gretchen looked increasingly uneasy. "But I still feel the Russians could threaten us, making it dangerous to be there."

"Everything's dangerous in this town," Vera warned. "So be prepared."

'With Wolf, and Peter or Victor, do you really need me?' Kurt considered asking her. It wasn't like he didn't want to help Guntar, it was just that the little strip of time between his future and the present was rapidly dissolving. And whenever he thought about how soon his togetherness with Bela would end, his throat tightened with a knot of helplessness, leaving his raw heart to stumble in the darkness.

"My dreams will soon vanish," he murmured, poking at the thought like he might have done with a walking stick on wet ground. And once again he saw himself reduced to the number on the pocket of his prisoner-of- war shirt. *With the Tommies shackling me to a seat in a train car until we reach the prison camp.... And while this train speeds through the British countryside taking me back to the men I've trained with, I'll close my eyes trying to sleep, with occasional spirit-kisses of remembrance from Bela finding their way into my dreams.*

Misery gnawed at him. *Not too many hours left before the sun drops below the horizon,"* he reflected. *And after we get to London, Bela and I will part company. And I'll not see her again.*

He lowered his head as he imagined he heard the rapid ticking of the Black Forest clock in the foyer. *Something else to remind me that the distance between Bela and me is widening... and we'll soon be very far apart.*

* * *

Vera headed back into her cellar with Wolf and Kurt. "I've made Guntar's predicament clear to his family, so now's the time to confront our two N.K.V.D. agents."

"What's the plan to get von Lehmann to London?" Wolf asked her before she started up the steps. "The OSS said you and Franz are supposed to have worked something out— however, we have no idea what it is."

"Since we know now von Lehmann is *who* he says he is, then his departure should happen next week."

Wolf gazed at her with uncertainty. "But what's to keep the Russians from shipping him back to Moscow tomorrow?"

"Nothing… although Carl's treatment program is working so well it's unlikely."

"Still," Kurt spoke up. "You've got to get him out of the hospital without Carl being arrested."

"Which we will," she assured him. "Because all von Lehmann has to do is tell Carl he's suddenly remembered some papers he's buried in something like a secret capsule, close to where he was launching his model rocket." She smiled briefly. "And then Carl will call Colonel Sokolov, who'll send over some soldiers to escort von Lehmann to where he thinks the papers are buried."

"And when they get there, then what?" Kurt asked. "Will von Lehmann get kidnapped?"

"By some Wehrmacht soldiers who're trying to get out of Berlin," she informed him as she stood in the shadowed doorway. "They'll kill the Russians, grab von Lehmann, and get to Lake Wannsee, where a previously arranged amphibian aircraft should be waiting to fly them to Stuttgart."

"I don't like it," Wolf remarked. "Because it's much too dangerous for a man of von Lehmann's age."

"It is," Vera agreed. "But it's all we have."

Kurt's gaze shifted between them. "I'd like to accompany the pilot, but I doubt the Tommies will let me."

"They won't." She shook her head emphatically. "But let's bring Jaclyn and Bela down here and see what Gretchen and her family think about our two *very* talented musicians."

"Good idea."

* * *

A few minutes later, when Vera opened the door to her living room, Jaclyn and Bela were sitting on the sofa next to where von Lehmann—in deep concentration— was attempting to finish some of his drawings and equations.

"You two should be doing some more searching," Victor told Jaclyn and Bela in an authoritative tone.

"More searching?" questioned Jaclyn, her chin resting on her hand. "In case you haven't figured it out, Bela and I are *not* the maids."

Forced to face off with this disgusting Bolshevik, Vera said, "But right now we seem to have a bigger problem."

Her shift in conversation immediately drew his attention, as it did von Lehmann's, when she gave him a blow by blow account of her predicament.

"Interesting a relative of yours has been shot and is about to die," remarked Peter with a cool detachment. "And you really believe this wound of his is from a sniper's bullet?"

"It's *shrapnel*. "She bit off the word. "I should know, since I've seen enough of it in the hospital—"

"And they're good people," interrupted von Lehmann. "Because I met them in the hospital after poor Boris died."

"Then I'll see what I can do," said Victor heading toward the front door.

A moment passed before he pointed at a truck across the street. "If there's a radio in it, I'll have the truck's driver contact the colonel and see how he thinks we should handle this matter," he informed her before stepping back outside.

But after he returned, several minutes passed before the driver came to the door and announced, "I'm unable to make contact with the colonel."

Anxiety spurted through Vera. "What's the problem?" she asked Victor,

"I have no idea," he said, his mouth twisting with reluctance like he hated to admit there was something he didn't know.

"Then have the operator contact Franz and see what he knows," she pressed. "Or—"

"What?'

"My pulse will explode."

Victor grinned slightly. "Then I suppose I'll have to."

So they all waited, until the driver came back and informed them, "The colonel's in a meeting with Marshal Zhukov and Major-General Volkov, and has left orders not to be disturbed."

"Now what do we do?" asked Vera, agitated. "Guntar needs to get to the hospital and—"

"We *wait*," Victor cut her short, his stern-expression forbidding any more questions.

She gave him one of her icy stares. "While my cousin dies?"

His jaw tightened. "Sorry— but it can't be helped."

"Then I'll have to introduce Jaclyn and Bela to Gretchen," she said, making no attempt to mask her irritation. "And I'll see if they want to come with Kurt, Wolf, and myself as we help Gretchen and her family carry Guntar, on his stretcher, to the hospital."

With a surprised look, Victor sprang to his feet. "But without protection that's dangerous, *Frau* Dietrich or Tovarishki," he reminded, with a hint of mockery." Which *you* of all people should know."

"Of course I do. But if we don't hear from the colonel soon, we have no other choice. So, if Jaclyn will be so kind to get her autographed pictures from her briefcase, then it'll be a pleasure for me to take them to the cellar and introduce both she and Bela to my family. Which perhaps will relax them for a brief time."

Grinning, Jaclyn went over to the briefcase and removed the pictures.

* * *

In the cellar Bela and Jaclyn took as much delight in meeting and exchanging hugs with Gretchen, Liesel, and Claus as they did. "You're both so-o beautiful," Liesel exclaimed. And taking Bela's hand, she told her that her golden- hair made her look like a princess in a fairy tale.

Bela was humbled by the remark. But when Kurt said he agreed, her cheeks burned.

Gretchen also clutched Bela's hand. "We didn't know about those camps like you were in until it was too late. And we wanted to do something, but Vera said it was so dangerous we'd have to wait until after the war and concentrate on helping the survivors."

"Which gives me reason to believe that today you were spared so you could do just that," Vera replied, smiling hopefully.

"We'd like to think," said Claus, before turning to Bela and asking, "Did those trains pull straight up to the ovens?"

It was a question Bela didn't want to answer but felt obligated to do so. "People were sent to the gas chambers first," she said, a firestorm of emotion threatening to shatter her. "But since they'd been crammed in cattle cars for several days, they were covered in excrement—"

"My God!" Claus exclaimed. "Then they were taken straight to the ovens?"

"No *showers*—as the S.S. called them," she clarified, remembering *Herr* Wallenberg's words.

Suddenly Gretchen began sobbing. "And *you* saw all that?"

"Not really." Then catching her breath on a sigh, Bela added, "Since I wasn't in that kind of a camp."

"Was there another kind?" asked Claus, looking surprised.

"Yes," Kurt spoke up, the familiar sadness returning to his eyes. "Close to the front." He paused as if struggling to keep his emotions at bay. "But it's something we'd prefer not to discuss."

"It was something I told him in confidence," Bela quickly said, not wanting to arouse any more suspicions with Wolf and Jaclyn than they already had.

Her response brought fresh sobs from Gretchen. "The front," she choked back a cry. "W...why a camp out there must have been almost as horrifying—"

"It was, but in a different way."

As tears kept pouring from her eyes, Gretchen insisted that she, Liesel, and Claus each gave Bela a hug for her bravery. Who deeply touched, didn't hesitate to return their affection.

Sensing Kurt's pain, Bela put her arms around him. "Remember, Kurt, you switched sides."

"At the last minute," he remarked in a disgusted tone. "Which makes me angry for not doing it sooner."

"Doesn't matter." She gave his hand a loving squeeze. "As time goes by, some good will come from it. Just wait and watch—"

"Time to get back to my living room." interrupted Vera, taking a step toward the connecting door between her cellar and Boris's. "But before we go back, I need to tell Jaclyn and Bela about our plan to kidnap von Lehmann and fly him to London."

They gathered around her as she described it in detail. And like Wolf, they both agreed it was quite dangerous for a man of von Lehmann's age.

"Is there no other way?" Jaclyn asked.

"Afraid not." Vera sighed, avoiding her gaze.

"A pity.

When they finally reached the door, Kurt stopped Bela. "We don't have much time left."

"Something I'm trying not to think about."

"Like me. But tell me, will Victor get upset if you wait here with me until he makes contact with the colonel?"

"He might." She lifted one shoulder in a shrug. "But who cares?"

"I'm going back to bring some food down," Vera told Bela from the door. "So if you and Kurt want something specific to eat or drink, then let me know."

But after an exchange of looks, they shook their heads."

"I'll be happy, Vera, to pack some of that good food in the basket for your family," Jaclyn volunteered. "Since that way all of them will have something to eat at the hospital."

"Smart thinking, *Frau* von Friesen." She smiled, holding the door open for her. "As long as Victor and Peter don't take more than their share."

"Which knowing them, they will," Wolf grumbled.

* * *

When the door closed, Kurt ushered Bela over to the workbench in Boris's cellar.

"You can sit here, *liebchen*," he said, pulling out one of the stools for her.

A yellow glow from the two additional candles Vera had brought earlier enveloped the workbench in a soft light.

Without electricity she'd deemed the candles necessary, after Guntar had been moved into the former upholstery shop... even though the open section of damaged roof there was *now* similar to hers. 'I was told the roof was hit last week,' Vera had informed everyone. "And there's a little light coming from the holes in the floor and ceiling above, but it's still not as much as I'd like. So we'll need some more candles.'

Under this warm candlelight, Kurt looked at the picture in his wallet of his fair-haired wife and little boy. Then, looked again at the rocking horse with its merry-go-round pole.

His grandfather, Carl, had insisted the wood on the pole was too fragile. So he'd paid the carpenter extra to make a carved, outside pole that screwed into the horse's back in front of the saddle.

"Will you tell me about your son?" asked Bela, her soft voice cutting through his sorrow.

"Our little one. "He shoved his wallet back in his pocket. "Who I never got to hug, kiss, or play with enough. And I was with his mother when he was born—"

His voice broke, so he quickly shifted subjects. "Will you write to me, Bela?"

"Of course," she said, the sadness of their departure clearly weighing heavily on her. "Until you're happily married and have a little boy."

Little boy? Pain stabbed him. *He wasn't worthy of another little boy, any more than he was worthy of Bela. God was testing him when he'd been forced to witness the shooting of Ivan's partisans. And he'd failed Him when he hadn't tossed them his pistol and given them a fighting chance. True...they would have probably killed him, but then his death would have canceled it all.*

"Where will you go when we get to London?" Bela asked, returning his attention to her.

"Supposedly Albert will be waiting to take me to Switzerland but—"Again he stopped speaking, clamping his mouth to lengthen the moment.

"But knowing the Tommies, I'm sure they have a special plan for me."

Time continued to close in on them...and life will soon part us.

The grief of their upcoming departure breaking his heart with a loneliness as cold as the void between stars....She would go to Palestine, but God knew where he'd end up after the Tommies finished with him. He still doubted he'd be at Albert's, even if he'd been assured he would be,

"Drinks and refreshments," announced Vera, returning with a large tray. "So indulge yourselves while you can."

She went over to her family, but they shook their heads. "I understand, Gretchen," she told her." But no matter, because Jaclyn is packing a basket to take with you."

"Victor and Peter packed some food in my rucksack," Kurt reminded Vera. "Which can be used instead of the basket, since it has a zipper."

"And you don't need it?"

He swung around. "If I did Victor wouldn't let me take it back to London...but here." He handed her the black, straw hat he'd found between the cardboard boxes.

"Pretty, but not mine." She smiled, not even looking mildly curious about whose it had been. "So give it to Bela."

"But I've nothing to put it in," she pointed out. "Especially since Victor and Peter are so afraid we'll find those papers and hide them, they won't let us carry anything but Jaclyn's briefcase. Which they're closely watching."

"Then wear it," Kurt suggested. "Because it will complement that lovely dress you have."

"Guess I'll have to." Bela grinned, putting it on. "Since I've always liked hats."

Vera reflected her grin. "It looks good on you and helps to wipe those sorrowful expressions off your face and Kurt's." She set her tray down on the workbench. "Two wine goblets and some fine cognac—all for your enjoyment."

But they declined.

"My goodness," she said. "What's the matter with you? Life is short so follow your hearts."

Her implied meaning was obvious. So Bela joined Kurt in accepting the cognac.

Then here's to following our hearts," he said, his goblet echoing against hers with the sentiment. And taking her hand, a deep pang of longing pierced him when her eyes met his and held them.

His desire ignited as he sipped the cognac and brushed her legs with the hardness of his thighs. "Let's not be shy."

"Let's not."

And squeezing her hand, he felt her tingle from his touch.

O-oh, how he'd imagined this moment.

* * *

Bela shook with emotion as he took her face in his hands and kissed her open mouthed.

His lips parted again, only this time his tongue swept between hers as the comfort they'd given each other at the Love Camp surfaced again.

Her mouth blazed with fire at the voice in her head whispering, '*Kurt, my shield— who speaks the language of heartbeats with his sweet, tender kisses.*'

"What say we take our happiness where we find it?" he asked, speaking the words against her open lips.

Immediately, her heart thundered with excitement. "Where?".

"On the other side of that pile of cardboard boxes." He pointed at them. "And there's some old bedding and scattered pieces of clothing on the wooden, plank floor behind them. So it's not as hard and cold as it looks."

"But will anyone hear us?" she asked, shooting a covert look in Claus's direction.

"Not with that portable radio playing. And besides this is a big cellar, and Vera's people are across the room rooted in their folding chairs, staring at Guntar."

"With such solemn expressions it makes them look like mourners at his funeral," Bela replied in a subdued voice.

"I know. And like his father, I'm praying he makes it."

CHAPTER THIRTY-ONE

What Kurt wanted was her heart, which he could never have. But at this moment, all he could think was that she would at least be his for one more time. And the burning sweetness he felt when he held her on this lovely spring afternoon would have to last him through eternity.

"In case we get interrupted, I'll adjust my clothes," he said.

"But since you're wearing that lovely dress which buttons down the front over your sweater and slacks, you'll be able to put it on quickly. So all you'll need to remove is your sweater and slacks—"

"And my boots?" She looked down at them. "Do I leave them on or off?"

"Leave them— on just in case."

No one noticed them as they slipped behind the pile of empty, cardboard boxes. However, the space was so constricted they were barely a breath apart.

She tugged her sweater and camisole over her head. And his hands moved down her arms as he helped her discard them.

Afterwards, he kissed her on the nape of her neck; then ran his hands over the peaks of her smooth breasts as they ripened to fullness at his touch. "They're likecrested waves with rosy caps," he whispered, locking his arms around her so he could hold her in this very tight space as she stepped out of her slacks and panties.

"If only we could have skin on skin contact," he remarked with a pang. regretting he couldn't feel the shapely beauty of her naked body against his fully clothed one as he rubbed against her.

"Kurt." She let her head drop." The way we did it the first time... can we do it like that again?"

"When I flipped you?"

"It greatly aroused me. And you drove into me so hard that for an instant I felt like crying—but then it got better, *much* better."

"*God*!" he blurted, all pleasure suddenly leaving him. "Then unlike those other brutes at the Love Camp, I must have hurt you without meaning to."

"On the contrary." She brightened, her heart clattering against his.

"The sincerity I saw in your soulful eyes, let me know that no matter *what*, you wouldn't hurt me. So I wasn't worried. Although, the delicious sensations from your powerful thrusts made me so desperate for release that the prolonged anticipation of it threatened to send me over the edge."

"Then, *liebchen*, I'll do whatever you think is good for you. Because your blood is so hot, I get hard just thinking about it." He smiled again, his hand massaging the smoothness of her bare bottom as he continued to admire the stunning beauty of her naked frame. "But for now remain the way you are, since I want to kiss you in places I didn't have time to do before— plus the places I did."

He held her in a tight embrace as he slid his knee between her thighs.

And searching her eyes, he allowed a few seconds to pass before imprinting a series of delightful, shivery kisses on her shoulders, breasts, and belly. And once again pressing a kiss at the pulsing hollow of her throat. "I love you more than you can imagine."

* * *

"How well I know," Bela murmured.

"Which greatly pleases me." He eased one of his fingers in her pleasure point, and sliding it in and out. And she moaned aloud at the intimacy of his touch.

Then kneeling, he sent her to higher levels of ecstasy by stroking the delta of her desire with his thrusting tongue.

Caught up in this sweeping current of growing arousal, her anticipation made her anxious to reach the peak of delight as she responded eagerly to the seduction of his mouth.

"I'm burning inside," she said against his lips. "Which several of your vigorous thrusts should easily assuage."

"Several?" he asked with a grin. "When I'm ready to turn your burning center into a crimson comet blazing across the heavens?"

The beat of her pulse in her throat skyrocketed. "And make me continue to grow weak with need?"

"Absolutely."

His lips touched hers with a drugging caress as he thrust his tongue in her mouth, allowing her to taste the essence of her burning center. And she breathed deeply between her parted lips, powerless to resist the passion of this magnificent kiss.

He reached for her dress. "Here. Slip this on so you'll be prepared if someone barges in," he said, helping her into it. "But forget about the tiny buttons."

"What if the dress slides off?"

"It shouldn't if I'm holding it."

She smiled at the thought. "Should be fine as long as you don't forget to hold me too."

"Impossible."

Desperate to feel him inside her, she got down on all fours with her knees on a piece of the bedding.

"A tantalizing temptation impossible to resist," he said, playfully lifting her thin, cotton dress above her hips. "And seeing you waiting for me gives me great joy," he added, giving her several love pats before unzipping his fly and aligning his lower body to hers.

More surges of excitement followed. But when he trust into her like he had the first time, the jolt of his hard flesh was explosive... shaking the roots of her being as he stroked her pleasure point from behind.

Then he gave her several more energetic thrusts, before putting his arms around her waist and turning her over to face him.

"Although I do have a question," he said, his hands resting casually on her shoulders. "If I'm not around, then who will ease your burning center?"

Her dress slid from her shoulders. "If you're not around, then I won't have a burning center."

He ran his over her breasts before they joined again.

"Oh my *liebchen*," he whispered, warming her face with his breath.

Arching her back above the wooden floor, she closed her eyes briefly while tangling her fingers in his dark hair and inhaling the warm scent of his hard body on top of hers.

A storm with the fury of a rolling locomotive raged between them as he positioned his knees inside hers. "Are you ready to blaze across the heavens with me?" he asked, with one of his enchanting smiles.

"Yes."

Her desire for his hardness was so overwhelming, it was like a warm river rushing through her when he lifted her hips higher and pushed himself into her with an urgent thrust.

She wrapped her legs around him, and the boundaries between them dissolved. Returning her to the lusty memories of his body against hers when their melting hearts had joined, and his warmth had flowed into her like a dissolving taper's.

"Bela," he said her name softly, returning her awareness to him." I could hold you like this forever."

"Same as I could you," she whispered. Meeting him thrust for thrust with eager anticipation as the clean brightness of her former Viennese world rushed into her, like she sensed it was rushing into him. *How great it was to experience pleasure with him.*

He lifted her again, so he could push faster and deeper... a sensual onslaught that enabled her to reach a fevered pitch in her spinning world. Even if it did seem an endless moment before the sensations buffeting her, turned her burning center into a blazing comet.

And when it did she grinned with delight at this tempo that bound their bodies in sheer joy.

Warmth circled her heart, and she closed her eyes an instant before this blazing comet pulsing between her legs, erupted in a downpour of fiery embers."My precious Kurt." She moaned... the delicious aftershock shattering her.

Sparks continued to splinter through her from this erotic assault until Kurt, joining her in this ebbing bliss, kissed her forehead so tenderly, those sparks became a glowing star.... *That lifts my spirit, with a brightness shiny enough to ease the sorrow of the words Feldhure branded between my breasts.*

Now filled to overflowing, she marveled at the deep tremors of Kurt's release...for his lovemaking had been more glorious than a tropical island perfumed with the spice-scented blooms of exotic plants.

"At least my burning center got eased quicker than my burning bottom did," she said, snuggling against him.

"*Liebchen,* if you'll recall I know all about burning bottoms. Which means that when the opportunity presents itself, I have every intention of taking this ObersturmFuhrer Helmer out for beating you."

"No, Kurt, it's too risky. So don't do it on my account."

"We'll see," he replied, raising a brow as if contemplating it. "Once those *damned* Tommies release me."

"All I can say is they'd *better.*"

"Yes, *indeed,*" he whispered, his breath warm against her cheek.

Some minutes passed as she lay sheltered in the warmth of his limp arms, uttering his name lovingly several times.

"The way you speak my name feels like redemption for all the deaths I caused, fighting for the wrong side," he said, pressing a reverent kiss against her forehead.

"I'm pleased you feel that way," she said, savoring the feeling of satisfaction.

After becoming lovers once again, his extraordinary kisses and touches made her runaway heart want to tell him, *'I know now that I can be strong and always give you the love you deserve but—'* She could never give him a little boy of his flesh, even if he didn't expect her to. *Because he's a man who loved being a father and needs to be one again.*

And then a new revelation dawned on her; Fate's diabolic joke was not about *her* but about *him....* A man who'd supported a cause which prevented her from being able to give birth.

Though the thought quickly fragmented when his fingers, stroking her hair, prompted her to kiss him. "Is it standing up in several places?"

He nodded.

"Doesn't matter."

"Still, I'd better fix it in case Wolf comes looking for us," he said, taking his comb and gently smoothing it.

She allowed a smile to blossom on her lips as she sniffed the air." It smells like sex in here, does it to you?"

"Of course." He beamed. "Since as we're both aware, that's what happens when people get excited like we did, but—"His voice was soft against her hair." I am concerned about one thing."

"What?"

"That you might be sore."

"I'm not," she assured him, her lips feather-touching his chin. "But even if I were, your lovemaking is so wonderful it would just be a lingering sweetness reminding me of the beauty we've shared."

He gazed at her with a look as warm as his lips on her mouth. "You make me feel the same way...but glancing at my watch, we've still got some time, so shall we begin again?"

"Absolutely. "Continuing to hear nothing but heartbeats... *then more heartbeats,* each time she buried her face against his chest.

"This time, I'll try not to mess up your hair."

"I'm not worried, since I can always put on that straw hat."

He laughed rubbing her naked spine. "I'd like to see Wolf's expression if you do."

"He would probably look like he did when Vera told him that each German girl who received food from a Russian soldier in exchange for sex, called him her *Wolf.*"

"Definitely surprising." Then redirecting the conversation, he smoothed his fingers over her face. "No matter what, *liebchen,* we need to stay together."

"We will with our letters," she reminded, fighting back tears.

"But you'll see as time goes by, you'll meet someone who'll make you happier than I'll ever be able to."

He reached for her dress on the floor. "Something I doubt because if you're in Palestine after the Tommies release me, then I'm going there."

"Kurt—please." She lifted her hand to silence him and then put her arm around his shoulder. "Promise me you'll give yourself a chance with someone else before you do."

"No—absolutely not!"

"But, Kurt, I'll always care about you, which is why I want so desperately to do this." She fastened several of her dress's buttons. "So, please sit on that stool and let me show you—"

"Show me what?"

"How much I want to give to you," she said, admiring the sensuality of his physique before pushing his legs apart and kneeling between them. "And besides, I love your impressive length." His fly still unzipped, she reached for it.

"My God, Bela!" he gasped. "What about *your* pleasure?"

"Doesn't matter," she said squeezing his hand. "Because I want you to realize that even after what your kind did to me and my father, when someone feels as strongly about your happiness as I do, that you should listen to them."

He started to say something, but before he could she bowed her head and her tongue swept against his organ, caressing and stroking it.

"Bela, sweet love, you don't have to do this—"

"Yes I do," she insisted, running her fingers across the purplish skin around his genitals. "Since your happiness is at stake. Which means *if* it makes you happy,

I'd let you take me that perverted way those soldiers took me at the Love Camp." She eased closer to him. "And I might even kiss your feet if you weren't wearing those boots."

* * *

The words had a profound effect on Kurt. "B... but, Bela—"he gasped, unable to finish the sentence as the heavenly sensation of her mouth moving over his shaft, took his breath away.

He leaned back against the wall, his heart racing as he savored her very soft and very warm mouth. *Was it possible that in the Prometheus myth the fire was not really fire but a woman like Bela he'd stolen from the gods who could make the fire within?*

And losing himself in her thoughtfulness and beauty, Kurt closed his eyes, remembering a magician years ago with fireworks that cast images of butterflies, ballerinas, gold rings, and white birds with giant wings, waiting to transport him to a world of endless possibilities... like his world now, with Bela's mouth on him. Which instantly made the war, with its rattle of machine guns, incoming artillery, Russian tanks rolling over people, and the *Katyushas*—Russia's howling rockets with their echoing rhythm—cease to exist as her lips, warm and wet against him, filled him with an amazing sense of completeness.

And for several minutes he felt quite strong... without pain, without loss. "Bela, sweet Bela, the uproar's gone, and the battle no longer rages."

He looked at his clothing but couldn't recognize his uniform because his great *transgression* of fighting with an army that supported concentration camps and mass extermination, simply drifted away. "Everything feels *so* right," he uttered as an amazing calm settled over him.

His ardor heightened when her mouth began stroking him faster and harder, bringing him to higher levels of ecstasy. And clutching her shoulders, his eyes caressed hers as he shuddered his release with a pleasure that was almost more than he could bear. And he pressed a kiss in her palm, before drawing her to him in another embrace.

When —suddenly —a thunder of blasts coming from the next block rocked the floor like it would have done a small boat on a turbulent river.

The 'tack tack' of Russian machine guns stuttered. up and down the street, followed by German ones.

Bombardment! Barrage! Mortar shells exploding!

"Stay down, Bela!" he yelled, throwing his body over hers as bricks toppled from the chimney.

A fusillade of small-arms fire sounded like it hit the building next to the tailor shop. "What's happening! "she cried.

"Probably some die-hard Hitler boys refusing to surrender."

Then a pocket-torch flashed, spilling a burnished light into the semi-darkness when the cellar door, connecting with the tailor shop, slammed open.... It was followed by the stomping of steel-shod boots.

"Sounds like *Ivan,*" Kurt whispered, pushing aside one of the boxes.

"What do you see?" she asked, on her knees behind him.

"A drunken, Mongol soldier is standing in front of the half-open door to the tailor shop.

And his hand's shaking, but he's holding a revolver."

CHAPTER THIRTY-TWO

"Want woman!" this Mongol soldier shouted at Gretchen above the rattle of the machine guns and the other guns firing...*"*woman come to me— *Frau Koman.*"

Gretched screamed as he staggered, wobbly-legged, toward her, pointing his revolver.

"*Unten Koman,*" he snapped.

But when she just stared, horrified, he back-handed her so violently she fell against the floor.

Hiding behind her chair, Liesel also screamed; prompting the soldier to turn and go after her.

Gretchen begged, "Take me—*please*—she's just a little girl!"

"I... I'm still a child," she sobbed, tears in her voice.

Shouting above the sound blasts outside, Claus struggled to make himself heard as he pleaded over and over, *"Leave her alone! Leave her alone!"*

But the Russian Mongol, grinning with malicious amusement, drew back his fist and punched Claus in the face.

Guntar attempted to rise from his stretcher, but shouting curses, this brutal soldier kicked him in the ribs with his boots, grabbed his stretcher, and shoved it over.

"Fucking Russian!" Guntar hollered as it slammed on top of him.

* * *

Kurt's eyes focused on the Mongol.

"If I have to, I can distract him from raping Gretchen and Liesel," said Bela, wiping her cheeks with the back of her hand.

"I know." Kurt said, the thought squeezing his chest like an enormous tentacle was wrapped around it. "But God forbid if you have to—"

"Still, he has a gun, and *you* don't. So what are you going to do?"

"He's drunk. And there's not much light. So with luck, I'll be able to catch him unaware—"

"Even so, I might be able to distract him," said Bela.

"And put you at risk...? Absolutely not!"

Liesel lifted her arms to cover her breasts as the Mongol, oblivious to her whimpering cries, tore at her skirt and grasped at her face. A distraction that aided Kurt when he took the several steps toward little Erich's rocking horse and quickly grabbed it.

Then, advancing toward this wild-eyed soldier, he slipped up behind him and delivered two hard blows to the back of his head with the horse's long, wooden pole.

Struggling to regain his balance, the Mongol teetered from side to side before firing three shoots in Kurt's direction.

Fortunately, they all missed.

And that was when Kurt snapped the pole from the horse's back and clubbed him so violently, he dropped his revolver.

The Mongol moaned in distress, swaying slightly as he grabbed at Guntar's stretcher.

"I've got his gun!" shouted Claus, stepping away from him. "So give him another blow, Kurt."

"What I was planning."

He lifted the horse's pole but before he could hit him, the wood on both the outside and inside poles split— "My God!" Kurt gasped as bound, rolled up papers flew out and landed at the soldier's feet.

"*P... papers... no writing,*" he stuttered, as he grabbed them and began flipping through them.

"Boris must have known the horse's inside pole was hollow," Kurt remarked, snatching the bound papers from the soldier.

Blood was streaming down Claus's face, but when he aimed the revolver at the Mongol, Kurt grabbed his wrist and held it with the fierce grip of a Rottweiler's jaw. "This soldier is one of Berlin's conquerors. And the Soviets have warned us that if you kill one of them, then you'll either be hung or sent to Siberia—"

"Still with all that commotion going on in the next block I suspect he's AWOL. So what would it hurt?"

"Don't tempt fate by finding out."

The Mongol's grunts of pain and choked gasps grew louder, and Kurt gazed at Claus. "What say we put him out of his misery for the time being?"

"How?"

He gestured at the sleeping pills on the table Vera had laid out for Guntar. "Two of those with a swallow of coffee."

"Great idea." Claus smiled, reaching for them and a coffee cup.

Kurt eyed the Mongol with a partial grin. "Since you Russians are befriending us Germans, then here's something to ease your pain."

Obviously, not in full command of himself, the Mongol's numbed mind seemed to have trouble for a moment grasping he was being offered deliverance from his pain. But the instant it did, he grabbed the pills and swallowed them with the greed of a hungry person gobbling food... and then he drank the coffee.

A sudden silence fell over the cellar as he toppled, limp as a sack of straw, facedown against the floor.

Claus looked at him in wonder. "Never saw sleeping pills work that fast."

"I think those licks on his head helped speed them up." Kurt chuckled.

Seeing the Russian fall, Bela rushed out in her half-clothed state to assist Kurt with Guntar and the bleeding Gretchen and Claus.

When to Kurt's surprise, Vera and Wolf appeared on the scene with their pocket-torches.

"What the hell!" Wolf barked at Kurt and Bela. His double meaning striking Kurt like a rifle butt as he stared at his suspenders hanging below his vest and his fly unzipped—and Bela... with nothing covering her, but her half-buttoned dress.

"Although, those die-hard Hitler Youth boys are still shooting, we're down here because von Lehmann, who's hiding in the understairs storage space, is so worried about you, he told Victor he can't finish his drawings."

Kurt swallowed nervously. "Good thing, since *Ivan's* paid us a visit."

"God in heaven!" Vera's face paled as she flashed her pocket-torch at Gretchen, Claus, and the unconscious Russian soldier. "We've got to get *him* out of here!"

"Especially since we found the papers," said Kurt, holding them up.

Vera and Wolf exchanged looks of disbelief. "But where were they hidden?" they asked, practically in unison.

"Apparently Boris had put them in the inside pole on little Erich's rocking horse," Kurt said, staring at the broken pieces. "And when I struck the dazed Mongol with it, the papers fell at his feet."

"What irony." Vera shook her head. "But do you think he'll remember?"

"Don't know." He darted another glance at the soldier before handing Wolf, von Lehmann's papers. "Because that no account piece of scum picked them up and mumbled something about them, so we can't take a chance."

"No we can't," Wolf agreed, putting the bound papers on the workbench and covering them with his coat,

Embarrassed, Kurt turned to zip his fly.

"I'll grab my raincoat so I can help you with Gretchen and Liesel," Bela told Vera, before rushing over to the boxes to get it.

"Do you think Jaclyn and von Lehmann will be safe upstairs while we move that Russian?" Kurt asked Vera.

"She's in the understairs storage space trying to calm him."

"Good." Kurt's tight expression relaxed. "But were you crammed in that storage space with him and Jaclyn?"

"I was."

"And Wolf?"

"Victor had an extra pistol to lend him. So he stood with the two agents ready to fend off possible attackers—"

"Sorry to interrupt," said Claus, blotting the blood inside and outside his mouth with a handkerchief, "but we need to get that *damned* Russian into the tailor shop."

"And I need to hurry and patch up the four of you," said Vera to Gretchen. "But is Liesel all right?"

"That sorry Bolshevik tore her dress and touched her," Gretchen snapped. "But otherwise, she's fine."

Vera picked up Gretchen's suitcase. "I presume she has fresh clothes in here. So, if she wants to change, she can go behind those boxes."

"She prefers wearing my warm coat for now," said Gretchen, rolling up its sleeves for her.

"Kurt is wonderful," Liesel said, sliding her hands in the coat's pocket.

Vera smiled. "I've always thought so—"

"We don't have time for you to patch us up," interrupted Claus, with a new-found authority. "Because that sorry bastard over there has *got* to go." He turned to Kurt and Wolf. "So hide him in the tailor shop and dress him in Guntar's Wehrmacht uniform, that looks like it might fit him." Then with a note of mockery, he added, "Which, hopefully, will cause these conquerors of Berlin to shoot one of their own and not know it until it's too late."

Liking his plan, Kurt and Wolf quickly began following his directions. "What should we do with his gun?" Wolf asked Claus.

"Give it to me and I'll put it in the false bottom of that metal chest in here, with his Russian uniform and personal effects. Because we can't risk him being identified."

Kurt stepped over to Vera. "Of course most uniforms are tighter than regular clothes. So getting *Ivan* in and out of one, will be harder for Wolf and I than it was removing Guntar's uniform and putting those looser clothes on him."

"I know," Vera replied. "But work as fast as you can, since it'll be better to hold the heat under von Lehmann's invisible-ink papers with your cigarette lighter or Wolf's, rather than using a candle that's apt **to** drip on them.

"That it will," Kurt agreed, fishing in his breast pocket for his lighter. "Just pray there'll be enough time to identify what's on those papers."

"Exactly," Vera agreed, helping Guntar get back on his stretcher.

CHAPTER THIRTY-THREE

"**W**as that Russian wearing a ring?" Bela asked Gretchen, smearing iodine on her facial cuts.

"Yes. A very large one, which was probably stolen like all those watches he was wearing," she remarked, in a voice heavy with sarcasm. "Since it's been my experience, those Russians only take what's easy for them to carry." She put her arm around Liesel. "But at least my little girl's safe."

"Except for his ribs, your brother's the same as before," Vera told her. "However, he needs a doctor to examine him at the hospital— like all of you do." She looked his cuts over before applying bandages. "Because something could easily be broken."

"But how will these N. K.V. D. agents get us there with all this fighting?" asked Claus, holding his handkerchief against his blood-smeared face as he waited for Kurt and Wolf to return from the tailor shop.

"It's simple. We *now* have a triple emergency. So I'll tell them you and Gretchen got severely injured when chimney bricks fell on you from the explosions." Vera's face filled with urgency as she motioned at Bela to hand Claus an iodine bottle and tape. "Which means we need to leave within half an hour."

"Half an hour?" Claus shot Vera a questioning frown. "But with all the shooting in the neighborhood, we'll need a truck to get us there safely."

"There's one parked at the end of the block—" But before Vera could finish, Gretchen hollered like she'd been hit in the head with a brick.

Attempting to reassure her, Bela was holding Liesel's hand in the silent, devoted way of a fellow sister when Gretchen, groaning, hunched toward them, holding her head. "I...it hurts," she cried.

"Then take some of Guntar's morphine pills," said Vera, rushing over with them and some coffee.

But she refused. "He needs them more than I do."

"Once we get to the hospital, there'll be enough for both of you. So *please* take what you need."

Liesel held the coffee cup for her while she swallowed them. "After the war, mama and I want to go school and study to be nurses like you," she told Vera. "So we can help the Jews who survived those terrible camps, as well as other people."

Vera hugged Liesel with great affection. "This world can always use more nurses, little cousin."

"True." Bela agreed. "But if you'll excuse me I need to get my sweater and slacks."

She started toward the boxes to change when Vera stopped her.

"I'm glad you and Kurt decided to follow your hearts."

"With our impending separation *hope* is evaporating for us, so—"caution made her reflect a moment before admitting the somber inevitability, "Since our time together *here* was all we had."

"Wait a minute!" Vera grasped her arm. "What do you mean *hope* is evaporating for you and Kurt? You may be separated for a time, but surely it's not forever. "

"Y...yes it is," said Bela, on the verge of losing her control. "Because I was sterilized at the Love Camp and can't give him children."

"And you think he doesn't want you because you can't give him any?"

She felt cornered. "He says he doesn't care."

"So what's the matter?" asked Vera, taking her hand in hers." Don't you believe him?"

"But he lost his son."

"I've known Kurt for a long time. And believe me, he doesn't say what he doesn't mean. So if he wants *you* more than children, then take him at his word."

"I do." Bela nodded. "But it still doesn't stop me from wanting him to find someone who'll give him the little boy I can't."

"*Bela, oh Bela.*" Vera sighed, embracing her. "You remind me of a sweet, innocent kid ready to go off the deep-end."

"So I'm a fool?"

"Not hardly. But you need to listen to your heart. Because my *whispering muse* is saying is that your heart is aligned with Kurt's—which makes his adoration of you quite obvious." She gave her arm a gentle squeeze. "Just know he's sincere and without each other, that beam of light shining on the two of you will quickly fade into the silence of the night."

Struggling to accept what Vera's poetic voice was telling her, Bela gulped hard.

"I'll do my best to do what's right for him."

"Then make sure you don't sacrifice yourself for him." Vera paused. "Because the irony is that if you *do*, you'll end up sacrificing *him*."

Bela was in a vise. With her poetic voice telling her the alarm bell ringing inside her was as mournful as the one at St. Stephansdom's Cathedral. *Isn't this what I've feared all along? But been hesitate to admit.*

Her heart would always belong to Kurt's as his to hers— making it impossible for them to ever be separated. *Our intense lovemaking earlier proved that.*

Which, in light of our impending separation, was our desperate way of trying to keep each other close.

In their brief time together she knew him like she'd never known another. For here was a man,who even amid the loud debauchery of the Germans coming to sate themselves at the Love Camp, had washed away some of her shame with his kindness and respect. And made *her*— a field-whore— feel like a decent young woman because he'd become the first man to treat her like a lover and not a prostitute.

While in the other beds, ribald drunken soldiers were devouring the girls like rats on top of a loaf of bread. But through it all, she and Kurt had managed to cross the boundaries of war and prejudice. Becoming comrades in arms, with a *déjà vu* feeling deepening their togetherness and cementing this remarkable unity between them.

For they'd been *united* at the Love Camp. *United* when artillery fire broke the coupling on their train carriage, *united* in the woods, and *united* when they'd battled that sadistic major. And now on this highly dangerous mission, they'd been *united* in their lovemaking with explosions from the outside forcing them to confront the ferocity of a Russian Mongol with a revolver.

O-oh the war had taken away her ability to bear children, but even so, it had given her Kurt.

And without their union there was no hope for either of them, with their lives being irreparably damaged.

"Then do what's right for *you* and for *him* and get married," Vera urged.

Get married. Bela pondered her words as reality struck. "And you're certain that without children he won't regret it later?"

"He won't, I know him too well. So tell him you'll marry him before you leave Berlin. Because if the OSS decides to go back on its word and returns him to some British prisoner- of- war camp, then for his sake and yours, you should be married before they do."

Bela flashed a smile at her. "I'll tell him at Gatow before we board the plane."

"Good," Vera said, nodding. "But why not tell him now?"

"Because our mission comes first. And we can't have any distractions until Wolf has safely got von Lehmann's papers on that aircraft."

"Makes sense."

"But one more thing—" Bela hesitated, still not convinced." The British will be waiting for Kurt when we get to London. So what do I say if they decide to return him to a prisoner- of- war camp?"

"That you're pregnant and have to be married before they do."

"And you really think they'll listen?"

"They should, after risking yourselves on this mission."

"Still they beat him badly when they took him prisoner."

"Beat him?" Vera looked crestfallen. "*Damn*— that's awful! Although nothing surprises me where the British are concerned."

"My feelings exactly. Which means I'll be spending a good amount of time in prayer if he's returned to them... but here, Vera, take this—" Bela reached into her raincoat's hidden pocket and removed three of the one- hundred-dollar bills.

"What on earth?" Vera blinked in surprise as Bela shoved the money in her hands.

"I can't take this from you and Kurt."

"Yes you can. Since you're apt to need it for Franz, Gretchen, or yourself."

Vera's brown eyes gleamed. "Well other than '*thank you*,' I don't quite know what to say."

"That you deserve it after making me recall what my father once said—"

"Which was?"

"That love often happens when you throw reason to the wind and follow your heart... something I'd forgotten until you forced me to look at the mistake I was about to make by not marrying Kurt." Bela put her arm around Vera. "Just don't say anything to Wolf about this money, because we don't want him to know how we got it."

Looking dismayed, Vera cocked her head to one side. "Now you've got my curiosity going. So just how *did* you get it— if I may dare to ask you?"

"Our adventure in the woods with those die-hard Germans."

"That you took care of?"

"The spoils of war." Bela smiled, hugging her.

She returned her hug. "Wasn't expecting any to come my way... but do I thank Kurt with Wolf around?"

"Just give him a hug like me, and I'll whisper why—"

But Vera stopped her before she could finish as Wolf and Kurt, returning from the tailor shop, handed Claus the Mongol's uniform and personal effects so he could stash them out of sight.

* * *

"Our AWOL Russian's still passed out cold," said Kurt in an urgent voice. "But for how long is anybody's guess?"

"Which means we've got to hurry and find a way to smuggle these papers out of here," said Wolf, reaching for them under his coat on the workbench. "But before we do, we really need to make sure those blank pages are written in invisible- ink, like von Lehmann claims."

"And this should tell us," Kurt remarked, holding up his cigarette lighter.

Eager to glimpse what was on the pages, Wolf, Bela, and Vera crowded around the workbench as Kurt, knowingly, angled his lighter a slight distance beneath them.

"My God!" Wolf exclaimed, his body stiffening in shock as the faint light illuminated images not seen before except in comic books like *Buck Rogers.*

"What is this?" Vera asked." Some kind of joke?"

"Hardly," remarked Kurt, with a dawning awareness of what they'd found. He gave von Lehmann's papers a closer look. "What you have here seems to be a design for a spherical form orbiting the earth." He studied it for a minute before scanning the rest of the pages. "And this spherical form appears to have been launched from a rocket."

"In other words *an eye in the sky,*" Wolf clarified.

"No wonder the Russians were so anxious to find those papers," Vera said, touching them. "Since putting a man in space before the end of the century is something they're quite anxious to do."

"On the contrary," said Kurt," they thought they were looking for the preliminarydesigns of the improved long-range V-3 Cannon Rocket, but this—"

"—is more than they ever expected," Vera finished.

Wolf continued to gaze at them. "Even so, I find it odd that these preliminary designs and equations for this orbiting device aren't taking up all the space Jaclyn's music is occupying in her briefcase."

"Like has been said," remarked Kurt, "with work from ordinary scientists—*yes.* But von Lehmann has such ingenious ways of doing things, that he's been known to baffle his scientific friends with his smaller designs."

"Which is really amazing,." Wolf said. "Which makes our problem of smuggling them out of here not as bad as we might think."

Kurt laughed. "Considering how we joked about not being able to find what *Ivan* couldn't."

"Why don't I tuck them in my pullover sweater," Bela suggested, tugging at her raincoat and covering her chest with crossed arms.

"Which you're still not wearing," Wolf pointed out, scanning her up and down. "But how will that help us when Victor and Peter will be patting down our legs and torsos?"

Bela gestured at the hole in the roof. "True. But remember Victor and Peter are to be informed that some bricks fell from the chimney and severely injured Gretchen and Claus during this unexpected attack. So regardless of the colonel, they'll now have to help Vera get her family to the hospital."

"And one of the agents will have to stay here while the other goes with us," remarked Vera in an upbeat tone.

An amused gleam sparkled in Bela's eyes. "And with the briefcase open for him to see at all times, I'll quickly remove the papers from my sweater and tuck them inside it."

"Still, won't the N.K.V.D. agent think it odd you're going through the briefcase?" Wolf asked her.

"Not if Jaclyn and I offer to play a piano duet for von Lehmann to help him finish faster." Adding after a long pause, "Which we'll pretend to take our time about deciding what to play."

"That's a great idea, Bela." Kurt commended her, as she handed him his tie, jacket, and overcoat.

Wolf's lips twisted. "Has to be since it's all we've got."

"That Russian could wake up any time," Vera reminded. "So I'll go inform Victor and Peter of Gretchen and Claus's injuries."

She started toward the door, but Wolf stopped her. "Before you go, send Jaclyn down so we can let her know what's going on—"

"And one more thing," Kurt broke in. "Von Lehmann and I worked out a coded message if we found his papers—"

"Which is?" Vera asked with a narrowed glance.

"See if he wants a glass of white wine. And if he says *where*, then say little Erich's rocking horse got destroyed when some bricks fell on it."

Vera nodded her approval. "I like it because it won't make any sense to Victor and Peter— but I nearly forgot." She took a step toward Kurt before reaching up to give him a grateful hug.

"Now what's that for?" he asked, surprised.

"Ask Bela."

"What's going on, *liebchen*?"

"I gave Vera three hundred dollars and told her it was from both of us, "she whispered. "And she thanked me earlier. So now she's thanking you."

"Good." He grinned. "I was going to suggest we give her something from our stash."

Wolf glanced at his watch." Vera, before we get Gretchen and her family to the hospital, you'll need to have Victor radio Franz and tell him what's happened here with those Hitler Youth boys. And emphasize we're in danger the longerwe stay here. So, see if that British amphibian aircraft, *Grumman Goose,* on the Elbe can fly into Gatow and pick us up within the next hour and a half."

"I'll certainly try."

Kurt's pulse pounded like a Spandau submachine gun. "It's imperative we get out of here as quickly as possible. Because not only will those Hitler boys keep on until their ammunition is gone, but as we know,

Ivan could wake any time. And we have no idea what he'll remember about those papers falling at his feet."

PART III

HARBORS

CHAPTER THIRTY-FOUR

Vera combed her hair while Bela changed into her slacks and sweater. She slipped her dress and raincoat over them, then grabbed her straw hat and hurried back to Kurt and Wolf.

"Think they'll suspect anything?" she asked, appearing to be keenly aware of their scrutiny as she tucked the papers inside her slightly low-necked sweater.

"It looks good to me," Wolf replied, meeting Kurt's gaze. "But what do you think?"

He tipped a brow her way. "I can't tell she's hiding anything."

"Then I'd better get Jaclyn and bring her back down here," said Vera. "So she'll know about the duet she's playing with Bela on my badly tuned piano." She looked over at Gretchen and Claus. "Because they need to go to the hospital, since we're claiming some bricks fell on them."

"Three injured people caught in middle of a maelstrom of lead," said Wolf. "Somehow I don't see how Victor can refuse medical aid for them, even if he can't reach the colonel."

And he was right.

"I'll see if that open truck with those two soldiers has returned," Victor told Vera, stepping to the front door. "Since earlier I had the driver leave to inform Dr.Grossklos that von Lehmann was doing well."

It had returned and was now parked less than half a block away, easing Vera's tension when she saw how close it was to them. "On more thing—"

"What?" Victor glanced back at her,

"Contact Franz and see if he can arrange for that *Grumman Goose* on the Elbe to fly into Gatow within the next hour and a half and pick up our four guests." She went over to the window. "Because with those die-hard Hitler Youth boys still out there, we don't know when they might attack again. And I don't think Colonel Sokolov would want to endanger these four British agents he's responsible for. "

"True." Victor jerked a nod, showing no signs of reluctance. "But since we're in a hurry, I'll contact Franz once we're in the truck."

"And don't forget," von Lehmann told Peter, "Colonel Sokolov said I could go with Vera to Gatow and see everyone off."

"I remember." He sighed, like there wasn't time to object. "Youand *Fraulein* Tovariski are supposed to go in the truck with our visitors, and afterwards return to the hospital."

Recalling the *code* Kurt had given her, Vera went over to von Lehmann. "Would you like a glass of white wine?"

He looked startled, but covered it well by frowning and reminding her with a hint of censure, "Don't you know by now that I only drink red wine? But where?"

"Where *what*?"

"Where's my red wine, sweet Vera?"

"I'll get it. But I'm still quite nervous, since some large bricks falling on little Erich's rocking horse struck it. And if they'd struck Gretchen, they might have killed her," she said, saying a silent prayer that with an unconscious,

Russian soldier in the adjourning cellar, Victor or Peter wouldn't insist on having a look at the damage.

"A pity," said von Lehmann. "Since I used to watch little Erich rock on it."

Vera nudged his thigh with her knee. "Because we're in a hurry, won't a piano duet from Jaclyn and Bela help you finish your drawings quicker?"

"Why absolutely," he said, catching on. "Because if I don't have that music, then I'm liable not to finish this last drawing with its equation."

"Are you willing to let Jaclyn make a selection from the briefcase?" She nudged his thigh again. "Or do you have a selection in mind?"

"I'll let Jaclyn choose."

"Then she should do it after I leave with Kurt, Wolf, and Victor to take Gretchen's family to the hospital."

"That's right—"

"Think this will do?" Jaclyn interrupted, stepping from the kitchen with the basket of food for Gretchen and her family.

"It looks good to me," Vera said. "However, there's more food in Kurt's rucksack that Victor's holding. So since it has a zipper, he said for us to use it instead of the basket."

"Then I'll repack it *Frau* von Friesen," said Victor, taking the basket.

"And I'll hold onto the rucksack until we get to the hospital." He turned to von Lehmann.

"But for now get him the wine he's requested."

Jaclyn looked Victor over. "And for now, get me a cigarette."

Frowning, he also looked her over, before slowly removing his pack from his pocket and handing one to her.

"And one more thing," said Victor lighting it for her. "Go down and tell Gretchen a truck is waiting to take her and her family to the hospital."

She gazed at von Lehmann before adding, "And while we're at the hospital, he's requested Jaclyn and Bela play a duet so he can finish his last drawing."

Acting affronted at the way things were going,

Jaclyn turned to Victor, "So after all that shooting, we'll be here without protection?"

"Peter will be staying." He shot a quick glance at the foyer's Black Forest clock." But please—we must go now since it's fairly calm out there."

"Then let's hurry and bring my people up," Vera told Jaclyn as she headed toward the cellar door.

* * *

For the next fifteen minutes a surge of lightening-fast activity filled the house as Vera helped Gretchen's family scramble to gather up their things.

Claus grabbed the family's one small bag, and Gretchen slung their portable radio— still playing very softly— in a knapsack over her back.

"We have to listen to the news," she reminded, watching Wolf and Kurt carry Gunter on his stretcher up the cellar steps.

On their way out, Claus and Gretchen waved at von Lehmann, and he waved back.

"Don't forget my dog," Liesel told Vera.

"I'm headed for his crate now."

The truck they'd seen earlier was now in front of the house, and with help from the two soldiers in it, Wolf and Kurt got Guntar in the back of it quickly.

Everyone crowded around him, listening, as Victor radioed Franz to request the British to send the *Grumman Goose* to Gatow as soon as possible. He didn't see a problem in getting an answer from the British communications near the Elbe, within the next ten minutes.

"Good," Victor told him, "since word has it the fanatical Hitler Youth boys are getting ready for another skirmish."

Also, Franz radioed the hospital that Vera and the wounded Guntar, on his stretcher, were coming.

"The smell of death on the street is stronger than ever," Vera told Franz on the radio. And she trembled each time the frightened Gretchen and Liesel jumped, when this truck—— bumping along the shell-marked road— plowed over the smaller piles of debris with a high-pitched screeching sound.

But fortunately within less than five minutes, the truck had pulled up atthe hospital. The driver parked in front of the lobby. Making it easy for the two soldiers with their submachine guns, to help Wolf and Kurt hand Guntar over to the two hospital people waiting at the door for him.

"I'm also sending a radio message to the British," Victor told Vera.

"Good idea."

He stared at her until she was safely in the lobby before he handed Gretchen the rucksack and indicated that the rest of her family and Shay get out of the truck.

Which they did... darting past Kurt in the lobby as Carl rushed up.

"Didn't expect to see you again this soon," he said, warmly squeezing Kurt's arm. "And I was pleased to hear all of you at Vera's survived those Hitler boys."

"They're still out there, but what about the hospital? Did it take any hits?"

"Just some minor roof damage."

"I'll see after your family," Wolf told Vera. "Because you need to ask Carl about Shay."

"Which I was about to," she said, stepping over to him. "My family has a puppy with them, so is it all right to keep him here?"

"Of course." Carl looked genuinely pleased. "A welcome distraction. And we'll keep him safe so no one steals him... but what happened to Claus and Gretchen?

From the glimpse I got of them, it looks like they were belted in the mouth."

"They were," Vera informed him. "And by an AWOL Mongol with a revolver."

Looking startled, Carl's breath seemed to quicken. "Where— at your house?"

"In Boris's cellar."

Immediately Carl tensed. "And right now that Mongol's where?"

"Thanks to Kurt, he's out cold in the tailor shop."

"Good thing," Carl agreed, staring at Victor radioing from the truck before turning to Kurt. "But how'd you manage to subdue that Mongol when you didn't have a weapon?"

"The pole on little Erich's rocking horse... I clubbed him with it—"

"But that's not all," Vera interjected," because to Kurt's astonishment, von Lehmann's papers flew out and fell straight at that *damned* Russian's feet."

Carl's startled look returned. "So that's where they were hidden but—"

"What?" asked Vera.

" Do you think that soldier will remember?"

"Claus and I got two sleeping pills down him before we moved him to the tailor shop," Kurt answered. "And then we put Guntar's Wehrmacht uniform on him."

Carl smiled unsurely at him. "Which let's pray makes his fellow soldiers mistake him for one of those White Russians in the Wehrmacht and open fire on him. Because don't forget, Colonel Sokolov's offering a reward for information about von Lehmann's papers."

"Frightening, isn't it?" Vera frowned, recognizing his fear. "And although Victor doesn't realize it, we're more afraid of *Ivan's* Mongol soldier waking up in the tailor shop than we are those Hitler boys."

"And right now," said Kurt, "Victor's doing a follow-up radio request to the one Franz sent the British, to have their *Grumman Goose* on the Elbe fly into Gatow within the hour and pick us up."

"Want me to go out to the truck and see what he's found out? "Carl asked Vera.

"No, I'll do it."

She quickly left the lobby and went over to the truck. And she and Victor talked briefly, before she came back and announced, "He's just informed me the *Grumman Goose* will soon be headed our way."

"Then grab Jaclyn and Bela and get out of here," Carl urged Kurt.

"The doctor says Guntar stands a good chance of making it," said Wolf, returning from the ward. "And Gretchen and Claus are being examined and told they can stay here with Guntar until he gets better."

"Then we'd best get back in the truck," Kurt pressed.

He started toward it, when Carl grabbed his shoulder. "Don't worry about anything but getting out of here," he said, giving him a hug. "And take special care of Bela— she's frail."

"Always."

* * *

Back at the house, Bela and Jaclyn thumbed through the sheet music in the briefcase as they debated on what to play for von Lehmann. They took longer than expected, arousing Peter's impatience.

"Hurry up and decide," he barked.

The rise in the volume of his voice appeared to be a signal to von Lehmann to drop his T-square. "My knee's gotten stiff from all this sitting while I'm drawing, so will you get it for me?" he asked Peter.

Present circumstances being what they were, it left him no choice but to bend over and pick it up.

Staring at Peter, Jaclyn grabbed two Strauss waltzes, one of which was the "Emperor's Waltz." "How about this?" she asked Bela.

"I suppose," she said, quickly stuffing von Lehmann's invisible- ink, bound papers between the two music books in the back of the briefcase.

Peter turned to Jaclyn."Are you ready?" he snapped, handing von Lehmann his T-square.

"As ready as we'll ever be," she said, following Bela to the piano bench.

"Then begin, *Frau* von Friesen."

She flashed him a crooked smile as a Strauss waltzbegan echoing throughout the house with its lilting melody. And von Lehmann seemed so impressed, he stopped working and applauded them.

The truck pulled up in front of the house. And immediately Victor jumped out followed by Vera, Kurt, and Wolf.

"Are you finished with the designs on that drawing?" Victor asked von Lehmann, pointing at it.

"I've finished it, but I'm at the end of this final equation," he remarked, clearly annoyed. "So give me a moment."

"How long is a moment?"

"Right now," he said, grinning at Victor's exasperated expression.

"A relief," Victor replied sarcastically, before turning to Peter and ordering, "Gather up his drawings because we have to leave right away."

"What about the car headlamps?" Vera asked Victor. "Are you leaving them here?"

"I can't be bothered about them since I'm required to search everyone for those papers."

Fearing he'd find the American money in her raincoat, Bela waded the coat upin front of Victor before tossing it in a chair.

Von Lehmann then asked Victor if he might slip a personal letter in her raincoat with the words scribbled across it, *"Bela, desperation can open doors we believe to be closed."*

"You can read it if you like," he told him. "As can Bela."

Though Victor shook his head like he didn't have the time nor the interest. "Because you're British agents, I'm required to do a quick pat-down body search of your arms, legs, and torsos," he informed them. "So don't be offended, since we're allies."

"Exactly," reminded Wolf. "Which brings me back to the unanswered question of how we were supposed to find something *you* Russians couldn't?"

But Victor, saying nothing, proceeded to do the quick pat-down of his four visitors.

"See, you still don't have an answer for my husband's question," said Jaclyn, throwing back her head and resting her hands on her hip.

Once again not answering, Victor went over and shut the briefcase. "Take it. He directed Wolf.

He had it secure in his hands, when von Lehmann reminded, "I wish to say good-bye to my son *here* and not Gatow —as well as everyone else." He took several quick breaths before wiping his eyes and turning to Vera. "Because at Gatow there will be no time."

"He's right," she agreed.

Pointing at von Lehmann's trembling arms, Kurt implored Peter and Victor,

"So please honor his request."

They didn't argue, since it was quite apparent von Lehmann was not only weak but tired. "Five minutes—no more, *Herr* Ulrich," said Victor.

Von Lehmann's eyes glinted with emotion as he put his arms around Kurt's shoulders and gripped them. "S...son, "I'm so very sorry for my failure to—"

* * *

"Don't say it," Kurt stopped him, guilt with a bayonet sharpness stabbing him in the heart. "What I did was worse than your refusal to marry my mother on her deathbed when—"

A lump rose in his throat. "I became involved with a gang of murderers, who destroyed innocent people like Bela."

The sudden silence falling between them was final as if the world they knew, was about to end.

"No, no, no!" insisted von Lehmann in a choked, desperate voice. "Hear me out.

You'll become an *avenger,* who'll bring many of those Nazi criminals to justice." He swallowed hard, biting back his tears." I know. Because my meditations have put me in contact with a higher intelligence, which you may not understand now, but know this... I didn't marry your mother and risk *you* because I'm part Jew. And even if *my* mother wasn't Jewish, my Jewish father made me understand that, regardless, the Jew-haters in the world would still consider me a Jew—"

"A Jew!" Kurt blurted, astounded. "Never in my wildest dreams would I have imagined you to be a Jew."

"I know," Von Lehmann said, giving him a very long look. "But Albert's father was quite ill before he died. And our mother needed money, so she had an affair with a wealthy Jewish man— my *real* father—whom both she and I came to love in secret."

"I can imagine," said Kurt, his vision blurred from the tears welling in his eyes.

"He's the reason I had money. And unknown to my brothers, they too had money."

Von Lehmann's grip tightened on Kurt's shoulders. "I...I would have given you money for a business, Son, but you never asked me."

"I didn't. Because although you had some financial assistance, you still had a good many projects to fund— He faltered. "And your experiments were so valuable to the world that you needed all the money you could get."

"Doesn't matter now since I've left you a great deal of it. So take it and enjoy it... and buy Bela some expensive gifts."

Kurt didn't know what to say. So he pressed his cheek against von Lehmann's— praying— this *wizard*, this *magic man*, whose knowledge was capable of making the world a greater place, would sense the change and transformation in him—"

"Something's on fire in the neighborhood!" came a sudden cry from Wolf as a cloud of dark smoke, mingled with the dusk of the early evening sky.

"We leave now!" Victor shouted, waving everyone toward the truck.

"From the looks of it we're about to have another attack by those Hitler boys, "yelled one of the Russian soldiers from the back of the truck. He quickly checked the bolt on his submachine gun before gesturing at Victor and Peter to take their seats in the cab with the driver.

Weighted down with the briefcase, Wolf was the last to climb in the truck.

Jaclyn and Vera reached out their hands to him. And at their urging, he took the seat between them.

Across from them Kurt sat between von Lehmann and Bela, clutching their hands.

"Looks like we're going to have at least one more night together, *liebchen*," he whispered, straightening her straw hat she'd knocked askew in her rush to get in the truck.

"Makes my heart perk up." She smiled, linking her arm through his as the driver pressed down on the accelerator, and the truck lurched forward.

* * *

When the Mongol soldier sat up on the cellar's dusty floor, he remembered a civilian man had done a great wrong to him. "Damn it!" He cursed, angry at himself for being weak and falling prey to someone like that. *And he stole my watches and ring.*

His chest tensed with flashes of memory... artillery overhead... a pole hitting him... bound papers at his feet.

There was something important about those papers; although he could see no writing on them. And some high-ranking officer was offering a reward for papers written in invisible- ink.

"But where are they? And where am I?" he murmured as he mentally stumbled back to the present.

Rising from the cellar's floor, he made his way slowly toward the door. He coughed several times in the hopes of clearing the red dust clogging his throat.

He *had* to think. Was it Sokolov who was offering the reward...? Had to be since that was the only name coming to mind.

So, despite his failing strength, he took another halting step forward.

There was dried blood on his uniform. "No doubt from the beating I received," he said, touching the swelling on his cracked lips. However, this tight uniform made him wonder if it was his or someone else's.

Someone else's, he decided, wobbling out of the dank-smelling cellar.

He was having difficulty standing erect, so he gripped the banister of the cellar's outside steps. The early evening sky was still smoke-blackened from the roaring bomb explosions, with hissing bullets and rifle fire echoing and re-echoing on the street behind him.

However, on the opposite side of the street, two Russian soldiers glared at him. And from what he could make-out, they were babbling about a Wehrmacht soldier being stupid enough to show himself, after the Freedom Marcher's massacre today.

"Certainly not one of the Hitler boys," remarked one of the soldiers, taking aim and firing two shots at him.

"Perfect shot," shouted the other soldier, rushing across the street to him.

Life was leaving the Mongol, but nevertheless as he toppled over he managed to say, "*Found papers... in broken horse pole...*"

The soldier who'd shot him asked in an alarmed voice, "Who are you? A Mongol fighting with the White Russians in the Wehrmacht."

"No... " he gasped. Then, crashing in pain as he took his final breath, he said brokenly, "Tell... Sokolov —"

A Russian officer now standing over him shook his head. "What do you make of that?" he asked the soldier who'd shot him.

"That he was talking about the reward Colonel Sokolov's offering for some missing papers."

"Then we'd better radio Major Petov and see if he can contact him."

CHAPTER THIRTY-FIVE

Sokolov was in a canvas truck headed toward Gatow to say good-bye to his four visitors, when Franz sent him a radio message he'd just received from the airport. '*Wehrmacht soldiers not honoring surrender——reinforcements needed—unable to contact Goose.*'

Since Major Petov and his Red Army were continuing to fend off some more attacks from the Hitler boys nearby, Sokolov quickly radioed him that he was coming to pick him up—plus ten of his most experienced soldiers.

But when the truck reached the major and his soldiers, noise from every direction came at them. Shouts, bullets, machine guns, explosions—not letting up for a minute.

However, once the soldiers climbed in the truck, the major mentioned a radio message coming through about *papers* and a *broken horse pole*. And immediately there was a minute of silence.

"They've got those papers!" Sokolov shouted in a triumphant tone. "I know because I saw that horse with a pole during a search." *Act fast—very fast*, was all he could think as he unsuccessfully attempted to radio Victor for the second time. Then, through the truck's speaker, he ordered Franz to radio Victor and keep this line open so the major could hear too.

Although, with all the static crackle on both the speaker and ear phones, it seemed that Franz was also having difficulty communicating with Victor. "*Franz* to *Victor—avoid Gatow*," he kept repeating. Sokolov heard the words the first time, but after that it was more like a gasping breath on the other end.

Until—suddenly— this gasping breath became a desperate murmur.

"It's too late— the runway's in front of us!"

Then a boom like a thunderclap followed, and the radio went dead.

* * *

Guns from German fire. German weapons.

On the truck's floor, Kurt had his arms wrapped around Bela and von Lehmann, the same as Wolf had his wrapped around Jaclyn and Vera.

The radio in the truck had gone dead with the first bombardment. "Everyone in back take cover!" Victor shouted.

"More Hitler boys?" Wolf yelled.

"Hardly," said Kurt. "Since from what I glimpsed these are men in pant- legged combat gear." His blood ran cold at the number of grenade bursts there'd been since their arrival at Gatow. Was it ten or fifteen? It sounded more like fifteen.

Good thing the Russians guarding the shell-marked runway were on general alert.

The twin engine *Grumman Goose* had already touched down and made itsreturn to the end of the runway, so it was facing into the wind.... And preparing for an instant take-off, the pilot had turned it into position.

Relief now overrode Kurt's tension for the moment as the truck got within a hundred meters of the aircraft. "I'm not about to leave you," he told von Lehmann. "So you'll have to scramble on board the plane with us."

But he said nothing as grenades continued to whistle and explode in the air. Then, Kurt added, "But if you can't make it, I'll carry you."

Some Wehrmacht soldiers appeared in the distance, their machine guns hitting the runway so the bullets ricocheted.

They had the range, and their shells whistled close to the truck.

Amid this hailing of sporadic rifle fire, the outnumbered Russians returned fire from behind a mobile generator and some stacked aircraft tires.

Several German grenades flew in front of the truck and exploded on the runway.

It shredded its front tires, creating an imbalance which made the driver lose control in the middle of a turn, causing the truck to flip over on its side.

Crawling out of the cab, Victor ordered the two soldiers in back, to take cover and return fire.

But the onslaught was already unbearable. The driver had been fatally wounded as had the two soldiers.

Stepping over to one of the dead soldiers, Victor grabbed his submachine gun and bellowed at Wolf to grab the other.

The briefcase was now in front of Wolf, so he kicked it over to Kurt, before jumping out and reaching for the gun. "Stay close to Bela and Kurt," he yelled at Jaclyn.

"We've no driver!" Peter informed Vera, his revolver drawn.

Kurt's arm was still around von Lehmann. "He's deathly pale but wasn't hit."

"Good," said Peter. "Since I 'm under special orders from Marshal Zhukov to look after him." So turning to Vera, he directed her, "Take his pulse!"

"Which I was just about to do," she snapped, clutching her medical bag.

"Son, take the briefcase and all of you *go*—" said von Lehmann in a panicky voice.

"You're the best father ever," Kurt told him, "but those Germans are reloading for their next assault—"He turned to Bela and Jaclyn. "Which means we have to get to the plane!"

The co-pilot of the *Grumman Goose* was reaching out to them with waiting hands. "Hurry! "he yelled. "Another attack's coming!"

Rifle fire from the Russians shooting at the Germans continued to hit the runway.

"I'm the rear guard, and you're the point," Victor hollered at Wolf, above the engines' roar.

* * *

Bela crawled from the truck. "We have to stay together— *always*," she shouted at Kurt.

"Yes always, *liebchen*." His voice rose in volume as shells continued to strike close by. "But hurry and catch up with Jaclyn because I'll be right behind you."

Bela knew the odds were slim of his keeping up with her while running with the heavy briefcase. And twice she glanced back at him.

However, undeterred, he was picking up speed when another line of bullets hitting the runway, struck close to the *Grumman Goose's* tailwheel.

"What the hell!" hollered Victor. "Why are they shooting at the *Goose* if they're trying to steal it?"

But then a blinding flash followed by the roar of another explosion, ignited the gas tank on the mobile generator next to where most of the Russians were firing.

It burst in a ball of fire, and hideous cries rang out as bodies were flung in all directions.

Bela stared, dazed, her sensibilities vanishing as Wolf stepped forward with his submachine gun. But instead of scanning the perimeter for imminent threats, it looked for a moment like he was pointing it at Kurt. *'If she stays with you, she'll never stop thinking about the Love Camp,'* she could have sworn she heard him say.

'Do you mean to kill him?' She opened her mouth to holler— but when she heard a cry and dull thud, she gasped. *Did Kurt get shot?*

It was frustrating not to be able to tell the direction of the return fire so in the middle of this fresh wave of attack, she dared to turn and look.

Kurt had fallen, the briefcase on the ground beside him. "No!" she screamed.

He appeared to be in terrible pain but was conscious— with a chest wound bleeding fast. And trying to get to him amid the hail of splinters from this fresh attack was absolute madness.

But what does it matter? The Gestapo slaughtered my soul so if I get shot, I'll at least die trying to save Kurt—

A fierce storm of shots lashed around her so violently, it made her wonder if she was still alive. *Have I been hit? If I have, I don't feel it.*

Then suddenly she saw the tree. "A tree in the middle of Gatow's airfield?" she said aloud, puzzled.

But then this was not Gatow but the woods. And there were wedge-shaped stone steps circling this very tall tree.

Stairs in the forest? Did it mean what she thought it did?

The horizon dimmed as the tree and stairs, now bathed in a blazing white light which jolted her, became all that was visible. *'Only those with nothing to lose climb those stairs,'* Kurt had told her earlier.

Although, since he's nowhere to be seen each time I look back, I'll climb them. She felt strangely empty. *But then von Lehmann had scribbled on Kurt's letter — "Desperation can open doors we believe to be closed." So maybe if I* **proceed**...? But putting her foot on the first step, she could feel no substance. "Not what I was expecting," she said, sensing something very important was waiting for her at the top. *Which lets me know I should hurry.*

And since these steps had no substance, and she felt oddly weightless, it was merely a matter of soaring straight into the heavens, like Jacob had done with his ladder.

Although, when she reached the top of the tree, she was surprised to find a landing with a blazing, blue sky above it. "Like the heavens of Galilee after a storm," she said, recalling the color of her eyes and her mother's.

An outline of a tall angel hovered above the landing.

"Are you a door through which all things pass?" Bela asked, viewing her surroundings.

"*Yes,*" came a strong male voice behind her.

"Pa!" She whirled around. "Is this the hereafter?"

"No." His head jerked up. "I'm only standing in this place because of the great danger surrounding you."

"Danger?" she questioned. "But I've nothing to lose."

"I beg to differ." He took her hand. "Since you have the beginnings of a family in your womb."

"*M...me?*" she questioned, her voice rising in surprise.

"Yes *you*, Daughter. Because in your womb is the little boy you so desperately want." His pewter-colored eyes caught hers and held them. "Who'll rise to great heights in the new Israel."

"But, Pa—" A tear rolled down her cheek. " I can't have a baby after what they did to me?"

"God has not abandoned you. And if you don't believe in miracles, I suggest you look behind you."

She turned then and saw Kurt in his Wehrmacht captain's uniform. "Bela," he called softly, opening his arms to her.

"Kurt!" Her heart leaped. "What are you doing here?"

"He's here because he was sent to you," Haral answered for him. "So I'd say a wedding's in order."

"Absolutely," Kurt agreed, getting down on one knee. "Which tells me I should do it formally." And taking her hand, he bowed his head. "I love you, Bela. And have no life except for you. So, please become my wife."

Basking in the warmth of his gaze, she waited a moment beforeanswering, "Since I love you and have no life without you, Kurt, I will accept your offer."

CHAPTER THIRTY-SIX

"We're surrounded!" a voice shouted.

"Surrender or die!" yelled a louder voice in the distance.

"Lower your head, Bela!" hollered Kurt, pulling her down on the runway beside him.

Her heart pounded at the rapid bursts of gunfire. And she clung to him as German soldiers, less than a hundred meters away, ran bent over to avoid the explosions of hand grenades.

When suddenly moving onto the runway, a truck filled with soldiers came closer and closer. "More *Ivan's*," said Kurt in a hoarse whisper.

The sound of Russian rifles and submachine guns opened up as these soldiers in it, jumped out. And fighting a rear-guard action, they fired at the fleeing Germans with the fury of a storm.

"Their fire power's loud enough to shake the sky!" cried a frightened Bela.

Kurt tightened his grip on her arm. "A...are you all right, *liebchen*?" he asked, his breathing labored. "You were so cold when I grabbed you, I thought you were going into shock."

She ran an appraising finger over her chest. "Did I get shot? If I did, I'm not feeling any pain."

"A bullet shot the hat off your head. And with God's help when I saw you fall,

I crawled over to you."

Although, glancing at the red streaks of blood on her sweater and raincoat from his shirt, she realized it was *him,* not *her,* he should worry about. And she opened her mouth to tell him but reconsidering, simply said, "Kurt, we're having a little boy—"

"I know. And I proposed, and you accepted."

"But how could you know?" she asked, mystified.

"Because I was inside your heart."

'*Why that's amazing,*' she started to say. When in the midst of all the noise, a sudden awareness made her heart lurch...for it wasn't the machine guns she was now hearing, but the great confusion of voices surrounding her.

"Kurt," said Vera in a rush. "I've got to wrap this medical dressing tape around you."

And getting on her knees, she began removing his overcoat, jacket, vest, and tie before pulling down his suspenders and cutting off his shirt.

"What's the matter?" Bela asked her.

Vera's bloodshot eyes fastened on her face. "He caught shrapnel in one of his lungs, and he's in pain and on the verge of passing out again. But you two were momentarily dazed, and *talking, talking, talking....*"

"Did you hear what we said?"

"No. And that was weird because it was almost like time was suspended for a moment."

"*V...von Lehmann*—"Kurt broke off, struggling for breath. "Is he all right? And the briefcase. Where is it?"

"Von Lehmann's dead, and I have the briefcase," came Sokolov's deep, composed voice.

"Von Lehmann's heart was failing him when you grabbed the briefcase,"

Vera was quick to explain. "And I kissed him on the brow and said, 'We all love you,' as he took his final breath."

"I see you were about to abscond with these invisible-ink papers of von Lehmann's," said Sokolov, holding them up. "So, if you go back to the British I'm certain they'll have some long-term plans for you."

"You've got what you wanted, "Kurt gasped. "So let me worry about the Tommies."

"And what will you tell them?" Sokolov asked. "That a dying AWOL Russian soldier mentioned *papers* inside a *horse pole.* And if he hadn't, you'd have pulled it off in the middle of all this excitement. So it was a good thing I'd seen that horse and its pole and knew exactly what he was talking about." He sounded exceptionally pleased with himself. "With the soldiers fighting in the neighborhood, quick to remember the reward I was offering for those papers."

"Which allowed you to find what you were searching for," remarked Vera, with a tinge of bitterness. "But right now you need to help Bela hold Kurt up while I wrap this medical dressing tape around him to stop the bleeding."

Sokolov didn't hesitate to aid her. "We must get him to the hospital, since he's in dire need of Dr.Grossklos's medical skills."

"But in his condition, moving him without the doctor present could be extremely dangerous," Vera pointed out. " So order Major Petov to radio for a vehicle and have the good doctor brought to us."

"With General Volkov on the way," said Sokolov," we'll do whatever you think is best—"

"Then let the doctor know von Lehmann died of heart failure," Vera cut in sharply. "And that you have his missing invisible- ink designs."

"Will do—but anything else?'

"Help me keep Kurt warm and his feet elevated," she directed, placing them over the discarded briefcase. "So hopefully, he won't go into shock."

Bela removed the gray scarf from her raincoat's collar and wrapped it around his head like a Wehrmacht toque. "His overcoat's not very warm, so this should give his body more cover," she said, unbuttoning her raincoat and dress and striping off her sweater for him. She was so worried about Kurt that she didn't notice the words *Feldhure* were now visible on her breasts, until she put her dress and raincoat back on.

"One more thing," said Vera to Sokolov. "Where are Wolf and Jaclyn? The last time I saw Wolf he had a submachine gun."

"He did." Sokolov nodded. "But Victor took it from him. And now he and several of my men are holding the couple while we locate a stretcher for *Herr* Ulrich."

"Wolf and Jaclyn need to help me take care of Kurt," Vera's voice ripped out.

"So—*please*— get them over here *now*!"

A terrible blinding fear seized Bela. "Why are you holding the couple in the first place? "she asked Sokolov. "Have you lost your mind?"

"Hardly." He gave an indifferent shrug. "Since Kurt is now *our* prisoner."

"Your *prisoner*!" she exclaimed, springing to her feet.

"Yes. Our prisoner. And once the doctor arrives, then you, Wolf, and Jaclyn will take off in the aircraft, before those *Freedom Marching* Wehrmacht soldiers make another attempt to steal it."

One problem on top of another. Which means I *have to redirect my focus—and quick*! "You're acting like Kurt stole those papers when, in reality, he was just trying to get them on the plane so they wouldn't be destroyed."

"Really now." Sokolov chortled. "Do you take me for a fool?"

"Not in the least." She stuck her hand deep in the secret pocket of her raincoat.

"But we need to talk, so find a place where we can be alone."

"I knew you'd come around." He smiled, the double meaning of her words clearly giving him cause to think otherwise. "So follow me."

"But I'm not offering myself." She shook her head sternly. "Although, believe me, you'll like this offer better."

"Better than *you*?" he asked, pinning her with his steady gaze. "I saw the words *Feldhure* tattooed between your breasts, so I doubt it."

She stood motionless for a moment, thinking about having those words removed after the war. "And you thought me willing because I allowed the Germans to make an army whore of me rather than die?" she asked, struggling to hide her anger.

He narrowed his eyes as if measuring her. "The words did imply you were available.

But if I misunderstood, then please accept my apology."

"You saw those words by accident. But there are many out there who would willingly condemn me for allowing the Gestapo to make a whore of me rather than kill me."

"I suppose." Sokolov replied with a taut jerk of his head. "But besides *you*, what are you going to show me that's so extraordinary?"

"This." She removed one of the oilskin- wrapped bundles of American one- hundred- dollar bills from her pocket. "And you can keep it if you'll let Kurt go. Because if it hadn't been for him, I wouldn't be alive."

Sokolov was amazed at all the money. "Where'd you get it?"

"From some Germans trying to make their way to South America."

"And you killed them?"

"With their own submachine gun they had aimed at me."

"Now that surprises me, Bela—if you don't mind my calling you by your given name."

"I don't, but it shouldn't surprise you. Since after what the Germans did to me, I became quite a survivor."

His dark eyes reflected admiration. "Knowing that, it's a shame I can't find a way to keep *you* and *Herr* Ulrich here, so you can help me with these Germans who refuse to surrender."

"With two such loyal agents as Victor and Peter, you won't need us."

Sokolov appeared to collect himself. "So they knew von Lehmann's plans were in the briefcase?"

"And were terribly concerned when we found ourselves in the middle of a battleground," she lied.

"Then I'll give them each a one- hundred- dollar bill from this bundle."

"But before you do, take this?" She held out another bundle.

"*More?*" he questioned.

"If you'll let Dr. Grossklos come with us."

"Of course... since *Herr* Ulrich will need him."

"And this." She handed him another bundle.

"What's that for?"

"To keep those Russian soldiers guarding Franz from mauling Vera—"

"But I've given specific orders to them not to rape her," Sokolov countered.

"They're *not*, but they're fondling her."

"Then I'll see it's stopped immediately... but here, Bela, keep this last bundle of American bills you just gave me."

"I don't want them." She stared at them, then at him. "Just keep your soldiers close to Vera and her family and see they come to no harm."

"Which I have every intention of doing," he assured her, continuing to act overwhelmed by her generosity. "But am I taking all your money?"

"A good portion of it." She stole a last glance at it. "Though it doesn't matter—"

"I can't believe I've fallen heir to such a fortune," He beamed with delight, grabbing her hand and kissing it. "Do you have any idea what this will mean for me?"

"A better life."

"A much *better* one," he replied, not letting go of her hand. "Although, I do have another question for you—"

"What?"

"Do you by chance have any idea where that AWOL Russian's uniform and personal effects are?"

The unexpected question came as a surprise. And she hesitated a moment before asking, "Why is it important to you?"

"Because I mean to make an example of him to General Volkov and the Asiatic troops." He raised his hands in supplication. "So, if you know, I'd appreciate your telling me."

"And you won't blame Vera?"

"Of course not. I just need her to help me gather his things."

Bela relaxed a little. "They're in a false-bottomed, metal box in Boris's wooden chest in his cellar."

"Perfect." Sokolov smiled again. "Then I'll give her a bag after we leave and wait in her foyer while she packs it with his things."

"And I'm sure I can trust you?"

"I've been infatuated with you ever since I saw a picture of you in an old, society magazine. And if something happens that prevents you and *Herr* Ulrich from being together, then I hope you will consider me."

"I don't want another man but Kurt."

"I know. Which is why I'm doing everything in my power to save him. And if that's not enough reason to trust me, then I don't know what more I can do."

"Not much other than bringing Victor and Peter over and letting me thank them—"

"Of course." Sokolov's breath quickened. "And I'll give them each a one- hundred-dollar bill, like I said."

"Which should please them." Bela smiled, continuing to think fast.

After lying to the colonel that Victor and Peter knew about von Lehmann's designs in the briefcase, then if General Volkov questioned them about it, they would have no knowledge of the designs.

Because regardless of Colonel Sokolov's feelings for her, if the word somehow got out before she departed, that Victor and Peter didn't know about von Lehmann's designs, all her efforts would be lost. And Kurt could still wind up being a Russian prisoner.

"I'm more than pleased to reward my two agents," said Sokolov, summoning Victor and Peter with a wave.

CHAPTER THIRTY-SEVEN

B ela also waved at them, hurrying toward them before they had a chance to get to Sokolov. "I told your colonel how you saved von Lehmann's designs by ordering us to put them in the briefcase. So, he has a special gift for you—the same as I do." She shoved a one- hundred- dollar bill in each man's hand.

"A special gift like this?" Peter asked with a curious expression. "Now what's that supposed to mean?"

But quickly catching on, Victor gave him a good-natured poke in the ribs.

"You make us both proud for helping save those designs."

Peter still looked confused, but he followed Victor's lead.

Coming over, the colonel also gave each of them a one- hundred- dollar bill. Now smart enough not to ask questions, they simply bowed and thanked him.

Seeing Bela's straw hat on the ground, Peter picked it up. "It has a bullet hole in it, but even so, it makes an interesting souvenir," he said, handing it to her.

She put it on with Sokolov helping her straighten it. "Did you get a chance, Bela, to look at von Lehmann's designs?"

"I did. And they didn't appear to me to be about a V-3 Cannon Rocket, but rather an orbital, intelligence gathering device."

"Why that's even better." Sokolov grinned, clearly amazed. "Because that should put us Russians ahead of the Americans in space."

"And increase your rank to general," she added, with a vague hint of disapproval.

His grin widened. "Which couldn't happen at a better time."

Bela turned as the truck with Carl arrived. And within seconds, the speedy footsteps of two Russian combat medics crunched across Gatow's shell-marked runway with a stretcher for Kurt.

Carl hurried over to Vera "How is he?"

"I've put medial adhesive tape on him to stop the bleeding, and I'm trying to keep him warm with whatever cover we can find."

"When I learned of his condition, I grabbed two heavy blankets and put them on the stretcher," Carl informed her. "And Sokolov just told me I'm to fly to the Elbe with Kurt."

"Something that should really help him," said Wolf. "Since all he has over him right now is his jacket, overcoat, Bela's sweater, and our lightweight coats." He nodded at Jaclyn.

"I suppose it's better not to ask why we're taking him to a field hospital on the Elbe for X-rays and possible surgery rather than *your* hospital." She sighed, standing beside Carl and Wolf as they covered Kurt with one of the blankets.

"That's correct," Carl agreed. "Because the farther away we can get from this dying city—the better."

Wolf handed him the other blanket. "I'm here to do whatever you need, Doctor."

"Just pray hard that the shrapnel in his lung won't collapse it." There was silence for a moment as he turned toward the *Goose*. "Because we need to get those tubes pushing against the space between his chest and ribs as quickly as possible to relieve the pressure from the blood, air, and other accumulated fluids in his lung sack."

The colonel followed Bela. "In case you didn't hear, General Volkov has just arrived with his personal combat medic to view von Lehmann's body and confirm he's dead."

"He got here quickly," Jaclyn said, surprised. "But what about afterwards?"

"We'll bury him wherever *Herr* Ulrich wishes."

Carl turned to Kurt. "How about close to Fresa and little Erich?"

"Y...yes."he said brokenly, his breathing harsh and uneven.

"And I'll see it's taken care of," Vera promised.

"Good." Carl nodded. "And be sure to see the hospital remains as is, since I won't be coming back until the Americans are here." He reached into the pocket of his white-lab coat and removed a wallet. "But you'll need some money for von Lehmann's funeral, so take some of these British pounds I stashed before the war—"

"Vera can handle the arrangements, but I'm paying for them," interrupted Sokolov, surprising everyone with this silken assurance. "And we'll all be keeping in touch through Franz, so you'll know exactly when it happens."

"That's very thoughtful of you," said Vera, with a look of utter disbelief. "But what about our hospital with Carl gone?"

"I'll make sure it continues to serve as a model for these hospitals in such dire need." Sokolov smiled, bowing slightly. "Which Marshal Zhukov assured me, will receive some medical people with supplies from Moscow no later than next week. And don't worry about those soldiers who've been bothering you because I'm taking care of them." He stepped toward her. "Just don't go anywhere by yourself without the N.K.V.D. agent I'm assigning you."

The medics were lifting Kurt on his stretcher into the plane.

"It's a short flight so we shouldn't be in the air more than fifteen minutes," said the co-pilot, now on the tarmac with them, "Even though this plane did take a few minor hits from small arms fire on the ground, by what we suspect were probably some of those Hitler boys outside the city."

"Assuming those Wehrmacht soldiers could all crowd into this aircraft, theywere probably planning on flying low," Wolf told Carl.

"And because it's not that far to the Elbe, my guess is they'd have made it," said Carl, before turning to Vera. "Guntar continues to do a lot better. And since your people will be staying at the hospital, then inform my staff that if you want to put some cots in my small room for Gretchen and Liesel, then it'll be fine."

Vera tipped her head in acknowledgement. "Gretchen and Liesel have offered to work with your staff at the hospital. So, I'll pack your things and hold them until the other allies arrive... but what about Claus and Guntar?"

"Once Guntar gets better tell my staff *all* your people will be staying on to help them."

She gave Carl a hug. "I certainly appreciate what you're doing for my family."

"Glad I can do it." He patted Vera's arm. "Because I've always admired Gretchen and the way she's taken such good care of those two special men in her life."

The co-pilot's hands motioned for Carl, Wolf, and Jaclyn to get in the plane. "Where's your sister, *Frau* von Friesen?" he asked her, looking around.

"Saying good-bye to me," answered Sokolov in a loud voice.

He handed Bela a striped, pajama top that had belonged to a male concentration camp prisoner. "My men took souvenirs. So keep it and remember it was *we* Russians who liberated Auschwitz...and also when von Lehmann was in the hospital, he gave *us*— not the British— those invisible-ink papers."

Bela looked away. "Then so be it, even though—"

"No, let me finish. We've lost a tremendous amount of Russians in Berlin. And the American General Eisenhower wanted to spare the western allies and let us Russians be slaughtered."

"Not exactly." She turned toward the co-pilot's extended hands. "The other story was Stalin wanted the Russians in Berlin *first*...! It was a matter of pride."

"*Bela— please*!" Sokolov shouted above the engines' roar. "You, Kurt, and I must keep in contact, because my instincts tell me that in a different time and a different place, we'll meet again."

"Could be. But for now Kurt's in danger, so I have to go!" And turning once again toward the co-pilot's extended hand, she wasn't prepared for the sweep of Sokolov's strong hands on her shoulders.

"I'll never forget you, "he said, before kissing her soundly on the mouth.

The engines were quite loud now and getting louder. "Wolf von Friesen,"the co-pilot yelled. "We've got to take off!"

"But we can't without Bela—so just where the hell is she?"

"Being kissed by the colonel," Jaclyn gasped, staring at them from the plane's doorway.

The co-pilot turned to her. "Since that Freedom March ended so badly, those Germans could return any minute," he reminded in a anxious tone. "So you'd better get your sister in *this* aircraft at once or else— we're taking off!"

"*This plane's* not leaving without me!" shouted Bela, pushing the colonel away.

Then turning, she quickly grasped the co-pilot's hand and clambered into the aircraft.

Almost immediately the aircraft commenced take-off. And gaining altitude, it began climbing steeply as it headed toward the Elbe.

"How's my soon-to-be husband?" she asked Kurt, kneeling by his stretcher next to Carl. Their emotion-filled gazes were fixed on the window as they stared at Berlin, engulfed in a gray cloud of defeat and death.

"I'm as easy as Carl can make me," said Kurt, his breathing slow. "But I heard Jaclyn say the colonel kissed you. Is that true?"

"He kissed me, but it was just his way of thanking me for giving him half ofour money to keep you out of Siberia."

"For which I'm eternally grateful...but what about that striped, pajama top you're holding? Did he give it to you?"

"As a reminder the Russians liberated Auschwitz."

"A...a sad souvenir," he uttered, his breath taking effort." But nevertheless, one that should be in a museum some day."

"Did you hear the story that the S.S. changed into the striped pajamas, so the Russians would think they were prisoners?"

He nodded. "A tale being spread around that claimed, since these S.S. men had more meat on their bones than the prisoners, the Russians shot them and—"

Carl stopped him mid-sentence. "Kurt, you shouldn't be talking this much."

"I know... but just a few more words," he said, struggling for breath.

"However, what I'm told really happened was that when the Russians arrived at the camp, there were nine thousand weak, half-starved prisoners, but no S.S."

"That's because the S.S. sent the stronger ones on a death marches from Auschwitz to the Bergen-Belsen camp, and other camps to hide what they'd done," Bela added.

"What the British told us."

"And also," she continued, "they needed workers they could hold for ransom when the allies arrived."

"Which— if they haven't already— the allies are liberating as we speak." She ran her fingers across the striped, pajama top she was holding. "You know, the colonel didn't really need to give me this."

"Nor kiss you good-bye."

"I wasn't pleased, but what I disliked even more was his request to court me if something happened to you."

Kurt looked faintly amused. "Which with my good father-in-law here, nothing will."

"That's the spirit," said Carl, gently squeezing his shoulder. "As long as you finish what you have to say and be done with it."

Kurt took Bela's hand and held it loosely. "But what else did the colonel say?"

"Simply that he's planning on writing us."

"Well now... I wasn't expecting to hear that," he remarked, closing his hand over her arm. "Though I guess we should let him because we need to keep our enemies in front of us."

"True. Especially since he's going to get the Russians to give more aid to the hospitals here." She turned back to Carl. "Which reminds me, I mean for you to stash the rest of this American money, in case I get searched during my debriefing."

She dug into her raincoat's pocket and handed the remaining oilskin-wrapped packets to him.

"That's a lot of money," he remarked, quickly counting it. "And a German you killed was carrying it?"

"Yes indeed. And he was meaning to do us harm. So if this money will help pay for Kurt's London hospitalization, then you're welcome to use it."

"I'll give it back after your debriefing. Since once I get to the Elbe's field hospital, I'm going to make arrangements to put Kurt in the London hospital with some of the doctors who helped me place the Jewish children in British homes."

"And will you be staying at the hospital?"

"Probably." Carl's eyes swerved back to Kurt's. "Watching your soon –to-be –husband and helping out wherever I can."

Bela leaned over and kissed him lightly on the cheek. "We both love you so very much, Carl, and are extremely grateful for all you've done."

"Which gives a measure of relief to the ache in my heart."

"Like Kurt gives mine." Then turning, she gazed out the window as darkness fell, leaving no sign of Berlin....

It was in this city she'd exchanged declarations of love with her former enemy... love without regrets... "*knowing in my heart these declarations will not fade with the passage of time,*" she looked forward to writing in her journal.

"Bela," Wolf called, catching her off guard with a paper he was waving at her. "It's a message I've given to the co-pilot for transmission to Albert. So, please look it over and see if there's something more I need to add."

It was a short message that informed him what had happened to Kurt.

And then advised him to wait at the chalet until they got word to him from London, about where they were staying.

"This will do for the sake of brevity," she said, folding the paper and handing it back.

Moving closer to Bela, Jaclyn gave her a fierce hug." Wolf has been quite worried about you and Kurt."

"I know," she said, remembering how scared she'd been. "But for a moment the way he was pointing his submachine gun at Kurt in the middle of that battle, I thought he was going to shoot him."

"You know he wouldn't have done that," said Jaclyn, squeezing her arm affectionately. "However, he did have a premonition something bad was going to happen to the two of you." She touched the bullet hole in Bela's straw hat." So, after that explosion he was beside himself as he scanned the area for more threats. And when it looked like the two of you were dead—"

"*Which we were,*" Bela broke in.

"What?" Jaclyn asked, raising her brows. "I...I mean I've heard of such things, but what was it like?"

"That Kurt and I had a spiritual fusion for an instant." Bela paused, recalling how it seemed time was briefly suspended like Vera had said. "And Haral spoke to us."

Jaclyn looked flabbergasted. "S...spoke to you, "she repeated. "God in his mercy what did he say?"

"He had some good news—"

"Which was?"

"That through the grace of God I'm pregnant with a little boy."

"Oh, Bela," Jaclyn exclaimed, her eyes shining with tears. "You and Kurt have experienced a *miracle*!"

"I know." She reached for Carl's hand. "And I'm naming him *Erich* in memory—"

"Erich," Carl repeated, looking thunderstruck.

"Yes— Erich. And I'm making sure the picture of your daughter holding the first Erich is in his room, along with yours— his grandfather."

Tears fogged Carl's eyes. "Is this really happening after *I*—as have all of us, lost so much?"

"It is," Bela assured him. "As was my father's foretelling of the new Israel... a miracle in its self. Which to me, ironically, is the result of the mistakes seeded by this terrible war."

CHAPTER THIRTY-EIGHT

BELA'S JOURNAL
LONDON, A WEEK LATER

" *The OSS has informed us that Berlin will be divided among the allies; which gives us another reason to be thankful we're not there.*

Franz has sent us word that von Lehmann has been buried close to Fresa and little Erich. And that Colonel Sokolov is taking special care to look after Vera and see she's safe. And why? Because talk has it that Stalin is so impressed with the way he's put the Russians ahead of the Americans in space that he'll soon become a general— like we all predicted.

The news of Vera and von Lehmann has given Kurt peace, and we're all pleased.

And Wolf and Jaclyn are buying new clothes and shoes for the four of us— plus Carl. With a special pair of bedroom slippers for Kurt and a robe for his hospital stay. Plus some fancy lace lingerie for me, Jaclyn maintains I need… for future use, I suppose?

Kurt insists he intends to pay for everyone's clothing out of some of the money von Lehmann left him, but Wolf and Jaclyn say there's no way they're going to allow it.

Fortunately, like Jaclyn, Kurt has stopped smoking and is getting much stronger, making Carl and I breathe easier. But he's had a rough time— especially when it came to his debriefing.

The OSS is claiming they received a cryptic message saying the Russians paid him to drop the briefcase. And the fact he caught shrapnel is unfortunate. So, at present he's still a prisoner. And never mind that regardless of what Carl says, the OSS has insisted Kurt be put in a crowded ward, rather than a private room, claiming it's their responsibility to foot his bill.

It doesn't bother Kurt, but it does bother me. Because it seems like the OSS is getting their claws into him deeper.

'Didn't I say the British would go back on our agreement and not release him?' Albert keeps reminding me. 'And it makes me angry because this sending reliable prisoners of war on dangerous missions is supposed to be an American operation, they're letting the British run—like we've said.'

'Almost like they're turning a blind eye,' Wolf is always quick to add.

Which prompted me to tell Carl about the terrible beatings Kurt received as a prisoner- of- war. He was shocked and promised me he'd do whatever he could to get Kurt released.

Still, like all of us I'm worried—as are the two Jewish gentlemen from Palestine who've arrived on the scene. These men helped the doctors save many of the children bound for Auschwitz. And we're all very happy to have them on board with us here. 'We'll help you any way we can,' they've told me, surprising me with their concern for Kurt.

'What will become of him if he's made to go back to being a prisoner- of-war?' I dared to ask them—and Albert when he arrived in London. 'Will he go back to the regular German prisoners, who'll probably kill him for being a traitor or—'

'No.' Albert answered. 'I'm assured he'll go back to the other German prisoners he trained with. A good many of whom will be loaned to the Americans to assist them with their Marshal Plan in Germany.'

'But for how long?' I asked.

Albert eased out a breath. 'There's no telling.'

When I mentioned it to Carl, he explained it like this. 'You see the Germans bombed Britain so badly, the British are planning on keeping their prisoners longer than the other western allies. Since it's a question of rebuilding the damage that was done.'

'And Kurt's an engineer so obviously they need him,' I concluded.

And Carl agreed."

* * *

Later that afternoon Kurt reminded Wolf and Jaclyn for the hundredth time, "Whether I'm to remain a prisoner or not, Bela and I *have* to get married right away."

"I approached Carl this morning," Jaclyn informed him. "And he thinks you'll be strong enough next week to sit in a wheelchair and go through the ceremony. However, the other doctors here still haven't said one way or the other."

After Jaclyn left, Kurt sighed and folded his hands over Bela's. "Did the doctors tell you that even if the British do decide to release me, then there's a possibility we'll not be able to have sex for several months?"

"They said it might put too much pressure on your lungs, and I agree. Since a lifetime of adventure awaits us in the bedroom."

Disappointment swamped him. "Even so it's *our* honeymoon— so why would being celibate for several months not upset me?"

"Just be thankful you're alive," said Bela, rubbing his arm. "Since the way I look at it, is we've already had our honeymoon."

"On a cellar floor in Berlin with *Ivan* storming through the door to rape Gretchen and Liesel," he remarked in a bitter tone.

"As you know I'm pregnant, Kurt," she whispered, leaning over and kissing him. "So I couldn't ask for a better honeymoon."

"And you'll be showing in several months."

Her mouth curved with tenderness. "With the baby discovering he has romantic parents."

"Which is as it should be." He grinned, adjusting his wrinkled pajama top.

Jaclyn had bought the pajama set for him because it had prints of elephants on it. 'Safari pajamas,' she'd informed him. And he'd laughed.

Bela straightened the collar on them. "We should be able to restrain ourselves because we do have a spiritual connection that— at times— seems to transcend our physical one."

"Of which I'm very much aware," he said, returning her kiss. "Because your nightmares don't seem nearly as bad, when I'm holding you."

"They're not. So it's lucky Carl has at least put a cot in here, that allows us to fall asleep holding hands."

"Still, Jaclyn tells me, that like she and Wolf, you have a room at a bed- and-breakfast place several blocks away. So if you slept there, you might get more rest."

Bela's hand slid from Kurt's shoulder to his arm. "What she keeps saying," she said, stroking his arm. "Although I rather doubt it."

"Doubt it? After she's promised me she'll see you eat well and get plenty of rest?"

"Kurt, I'll do anything you want me to do—even if it means sleeping at that bed and breakfast place."

* * *

"Bela, what I want is for you to follow your heart —and do what *you* want." He gazed at her as if staring at the sun before asking, "Don't you know me well enough by now to know that?"

"Of course. It's just I suspect I have so many buried feelings from the war that part of me is still attempting to step from the darkness into the light. Yet, it doesn't matter because I very much want to please you."

"Then you'll understand the only reason I'm not fumbling in the darkness is because I'm guided by *your* light." He buried his hands in her hair. "So the best way you can help yourself and me, is by following yourheart... but tell me, do you ever have a good dream any more?"

"Last night."

"And you didn't tell me?"

"I was saving it as a surprise for our wedding day."

"Then it must have been something really *good*."

"It was. Since I heard our son in my womb whisper his love for us."

"Well now." Kurt beamed. "That must be because he knows how much *we* love him."

"It really is. Which is the reason I want the best for him and have asked Carl to come to Palestine and deliver him."

Kurt patted her arm. "Exactly what I was thinking. Because if the *damned* Tommies won't release me, then with Carl there, I won't worry about you and little Erich so much."

"If the British won't release you, I'm staying here until they do."

"No!" he said firmly. "We want our son born in Palestine.

And Jaclyn and Wolf will be with you— even if I can't be."

"Still I won't leave you."

"Bela, please—someone must watch after you. And Wolf and Jaclyn are your family. So you must stay with them."

"With Jaclyn and I working together, we're usually not apart, So I doubt she'll leave me."

"She'd better not."

"Albert's doing everything he can to get the OSS to release you to him as promised."

"I know. And Wolf's working overtime with him, to get the Tommies to allow me to do some drafting work for them— if I'm lucky enough to convalesce in Switzerland."

"How's Wolf helping Albert?"

"It's something of a secret, but Wolf admires Churchill and insists if it hadn't been for his fighting spirit, the Germans would have won the war." Kurt stopped long enough to catch his breath before continuing, "So if you can believe it, he's volunteered his services as an engineer and agreed to work for them with *me* at Albert's chalet."

Excitement rippled through Bela. "Now that's an offer too good to refuse."

"What Albert says. So stand by, Bela, until three o'clock this afternoon when we're supposed to hear something."

"Will do. "She nodded, checking her watch eagerly. "But in the meantime I'll be praying the news is good."

"Same as me."

The suspense built as they waited. With she and Kurt exchanging helpless looks several times as three o'clock came and went, without so much as a word from anyone.

Then when five o'clock came, Albert rushed into the ward with the announcement that the British had taken Wolf up on his offer to work with Kurt at the chalet.

"Hallelujah!" Kurt shouted, putting his feet on the floor.

Lucky for him, Carl was nearby. "If you don't calm down we'll have to put off your wedding until week after next," he cautioned.

"Can't have that now, can we?"

"No we can't. But hopefully after your evening walk with me in the hall, you'll relax."

"I'll try my best."

As was speculated Carl's doctor friends were so anxious for him *not* to return to Berlin, they'd given him a small room in the hospital like his in Berlin. "They didn't need to go and do that," he reminded again, "because they know I'll have to get back with this talk about the city being divided among the allies."

"And Wolf just told me in the hall that his sources are claiming, Potsdam is expected to become one of the sectors of Berlin occupied by the Soviets."

"Which means that sadly, plans to do so are probably being made as we speak," said Wolf, joining them.

Carl shook his head somberly. "Sad indeed."

In the face of the stony silence following, Wolf turned to Kurt.

"The two gentlemen from Palestine who worked with the British and Carl are waiting in the hall to see you."

His eyes widened. "Whatever for?"

"I'll let them tell you."

After Wolf and Carl headed toward the hall, Kurt looked at Bela with glazed eyes. "If they ask me if I murdered innocent people, then tell them I'm guilty on all accounts by association."

Dismayed, she stared at him. "Kurt—for goodness sake, don't upset yourself. They're probably impressed you switched sides."

"I doubt that," he said, stepping into his slippers. "Since if they know much about me, then they'll know the war was almost over when I did."

* * *

There was just a little light outside when Kurt followed Wolf and Carl into the hall where the two gentlemen from Palestine were waiting.

Carl beckoned to Bela, standing in the door, to come over. "You'll need to hear this too," he said. "And help Kurt decide whether or not he wants to move, to Buenos Aires and work in the future, for the new Israel—like the British have promised the Jews."

"Buenos Aires?" Kurt questioned "Who told you we were planning on moving there?"

The older, fatherly- looking man turned to Wolf with a broad smile. "He did."

Kurt moved closer to Bela. "And did Wolf *here* explain why?"

"It goes back to your planning to kill ObersturmFuhrer Horst Helmer—"

"Who we just learned from these gentlemen is dead," Wolf announced with a roguish grin.

Kurt was astonished. "How on earth did we get so lucky?"

"By the Americans sonar tracking the U-boat he was on, and sinking it with a depth charge."

Kurt placed his hand in the small of Bela's back. "Because what that tells me is that half your nightmares should be over."

"Which I certainly hope."

"Couldn't ask for a better wedding present." Wolf smiled. "So why not invite these two gentlemen to your wedding?"

"No reason not to." She turned to them. "It's a civil ceremony, but even so I'd be honored if you came."

"And we'd be honored to come," said each man.

The younger man moved closer to Kurt. "But tell us more about your plans and your wife's plans for the future."

"Even if they're complicated?" he asked, putting his arm around Bela.

"Doesn't matter, just proceed."

"Well." Kurt hesitated, wishing he could evade the question, since he hadn't discussed everything with Bela. Though, looking deeper into her blue eyes and seeing the encouraging expression in them, the answer to the older man's question rushed out with the swiftness of a glacier- fed torrent. "First we'll return to Switzerland. And after things settle down to our satisfaction, then hopefully we'll return to Vienna where von Lehmann left me two houses in the Vienna Woods."

"But with the Russians in Vienna are the houses still standing?" Carl asked.

Kurt shrugged. "They appear to be from what the OSS has told Albert."

"Even so," Carl remarked in a voice that held some suppressed emotion, "the Russians are saying they're planning on staying in Austria, like they are in Hungary."

Wolf's lips curved. "Hopefully not? Since the way things are shaping up, there's a good chance the British and Americans are making plans to take care of them."

"If the political situation goes the way we want, I'm giving Jaclyn and Wolf one of the houses," Kurt informed the two gentlemen. "Because as you've probably already figured out, Bela and Jaclyn need to remain close because of their music."

"That's understandable," said the older gentleman, turning to Wolf. "But what about Palestine? Will you be living there part of the time?"

"A good possibility," Wolf answered. "Since our wives are planning on giving charity concerts for the benefit of the refugees expected to arrive." He turned to Jaclyn and Bela.

"In what the British keep saying will soon become the new Israel."

"And Buenos Aires?" asked younger man, directing his question to Kurt." What about it?"

"Don't know, now that ObersturmFuhrer Helmer's dead."

"Still there are others like him in the escaping S.S. who have either moved or will be moving there. Bribing those in charge to give them a measure of power in that country."

"So in the future we could use you," said the older man. "Since you've been in the Wehrmacht and have an opportunity to connect with the S.S." He gazed at Kurt with a thoughtful look before adding, "And possibly ferret out some information from them as to where some of their death camp murderers are living."

"Von Lehmann said I'd become an avenger," Kurt recalled, thinking how at times the man's intuition was like a seer's. "But without Bela, Wolf, and Jaclyn agreeing to come with me, then I'm afraid it wouldn't be possible."

"Before the war the Conservatory in Buenos Aires was begging Jaclyn to become an artist-in-residence and perform and teach there," Wolf informed the older man with pride. "But she chose to marry me and was pleased to spend her time at the *embassy* when we worked with *Herr* Wallenberg later."

"Which in those dangerous times was a wise choice," agreed the older man. "But for now, how about the four of you discussing it and getting back with me?"

Kurt turned to Wolf. "Sounds good to me."

"We've time," he replied. "Since I don't see much happening until the British honor their promise about the new Israel."

"That's what I keep saying," remarked the younger man in a somewhat despondent tone." But regardless we'll be talking with you again."

* * *

The future move to Buenos Aires was decided quicker than Bela had expected. With Wolf, Jaclyn, and Kurt agreeing to it as long as she did. "Which I do," she assured them. Knowing how Kurt could not forgive himself for the regret he had at his inability to penetrate the mask of the *Fuhrer's* deception, unless he became an avenger.

At the hospital, Jaclyn's plans for the wedding in such an unusual place were coming together in an amazingly short amount of time. And she even took the liberty of picking out a wedding dress, which Bela declared was not only fit for royalty, but something she could wear when she performed with her.

It was a creamy-white dress with a fairly high, square neckline. And its skirt was long and covered in lace ruffles, the same as its short sleeves and torso. "The pearls I'm lending you will look lovely with your dress," said Jaclyn. "And you'll have a veil in back with white flowers on top of your hair, matching your bouquet."

"Which will truly make you a sight to behold." Carl grinned, adding, "Even if you are walking down the aisle of a hospital ward."

"Which the patients are telling me will be exciting," said Bela, anticipating it. "Because they're looking forward to a slice of the huge cake and non-alcoholic wedding punch, Wolf and Jaclyn are having prepared for everyone here in the hospital."

"But who's serving it?" Carl asked.

"They have some volunteer helpers."

"And Wolf's walking you down the aisle?"

"If he is, he hasn't mentioned it."

"Well," Carl began, cocking his head as if thinking about it. "I lost a daughter—"

"And I a father."

"So if you want, I could walk you down the ward's aisle and give you away,"

Bela touched his hand. "Which would greatly honor me."

Carl's grin widened. "Then by all means, I will."

* * *

The rest of the week passed quickly. And the following week when the day of the wedding finally arrived Bela was so excited, Jaclyn teased her about the scarlet stains on her cheeks.

"Better slow down," she warned her.

She exchanged a smile with her. "I would if I could."

Because it was a civil ceremony the words were few, so she and Kurt wanted to add some of their own. However, due to his health, the doctors didn't think it wise for him to talk much.

A situation that prompted Jaclyn to hire three musicians to accompany her. 'That way the wedding won't seem so rushed,' she'd explained.

Carl wore a tuxedo that matched Wolf's. And Kurt, also wearing a tuxedo, sat in a wheelchair with a blanket thrown over his legs.

Bela stood behind him, smiling at the garden trellis Jaclyn insisted the wedding needed. It detracted from Kurt's injury and gave their togetherness an unexpected attractiveness for the photographer snapping pictures. One of which would be used for the oil painting Wolf had commissioned an artist to do as his wedding present to them.

Also the garden trellis served another purpose. Since covered in fresh flowers, it enveloped the hospital's ward with a carnation smell that quickly eliminated its antiseptic one.

Albert had returned from Switzerland the following evening with the diamond wedding band Haral had given Jaclyn's mother.

It was the best that could be done on short notice. Although Kurt did promise Bela that as soon he got better, he'd buy her another large diamond. Something she was quick to insist she didn't need. But he disagreed. And smiling at her craftily, he remarked, "We'll see."

When the ceremony ended Wolf and Jaclyn toasted the couple's health and happiness with the wedding punch as Bela leaned over to Kurt, so he could seal their vows with a kiss.

In the background Jaclyn remarked to Wolf, "Later, they must be sure to put a lock and key on a bridge in Paris like we did, to symbolize their everlasting love."

"Absolutely." Wolf agreed. "Because they really must have met at Demel's or otherwise they couldn't be this happy."

"Didn't I tell you?" Jaclyn reminded, in a slightly uppity tone.

"So whatever made you believe that Gestapo man in the first place?"

"The desperation of the times, I suppose. So, all I can say is so much for not recognizing it as a lie."

"Glad you're seeing the light," Jaclyn commended him.

Lifting his head, Kurt asked Bela in a soft voice, "Do you think when Vienna gets put back like it was, we should make our lie about Demel's the truth?"

"Absolutely," she whispered, kissing his ear.

"Then if we do make it back, I'll spill cold coffee on your skirt at Demel's."

"Which won't bother me in the least." She grinned, once again crouching to his level.

"Maybe not— but know this, once I do it, then I'm going to buy you four of the most beautiful skirts in the city."

"Now, *Kurt*—" Embarrassed, she cast her eyes downward. "That simply won't be necessary."

"Now, *Bela*," he said. "We've seen how our souls are joined, which makes *you* a gift to me." He broke into a wide, open grin. "So promise me this on our wedding day, that you'll allow me to spoil you so long as we both shall live."

Overcome by such a beautiful thought from this man who'd changed her life, her eyes misted. "When you put it like that," she replied, as if drawn by the complex memories of their past. "Because like my father told me, it was *God* who sent *you* to me."

"Which was more than I could ever imagine—much less deserve," he said, a lingering huskiness in his voice as his hand covered hers and stroked it gently.

Dear Reader: If you enjoyed *THE FIRE, THE ROSE, AND THE CITY, a review* on Amazon would be appreciated. For those who are interested there are discussion questions for book club review.

Also by Kymberly Hastings, *THE FLOWERING EUCALYPTUS: A CONVICT'S TALE*

Actress Lily Kendall hurrying to aid a poor widow, is captured by escaped London Newgate convicts. But when sea captain, Jake Ravin, rescues her, it's love at first sight. However, after he's arrested for being an Irish freedom fighter and sent to Australia, she and her family follow him. Although upon arrival, the wicked Governor Darling and his cousin obstruct them at every turn

AN ACKNOWLEDGEMENT
FROM THE AUTHOR

At this time I deem it appropriate to mention Ruth, a young German girl in her early twenties, who'd married a soldier during the American occupation. I met Ruth while I was in my teens, and we enjoyed talking to each other, since I was anxious to visit Europe. So one day she told me about a lady —her best friend in Germany— who lived across the street from a very romantic married couple.

These two had met briefly during the war and afterwards, through a twist of fate, had met **again**. In **my** no**vel** I've named this pair Kurt and Bela.

They had a secret, and Ruth's trusted best friend knew it— yet, never revealed their **names**. "But what could this secret be?" I was curious to know.

And closing her eyes, Ruth answered in a solemn tone, "It was the shame of this couple meeting in a brothel for front-line soldiers."

"Brothel!" I gasped, stunned.

Apparently the man was a Wehrmacht officer who was visiting it, and the girl, a young woman the S.S. had forced into prostitution. Although unknown to the S.S. she was Jewish.

Immediately I pondered the incredibility of this young woman's degradation. "Would a secret such as hers be taken to the grave?'" I asked Ruth.

And she quickly said, "No doubt."

An unhappy marriage eventually forced Ruth to move back to Germany, and except for Christmas cards, we had little contact. "Life has separated us," I remember writing on one.

So I made a rushed Cook's tour of Europe on a bus and visited Germany. And Ruth was planning on taking a train and meeting me in Cologne, but at the last minute, a family illness prevented her from doing it.

Then much later her brother wrote me that she was dying of cancer and suggested I fly over.

Which I did.

Ruth's trusted friend had passed on. "But what about this couple with the secret? Had they passed on too?" And Ruth nodded, adding, "With their names and secret never being revealed publicly—like they wanted."

However, after I returned home I felt the world needed to be aware of the amazing love between this former Wehrmacht officer and Jewish girl. So after much thought, I added a considerable degree of action and adventure to their love story to insure their privacy.

*If you wish to read more about Kurt and Bela, then please turn the page for **BELA'S JOURNAL AFTERWARD**.*

Our dear little Erich, a true miracle from heaven who sweetened our lives.

"As planned, Kurt and I found ourselves in Palestine with Wolf and Jaclyn when our special little angel was born. The rest of our friends were there, with Carl delivering him and Vera assisting.

Vera and Franz were now married. However, they felt the same as Wolf and Jaclyn about having children. 'There's no need,' Jaclyn told them. 'Since you can always be godparents, like we are.' Which of course, meant she and Wolf would be keeping little Erich frequently.

Kurt and I both know that neither Erich nor I would be alive if it weren't for them, so we had no objections.

Gretchen, Liesel, Claus, and Guntar were also present at Erich's birth. Which came as no surprise, since Carl and Gretchen were now married, and— with the help of Vera— he was training her to become a nurse in his new hospital. And all thanks to Colonel Sokolov who'd pulled the strings that allowed them to move to a sector of Berlin occupied by the western allies. A kindly act that enabled Carl to send Liesel to a boarding school in Switzerland, so she could hurry and get into the university and become a doctor. 'I love babies and am looking forward to holding little Erich,' she declared as she anxiously awaited his arrival.

Claus and Guntar came with them to Palestine, because they'd always wanted to see the Holy Land. And Carl and Gretchen saw no reason not to indulge them... especially with Guntar now working with Franz in communications.

I arranged for Carl to meet Yanni's father. And they immediately became good friends. In fact, he assisted Carl and Vera when little Erich arrived.

Naturally Kurt was with me at the time.

'I do believe we have a little boy,' Jaclyn exclaimed later to Wolf, Claus, and Franz in the lobby. 'And he has Kurt's dark hair and his mama's blue eyes.'

'*A perfect combination,' said Wolf, applauding so loudly with Claus, Franz, and Guntar that Vera had to step out and shush them. At Kurt's request she'd brought the first little Erich's remaining baby clothes, toy giraffe, and blanket. 'A gift from his namesake,' she said, after she'd wrapped him in it.*

Kurt smiled as he handed our tiny son to me to nurse. And tears of joy rolled down my cheeks as I held him. 'Our magic time begins, Kurt,' I whispered, loving the strong bond I could swear was already developing between them.

And he nodded, his eyes gleaming as he took one of his handkerchiefs and gently blotted my eyes."

* * *

"*Several days before Erich's birth, the two Jewish men from Palestine, who'd attended my wedding, introduced me to a considerate rabbi, who asked me if there was anything he could do for me, since I had been through so much.*

There wasn't. Although I could tell by the way he fidgeted he wanted to ask me another question.

So I finally said, 'Is there something more you want to know?' And he nodded. 'If you're willing to answer.'

Which I was. Since I could feel he needed to get his question off his chest.

'Well,' he began, 'because you were one of the people the Germans mistreated, do you hate them now that you're married to one?'

I'd been asked the question before, so I answered it as best I could. 'Their evil was so overwhelming, it was too vast for me to know exactly where I should put my hatred.' Then hoping to simplify it for him, I added, 'Making me feel at times like I was looking into a well so deep, I couldn't see its bottom—'

'That you very much wanted to see?' he asked, searching my face.

'Yes.'

'You sound to me like a lot of survivors who aren't sure what to do. So, I'll pray for a ray of light to pierce this darkness of your deep well,' he said, dropping his eyes like he was already in prayer 'And rest assured, my friend, it will happen.'

Which on the day my Erich was born, it did.

Exhausted from giving birth, I hadn't been asleep long when Madam Kollar appeared to me in a dream. She told me there was a snake in the bottom of this deep well, which had narrowed the vastness of my hatred down to a group of unnamed soldiers.

'But where are you, snake?' I asked, leaning against the well. 'Haven't I had enough nightmares, so please show yourself—'

Then a shadow passed over the well and my heart beat faster. For clearly the deafening silence of the well's surface was the only answer.

Stagnant water with glimmers of light, made it clear the snake had vanished. So now, I'll never know the names of my demons.

'Because condemning those names will not be enough,' I could have sworn I heard Madam Kollar say.

However, I suspected the snake's list was made up of the names of those often angry soldiers— particularly the murdering S.S. men with the devil's snake eyes — who planted themselves in my body night after night at the Love Camp. Men I tried not to remember, but at times couldn't keep from it. With Kurt being the only one of those men I'd been given the chance to kill, yet hadn't.

It simply hadn't crossed my mind until he'd asked me, 'Why not?' A question that surprises me even now. But not my answer, 'You were suffering too, the same as me.'

Still, as time has passed, and I've given it more thought, today my answer would be, 'You aroused something in me, because you were so much better in so many ways... that you were able to guide me from the darkness of my despair toward the light. Whose vibrant radiance gave me hope.'

'With its glowing brightness capable of melting ice for eternity,' Kurt would say. 'Which hopefully, at some point, should ease your pain of looking at Yanni's picture.'

Even if there were still many times on foggy dark nights I'd awake trembling. So, I'd gaze outside the window beside the bed Kurt and I shared.

The fog's thickness had the power to make it easy for another round of painful memories with those ribald soldiers and snake-eyed S.S. men at the Love Camp to enter them. They—the murderers of my people—would look at me like I was vermin to be crushed. And frightened, I'd swallow hard each time they pointed at my bed.

Then my anxiety would awaken Kurt, whose protective arms around me were the miracle he'd use to keep the night's blackness at bay and drive those murderers back to their nothingness... for a time at least."

* * *

'In a different time and a different place, we will meet again.'
"Colonel Sokolov told me that in Berlin before we parted on May 2, 1945.

The years have passed quickly, but I've forgotten nothing. And although Kurt has bought me an expensive sable coat, I made sure Madam Kollar's mink coat always hung next to it, with the note in its pocket reading, "Only one of the nineteen girls at the Love Camp will survive."

I guess she knew it would be me and was depending on me to tell what happened— or otherwise its history would be lost. And the reason? After the war at the Nuremberg Trials, it seemed the Nazi Love Camps were a taboo subject. So this part of Hitler's scheme was dismissed.

Vera volunteered to speak out about it for the sake of women, but was told in a letter, the Nazi Love Camps could become a distraction that might sidetrack some of the Nazi's bigger crimes.

Kurt and I didn't agree, but we had no choice other than to accept the decision.

After all, I supposed, there were only a handful of survivors who shared my secret. And like me, feared people would ask if they knew, 'Aren't you ashamed of yourself for becoming a whore?'

Which possibly was one of the major reasons a good many of these women— the Germans had turned into army whores— had ended up committing suicide. Something that made me realize even more, how truly blessed I was to have found Kurt. Which is why, for time the being, I thought it best to let the matter rest.

Though several years later, a book from an Auschwitz survivor did describe how a relative had been forced into prostitution before being killed. However, since he could provide no real proof, it was dismissed as fiction.

After that— Stalag novels— paperbacks about German soldiers forcing Jewish women to have sex, and glamorous German females forcing captured American pilots to have sex, flooded the markets until after the Eichmann trial. Young people in Israel and other countries, eager to learn all they could about sex, read them avidly.

Were there other women survivors from Europe's Love Camps besides me, I continued to wonder? If there were, it did not appear any—other than myself— had come forward. (And I never revealed my true name.)

In the book by the concentration camp survivor whose relative had been forced into prostitution, there's mention of a German soldier becoming infatuated with one of the girls. Also, in my Love Camp there were rumors that the S.S. didn't want the rank-and-file soldiers— who were frequent visitors to the Love Camp—selecting the same girl each time they visited the camp. So, did the S.S. fear a growing attraction for certain girls and soldiers?

However, with Kurt being an officer, it wasn't supposed to matter— even if it was never put to the test. So fearing my story would be viewed as a Stalag novel, I once again chose to let the matter rest.

But now with sexual abuse on the rise, some questions continue to haunt me....

The newspapers frequently write about women, taking men in the film industry and other businesses, to court for accosting them sexually. And it makes me wonder what if my story had been in their possession. Would they have filmed it? Or simply looked the other way like the Nuremberg Trials, when they'd implied women's degradation was not important?

And would we have a better world for women if those Nuremberg Trials hadn't looked away...? I'd like to think so.

Pursing the matter further, I question what if one of those filmmakers, being dragged to court by women for sexual assault, had filmed my story? And what would the courts have to say about this dichotomy? Guess I'll never know, even it does continue to raise questions?

But at least the world knows what the Nazis did to me—as well as the other eighteen girls who died at the Love Camp, for whom I'm their voice.

Once again then I say, if it hadn't been for Kurt and the strong love bond that developed between us on our Berlin mission, I doubt I'd be alive today... even though we did lose von Lehmann and his preliminary designs.

So, definitely I'm meant to tell this tale, but under a pen name."

* * *

"My editor was so impressed with my book that it immediately went to press, with the title, 'The Private Journal of a Woman Who Lived Through Hell.'

'So tell me, Bela,' she said one day. 'What happened next?'

'Next?' I questioned.

325

'With you, Kurt, and Erich,' she said, pointing at my manuscript. 'Which I'm sure is all written down in that journal of yours, I've never seen.'

Of course it was, but I had no intention of giving it to her. So I compromised. 'I'll write you a summary of what happened next as long as you give your word you won't publish it.'

Which she did. 'But please—Bela— begin at the beginning.'

'After little Erich's birth?' I asked.

And smiling, she gave me a big nod.

So thumbing through my journal, I began copying the parts I felt best described our lives from that day forward."

* * *

"After Erich's birth in Palestine the five of us returned to Albert's chalet where we stayed with him,! at his invitation, until times changed.... In 1947 Israel was founded, and in 1948 the state of Israel came into being on May fourteenth.

We frequently visited the graves of Fresa, Erich, and von Lehmann in Berlin.

And Kurt and I, along with Wolf and Jaclyn, often talked about moving to Vienna. But since there was still so much wrangling between the western allies and the Russians over who would control what in Vienna and Austria, we decided against it.

In the end we agreed to wait it out and allow the caretakers of our estates to let some of the more important men in the military be housed in them."

* * *

"Under assumed names Jaclyn and I often gave concerts in Israel to benefit its refugees. And a certain comfort would swell inside me when I sang in Hebrew, and she accompanied me with a group that specialized in music from ancient Israel. It was during one of these concerts the two men who'd approached us to move to Buenos Aires, informed Kurt and Wolf it was getting close to the time, and we should do it in the not- too -distant future.

Wolf and Kurt were eager to open an aircraft parts factory there. And as mentioned earlier the music conservatory, in conjunction with the university, had long wanted Jaclyn (and now me) to be artists- in- residence and give concerts and teach their more exceptional students. So, in the middle of 1950 we made our move.

Albert, Carl, Gretchen, Vera, and Franz, were sad to see us leave, but with twenty-seven weekly, westbound commercial flights now being offered, they promised to visit often.

We were eager to move, because rumors had it that the Vatican had issued over a thousand visas to Nazis, so they could emigrate to Paraguay and Argentina.

'War criminals who escaped punishment must be dealt with,' Kurt insisted. 'So I'll do whatever it takes to find out where they are and what they did. And then pass the information to the Israelis.'

Kurt was a good Catholic, but after hearing this he began to view his religion with concern.

'The same as me about Judaism,' I'd say…who like many Holocaust survivors was on the verge of walking away from all religion.

But after giving it more thought, Kurt maintained we needed some degree of spirituality, so he suggested we remain who we were. 'Since after all, you and I shared a near-death experience.'

Then he reminded me, 'And when I ended up becoming a Tommie prisoner-of- war, the only way I could help you was to pray to God to keep you safe and let me know you survived.'

That was all it took to get me to agree to whatever he wanted.

So I remained a Jew— but role-played a Catholic, who like little Erich had been baptized, because I was quite fearful of the anti-Semitic feelings so very close to Israel. Even though I knew that in my faith this faked conversion was frowned on.

However, our Israeli friends who were helping arrange for our move to Buenos Aires argued with a rabbi.' If Kurt is hunting war criminals, then he won't be able to do it with a Jewish wife. So what do we do? Just let them get away?'

This rabbi had no real answer, other to frown and say, 'Then do what you think you must—but revenge is still looked down upon by many who suffered in the holocaust.'"

* * *

"We celebrated both Jewish and Christian holidays, but cautioned Erich not to chose between the two religions until he was at least twenty-five.

Kurt gave me a diamond cross and a diamond Star of David. And I'd wear the cross to mass when I went with Kurt. And Jaclyn would tease me and say that even Jesus would think I was a devout Catholic— and I would simply say, 'Oh.'

That prompted Wolf one day to tell Jaclyn, teasing me like that was sacrilege. And Kurt—he was certain— would agree.

But I never mentioned it to Kurt, because he liked me for who I was. And saw to it I had kosher food whenever possible. Even though he never asked me to cook the pork he loved. 'Because if you're not allowed to eat it, then you shouldn't be cooking it,' he would say.

But I'm getting ahead of myself, so I need to redirect my attention to little Erich's babyhood and his early years.

Of course, Jaclyn and Wolf loved him so much they insisted on helping us take care of him. And whenever Gretchen and Carl would visit, they took such good care of him, they hardly let him out of their arms.

When Erich was six months old, we received a letter from General Anton Sokolov—of all people. He had married a beautiful doctor, Manya, whose elite family had positions in the Russian diplomatic corps. He sent us a wedding picture, and Kurt swore that Manya looked enough like me to be my sister.

We responded by sending a picture of our Erich. It was a good picture with me sitting on the couch giving him his bottle, and Kurt's arm wrapped around my shoulder.

It was also the beginning of a penpal-like correspondence between us and General Sokolov. And at the end of each letter Anton would scribble something in Russian to Kurt, and he would do likewise.

From time to time Anton and Manya sent us gifts. So naturally we felt the need to reciprocate—especially a year later when their daughter, Katya, was born. We sent her a teddy bear and some hand-embroidered dresses with a card inside the package that read, 'May she bring as much joy to you as Erich is bringing us.'"

* * *

"For truly Erich was amazing. And though it wasn't necessary, Albert hired a nanny for him who spoke Spanish. He was a good baby who rarely cried. But even with a nanny when he did, it was a race between Kurt and me to see who could get to him first.

The bond Kurt and Erich shared was like nothing I'd ever seen between a father and son. And as Jaclyn had predicted, he looked like Kurt— except for my blue eyes.

Erich became a very well-behaved young man, who spoke German, English, and Spanish by the time he was nine. And of course French with Jaclyn.

Carl described him as his genius grandson and wanted to set up a trust fund for him. But Kurt and I didn't want him doing it alone, so Wolf and Jaclyn suggested the five of us set it up...which we did.

Erich was six years old when Kurt taught him how to ride a pony, plant a garden, swim, and ski. Kurt loved to swim and ski... however, I taught Erich how to play the piano.

But the thing Erich liked best was riding in our motor bike's sidecar.

Kurt would laugh and say, 'I guess I know who's going to end up with this souvenir of our misadventure.'"

* * *

"Erich was seven when we moved to Buenos Aires. Where at long last Wolf and Kurt got to open their aircraft parts factory.

Those in the S.S. who'd escaped with stolen gold from Germany had a strong hold in the country under the Peron government. And they seemed quite impressed to see Germans, with two outstanding musician wives, re-locating in the city.

The door was opening for Kurt, and he didn't hesitate to seize the opportunity. He didn't talk too much to these former murderers, but it didn't matter. Because it was his silence that got them to open up and throw out the bits of information the Israelis were seeking.

Times were tense, so at Jaclyn's suggestion Kurt and I worked off some of the tension by learning to tango. With people liking our dancing so much, we frequently got asked to perform at parties.

Twice a year before heading to Israel, we'd visit Albert, who in declining health, couldn't visit us."

* * *

"*Carl, Gretchen, and Vera, would meet us in Israel and help Yanni's father provide medical services to the refugees crowding into the country. Liesel was now a doctor married to a doctor, and when she could, they'd meet us there with their two children. And if they couldn't, then they'd visit us in Buenos Aires.*

Once a year at Christmas, Yanni's father along with Carl and Gretchen's family— including Claus, Gunter, Vera, and Franz— would come as a group to Buenos Aires and stay at our house. The men would often stay out all night, visiting with the former S.S. And it was amazing the snippets of information they gleaned from them. Which Kurt, with a big smile, would readily pass to his Jewish friends.

Nothing got past our growing Erich, who soon caught onto what they were doing...the only problem was he wanted to be included.

He was quite aware of the holocaust. And on some of the Jewish holidays we'd celebrate in our home in secret, he'd wear the striped, pajama top from Auschwitz that Anton Sokolov had given me. 'One day it should be in museum,' I'd remind him, and he'd nod his agreement.

Erich wanted to read my journal, but I told him he'd have to wait until he was thirty-five.

'No—make it forty,' Kurt told me.

To which Erich sighed, adding, 'I have overprotective parents and godparents.'

'But only because we've lost so many of our loved ones,' Kurt would quickly say.

And Erich would say nothing, aware of the loss of Haral, Fresa, the first Erich, and von Lehmann, whose pictures we always kept close."

* * *

"*When Erich was eleven, he managed to glimpse the words Feldhure beneath the scarf I wore. Since I was a survivor, it was suggested survivors keep their tattoos, so the world would believe the holocaust, should someone say it never happened.*

My son said nothing to me, but double- checked his German dictionary before approaching. Kurt. It was the right thing to do, since the two shared such an extraordinary bond.

Kurt never lied to him. So without reading my journal he soon knew what was in it. I was sad when I learned he knew. Still, I had enough faith in Kurt to know he'd handled the situation correctly.

Erich wanted to go to military school. Something Kurt and I had not expected. So we discussed the pros and cons of it with him. 'Von Lehmann allowed me to attend military school before I went to the university,' Kurt reminded. 'So I guess we should let Erich make up his own mind.'

Which that being said, we did.

He immediately took to it. Because hoping one day to help the Israelis, Erich strove to be the perfect soldier. And while still in his early teen years, Kurt declared Erich to be an excellent shot with a rifle."

* * *

"In 1955 it was agreed the West would control Vienna. However, the four of us decided we'd probably wait until Erich was ready to go to the university there and study engineering like his father and uncle.

After all he was to inherit their aircraft parts business. And he was eager to invent something in the future connected with the business, that would greatly aid the Israelis—along with the rest of the world."

* * *

"Kurt and I never gave up trying to have another child, but it wasn't meant to be... reaffirming our Erich was truly a special gift from God.

Jaclyn and I continued to give concerts in many countries in Europe, as well as places like Rio, New York, Israel, and Puerto Rico.

Wolf and Kurt made plans to sell their business in the future and open another one like it outside Vienna— but of course they were in no hurry. However, to their surprise it sold quickly and for an extremely good price.

'But there's still a very Big Fish hiding in the Buenos Aires S.S. pond,' so the Israelis would whisper. Who like Kurt, couldn't put their finger on who this man was, because he was living under an assumed name. And apparently he wasn't wealthy like so many of the former S.S. living here were.

Then Kurt mentioned a strange dream he'd had. And the next thing I knew, he had a management position at Mercedes-Benz. (As to what happened next, I'm not allowed to discuss.)

Before we left the city, Kurt taught young Erich how to drive our Mercedes on a friend's ranch, since we were planning on buying him one when he came of age.

'But it's really not necessary,' he would insist. 'As long as I have my motor bike.' Which he'd drive all over our friend's ranch, with Kurt in its sidecar.

Guntar, who'd been the Berlin general's courier with his motor bike and its sidecar, fascinated Erich. So, whenever he'd visit us, Guntar would drive him all over Buenos Aires in our motor bike."

* * *

"My son was a simple fellow who liked to wear suspenders like his dad and didn't want us buying expensive clothes for him. So we'd buy him what he wanted, but slip in a few higher priced outfits to wear, so he'd be well-dressed when Jaclyn and I performed.

And as mentioned earlier, there are things I can't discuss— but the five of us had to leave Buenos Aires and return to Vienna sooner than we'd expected. Although four days before our departure, we had an unexpected visit from an alsatian puppy, a German shepherd breed, that showed up in our yard.

Erich and the dog immediately bonded. But Kurt had reservations, since he knew I'd seen a girl in the Love Camp torn to pieces by dogs like these. 'So what do we do,

Bela?' he asked me.

I didn't know how to answer until the puppy came over and began licking my hands. 'I suppose we should try and find the dog's owner,' I said. And Kurt agreed.

With our departure pending, we were concerned as how to go about it when, less than two hours later, the owner appeared. 'The last of my puppies,' he informed us. 'And I think he's lonely.'

Before I knew it, Kurt was opening his wallet and giving the man money for the dog.

'My lucky day,' the man said. ' So I'll bring his papers around tomorrow.'

Kurt had told Erich about a dog like that von Lehmann had given him when he was a boy. And Erich admitted he'd wanted a similar dog but was afraid it might upset me.

Kurt then turned to me. 'Wolf and Jaclyn will keep him for Erich, so you won't have to see the dog.'

But no sooner were the words out of his mouth, than the dog was in my lap covering my face with kisses. ' I want him to stay with us. So, what are we naming him, Erich?' And he grinned and said, 'Shadow.'

Jaclyn and Wolf were delighted with Shadow. 'Well I guess we now have a dog too,' they teased us. In fact Kurt, with help from the former owner, got the dog's shot records and papers together in an amazingly short amount of time. 'So there won't be a problem taking the dog on the ship to Italy with us,' Kurt told me.

'Right,' said, Jaclyn, grinning. 'As long as I get to walk him twice a day on deck.'

'He's going to love the Vienna Woods.' Erich smiled. 'Plus he's going to love riding in my motor bike's sidecar.'

Shadow was our newest family member, and we sent a picture of Erich holding him in a letter to Anton and Manya.

It brought an immediate response from them, and they sent a picture of Katya with her white Siberian husky, Natasha... which Erich framed.

We enrolled Erich in a military school in Vienna— like he requested. And he graduated with honors and entered the university sooner than we expected.

He wanted to get his pilot's license, and my overly protective Kurt agreed to it as long as he could get his too. 'I have to make sure Erich can safely solo,' was his reason— but he need not have worried.

When Carl visited, he was a little nervous when Erich offered to take him flying, However, after it was over he couldn't say enough good things about what an outstanding pilot his grandson was.

Of course the next step was parachuting. And before Erich did it, he advised Kurt to hold me tight so if I fainted, I wouldn't have far to fall... which I almost did.

But like Carl, I need not have worried, because all Erich's endeavors were done with upmost care.

Though I did wonder why after he finished the university, our tall and handsome Erich— who looked like Kurt— went out with girls but didn't have a steady girlfriend.

'It's simply that he's like me,' Kurt would brag, grinning. 'He's waiting for the right young lady to come along.'"

* * *

"Because of Erich's great interest in inventing aircraft parts which would greatly aid the Israelis— some strings got pulled while he was still in the university. That way he could spend his summers in Israel, learning Hebrew, and training and flying with the Israeli air force. And in combat several times— shocking us.

When he graduated from the university, Erich informed us he'd made his decision about our two religions. 'Which is neither,' he said. 'Since I have the two greatest parents in the world and choosing one of their religions over the other, is like favoring one of my parents over the other.'

So Kurt and I just looked at each other and said, 'Oh.'"

* * *

"The day eventually came when Jaclyn and I were asked to perform in Smolensk, in the Soviet Union. Kurt and Wolf were not particularly happy about it, but nevertheless had no intention of not accompanying us. After all, General Anton Sokolov and his lovely wife Dr. Manya Sokolov were rolling out the red carpet for us. 'So you and Anton will meet again,' Kurt would frown and say to me. 'Just like he said you would.'

'Manya's parents are in very high diplomatic circles,' I would remind. 'So I guess we'll just have to grin and bear it.'

Our twenty-three year old Erich was going with us. And for one of the few times in his life, he took some interest money from his trust fund and bought some expensive clothes and men's cologne."

* * *

"After the concert Anton kissed me on both cheeks.

Kurt wasn't happy about this traditional kiss, any more than when someone said to me,

'You and Manya look enough alike to be sisters.'

Victor and Peter were now Anton's bodyguards, and they seemed as happy to see me as Anton was.

Manya had a lavish dinner planned for us at an exclusive place for diplomatsnext door and the elite. And backstage, Anton saw to it that champagne was brought in from a small bar adjourning the theater and the place where we would dine.

While we talked and sipped champagne, I suddenly realized that two members of our party had disappeared— Erich and Katya.

Sensing my concern, Victor informed me they were sitting in the bar sipping Russian tea. And Erich was practicing his Russian with her, while she was practicing her English with him.

When Erich saw us, he said, 'I told her we'd be coming back here in a month.'

'We are?' asked Kurt, mortified.

'I guess I forgot to tell you,' I said, gently nudging him.

'Guess you did.' He smiled, shaking his head.

'Remember,' I whispered.' It's what Erich wants.'

'Well he has good taste.' Kurt smiled. 'Since Katya's a beautiful blond like you.'"

* * *

"It was a well-planned evening, with Anton suggesting Erich and Katya have their dinner in the adjourning area close to the dance floor where it was more private. 'That way they can continue to enhance their language skills and won't have to listen to us talk over old times.'

'Guess not,' I said, seeing the sparkles in Erich and Katya's eyes.

Dinner was lengthy, and afterwards Anton escorted us to the dance floor where a group of musicians were playing a waltz, with Erich and Katya dancing quite close. 'I don't think we have to worry about our handsome Erich not having a girlfriend,' I told Kurt.

'No we don't,' he said.

The six of us also waltzed, exchanging partners several times. And when the evening ended, Anton insisted we stay one more night so he, Manya, and Katya could show us some of the wonderful museums in the city that they knew we'd love. And in the evening, his chef would prepare a special dinner for us at his home, so we could meet Katya's dog, Natasha. In fact, Erich presented her with a small oil painting of the dog he'd paid an artist to do from the photograph in the letters, Anton and Manya had sent us. And Katya was thrilled and eager to meet Shadow.

What choice did we have, seeing how Erich and Katya couldn't take their eyes off each other?

'Mark my word,' Jaclyn whispered to me. 'We're going to have a Russian in the family—' And was she ever right.

Their engagement happened quicker than we could have imagined. 'Can you believe it?' Kurt asked. 'We're going to be related to Anton Sokolov, who was threatening to make me a prisoner and ended up with von Lehmann's preliminary designs.'

'But his wife and daughter are lovely,' I reminded him.

'And thankfully, you're a lot like them.'

'And Erich's a lot like you. So, he and Katya should be fine.'

'Manya nearly died giving birth to Katya,' Anton said. And though she wanted more children, the doctors advised her it wasn't safe. So regardless of what she wanted, he wasn't about to let it happen.

Kurt assured me Erich knew all about the physical side of marriage, because they'd been talking about it since he was in his early teens. 'And any questions I can't answer, we look them up together.'

Jaclyn had a six-carat -marquise diamond her father had given her mother.

She said it belonged on a young, pretty hand. And if Katya had no objection to it being her engagement ring, then she could have it. Erich believed he should buy her a ring, but he said, 'If Katya wants things this way, then that's the way they'll be. But first they'd have a talk with her about it.'

When she saw the ring, she said it was beyond her imagination, and she thanked Erich and Jaclyn and kissed them.

Katya was going to have to continue to work after they got married. Her university studies had centered around languages, preparing her for a diplomatic career. 'If I'm working with embassies, I have the freedom to live other places and move in and out of the Soviet Union, like few people living there can do.' Of course it helped her father was a famous general."

* * *

"As a wedding present, Kurt, Jaclyn, Wolf, Carl, Gretchen, and I pulled our resources together and bought the couple a lovely home in the Vienna Woods they'd admired.

Their wedding was to be in Vienna and their honeymoon in Israel with Yanni's father, who adored Erich, planning some entertainments for them while they were there.

Of course the wedding was to be a civil ceremony because like Anton explained, their grandparents had slipped out Manya, Katya, and himself when they were infants, to a Russian Orthodox church and had them baptized —since after all, only old people went to church.

So Kurt and I just looked at each other and said, 'Oh.'"

* * *

"The wedding was lovely, with family and friends from the Soviet Union given special visas to come.

Everyone in our family was there. Carl, Gretchen, Guntar, Vera, Franz, Yanni's father, and of course Liesel and her family. Claus and Albert had passed on, but like Gretchen said, 'They're looking down from above.'

Katya's dress was white with three -ruffled tiers that brushed her shoes.

And the flowers, seven-tiered cake, bridal bouquet, and music coming from Jaclyn and a string quartet, all helped to make the event memorable.

The couple read vows they'd written to each other. And after the ceremony, they stood in the middle of a huge friends and family photograph.

Anton kissed me on both cheeks. And afterwards Kurt whispered, 'What do you think he'd say if I kissed Manya like that?'

And I merely said, 'He's family now and loves Erich. And our son is quite happy, which is what we want for him. So, we just have to accept Anton for the way he is.'

Of course Franz was quick to tease Vera, when Anton told her how good it was to have her in the family at long last."

* * *

"Surprises continued to follow, because in just a little over six weeks, Katya announced she was pregnant.

'*Do you know what people will say?*' *Jaclyn asked Erich.*

'*Nine months and fifteen minutes after the wedding.*' *He laughed.* '*But believe me— this was all planned.*'

'*We both love children,*' *Katya added.* '*So we saw no reason to wait.*'

'*Especially since our parents never got to have all the children they wanted,*' *Erich said with a grin.* '*So we figured we needed to give them a hand.*'

And a helping hand they did. Because nine months later Kurt and I were the grandparents of twins— a boy and a girl.

'*It's great,*' *Kurt told me.* '*Even if we are sharing grandchildren with General Anton Sokolov.*'

'*Who's heard to be bragging all over Smolensk and Moscow about his twin grandchildren.*'

Manya was worried Katya would have a difficult time giving birth. So she, Yanni's father, Carl, Gretchen, Liesel, her husband, and Vera were all there. With Erich holding his wife's hands and mopping her brow when she gave birth.

Kurt, Jaclyn, Wolf, Anton, Franz, Guntar—who considered Erich his dearest friend— and myself waited outside, pacing back and forth. But thanks to God,

Katya had no trouble giving birth.

We all had tears of joy in our eyes as we held the babies. And Jaclyn declared she and Wolf were now Grand Godparents.

The little girl was named Sasha Bel and the boy Nikolai Sergei. And a month or so later, Kurt and I sat in our porch swing holding them with Shadow and Natasha at our feet, guarding them.

Kurt grinned. '*You know I think we did just fine having only one child,*' *he remarked in a teasing tone.* '*Or otherwise we might have had our hands full.*'

'*Could be?*' *I laughed.* '*But I think we would have had plenty of help from Wolf and Jaclyn—*'

'*Who'll be here in a minute to take these little angels from us…but I have a question. Do you think if you hadn't given Anton part of the money we took from that dead German, he would have done as well as he has in life?*'

'*I think if I hadn't given him that money, then we wouldn't be holding these little angels right now.*'

Once again he grinned. '*I agree. So I'd say you made one hell of an investment.*'

And me, what can I say...? Simply that the miracle continues as I gaze at the striking color of the babies' eyes. Blue— the color of the heavens of Galilee after a storm— handed down through many generations."

ENHANCE YOUR BOOK CLUB

DISCUSSION QUESTIONS

1. Did Kurt's denial of Germany's whispered atrocities make him unsympathetic?
2. In what way was Kurt not a monster?
3. How did the war change Kurt?
4. Were the German atrocities downplayed in this novel?
5. What did the war do to Kurt's soul?
6. Wolf says to Kurt that he always showed an indifference toward Vienna's Jews. And Kurt responds, "They were wealthy, and I had little in common with them." Then he adds, "Besides Goebbels never let the truth get past him." Is this an excuse?
7. What character in the story did you most admire?
8. Von Lehmann's refusal to marry Kurt's mother made him feel like a charity case, so Kurt joined the Wehrmacht out of bitterness. Do you think he overreacted?
9. The Nuremberg trials over looked women forced into brothels. Do you agree with Bela that things would have been better for women today if they'd brought them up? Why or why not?
10. Kurt was forced to admit he was fighting for the wrong side after he had sex with Bela at the Love Camp. What effect did this have on him?

11. How would *you* cope if you were Bela, trying to reconcile her feelings for Kurt, who'd been her enemy?
12. What about, "Desperation can open doors we believe to be closed?" Do you believe Bela having a son was a miracle?
13. How did becoming an avenger change Kurt?
14. What particular event in the story were you not expecting?
15. In your opinion what was the single thing that convinced Bela she must always stay with Kurt?
16. What do you think of Kurt's treatment by the British?

www.ingramcontent.com/pod-product-compliance
Lightning Source LLC
Chambersburg PA
CBHW051322190726
48290CB00001B/272